AM SCOTT

Author's Note:

Time Guild 1 is a follow-on to the Folding Space Series; I highly recommend reading the seven-book series, starting with *Lightwave: Clocker*, Book 1.0. Or if you prefer a coming-of-age story, start with *Quinn of Cygnus: Lift Off*, and read the four-book Quantum Fold Series. Both series are available in omnibus ebook and individual paperbacks at all major retailers. *Lightwave: Nexus Station* is a stand-alone prequel novella and FREE at all ebook retailers.

As in the rest of the Folding Space Universe, *Lightwave's* destinations are based on the eighty-eight classic constellations. That wouldn't work for real life space travel, but it looks lovely in the night sky! There are many star apps for your smart phone; I use the free version of Heavens Above.

Dedication

To the marvelous Gentle Beings who pledged to my Kickstarter!
You are AWESOME!

Chapter One

RUHGER

Saree jabbed a finger at "Doc" Holliday, displayed on *Lightwave*'s Command Center screen. "Tell the idiots from Gov Human to take a short walk out an airlock. They haven't supported the effort to test and find more fold clock maintainers in any significant way, so they don't get a say in the experimentation. Period. At their insistence, this is a Time Guild matter. And they're right. We will screen and train at our discretion."

Saree had been too patient. Ruhger would have yelled immediately. He wasn't sure why Doc was bringing up Gov Human demands for progress again. As usual, Gov Human offered no help. They could pre-screen candidates for security and suitability, provide psychological profiles, and transport candidates to *Quantum Fold*. But they didn't. Probably because they wanted to control the testing, which was impossible. Saree and Q were the only non-Sa'sa able to fully test candidates.

"I have told them that, in a slightly more diplomatic fashion, many times." Doc sighed. "The problem is, Gov Human noticed the Sa'sa Time Guild clock maintainers are now focusing on non-human systems in the fringe. The assigned clutches have remained in the large core systems, but those are mixed species." He ran his hand through his thick, black hair, lips clamped together.

"Oh." Saree frowned.

Ruhger hadn't tracked the other clock maintenance clutches, but it made sense. The Sa'sa kept pushing human problems to Saree, including all human-dominated systems. In their way, they were encouraging her to enlarge her clutch and capabilities. To them, that meant procreation; he was sure the Sa'sa didn't understand why Saree wasn't having children. Ruhger was more than ready to raise a family with her, but their lives were so dangerous. Having a child seemed reckless. Besides, Saree wasn't a Sa'sa queen; she couldn't birth and raise an entire clutch in a matter of a standard year or two.

Grant Lowe flopped back in his seat dramatically. "We're trying to do something that's never been done and we don't know how to do. We're under pressure from Gov Human and the Sa'sa. Wonderful."

Saree tapped on the table. "Well, they're going to have to be patient. We're doing the best we can."

"I've told everyone that, but you know how so many so-called leaders don't want to hear about problems, only solutions. Immediate solutions." Doc pursed his mouth like he'd eaten an Eridanus sour. "And speaking of immediate solutions, I've had an extremely troubling medico-led experiment floated to me. If it works, it would solve our problems, but I believe the chances of success are extremely low. However, turning it down will be difficult for all of us."

"Why?" Ruhger had remained quiet, supporting Saree during their weekly meeting with *Quantum Fold*. But anyone threatening Saree would regret it.

Doc sighed again. "Because it's from my father."

"No." Ruhger slammed both hands on the table, fury tightening his muscles. "Whatever it is, it's no. I'm not allowing some selfish medico to experiment on Saree or Q." He sucked in a breath, trying to regain control of his anger. "Experimenting on the only two human clock maintainers is incredibly shortsighted and foolish. We cannot allow it to happen." He'd say that about any medico proposal Doc considered troubling. But Doc despised his father, joining Gov Human military to avoid him and the family's "body modding to the stars" medico business. Bringing his father's proposal to them stank like a week-old Antlian puffer sandwich.

Ruhger raised his hand to disconnect the conference with *Quantum Fold*, but hesitated. Doc must be under a lot of pressure from his father, Gov Human, or someone more sinister. They had to know the full extent of the threat, especially since Q was flying to *Quantum Fold* in Beta shuttle.

"Normally, I'd agree." Doc nodded once, sharply. His normal smirk was missing, and dark circles under his eyes stood out against his pale Celtish skin. "But the proposal is relatively non-invasive."

Ruhger pinned Doc with a stare. "Define relatively and non-invasive."

"The proposed testing consists *mostly* of deep scans and DNA sampling. They're very similar to those required before body mods. That's why my father—Chief Medico Lorcan Holliday, I mean—is heading the investigative committee."

Saree sniffed. "Well, send me the proposal. I'll look, but no guarantees. I agree with Ruhger. Anything that takes me out of commission is a non-starter. Q is off the table, period. The previous trauma inflicted on her makes her ineligible for *any* experimental testing. And if this committee has expert medicos, they ought to know that. It doesn't give me a lot of faith in the completeness or effectiveness of their proposal." Her face remained composed, but Ruhger could tell she wasn't happy.

Ruhger's sense of danger deepened. "Everyone involved in this proposal ought to be very careful. There are laws concerning body modding for a very good reason." That was why they'd taken the chance on the Mensa body modders. The Mensians were not only experts, but uninterested in other species' laws or reporting requirements. In hindsight, his desperation was foolish. They'd been lucky to survive.

"Oh, they're fully aware of that." Doc's lip curled. "That's why Chief Medico Holliday is in charge. He's an expert in pushing the limits of those laws." He swept his hand through the holo floating in front of his face, highlighting a document and pushing it to his right. "Along with the proposal, I'll send you the Gov Human Medico Association's records on him and the rest of the coalition. There is a... pattern of concern."

"I bet." Saree rolled her fingers over the armrest of her chair, a faint drumming rising from the plas. "And some very expensive legal assistance, no doubt." She nodded sharply. "Anything else to share?"

"Nothing more at this time. If you don't mind, I'd like to discuss the details in person. Perhaps I can fly back with Q on Beta shuttle?" He raised a brow but immediately looked to his left. Probably at Q, conferencing from Beta shuttle.

Distrust simmered in Ruhger's gut. He'd never had reason to question Doc, but he wondered about the man's motives.

"I'm staying on *Quantum Fold* for a couple of days, Doc." Q's head, displayed in the lower left of the Command Center screen, tilted. "Are you willing to wait?"

He nodded. "Of course. It will take Saree time to dig through those documents." He returned his attention to Saree. "Please send me your questions. The proposal is dense. I've provided a summary, but you'll want to read the whole thing. Carefully."

"Very well. *Lightwave* out." Saree pointed at Grant.

Grant's fingers flicked through his holo. "Conference with *Quantum Fold* terminated. I assume you want to speak with Q?" Her face expanded on the main screen.

"Q, I'm not sure you should go to *Quantum Fold*." Ruhger's words almost surprised him. "I don't like this."

Q's shoulders rose, her tension clear. "I don't like it either. I've always trusted Doc, and I still do, but family complicates everything. Doc's got his own shuttle."

"Thanks, Q." Ruhger's relief crashed through him. "Between the pressure from Gov Human, the Sa'sa, and this proposal, my sensors are pinging like high-velocity micro-debris on a single-use suit. I wouldn't be surprised if a folder showed up, trumpeting that this is a done deal and we must cooperate immediately."

"I agree." Saree nodded, her brow creased. "I don't like the proposal or the way it came to us. I trust Doc, but there's a lot more here than he's saying." She scrolled through her holo. "I'm sending a link to this proposal to all of you. Please scan the whole thing, looking carefully at areas you're an expert in, and put notes in the document. I'm certainly not folding to Sirius until we get a thorough review of this proposal. Grant?"

"Yes, oh fearless leader?" Still seated, he bowed.

"Can you find Medico Pancea? I trust her and her associates. Offer to pay them well for their expertise."

Grant bowed again, his head almost touching the tabletop. "Your word is my command, clutch leader extraordinaire."

Ruhger huffed, but Grant's return to his old, lighthearted self was reassuring. Especially when it wasn't coupled with his previous playboy lifestyle. They didn't need manufactured drama when they had more than enough in real life. Ruth's recovery on Aljanah with the Guardians seemed to lighten Grant's worry.

Saree squeezed Ruhger's hand. "You're not immune to my request. There's a lot of statistics in this document, and you're our numbers expert."

"Blast and rad." Ruhger returned her clasp. "Don't worry. I intend to read every word, even if I have more questions than answers."

"Perfect." Saree maintained her grip but turned to look at the crew. "That's what we're going for. Lots and lots of questions. We'll ask for clarification on everything, which will buy us time. The summary of the Medico Association's complaints makes me question Holliday's professionalism."

"Money-grubbing mudhuggers, every one of them." Chief shook his wrench in the air. "They deserve a quick trip to a big black hole."

"Can I send this to the medico school on Cygnus Secundus?" Lashtar asked. "They'll probably have some brilliant questions, too. After the head trauma you sustained, they may object to you being an experimental subject."

Even though he and Lashtar didn't always see eye to eye, he was happy to have her along. She brought a fresh perspective.

"Excellent suggestion. Do that now." Saree pointed at Katryn. "Work with security on a transmission protocol. We don't want this leaking to the public."

"Not until it will help us." Tyron lifted a brow. "If there's something truly nefarious, and significant evidence of malpractice, then public opinion could go in our favor. With only two of you available, I don't think the trauma exclusion will fly, but publicity will make it hard for them to chance damaging either of you."

Grant shook his head. "These beings have a lot of credits. They can easily sway public opinion. We don't want to start a fight we can't win."

"Point. But it's still something to consider." Tyron turned to Katryn.

"Any other questions or concerns?" Saree asked.

Q waved. "I'm looking at the Time Guild priority list. I think we should fold when I get back. We'll say it's an emergency clock maintenance request and go. Because I've got a bad feeling about all of this."

Ruhger's alarm grew. They all knew Q had some sort of intuition, and added to his uneasiness, the equation wasn't balancing. He brought up command and control and the tractor beam commands. "Q, strap in. We'll make this quicker." He'd pull Beta shuttle in, then they'd fold.

"Copy that, Captain." Q fastened the straps over her body. "Ready when you are." She shivered. "Sooner is better than later."

Saree stood. "I'm going into ^timespace^. If Q's not happy, then we need to go."

Grant walked to the far side of the Command Center, his fingers flicking in front of his face. "I'll let *Quantum Fold* know we've got a priority request from the Time Guild."

"I'll plan the emergency fold while you tug Beta shuttle." Chief poked at his holo. "Attention *Lightwave*, prepare for fold."

"No!" The main screen split, and Loreli's face appeared, white showing around her deep brown irises. "You'll ruin dinner!"

Ruhger latched the tractor beam on Beta shuttle and drew it in, increasing the velocity slowly. "Sorry, Loreli, but Q thinks trouble is coming, and I agree."

"Oh." Her long, electric-blue lashes fluttered. "Well, in that case, carry on. I'll be secure in thirty seconds. Loreli out." She saluted and disappeared.

Ruhger calculated the pull of the tractor beam combined with Beta shuttle's velocity and increased *Lightwave*'s thrust. He couldn't accelerate too much because matching velocities required deceleration. But with Q certain something was wrong, and his instincts pinging, he wanted her back on *Lightwave* sooner rather than later. Good thing they'd practiced these particular maneuvers. He swept away the warnings from navigation; he knew the hazards involved better than the computer.

It was also a good thing Q was a more cautious pilot than he'd been at that age. Beta shuttle was well within range of the tractor beam.

Q scrolled through her holo. "Chief, if you don't have a great destination, Piazzi's Mistake is really high on the Time Guild list. And it's not a system high-credit types want to visit. With two galaxies colliding, it's too risky for the upper class." Her expression was unusually grim, showing her anxiety more than her words.

Ruhger recalculated again. He was right on target; any more acceleration would be counterproductive, no matter how much his fingers twitched to add thrust.

"Incoming folders," Saree said over the comms. "I think I can do the extended fold if you can, Ruhger."

"With the disturbances caused by the incoming?" Ruhger didn't want to endanger Q or Saree. "Let's do an emergency fold, dead system, Chief." The calculations popped up in his holo. Ruger didn't recognize the destination coordinates, but their specific target didn't matter; extending the fold field to enclose Beta shuttle did. He pulled up the fold field controls and pushed away the warnings about potential destruction. Then he extended the field to enclose *Lightwave*, the tractor beam, and Beta shuttle. He was pushing the limits; they had to pull Q closer.

"Three folders, in Delta One, Two, and Three," Tyron announced. "One is General Kerr's flagship."

"I can't believe they brought that into a Delta orbit." Chief smacked his wrench into his palm. "That's way too close for that enormous folder. It should be in Hotel or farther out."

"They're testing Saree, and they don't want us leaving. Which is an excellent reason to go now." Grant returned to his chair. "I'm refusing the request for comms from *Beautiful Perfection*, Chief Medico Holliday's folder."

Ruhger pushed the limits of the fold generator and their engines. "If we drop the shields, we can fold. We might lose a few exterior sensors."

"Concur, Ruhger." Chief raised his wrench. "Go."

"Concur. Give me thirty seconds and then go," Saree said.

He opened the ship-wide comms. "Voice objections to fold now." He watched the time count down; no one objected. "Fold in five, four, three, two, fold." Ruhger stabbed the fold button and navigation changed. He turned *Lightwave*'s thrusters off but didn't enter a counter thrust. "Q, are you there?"

She didn't answer.

"Tyron?" Ruhger's muscles tensed and dread shivered down his spine. He pushed away the fold controls, returning to the tractor beam, and decreased the pull. Mass remained on the end of the beam, so the shuttle was there, but he didn't know what state it might be in. If he'd killed Q based on a hunch, he'd never forgive himself.

"Beta shuttle is there," Tyron said. "Initial scans show the shuttle is intact. Reconnecting vid. Did Q enter ^timespace^?"

In the lower right quadrant of the main screen, Q lay limp in the pilot's chair. Ruhger's relief was immediate but short-lived. The shuttle reported she was alive. But he couldn't tell if Q was unconscious or in ^timespace^ like he could with Saree. "Probably. I'm not sure she's capable of helping, though."

"Saree will keep Q safe." Grant rose, trotting to the hatch. "I'll take the main medfloat and wait at Beta's hatch." The Command Center hatch seals hissed.

Grant's belief in Saree helped, but Ruhger wouldn't be happy until Q replied. He returned to the tractor beam, adjusting the velocity down. No sense in colliding with *Lightwave* or getting squished by g-forces the grav generators couldn't handle. He thrust away the ridiculous worry that the g-forces had surged during fold; if that happened, the results would show in the current velocity profile.

But no one knew what happened during fold, especially extended fold.

Loreli bustled into the Command Center, her skirt swishing. "Dinner is delayed by thirty-seven minutes." She carried a bev-tainer past him; a recovery shake for Saree.

Ruhger wanted to join them, but bringing Q in safely came first. He decreased the pull, slowing Beta shuttle's approach. Making micro adjustments, he flew Beta shuttle into the berth and locked it in place. "Beta shuttle secure."

"I'm fine, Ruhger," Saree said over the comms. "Go check on Q."

Ruhger ran to the passageway before she finished speaking. He pounded up the ladder, along the upper passage, and into Beta shuttle.

"I'm fine." Q sat in the pilot's seat, holding up both hands, palm out, facing Grant. "I was just watching Saree. I can't do what she does, even with soothing stones."

Ruhger pulled Q up and into a hug, relief letting his taut muscles relax. "Thank all the seven suns of Saga that you're okay. That's the longest extension we've done yet."

"Since you're all right, I'll send the medfloat back." Grant patted Q's shoulder, then left the shuttle.

Q squeezed him tight, then pulled away. "Is Saree okay?" She plopped into the pilot's seat and finished the shuttle docking procedures.

"She's fine. Told me to come get you." After Q finished, Ruhger signed off on the checklist completion, then led her back to their compartment at the far end of the Command Center. Saree sat on her personal medfloat, sipping.

"Q!" Loreli wrapped her arms around the girl. "There's a recovery beverage waiting in the kitchen. I'll get it." She released Q and left.

"I'll get it later. I've got questions." Q faced Saree with her hands on her hips. "Are you crazy? That was a really difficult fold."

Saree shrugged one shoulder. "No choice. Between your concerns and Ruhger's, we had to do it. I don't know what you two felt, but you're not prone to exaggerate. I trust your warnings. You saved us and a lot more beings in Old Earth orbit when the Librarian version of Galactica blew up the planet."

Ruhger sat on the medfloat and slid his arm around Saree's waist. She leaned into him, her supple warmth comforting. "I don't know what I felt, either, but combined with Q's intuition, everything in me was screaming 'get out, now.' It was intense."

Q wrinkled her nose. "Maybe we're magnifying each other's fears?"

Ruhger shook his head. "I don't think so. You know I'm not easily worried. Or terribly imaginative."

"I've got enough for both of us." Q shivered. "But you're right. The menace wasn't at the level of Old Earth, but it was still strong."

Saree tilted her head. "That makes me wonder all the more about Doc and his connection to the proposed experiment. Because you both announced your concern well before *Beautiful Perfection* folded in. Physical location may not matter for Q." Saree's fingers moved restlessly on her thighs. "She's connected to the whole universe through ^timespace^. But who knows if that's true for you, Ruhger?"

Ruhger huffed. The idea of him being like Q was absurd. "I'm the last person I'd ever tag with intuition. I'm a solid block of cerimetal. But we faced menace. I'd swear it on the giant black hole of Andromeda."

"Cerimetal can be modified and molded." Saree squeezed his thigh. "Perhaps it's more of a math and probability calculation. You're constantly assessing the odds of something happening at the physical level, so why wouldn't you do that for people's reactions? And an AI should be even more predictable. You know Galactica is probably behind all of this."

Ruhger couldn't hide his relief. "That makes a lot more sense. I just couldn't understand how I could possibly be intuitive or psychic or any of that. It's a ridiculous notion."

"What isn't ridiculous is being hunted for our genes." Q scowled. "Surprising it happened so fast, though."

Ruhger scowled. He should have thought of the possibility but hadn't; while evil was familiar to all of them, coming in the guise of medicos wasn't. "Wise hunters stalk, hide, and then pounce. That's how it works. Plus, we're not plugged into the upper echelons of human society. You can bet that Doc's father is only a tool. There are some big credits behind this proposal. Someone wants control of a fleet of human clock maintainers."

Grant appeared in the hatchway. "If you dig into this proposal, they could be trying something a lot worse. I think they're trying to clone Saree and Q."

Revulsion made Ruhger swallow hard, his stomach rising. "Clones? Those are outlawed. It's immoral."

"Because clones don't work." Grant leaned against the bulkhead. "They're mindless and must be cared for like a baby. Worse, because there is nothing there. No instinctive cry when they're hungry, dirty, or cold. A block of meat, lower than an animal. And that's true for every alien species, too. But what if someone could create a set of mindless clones with the talent for smoothing ^*timespace*^ and install them in medfloats in every fold clock along with soothing stones? Self-smoothing fold clocks." Grant spread his hands apart. "Ta-da." He swallowed hard.

Nausea rocked Ruhger. Saree shuddered violently, and Q's golden skin paled. "That's disgusting." He pulled Saree closer.

Saree pressed against him. "I don't think it will work. I have to think, concentrate. So do the Travelers."

Grant nodded. "It probably won't work. But if keeping a being alive in a medfloat permanently smooths ^*timespace*^ around every single fold clock, it will happen, fast. They almost have to try."

Ruhger bounded to his feet, turning to Saree. "They want your eggs, Saree. They know you had them harvested and stored. That's the best source of genetic material for cloning, right?" They'd hidden her storage container inside a false plas crate labeled "live plants" in the main cargo hold.

Saree nodded, her face grim. She gripped Q's forearm. "Q, did you have that done?"

The girl shook her head. "No. I had no intention of working in space. I went to Adzari Net Academy to find employment on a planet, not a station or ship." She wrapped her arms around her waist. "But I've gotten a lot of suit time since then. Maybe enough for genetic mutations, right?"

Grant stepped to Q and hugged her tight. "I don't think so. The human body is remarkably resilient. You've been checked out a lot, and the medicos would have said something if it was an issue.

Besides, they can body mod out most genetic mutations." He let go and faced Saree. "I suspect they encouraged Saree to do that more because of her profession and location. She'd be working directly with transuranic metals, living and working in space."

Saree's mouth twisted. "There was probably some prejudice as well. I was a foster kid. Poor. I'm sure those well-meaning medicos thought they were doing me a favor because they thought I'd never be able to support a child." She shrugged and lowered her voice, imitating an officious man. "Why leave the girl any chance of an oops baby? If she earns enough to support a family, these eggs will be healthier. The artificial hormone implant is better than the real thing, anyway."

Ruhger snorted. "You've got more than enough credits and an extended family thrilled to help you." He'd be first in line, whether or not Saree chose his genetic material to assist. Holding her child would be an amazing privilege, but it was her choice. "So, we'll have to protect not only you, but your ability to procreate. Because if they could have cloned or body modded your abilities from skin or other samples, they would have by now. They could get your genetic baseline from many places, including Gov Human military, against regulations or not. You've been in their medico facilities enough, and with enough pressure, rules go out the window."

"Suns, they could get my genetic material from *Quantum Fold*." Saree snorted.

"Mine too. They practically rebuilt my heart." Q tapped her chest.

Grant straightened. "I'm sure that's all supposed to be destroyed or safeguarded against misuse. But if we're right, there are a lot of credits at risk. And when that happens, the rules get ignored."

"Your speculation is correct." Tyron leaned past Grant. "Why don't you come back to the Command Center, rather than all of us shoving into your tiny compartment, and we'll go over what we've found already. I've called the entire crew in and given them a synopsis. Doc was right, and so is Grant."

Ruhger ground his teeth. Whatever was coming, he'd protect Saree and Q, no matter what it took.

Chapter Two

SAREE

Saree marched to her chair, fists clenched and fury raging through her like a geomagnetic storm in the Ghost Nebula. If their speculations were correct, Gov Human had gone way too far. Under human law, they had no right to her genetic material. Plus, she worked for the Time Guild. Humanity insisted on keeping fold clock maintenance separate from species politics. If she had to declare herself no longer human, she would. Her genetics might even back that idea—but that could be a double-edged sword. If Gov Human decided she wasn't human, then they'd have a lot less trouble experimenting on her. Humans demonized other humans to justify their abuse—aliens would be easier. Especially an alien that was working against humanity, and Gov Human would spin it that way. "Tell me what you've found." She sat, Ruhger joining her and Q plopping into the seat behind them with a loud smack of plas. "Bring everyone into a conference, please, Katryn."

"There's no direct mention of clones." Tyron swept a document onto the big screen, highlighting a section. "This clearly states they'll use 'adequate genetic material' to attempt *full* re-creation of the ability, both alone and by body modification. All volunteers, of course." He grimaced.

Q blew a raspberry. "Sure. If volunteering for a medical trial gets you off subsistence living on an overcrowded world, people will jump at it, no matter how risky." Her nose wrinkled and her mouth pursed.

"Just when we were getting along with Gov Human, someone has to blast it into rads." Katryn scowled.

Saree agreed. "The phrase 'full re-creation' certainly implies cloning."

"I'd wondered what they meant." Tyron pointed at Grant. "But when he brought up the possibility, it became clear. Doc's father must have attempted cloning or something close in the past or Doc wouldn't have sent us the Medico Association records."

"I'll look through the complaints and find the loudest objectors." Grant scrolled through a document on his holo. "The enemy of my enemy is my friend."

"Thank you." A religious argument was the last thing Saree wanted, especially after the Travelers and the Madras, but cloning would take them there quickly. "How could he get funding to support that kind of research? It's completely illegal for a good reason."

Grant shook his head. "You know wealthy beings are always searching for ways to extend their selfish lives. Historically, they don't hesitate to fund research that's morally gray or outright black. That research has contributed to the extension of human life, but extension isn't enough for the rich. They want immortality. I'm sure there are clone labs out there now, desperately searching for a way to transfer a dying being's consciousness into a youthful body. And I doubt they're using themselves as guinea pigs unless they're on death's doorstep. More importantly for us, Doc's family business serves many extremely affluent people who aren't famous, just super wealthy. I'm betting Daddy Holliday has at least flirted on the edges of cloning in the past, if not gone all the way there."

Ruhger gripped her hand. "There's compensation offered for the so-called suitable genetic material in this document, right?"

Tyron nodded. "A lot."

"Then if we turn it down, they'll move to confiscation or conscription through Gov Human next."

Grant raised his brows. "That's probably why they brought the fleet." He raised both arms and waved his hands around. "It's a critical issue for all of humanity! We must be free of the evil Sa'sa no matter what it takes! Clutch Saree is selfish!"

Saree sniffed derisively. J'ker Hanty and his so-called news show should fly straight into a black hole. "They conveniently forget that I'm part of the Time Guild. They insisted on the creation for their benefit." She stood, unable to sit still. "But what they keep forgetting is that I'm not a pawn."

"Would the Sa'sa care about clones?" Lashtar entered the Command Center, Chief behind her. "They don't care about their own young until they're clutch members. With the right explanation, clones would seem like immature beings, the unnamed. Or even an animal raised for food."

Q's face wrinkled. "Ew. That's disgusting."

"Even food animals have minds or they don't survive." Chief toyed with his wrench. "I'm fairly certain Saree could explain the problem to the Sa'sa leaders."

"Yes, I can." She was positive. "Egg stealers are evil, and that includes predators who would eat the recently hatched, unless they were defective. Those don't survive. The Sa'sa will definitely understand these people are trying to steal my eggs. And while the unnamed aren't worth the life of a clutch member, they are protected to some extent. Plus, if I explain this attempt is trying to create a presence in ^*timespace*^ with incomplete, defective life forms, they'd say it was a waste of resources. More than likely, they'd find such an idea anathema. It might even have a truly negative effect on ^*timespace*^. If it worked, which it won't, and these clones are like soothing stones, the Sa'sa would have to avoid them. Touching the mind of a living soothing stone might be just as bad or worse than they experienced with Q, before we got her trained. And clones could never be trained."

"Assuming we're right about all of this"—Tyron waved at the big screen—"what do we do about it? We can't hide forever."

"Again." Katryn smirked.

"Let's individually review the document after dinner, as originally planned. We'll talk about it tomorrow morning." Despite the shake, Saree's stomach rumbled with hunger. ^*timespace*^ combined with rage burned a lot of calories. "We'll need to be logical and calm, not emotional. Gov Human will use that against us." She wasn't in the right frame of mind for a full discussion, even if the rest of them were.

"Doc's father even more so." Grant pointed at the document on his holo. "Everything I'm finding says the man is a sociopath who covers his selfishness with charisma. He's very good at getting masses of people on his side, and he has the credits and supporters to buy the rest. There are very few people willing to stand against him, and most of those are too poor to matter to Gov Human. The Medico Association investigates medical violations, but few are reprimanded. They throw even fewer out of the Association; almost never unless they're convicted of an associated crime. Daddy Holliday has a lot of complaints but very few reprimands. I'm sure that's one of many reasons Doc doesn't want anything to do with his father."

"None of this is surprising." She strode to the hatch, determined to put the horrifying discussion behind her. "But let's talk tomorrow, okay? We'll have a family dinner, then split up and review this stuff and discuss in the morning like civilized beings." Or even better, never.

Ruhger caught her hand in his as they strolled the corridor to the dining facility. "You're right. We'll do a better job that way."

"Unless it gives us all nightmares." Q entered the dining room on their heels. "Pretty sure I'll have more than a few. But the thing that makes me positive it won't work? That's because if there was any way for cloning to work, the mudhugging slavers would have figured it out by now. There are a lot of credits at stake."

Tyron sat next to Q, Katryn sitting next to him. "Remotes can replace humans for most tasks in the short-term, but long-term, it becomes too obvious."

Saree sat next to Ruhger. "Except on the AI worlds, of course." They needed to stop talking about it. She wanted to enjoy dinner.

"Of course." Katryn sipped her water. "AIs want other AIs around. Why bother with short-lived, overemotional humans?"

"Because we're fabulous!" Loreli posed in the kitchen hatchway, one arm above her head, the other outstretched, holding a tray. "And inventive. Tonight's starter is a delicious confit of Secundus filet, with a lovely white wine I liberated from Friss on Geneva before the troubles started." She placed a small plate in front of each of them, redolent of smoked meat. Q followed, distributing wine. "Now, no more business, dahrlings! We must enjoy. Savor. Celebrate my amazing food!" She sat at the foot of the table and raised her glass. "To us and our triumph!"

"To us!" Gratefully, Saree echoed the group and sipped. Of course, Loreli was right on all counts. But as she sipped, dread pooled low in her belly. They'd faced off against Gov Human before, but Chief Medico Lorcan Holliday's wealth and influence brought a much bigger threat.

Ruhger squeezed her thigh. "It can wait until later, Saree. Enjoy what we've got now."

She nodded. He was right, and she'd worried enough. They were hidden, safe. It was her job to lead the way. "Q, tell us what you were going to do on *Quantum Fold*. Some sort of game?"

Q grinned. "It's so cool. No net stuff at all." She chattered, drawing all of them into the discussion, providing an excellent distraction. Before the end of dinner, most of the crew had agreed to join her in a beginner's game in the days to come.

Later that evening, Saree nestled next to Ruhger in the soft seating at the rear of the Command Center. Q lounged in a chair next to them, the rest of the crew nearby, reading. Chief and Lashtar sat in the command chairs across the room, watching the surveillance and planning the next few folds.

As she read the medico proposal, all the tension and concern Saree had pushed away during dinner rushed back. They'd been correct. Gov Human was attempting to take Saree and Q's genetic material. They were probably trying to take the advanced students', too, even though none of them had shown a full capability in *^timespace^*. Some could see *^timespace^*, or claimed to, but none had manipulated it yet. Saree was certain that wouldn't stop Doc's father from attempting to steal from all of them. She could only hope Doc could protect them. "I wish we'd taken all our students with us."

Ruhger's cheek pressed against the top of her head for a moment. "If we'd realized the full extent of this attempt, we would have. Why didn't Doc warn us? His father must have threatened him."

"Doc doesn't have kids, right?" Q scrolled through her holo.

"No, but that doesn't mean anything." Ruhger's fists clenched. "Doc left the family business and joined Gov Human military. There might be more reasons than Doc shared. Or his father could threaten Doc's brothers or sisters, or other family members or his military family, or who knows? Most of us have multiple pressure points. Even when we know the pressure won't stop, many of us can't handle the immediate stress or the optimism complying brings. Doc will know all this better than most, but that doesn't mean he's not susceptible."

"Too true." Gov Human could threaten people she'd grown up with on Sa'sa, or those she'd gotten to know on Aljanah. Oh, blast! "We need to warn the Travelers."

"Already done." Grant slashed his hand through the air. "I sent a message folder to *Tobar* and Aljanah Station after we figured out the possibilities. The Travelers can slip away from Gov Human military, but it's better if they can avoid interaction. Aljanah is harder, but they've held off a lot of attempts to take what is theirs."

Saree's shoulders sagged, the tension leaving her. "Thank you. The Travelers have enough trouble with Gov Human as it is. They don't need more."

"We need to warn Goldie at Bonfanti Station, too." Saree felt Ruhger's growl of frustration. "These people would think nothing of taking someone differently abled. They'd claim the station abused him or something."

"Ah, suns." Grant's fingers flew. "Didn't think of them. Bonfanti is a gray station; I'm sure they discourage Gov Human attention. But I'd bet the military keeps a watch on them as a potential hiding place for criminals."

"Or a desperation refueling stop." Ruhger huffed. "They're happy to use people they mistrust."

"Yeah, like us." Q bounded to her feet. "I'm off to do some y'ga. I can't sit anymore." She jogged through the hatch.

Saree couldn't blame her. "If I didn't have a lot more to read, I'd join her."

"We'll all break in an hour." Ruhger's tone was determined. "It's late, and we had a good meal. There's no sense in pushing anything when we're safe for now. We can stay here, take our time exploring the ramifications, and create a plan."

"Which will only meet first contact with the enemy." Chief adjusted a sensor, and the view on the Command Center view screen changed to a wide surveillance of the dead system surrounding them.

"Not our first solo flight, Chief." Tyron grinned. "Besides, what else is new?"

"Nothing at all." Saree smiled at her crew, her family. "We've survived and thrived no matter what's been thrown at us, and we'll continue to do so because you are all amazing, talented, and smart." She stood. "Rather than an hour, let's stop now. We'll start again in the morning, after breakfast." Reading this dry proposal, knowing the evil behind it, made her stomach churn. Despite that, she couldn't help but consider the full ramifications. Even if the chances were minuscule, if it worked, she was being horribly selfish.

Ruhger rose, wrapping an arm around her. "And coffee."

"Of course." Ruhger's hand slid down her arm, across her back, and grasped hers in his large, rough palm. Saree happily followed him to their compartment, eager to leave her worries behind for a short time. And if anyone could make her forget everything, it was Ruhger.

After another fabulous Loreli breakfast, they reconvened in the Command Center. Saree's breakfast sat uneasily; cloning and medico experimentation made her queasy.

Grant put the medico proposal on the big screen, comments and highlighting decorating the screen like an editing program gone wild. "I got up early this morning"—he rolled his eyes at the teasing exclamations of amazement—"and merged the comments and concerns. First, we're all worried about what the terms actually mean. I think in our reply, we should ask blunt, open-ended questions that make them define exactly what they're doing. Things like 'how does this differ from cloning?' or 'how are you ensuring the safety of the experimental subjects?' rather than yes or no questions."

Saree agreed, but her questions were more personal. "I'm more worried about what they'll say when I refuse to give up my eggs."

Grant nodded. "That's one of the first questions. Define what adequate genetic material means."

"Why are we bothering?" Ruhger glowered. "We already know what they want. Let's just write up a refusal with all our reasons. Gov Human can blast itself into a black hole."

"Ruhger, you know we can't fight Gov Human forever." Chief frowned at him. "But Saree, I figured out a way to win the battle, if not the fight."

Hope bloomed. "Oh?"

Chief nodded. "We build a small station, like a fold clock enclosure, with multiple layers of security and remotes to patrol around it. Then we park your so-called genetic material inside and put the thing in some back of beyond system no one knows about except us. Maybe shadowing a moon's orbit or inside a large piece of debris in a planetary debris ring?"

"Can we build something like that right now?" Ruhger looked skeptical.

Chief shook his head. "No, we'd need supplies. But we could probably pay the AIs to gather them for us, and they wouldn't allow us to be taken in Old Earth orbit. At least I hope they'd back us against Gov Human."

Saree wasn't so sure. "Would they? If they need a meat-form smoothing ^*timespace*^, I'm sure they'd rather it was mindless. Some of them don't think we have minds now. Besides, that only saves me. What about Q? And no, I don't think putting her through harvesting is a good idea."

"I'm certainly not going to hide out in a tiny box in the middle of nowhere, either." Q shuddered. "Done enough of that already."

"I didn't propose it as a complete solution, just a way to win one battle." Chief grimaced.

Saree nodded, grateful. "I understand. It's a good thought, and it's definitely worth consideration. But even if we can build something adequate, we'll have to hide our tracks in and out of wherever we put that small station. We're still not sure if the companies that build fold generators can track our folds or not. If they can, the idea is riskier than keeping the eggs with me."

"Possibly." Chief's lips flattened.

"It is a great idea, though." She had to encourage all the ideas, rather than shut them down. "We'll leave it on the list, and if we select it, we'll work on different ways to implement it. What else can we do other than request clarification? Because Ruhger is right. That's only a delaying tactic, not a solution."

Katryn raised her hand. "I think we should investigate the past cloning experiments. Let's revive the concerns among the general population. And if a genetic marker can be found and tied to ^timespace^ ability, beyond what you've already got, Saree, then anyone with that marker could be at risk. I think it's time we use the media rather than it being employed against us. I've got some ties from my old activist days."

"I don't see a downside with that approach. Anyone else?" Saree pointed at Grant.

"Only that if they want to, Gov Human and the people who are undoubtedly backing Chief Medico Holliday can easily counter or twist those reports to look the way they want. But really, we've got nothing to lose, so we may as well." Grant turned to Katryn. "I'll help. I've made a lot of contacts since I took on this job, and some of them are investigative reporters. True believers that the press shouldn't hold a bias." He shrugged one shoulder. "Of course, that isn't always a good thing for us."

The press had definitely been a mixed blessing. That idiot, J'ker Hanty, was still around, blathering his nonsense to his rabid followers. Cults of personality were the worst. But keeping the critics at bay meant working, keeping human systems connected to the wider universe. "So, how do we continue smoothing ^timespace^ without getting caught and show the general populace that we're doing everything we can for humanity and the rest of the universe?"

"But you're not." Lashtar held up her hand, palm out. "You could become a true Clutch leader if you started all your eggs right now." She shook her head. "I'm not serious, just saying what others will think."

Saree grimaced. That would take a fleet of nannies, and they simply couldn't trust that many people. Nor did they have enough room on *Lightwave*. She wasn't dropping her children off to be raised by others and would tell anyone suggesting such a thing that it wouldn't work. Obviously, she'd have to train them from childhood; she didn't care if the statement was true or not. "Okay, every reasonable thing for humanity."

"We can do the quick fold and tune we've done in the past." Chief pointed at the big vid screen. "I've planned out a series of folds that will take us to the worst of the clocks, bouncing around the universe, but not far enough that those folds cause you pain. At certain points, we'll need to send messages, reporting back to the Time Guild, There's no reason we can't put out press releases at the same time, announcing our accomplishments to the locals and a general update to the core every ten folds or so."

Ruhger moved to the edge of the seat, meeting her gaze. "I think we should take the fight to Chief Medico Holliday. Let's find his house of horrors, bring in some respected press, and expose him and his funding sources."

"And if it's not a house of horrors?" Grant shook his head. "I'm sure he's got public-facing research that's perfectly lovely."

"Of course he does." Ruhger glowered. "But if he's taking this step, going up against the Time Guild and alienating the only human maintainers, he's desperate. That means he's already got clones somewhere, and we know what that means. Even if they're all in medfloats, they're mindless. Soulless. Disgusting."

Chief pointed his wrench at Ruhger. "You're not thinking about this straight. If we go to a location under his control, we take the chance of getting caught. Then Saree and Q are right where he wants them. If he's doing cloning, he's got lots and lots of security. Probably mercenary fleets. That's what I'd do. A station around an uninhabited planet or moon, with remote protectors and mercenaries. If we're being tracked, then they'll know we're there. We can't sneak in and out."

"If Hal would help us, we could get a small team in," Ruhger said. "We'd leave Saree and Q on *Lightwave*, someplace safe."

Saree had learned splitting up was a bad idea. "No. Without all of you, Q and I wouldn't be safe. Yes, we could take *Lightwave* and fold away. But if we're attacked, we can't do an escape fold and fight at the same time. Even with the improvements you've made to *Lightwave*, she's old. Something will break at the worst possible time."

"She's right." Lashtar rubbed her artificial leg. "I could stay with them, but I don't know *Lightwave* like Bhoher does. But the bigger problem is this house of horrors you're looking for probably doesn't exist. There will be rows of medfloats, with healthy-looking humans sleeping peacefully. They won't be lying around in cerimetal huts, dirty and starving. That wouldn't produce good results for any medical experiment on any living being, sentient or not."

"Plus, specialized skills require more than adequate nutrition," Tyron said. "Anyone can be forced to do a task, but they'll do better if they've got adequate food, shelter, exercise, and security. More importantly, though, they're not trying to force Saree and Q themselves to do anything. They want reproductive material. Saree's is easy to get, already in a transport case. They'll make the argument that she won't use all those eggs, and she's simply being selfish not to help humanity. People won't care if a mindless body is stuck in a medfloat in the middle of nowhere. If it's mindless, it won't know." He raised a hand. "Unpopular opinion here, but if it actually worked, which I doubt, I'm not sure I'd care as long as it was treated decently."

Katryn smacked his shoulder. "That's disgusting."

"Yes, but the key here is it won't work." Ruhger got up and paced. "They're stealing from Saree for no reason."

"They don't see it that way." Tyron shrugged. "It's hard to prove a negative without experimentation."

Saree shuddered. Her children, trapped forever in medfloats for no reason at all. "Here's my problem with this entire idea. If they're using my eggs, they're my *children*. Period. They're not mindless. Now if they attempt to clone children born from my eggs, then those might be mindless, but my kids won't be. And I'm not leaving my children in the hands of a bunch of greedy, soulless, black-hearted experimenters who will put them in little boxes their entire lives. I may as well turn them over to Galactica."

"Sorry, Saree, you're right." Tyron rose and bowed deeply. "My apologies. I wouldn't want my children in the hands of unethical medico experimenters either."

Lashtar held up both hands. "Let's assume that all of us have good intentions. We must discuss the entire issue to define the problems. We've got to get it clear in our minds before we can inform the public. Gov Human courts have ruled, time after time, that genetic material belongs to that person unless it is deliberately turned over to another. The courts can force that to happen if the person involved has a record of child abuse. Saree does not have a record. Another thing in our favor is that many worlds have tried to raise children in creches as workers. It takes too long and results in poorly adjusted adults. Despite the desperate need for our orphanage on Cygnus Gliese, the Sisters of Cygnus struggled to provide enough adult guidance and love. Both Q and Katryn can attest that when love is taken out of the equation, the results are poor. The wealthy ought to know that better than anyone. When they pay someone else to raise their kids, those kids turn out badly, unless the paid person fully embraces the role of parent. And then the real parent resents that so-called intrusion. Most of these wealthy beings are the result of exactly that standard of care. Or non-standard. Not that they'd admit they were anything less than perfect."

"If the parents don't care at all," Chief said, "it still results in a messed-up human needing a lot of counseling. And probably not getting it."

"Precisely." Lashtar nodded sharply. "To me, the problem is these are children. Saree and Q's children. They should not be raised as experiments."

"Saree, do you know how viable your eggs are?" Chief asked. "You've hauled that case through a lot of severe environments."

Ruhger returned to her, reaching for her. Saree put her hands in his and gratefully stepped into his loving arms. She needed the comfort. "No. We'd just started talking about possibly having children. Until recently, our lives were too dangerous to even consider it." She leaned back, and Ruhger relaxed his arms slightly but didn't let her go. "We were discussing the timing and thought that once I had ten people trained to smooth ^timespace^ at a beginner level, then we could move forward. But this has put a stop to those ideas."

"Don't let it." Lashtar shook her head, a mournful look on her face. "Every life is fraught with danger, no matter where you are or what you're doing. If you're ready for children, have them. Don't wait, because the timing will never be just right, and you'll be old before you know it."

Chief put his arm around Lashtar. "Besides, you've got a folder full of help. I'll be a good uncle."

"I'll be the fun one!" Grant waggled his brows. "I can teach them how to get what they want with just a smile."

Saree put her head back on Ruhger's shoulder, listening to his slow, steady heartbeat while the crew joked. Lashtar was right. Seize the day because tomorrow may not come. But that thought didn't sit well either. Dying was bad enough, but leaving a child unprotected might be worse. Still, Chief was correct, too. She and Ruhger had a lot of support, the timing would never be perfect, and they weren't getting younger. "What do you think, Ruhger?" She kept her volume low.

"I'm ready for kids when you are. But the timing is up to you. As is the father." His bass tones rumbled comfortingly through her upper body.

She nodded, her cheek rubbing the material of his shipsuit. "I don't want anyone fathering my children except you." They'd discussed having children for quite some time, and they were both ready. "Let's do it. We'll need the right medico supplies because I see no reason to do this the old-fashioned way." Her eggs were already harvested. Putting them back in her body, where they'd all be at risk, seemed stupid.

"Smart. I don't either. It's too dangerous. Besides, I'd rather you were fully operational while we gestate and raise our kids. They'll need all of us protecting them." He loosened his arms and met her gaze. "How many?"

She shrugged. "Two or three?" For now. Maybe more later. Happiness bubbled in her chest, like Sirius Sparkler in a glass.

The corners of his lips lifted in his usual tiny smile. "Four? Two pairs means no one feels left out. And we have lots of diaper changers on board."

Saree grinned. "Okay. Let's do it." Happiness sparkled in her heart.

Ruhger released his left arm and moved next to her, facing the rest of their group. Their family. "We've agreed. Four kids, as soon as possible. Where can we safely go for medico supplies?"

"You're kidding me, right?" Lashtar shook her head, scoffing. "Four? All at once? My friend Miles did that, but even with lots of paid help, I think he regretted it. And, as someone who's raised a lot of kids, multiples are challenging. Plus, I'm not changing diapers." She tilted her head, frowning. "That's the parent's job, not the cool aunt's."

"Yeah. That's definitely not my job!" Q wrinkled her nose. "It will be a long time before I'm ready for motherhood."

Saree grimaced. Lashtar had some excellent points.

Tyron and Katryn stood and put their arms around each other. "Well, it may be a long time for you, but Tyron and I are ready. What if we both have two kids now and two more each in a standard year?"

Saree grinned. "Excellent idea! Our kids will be the best of friends from the start. Congratulations!" Everyone echoed her words. Tyron kissed the top of Katryn's head.

"Let's see how you're feeling after a year of no sleep before you plan the next set." Lashtar sniffed, smiling. "But congratulations to all of you."

Loreli entered, towing a train of grav generator trays. "Well, I'll plan a fabulous celebration for tonight and an even better one for the procreation and births! But for now, you'll have to make do with a basic soup and salad lunch."

Q helped her place dishes and food on the conference table. "I doubt it. You're not capable of basic, Loreli."

She put a hand over her heart, above the shiny white plas of her corset, decorated with tiny alternating bows in blue, pink, and yellow. "Thank you, dahlring. You are, of course, entirely correct." She pushed the trays to the far wall, taking a bottle from the last one. "Come eat and celebrate! The family increases!" The cork came out with a pop, and she poured bubbly wine into flutes and handed them around. "To Saree, Ruhger, and the *Lightwave* Family. May we always be fabulous!"

Saree raised her glass. "Here, here." She took a seat, smiling at her found family. They were indeed fabulous.

Chapter Three

RUHGER

RUHGER OPENED SHIP-WIDE COMMS. "Ready for fold? Voice objections now." He waited for a five-count. "Fold in five, four, three, two, fold." He checked the navigation and surveillance. "We've arrived safely in Piazzi's Mistake. Perform post-fold checks and report issues. Engineering, how far can we fold?"

"We've got enough power to fold to the closest constellations right now. Full regeneration in seven point two hours at our current rate."

"Thanks, Chief. Surveillance?"

"No concerns, Captain." Tyron pushed his view to the main screen. "The orbits have plenty of junk, but nothing with an unusual amount of velocity headed our way. If it becomes our problem, a quick laser strike will take care of it."

"Speaker for Lightwave Clutch?" Ruhger triple-checked the navigation. They'd arrived slightly off target, but it wasn't surprising. The fold clock needed tuning, plus the two interacting galaxies generated the unusual forces.

"No concerns for the clutch. Lots of automated requests for emergency transport coming in, along with tons of advertisements. I'm running a search for medical equipment."

"What's a ton, anyway?" Ruhger checked the surveillance near the fold clock; nothing unusual. With any luck, they wouldn't need to fly there.

Grant chuckled. "No idea."

"Says here, Captain, that it's a measurement of weight from Old Earth." Tyron pointed at his holo. "The ton varied by location and material being measured, but the most common one is about 900 kilos at Old Earth standard gravity."

Katryn snickered. "Our ancestors were weird."

"No doubt about that." Q wrinkled her nose. "And the customs that get carried on are even weirder. Sometimes, the people doing them don't even know why."

"Humans are creatures of habit." Lashtar shrugged. "We learn by rote and have a hard time changing. Think about how many things we do every day without knowing why. But that's what kept us alive before we had sufficient weapons to dominate our environment. It's difficult to get out of that mindset."

"Like the name of this system." Tyron smirked. "Piazzi was an ancient Old Earth astronomer, and he misnamed a star in Leo Minor, which created more mistakes. But the colliding galaxies that contain Piazzi's Mistake have nothing to do with him. He probably couldn't even see them, but they still named the system after him."

Ruhger didn't care about the ancients, he cared about Saree, who ought to be emerging from their compartment. He unstrapped, jogged to the hatch, and peered inside. Saree rested on the medfloat, eyes closed, body still, deep in ^timespace^.

Q entered, stopping on the other side of Saree. "She's still out there? Huh. Maybe the movement of the galaxies." She plopped down in one of the nearby chairs. "I'll go check."

"Don't do that, Q." Ruhger's concern grew. "If Saree's still working, ^timespace^ must be chaotic. You might get lost."

"She might need help. I don't think there are any soothing stones here." She spread both arms wide. "The first evacuees would have taken those."

Ruhger grimaced. "It's your decision, Q, but if you decide to go, please be careful. Suns, go get on a medfloat now, just in case. If you look around and don't see her immediately, or she looks like she's lost or in trouble, come back and let me know. I'll recall her."

Q bounded out of the chair. "Good idea. Too bad *Quantum Fold* isn't here. They've got all those soothing stones and plenty of comfy med loungers."

She jogged away, leaving Ruhger to brood. They finally decided that despite the dangers, they'd raise a family, and then the next fold puts Saree at risk. They should have known; two colliding galaxies could bend space and time, so ^timespace^ would reflect that to some extent. Or it could be completely unrelated. If only he could truly watch Saree's six. Q could, but between her impulsiveness and relative inexperience, that could be a mixed blessing.

He pulled up the acquisition list and added, "comfy med lounger." If Q thought their medfloats were uncomfortable, she wouldn't use them. He should have asked her previously, but that comet had left the system. Regret was useless.

"Hey, Ruhger?" Grant lounged against the hatchway.

"Yes?"

"I've been looking into the media here, and I believe the current exodus was manufactured. The galaxies have been colliding for centuries and will continue to do so at a ridiculously slow pace." He smirked. "Humanity will be dust before the beings in Piazzi's Mistake need to worry. So, who created the emergency and why? Most likely, there's something here that someone—or something—wants. Maybe Galactica; there's something about the progression of the messaging that makes me think about it."

Ruhger turned to Saree. "Maybe soothing stones? Perhaps that's why she's not back already." Ice shivered down his spine. "She got pulled into a world of soothing stones, and Q is out there too!"

Grant spun. "I'll bring back Q. Saree can call the Sa'sa, remember?"

She could. Ruhger breathed deeply, calming his body, while inspecting Saree for any distress. She appeared normal or as normal as she could be in ^timespace^.

"No, there's no soothing stones here." Q's voice carried. "There's nothing weird here at all. At least nothing I could see in the short time I was there. Can I go back now?"

"Sure, Q. Sorry, we were worried." Grant didn't sound sorry, and he shouldn't be.

"I understand. But stop bugging me. I can take care of myself, even in ^timespace^."

Grant's reply was too quiet for Ruhger to hear. Moments later, he lounged in the hatchway again. "You heard, I'm sure." He smirked. "She's not quiet."

"Thank the seven suns of Saga for that." Ruhger remembered the Q they'd found on Reane; he'd take loud over abused, wary, and scared every time.

"Agreed." Grant shrugged. "But maybe there's nothing to worry about. Saree hasn't been out that long."

Ruhger nodded. "You're undoubtedly right. But worrying is all I can do."

"Well, don't. Waste of time. I'm going back to my research." He shrugged again. "Maybe I can figure out what's here."

Saree shifted, stretched, and sat up. Ruhger put his arms around her, holding her close. She returned his hug, then pulled back but kissed him quickly first. "There is something here. Transuranics, a lot of them. Enough to affect the fundamental frequencies of the universe in the galaxy." She grimaced. "Or maybe affect is too strong a term. It's difficult to reach any of them except the dominate, americium. It isn't found in nature very often because the half-life is relatively short. It was probably generated by a recent star collision—recent by Galactica's timeline—and impacted nearby objects. There may be a source that can be easily surface-mined by remotes."

"Heavily shielded remotes, obviously." Ruhger imagined the radioactivity would keep most humans from investigating.

Grant snapped his fingers. "Of course. I found early reports of extreme radiation from a system relatively close to Piazzi's, but it doesn't have habitable planets, so no one here cared about it. But Galactica knows sentients are curious. So, rather than chance the system being discovered, it manufactured an emergency. But it didn't understand humans very well; few of us care about anything that will happen a thousand years from now." He turned his hand palm up and raised it to above his head. "So it ramped up the pressure and excitement with fake news reports over the last hundred years. Humans are so gullible."

"Diabolically clever." Ruhger shrugged. "We'll stay away from there. I never want to fold into another Galactica mining system, and we don't need large amounts of transuranic elements."

Chief shouldered Grant aside to sit on the couch. "I'm sure it's a target of opportunity. Galactica gets a valuable transuranic but more importantly, creates chaos and death for humans. Win-win."

"Seems consistent." Saree's fingers drummed on her thighs. "Well, let's find what we need, if we can, get it, and get out. No need to fire lasers at Galactica."

Grant turned. "Off to find sources. Keep building your lists."

Loreli pushed past him and dropped a bev-tainer in Saree's hand. "Really, dahrling, let me know about these little forays into ^timespace^ earlier. You're rushing my creativity!" She bustled away, a second recovery shake in hand for Q.

Ruhger chuckled. Trust Loreli to make everything about her and diffuse the tension.

Chief rose but also paused in the hatchway. "Why do you bother with a full compartment? You may as well bring Saree's medfloat back out to the main Command Center, rather than all of us squeezing into your tiny space." He stepped out and deliberately closed the hatch. "Lock it."

Saree grimaced. "He's got a point. I don't need silence and low lights to enter ^timespace^ anymore, so I should leave this thing out there. But at the same time, I'm not a fan of being on display." She smiled at him, jumped off the medfloat, and using her holo, locked their compartment. Then she stepped in close, wrapping her arms around his waist. "But I enjoy having a full compartment to ourselves occasionally, not just a bedroom."

Ruhger grinned, pulled her in tight, and lowered his lips to hers. He liked it too.

A standard day later, Ruhger fidgeted on the Command Center couch, Saree and Q lounging next to him. "We can't stay much longer, or Gov Human will find us. I'm amazed they haven't tracked us down. The news of our presence here has spread quickly."

"Maybe General Kerr likes Chief Medico Holliday's cloning proposal as much as we do?" Saree sniffed. "Because they should have found us."

"Unless they're busy stealing genetic material from our students." Q wrapped her arms around her middle.

"Children." Lashtar spat the word. "Let's use the right name. If they're taking eggs from your female students, those will be children, not clones."

"Unless they can clone the eggs before they're fertilized?" Tyron couldn't hold back a shiver, even though he was clearly attempting to be unemotional.

"Children. Besides, it won't work." Lashtar's tone was certain. "It's been tried. Clones aren't humans. They don't have a soul, so they don't have a mind. It's one of many reasons I believe in a higher power."

"I'm sure Chief Medico Holliday will try just about anything." Katryn sneered the title. "He needs the credits." She swept a spreadsheet to the big screen in the Command Center. "We've been digging. While he's wealthy, he's made some poor decisions lately. He expanded his business too fast, pushing into some systems without quite enough demand, so he's blowing through credits like air out a leaky hatch seal. Plus, he seems to have had quite a bit of income that isn't from his regular medico business. Probably those experiments we were speculating about. But when the ultra-wealthy don't get the results they want, they often withdraw their investments or turn on their former partners."

Tyron put a star map on the screen with a moving timeline at the top. As the last year passed, systems highlighted in green morphed into yellow, orange, and red. The remaining green dots were in human-centric systems in core constellations. "Something of that sort has happened because several formerly lucrative locations are sucking like big black holes. We believe he's been laundering illegal credits through his shops. His appointments are booked solid for a standard year or more, but when we checked nearby surveillance vid, there was very little traffic. His employees spend more time on gossip nets than they do with patients."

"Since he's got his own medico folder, there's no way for us to track his movements." Katryn scowled. "He could be going anywhere and hiding all kinds of things for all kinds of beings."

"He could even hide experiments on his folder." Q shivered. "Familia is good at that, so why not a medico? He could claim patient privacy to keep everyone out." She pointed at the screen. "Suns, if you look at when we broke Familia, you can see a dip in his income, so their dirty paws are in that mess."

Ruhger put his arm around Q's shoulder, squeezing her gently. "It's not surprising. Medico to the stars and the wealthy would include those with illegal credits. But those drops are small in comparison, so I'm betting they're body mod clients, not funding research. Or not a super-expensive research project."

Q shuddered. "Maybe. I couldn't guess Fatima's age. I'm sure she's done body modding, whether that's through Holliday or not. I'm even more sure she'd love to jump into a new body when modding and organ replacement quits working. Or right now."

Ruhger ran his hand up and down her bicep, trying to comfort her. Familia was never good, but Q saw them in the worst light possible. He didn't blame her, and she was usually correct, but they had to remember her bias.

"Lots of people would, and some for much better reasons, like disease." Lashtar grimaced. "If someone could figure out how to transfer a being's consciousness, cloning would be big business. I'd have a harder time arguing against it if we could cure fatal disease."

Chief shook his head. "Entropy wins. Death comes for all. There's no escaping it, no matter how hard you try. If you think about it, what would an immortal society bring? I think the majority would exhibit extremely selfish, hedonistic behavior. Few would have reasons to create anything new or help others. Species would stagnate, things would break, and before long, we'd recede back into the stone ages. Challenge is key."

"Maybe. With their hive mind, the Sa'sa are sort of immortal and they're doing fine. Although most don't maintain individuality." Saree shrugged. "I'd be pretty happy flying around the universe

smoothing ^*timespace*^ forever if I wasn't being hunted.
There's always something new to see and do. More discoveries.
Maybe only those inclined to be lazy would spiral down.
But either way, no one has figured out how to transfer a
consciousness. Lashtar obviously thinks it's impossible, and I
tend to agree. Soul or not, how could you transfer everything
that makes you who you are? Our brains aren't built on ones
and zeros."

Grant nodded. "There's still a lot we don't know about the
brain and plenty of legal studies into it. If Doc's father is doing
illegal research, it will come out eventually. Someone always
tells, either to reveal it or brag."

"Might not happen until the man has been gone for many,
many years." Saree shrugged. "Regardless, we need medico
supplies to gestate and raise kids. Did we find sources for that?
The bigger picture and problem can wait."

Grant, with his back to them, raised his finger pointer in a
"wait one" motion. After a few moments, he turned. "Found a
potential source. On the closest inhabited planet near a city
called Hanny, there was a big medico manufacturing area. Lots
of companies had factories there. But like much of Piazzi's,
those who could leave have gone. People still live there, but it's
a strenuous life. In the city itself, scavengers search for food,
water, and fuel. Beyond the outskirts, there are plenty of farms
and ranches and decent subsistence living."

Grant grimaced. "But the outskirts are a battleground. Both
the city and country residents make forays into the former
industrial areas, looking for food and working technology.
So of course, there are warlords who have claimed sections
and control the remaining goods. Some even operate the
automated factories. It's more a matter of who collected good
maintenance technicians early on and who's been able to keep
that training alive. In some places, that system has turned into
an apprenticeship model, passing the skills down methodically.
In other locations, it's become a quasi-religion. Then there are
pockets of pure scavenging where a warlord was overthrown,
no one won, and the entire section fell into chaos."

Ruhger's hopes dropped. Once modern technology disappeared, traditional roles from hunter-gatherer society appeared. Women became second-class citizens, valued for child-bearing and home-making skills. "Let me guess. Artificial gestation isn't high on anyone's list of necessary tech."

"Unfortunately, yes." Grant frowned. "But there is some hope, or I would have suggested we move on. The warlord in the section I found is a woman, one who seems determined to keep women in charge. She's kept her technology going and her society vibrant, but men are subservient."

"So?" Katryn sniffed. "That means Saree negotiates, me and Lashtar back her up, and we're good. In case you didn't realize it, we're led by a female, and you"—Katryn pointed at the men on the crew—"are second-class citizens here. It's true in Sa'sa, too. Queens run the clutches."

"I have no issue with that." Grant raised both hands, palms out. "I don't want to be in charge. But slavery is slavery, no matter who it is. Generally, we don't deal with slavers. And this society is based on slavery of males." He turned back to Saree. "Are you willing to deal with a slaver to get what you need?"

Saree shook her head. "No. We can order what we need through the Sisters' contacts on Secundus and get it shipped to us through third parties. Maybe the Travelers will do it." She smirked. "For a fee, of course."

Grant shook his head. "But Gov Human will monitor comms with the Sisters. And as many Travelers as they can."

Q snorted. "Good luck with that."

"Even with Saree's talents, we can't track them, so I don't think Gov Human can." Lashtar shrugged. "But if we can find a Traveler folder, we can make the request through them. No need to specify where they get the items, just be prepared to pay. A lot."

"And don't expect it quickly." Q's mouth twisted. "The Travelers work on their time, not ours. Something like this, they'll want to find the least expensive source, then mark it up to the higher end and add fees. It's the safest route, though."

Tyron raised his pointer finger. "Do the Travelers believe in using this kind of tech? And if we ask them to purchase things for us, are we exposing them to discovery by Holliday's crew? While the Traveler folders usually can't be held, Gov Human could bring enough force against an individual folder to capture them. Plus, they're vulnerable when they're on planets. And since we've already sent the warning, I doubt any of them can be found right now. They've certainly scattered to the far fringes where comms are iffy at best."

Ruhger's idea was likely to create controversy. "There's a different way. If the person controlling the goods we need is a slaver, then we roll in and take them. I don't feel bad about stealing from slavers."

"Normally, I'd agree." Grant's mouth twisted momentarily. "But the society is stable. They don't treat their slaves badly, exactly. Slaves are fed, housed, even educated. They're encouraged to form family bonds. They just don't have a say in what they do, when they do it, or in the society. It's no different than hundreds of societies on hundreds of subsistence worlds."

"Then why did you call it slavery?" Saree raised her brows.

"Because it is. No free choice means slavery." Grant raised both hands to the side.

Tyron slashed his hand through the air in front of his waist. "I think you're deliberately making a statement. There's something in this society you don't like. Is it our problem? And is our problem, finding medico equipment, so urgent that we can't wait a while and find a better source? You're manufacturing a crisis. All of you." He scanned the entire crew, then turned to Grant. "You're making it worse."

As Katryn reminded them, they were a clutch and Saree was the leader. His job was support. "You're correct." Ruhger gripped Saree's hand. "We've allowed our emotions to drive us. We aren't in a rush. While we've decided to move forward despite the dangers, we don't have to act immediately. We can wait for a more auspicious opportunity."

"Ooh, big words." Q snickered.

"And it isn't our job to travel the universe righting wrongs." Saree rose, crossed to Grant, and gripped his shoulder. "I don't like slavery any more than you do. But we have our own battles to fight and a war to survive. Why is this one important to you?"

Grant swept away the view on his e-torc. "It isn't. It's a cheap source of what we need, available now. That's all. We'll wait for our deliveries and go."

Saree bent, face to face with Grant. "Are you sure? Because if something is important to you, it's important to me. It may not survive the prioritizing process, but that's true of all of our wants and needs. After mission priorities, no one's preferences impact our decision making more than anyone else's."

Grant shrugged. "The orderly self-enforcement of slavery bothers me. It's bad enough when beings are enslaved. When the victims actively perpetuate the slavery, it's horrid."

Saree straightened, shivering. "I agree. But I have to agree more with Tyron and Ruhger. We have a mission, and interfering with a society isn't it."

"I agree." He nodded. "I really do. I got caught up in my feelings."

Saree gripped his shoulder again. "We all did. But your feelings are one reason you're so good at what you do. You are sympathetic. Beings see that, understand it, and believe in you. Don't shut down your feelings. They're important."

Grant nodded, smiling slightly. "You are correct on all counts. But especially that this battle isn't ours. I don't like leaving this society intact, but it's not our job, and it will stand or fall all by itself."

"It'll fall." Q smirked, shaking her head slowly. "Slavery can't last forever. Humans are stubborn." She swept her hands from her head to her feet. "Exhibit one."

"Determined, not stubborn." Saree raised her brow at Q in a perfect "Mom" look. "Determined, strong, intelligent, clever, fast. Those are your descriptors."

Q huffed a chuckle. "Stubborn isn't always a bad thing. Sure, I'm all those other things, too, but stubborn got me back here. It's what will keep all of us out of Holliday's hands, too. I'm stubborn, and I embrace that identity."

Lashtar sighed. "Well, mules are stubborn but smarter than horses, so I guess it fits. But even stubborn can take the wrong path. Mind your feet." She turned, gazing at each of them. "That goes for all of you."

"How about we mind our fold out?" Chief twirled his wrench on his fingertips. "Where are we going?"

Klaxons rang. Ruhger swept command and control forward, selecting an emergency fold at random. "Defense, report."

"Laser fire from the planet. The same location as that city Grant told us about, Hanny." Tyron's fingers danced. "Increased shielding planet-side."

"Scanning for additional threats planet-side," Katryn said.

"Scanning for non-terrestrial threats," Lashtar announced.

Ruhger brought up comms. "All stations, emergency fold in five, four, three, two, fold." He wasn't giving Loreli a chance to object; surviving a planet-based laser was unusual enough. Navigation changed and Ruhger compared the coordinates with reality. "We've arrived safely in Keere in Camelopardalis. All stations, perform cross-checks and report issues."

"Wow." Q sniffed. "This place is more back of beyond than Cygnus. There's nothing here."

"There's a G-3 star, an inhabited planet, a spaceport, people selling things..." Grant shrugged. "Looks better than Cygnus to me."

Katryn snickered. "Lots of advertisements for sex. No wonder it looks better than Cygnus."

Grant shot Katryn an annoyed glance but didn't reply. "There are lots of advertisements for personal specialty weapons, like high-end expensive stuff. Maybe for assassinations. Lots of hints, not much solid intel, so I'm guessing. If we stay, I'm sure we can find out more."

"Specialized medico supplies too." Katryn frowned. "Why would there be medico manufacturers out here in the far fringes? Transport costs to the core would be high."

Q shook her head. "I don't like it. Something is off."

"Are there gestation devices?" Saree asked, her tone hopeful but wary.

Katryn nodded. "Yes, oddly enough. High-end expensive ones, along with equally pricey medfloats and medico suites. Plus long-term medpods for people in comas or with life-threatening injuries."

"Everything you'd need for clones, actually." Tyron grimaced. "Maybe that's why they're out here."

"Let's settle in and do some research. We'll report in four hours." Saree assigned tasks.

Saree asked Ruhger to handle defense and planning the next fold. Which was good because researching purchases wasn't his strongest ability. With the warning about assassin supplies for sale on the planet, Ruhger spent most of his time on near surveillance but found nothing. In between scans, he tried to figure out why anyone in Hanny would fire on them. As a small folder, they were no threat. He brought up the surveillance records and searched. Eventually, he found a drone swarm nearing the attackers. But using a space defense laser for such a small target didn't make sense. Those took a lot of power. Maybe it was the only laser weapon they had left.

Four hours later, Saree stood and stretched. "Reports, please. Ruhger?"

"Nothing seen. Next folds are planned." He kept watching their surroundings.

Q on net, Chief on mechanical, and Lashtar on distant surveillance had nothing to report. Saree nodded. "On to the medico equipment. Katryn, what have you found?"

"Life Loom has factories here. They market hands-off medico care of all kinds to the upper class." Katryn's nose wrinkled. "You know, the kind of people who don't want to be bothered with long-term care or kids. Except they need an heir and a spare or can't afford to let a parent die for political reasons. Royalty, politicians, anyone who's driven to leave a legacy or dynasty and wants to prevent bad publicity."

"Their stuff seems good." Saree scrolled through her holo. "Reviews are very positive."

"They also produce mass-market models under the umbrella of IsoSafe, although they do their best to hide the association." Tyron swept an advert to a side screen. "HoldSafe, for long-term care, and SurroSub for gestation are used by many lower-end medico facilities. Their failure rate is significant, but few care. Those products are used on overcrowded worlds where medico care is rationed and births are discouraged."

Katryn placed the Life Loom model advert next to the SurroSub. "You can see the similarities under the branding. What you can't see is the dark secret behind the super-rich. Every auto-gestation device produces a healthier child when the mother—or a mother-surrogate—is actively interfacing with the machine. At the start, mothers should participate an hour every day. As growth slows, the time requirement lessens, with only an hour a week at the end. SurroSub doesn't have a mother interface option. The wealthy use surrogate mothers; they pay a healthy young woman to sit in the machine for twelve hours a day. They're all convinced that more hours are better, even though evidence doesn't support it. Too many influential people spouting off word-of-mouth that isn't true." She scowled. "And some don't pay those women. They promise safe lives on a luxury world but never tell them they'll be shackled to machines, unable to leave."

"It's one trick we warn our girls about." Lashtar sighed. "But there are so many schemes like that. I'd forgotten about that one."

"If it's too good to be true..." Chief shook his head.

Katryn's scowl etched a furrow between her brows, scrolling through something on her holo. "They keep the women healthy while they're in the machines, until their bodies can't produce sufficient hormones. Without proper medico care, they go into early menopause. If the employer is decent, they can live well later, but often, the girls end up as servants or worse, ancient before their time."

"What about normal women like us?" Saree asked. "I guess we need to do a lot more research before we buy anything."

Tyron shook his head. "No, Katryn and I already did. Mid-market or better machines recommend the mother interface with the surrogate womb for one to two hours a day during the first trimester. Then one hour every other day during the second, decreasing to twice a week during the third. More isn't necessarily better, no matter what the wealthy believe. But there are plenty of perfectly healthy children born with no mother interface. Some children will need gene editing to avoid common issues, but that happens with or without a mother interface. There is a small amount of hard evidence that suggests mother-interface children are healthier. There's also a small statistical difference in emotional intelligence scores, incarceration rates, and life success like schooling. But they can tie most of those to socio-economic factors. And those assessments aren't done until later, when parenting has far more of a role than gestation."

Katryn turned to Saree. "Really, the mid-level machines are great all on their own, if the initial priming is done properly and good nutrients are used. So, if something happened after the initiation, it's not a big deal. The baby will be healthy and just as well-adjusted as any other kid. There's also a tiny statistical probability that mother-interface machines do a better job of passing on immunities—although those are easily added later—and special talents. So, for you"—she waved across them—"if you want your kid to have ^*timespace*^ talents, you should use the interface."

Tyron shook his head. "I think it's junk science. Male talents are passed down just as consistently, and the only thing that happens there is fertilization. If there's no need for a father interface, there's no need for a mother. And there is some risk to the mother."

Katryn scoffed. "The same as any medico device that interacts with the blood stream. There's a minimal risk of infection, skin damage, nutrient depletion, and vein damage, but they're all avoidable."

The argument sounded rehearsed. Ruhger would bet they'd had it before.

"Hmm." Lashtar poked at her holo. "The wealthy think their kids come out better emotionally adjusted if there's a positive mother-interface. The surrogate woman must think positive thoughts, read intelligent books, listen to classical music, and feel love. Some use inhaled drugs to make the surrogates feel good, and then those substances are filtered out of the blood interface." Her face screwed up in horror, and she pushed the document away. "Don't want to read that. Some of these people are insane."

Ruhger needed to move the crew along. "Do we stay here and buy or move on? I don't want to get caught here. Not with the initial report of assassins. If we're not ordering, we need to fold."

"These are good medico machines, but they're super expensive, and I'd bet that the failure rate is higher than reported." Tyron shook his head. "Let's just move on."

"Why would you think the failure rate is high?" Katryn turned to Tyron. "These are top of the line."

"Because I'd bet the bottom and top lines are manufactured together. The only difference is the mother interface and the shiny exterior. The wealthy don't report the failures because they don't care. It's not them in the interface, and they simply start over with a new machine." Tyron snorted. "They couldn't be caught with anything less than the best name, even if it's not actually better."

Ruhger brought up the fold controls. "Good enough for me. Let's fold to a system we know has good medico manufacturers of all kinds. We'll need to upgrade our medico suite for kids, too."

"You should have decided that earlier." An armored figure stood inside the Command Center hatch.

Alarm shot through Ruhger. "Emergen—" His vision narrowed and wavered, and an alarm rang.

"A boring discussion." The voice sounded dispassionate. "When will I find someone interesting?"

Chapter Four

SAREE

Saree blinked but saw only darkness. Had *Lightwave* lost power? No.

Someone had invaded and most likely, stunned all of them. She closed her eyes again, hoping whoever it was hadn't noticed her movement. She floated, her body shifting slightly, as if she was being moved. If they were monitoring her vital signs, they'd know she was awake, so she tried to roll over. Her right arm was secured. Tugging gently, she found her left arm, legs, and torso were also secured but not with straps around wrists and ankles. A full suit in an isolation tank, perhaps? Or a specialty grav field, like they used for burn victims.

"You're awake." The voice was androgynous and pleasant, almost certainly run through an anonymizer. "Now, you are interesting, Saree of Lightwave Clutch. There are so many people who want you for so many reasons with such big rewards. But like most highly sought-after items, receiving the promised benefits is challenging. Will you be worth the risk? Maybe if you don't cooperate. Or maybe the risk is too much and I should fold *Lightwave* into a black hole."

Saree didn't reply. She wasn't going to help this individual. And getting *Lightwave* to do anything without the cooperation of one of them would be extremely difficult. But the being had boarded somehow. She recalled a voice telling them that they were boring. The only thing she'd discuss was payment for release of the crew and the folder.

"Fortunately, someone already on the wrong side of the law wants Quinn of Cygnus. Familia connections make transfers almost risk-free."

Staying silent was more difficult, but she'd expected the being to threaten Q. She was the obvious target. The rest of the crew expected it, too. Ruhger would have a harder time remaining quiet but would hold out regardless. She'd keep listening, but if the being demanded something dangerous, she'd drop into ^*timespace*^ and alert the Sa'sa.

"You've all been threatened and tortured before, so I'm not going to waste my time. If necessary, I will torture Q to get you to do what I want, but I'm sure you expect that as well. I hope we can come to an equitable agreement. If you pay, I go away, you go away, and we're all happy. Of course, I could come back at any time and demand more, but I probably won't. The risk isn't worth the diminishing rewards. So, the initial payment must be very large. Also, I'm not doing this on my own or for myself. There is a group of us working on a larger project, so even if you succeed in getting rid of me, others will follow. You won't find us either. I'm not some ridiculous villain to tell you all my secrets or motivations. I just need a lot of credits, then I'll release all of you. Simple."

For someone who claimed to not be a ridiculous villain, they were talking a lot. Saree stayed silent, waiting for him to name a figure.

Light bloomed. Saree squinted while tears dripped down her temples. She blinked the liquid away. The blur resolved into a list of bank accounts, including Lightwave Clutch's Sa'sa bank account, with identifying information. The list appeared to be correct.

"Leave sufficient funds in each account to stay open and not raise alarms. The credits will be transferred into the list of institutions I'll give you. Once I confirm the transfers, I'll let all of you go. Simple."

Saree doubted there was anything simple involved. She had no guarantee they'd be released.

"You have no reason to trust me. But keeping you contained becomes more challenging the longer it goes on. And while I could kill all of you after I get the credits, that would be a terrible disservice to humanity. You are the only humans who can tune fold clocks. The aliens aren't reliable, and the massive clock arrays in the core systems aren't affordable. I've studied all of you, and I know that if I kill anyone in your crew, you'll spend the rest of your lives hunting me rather than working, so I don't want to do that. I understand the same thing will happen if I permanently damage any of you or leave any tricky timers or medical issues behind, so I won't do that. This is a simple transaction. But if you try to stall, I'll cut my losses and kill all of you. There are other lucrative targets, and eventually, they'll come within reach."

Transactional, but not as cut and dried as the being claimed. Still, she had enough information to make a counterproposal. "I'll transfer all the funds into a third-party escrow account triggered by *Lightwave* folding to a destination of my choosing. Then I'll send a message from that system that *Lightwave* is intact and functioning correctly. Don't leave any traps behind, or we will hunt you down. I will not fold without my entire crew and clutch on board, in the same healthy condition they were prior to this encounter. If you take someone with you, or damage them, I will fight to the death, even if that means the destruction of *Lightwave* and everyone on it. Could I refuse to fold or report to the escrow company after folding? Yes. Is it likely? No. I keep my word. Is that a chance you're willing to take? Because the risks of me double-crossing you are much lower than the opposite."

"I accept. If you attempt to alert the institutions, the Sa'sa, or anyone else, I'll kill all of you."

"Agreed." Credits were relatively easy to come by and trying to break free of an unknown captor who infiltrated *Lightwave* so easily was chancy. She'd take the simple route. "I'm sure you're going to leave some sort of weapon in *Lightwave* to kill us after the credit transfer. I won't send the confirmation to the escrow company until we've searched every centimeter of *Lightwave*. Be patient."

"I will not injure or kill any of you or damage *Lightwave* if you deliver the credits. I won't leave anything behind, either. I trust your word. I have created an escrow with Sirius Central Bank, with the specified triggers. Proceed with the transfer by voice command."

The escrow account information appeared below the list of Saree's banks. She sighed and checked the escrow account's release criteria. It was correct, although she changed the notifying communications account from their common comms to one of their Gov Human comms. That should be harder to fake. She considered starting *Lightwave*'s lockdown procedures with a voice command, but secured in an isolation tank, it wouldn't do any good. She may as well transfer funds. "Sa'sa Bank, *Lightwave* Clutch account 170142..." It took depressingly little time to wipe out the clutch's savings. At least the being wasn't stealing individual crew member savings, not even her small personal account, which seemed strange. But desperation made people more determined, so perhaps the being was wiser than they initially appeared.

"Excellent. I'll leave you now, and you'll be released shortly. Please make your fold as soon as possible because you will not enjoy the results if you do not fulfill your word."

Saree sniffed. "If you kill us, it's likely the Sa'sa will abandon humanity and take their fold clocks back. I don't know what your organization's goals are, but unless it's being trapped in your systems forever, I recommend you release us. If you, or anyone else in your organization, attempt this again, or try to kill us now, you will not like the results either."

"Consider where you are at this moment. I could easily kill all of you, but I won't."

Saree listened but heard nothing. If she was in an isolation tank, the being had probably shut off her comms and walked away. She sank into ^*timespace*^; perhaps the being would leave some clue. But she ^*saw*^ nothing unusual.

Time passed. After two hours and twenty-four minutes, a click sounded, followed by a hiss, then a seam in front of her face unsealed. Ruhger glowered down at her, his expression morphing into relief when she blinked. "I'm okay. Just get me out of here."

"Working on it." He moved toward her feet, and the seam unsealed with a sticky pulling sound. "You're in an isolation suit in an isolation tank. An IsoSafe, as a matter of fact." He held out a hand. "You should be able to sit up now."

Still in the immersion suit, Saree took his hand and sat. Then she twisted to free her arms from the suit and let go of Ruhger to place her hands on the sides of the tank and pull her legs from the inner suit. "Everyone is okay?"

"Grant, Loreli, and Tyron regained consciousness about the same time I did. Chief and Lashtar are waking slowly. Q and Katryn are still out. I think the being used a stunner, set for an adult human male, so less body mass means more time before shaking it off. We put Q and Katryn on our medfloats, since they've both had medical issues." He stretched his hands to her.

She grasped his hands and jumped out of the isolation tank. "I told that being that if any of us were injured, I wouldn't release the funds." Ruhger's solid arms closed around her, and she hugged him tight, then pulled free to check on the crew.

Grant, already in his seat, pressed his fingertips against his temples. "This was a robbery? Really?"

"Yes." Her crew was safe. Loreli sat next to Grant, also rubbing her head. Chief and Lashtar were on the couch, Chief attempting to sit up and Lashtar twitching beside him. Tyron stood next to a medfloat, scrolling through his holo. Katryn's body lay slack on the medfloat, Q on the one next to her.

Saree trotted to the back for her armor. "The being just wanted credits. I transferred them into an escrow account. We have time to check for devices, although the being claimed they wouldn't leave any behind. Then we fold and send a message, releasing the escrow." In her armor compartment, she stepped into the lower half and made sure her group comms were on so they could all hear her. "I promised to release the credits. But I also told the being they'd better not leave any parting gifts. Since my e-torc was still on, I'm betting that the entire conversation was recorded."

"I'll pull that so we can all listen. Unless the being deliberately turned off the recorders, the vids in *Lightwave* should have captured everything, too." Tyron scrolled through his holo. "Then I'll start scanning the exterior, trying to figure out how that being got in here."

"Ugh. That's a big hit to our accounts." Grant sighed. "No new medico equipment for us. I'll start the interior scan."

Saree put the top half of her armor on, sealed it, and returned, stopping next to the medfloats. Both women were unconscious, but stable. "No, wait. Tyron, I want you to turn your exterior scan over to Ruhger, Grant, and Loreli, so you can start on the net. We've got to know how this being broke through *Lightwave*'s shields and security. When Katryn and Q recover, they can take the net. Chief and Lashtar can start scanning the interior when they wake fully."

"I've got the interior surveillance vids." Tyron pushed a vid to the big screen. "The being used a visual disrupter, but I've tracked them the whole way and added a green outline so you can see them easily. It's wearing full soft armor, so the chances of finding DNA are very slim."

A view of *Lightwave*'s Alpha airlock corridor appeared. A bod-pod interior hatch opened, a slight shimmer barely noticeable. Then bright green flared, outlining a figure. The being paused, then strode along the passageway, stopping at the Command Center hatch. It opened, they stepped inside, and the view switched to the interior. The shimmer turned off, and the being appeared in black, soft armor and spoke while firing a stunner. The being shackled everyone's wrists, then returned to their shuttle, towing the IsoSafe. It placed Saree inside, removed her shackles, and locked the IsoSafe. Then the being stunned everyone with a second dose, removed their shackles, and returned to wait near the IsoSafe. They appeared to read the IsoSafe screen, then remained standing in that exact position during the being's extortion of Saree. The being then returned to the bod-pod, closing the hatch.

A view of the exterior of *Lightwave* appeared. "I've sped this up," Tyron said. A small shimmering bubble flew to *Lightwave* and attached to the side, enclosing the entire bod-pod ejection port, then detached and flew away. "Doesn't appear to have dropped any surprises inside or out, but it's hard to tell. They shouldn't have been able to get so close to *Lightwave*, and they definitely shouldn't have gotten through our shields. Or been able to latch on, let alone get through a bod-pod. I've got a lot of questions and very few answers."

"Were you able to track the shuttle?" Ruhger flipped through screens.

"No. Or not yet. It remained cloaked, and I wanted to concentrate on *Lightwave*'s safety."

Saree took Q's lax hand in hers. "Grant, if you and Loreli can sweep the exterior of *Lightwave*, especially around Alpha, Ruhger can attempt to track the shuttle."

"Already got remotes set up to scan in a grid." Grant pointed at the big screen; the view of the shuttle bay must be live because a remote was flying into view. "Loreli and I will suit up and check it all in person. That being got through, so who knows what else he could do to our net?"

Her family was wonderfully competent. "Thanks."

Chief helped Lashtar rise from the couch. "We'll suit up and start on the interior scans. Initial scans show nothing, but the being could have dropped a cloaked remote. I've turned the interior sensors and defenses to maximum, so if you leave the Command Center, be sure you're in armor. All our suits are tied into the system, but no sense in taking chances. I've also turned the air pressure up. If there's a flying remote, it's likely to get swept into an air return." Taking Lashtar's hand, they walked to the armor compartments. "We'll have to turn up the air and scan in here, too, once everyone's in armor. And I've marked that bod-pod as inoperable, whether it is or not. And once we're in a secure location, we'll energize the hull."

"Excellent, Chief, thanks." Q's medfloat readout flashed—she was waking. Saree squeezed her hand. "You're safe, Q. We're all safe." She repeated the words because both women's hearing would return first.

Q's eyelashes fluttered, then snapped open. She put a hand to her head. "Stunner, right?"

"Yes. Got all of us."

"Blast and rad." She sat up with a groan. "I knew there was something wrong, but I ignored it. Sorry."

Saree snorted. "No need to be sorry. Multiple failures got us here. Go get a drink and a snack, then get your armor on. You too, Katryn. Take your time. Recovery will be slower for both of you because you got a full force stun twice."

"Ugh." Katryn rubbed her eyes. "No wonder I feel like sand scooter scat." Tyron helped her sit up, then pulled her off the medfloat and into a hug. They clung, whispering.

Q wrinkled her nose, jumped off the medfloat, and jogged to her armor compartment. "Back in a few."

Saree chuckled. No sense in telling Q to take it easy. Katryn followed, much slower, Tyron hovering. Time to handle the rest of the problem. Saree crossed the Command Center and sat in her chair. "Ruhger, let me know when we can safely fold out. I don't want to push this being too much or give anyone a way to question my word."

"Copy that, Clutch Leader." Ruhger lifted a brow, with his tiny smile lightening his countenance. "I've got multiple folds planned to systems with adequate comms. Just need a safety report from the interior and exterior scan teams. Remotes have found nothing."

"Understood." Grant and Loreli trod by in their hardsuits. Saree brought up the exterior vid on the Alpha side. "Grant, Loreli, I'll be watching while you're out. Use safety lines."

"Copy that, Queen Bee. I'm in no mood to play." A personnel hatch on the crew level opened, and two figures stepped out, fastening safety lines to the exterior. Bouncing slightly, they crossed the Alpha passenger level, walking one meter apart, then turned around and covered the same territory on a diagonal. The careful scan took time but was necessary. "Nothing to report, Captain, Clutch Leader. We scraped off some oxidation on a sensor, but I don't think that had anything to do with the intruder."

"Copy that, Exterior Team. Return now." Saree tracked her crew members until both stood in the crew passageway. She turned to Ruhger.

"Interior team reports nothing found except a couple of flying remotes, found crushed in an air return garbage bin. They were tiny and too mangled to figure out what they were. Vid, for sure, but beyond that is unknown. I've contained the remains and will look for manufacture marks later. We're letting the system analyze other debris for DNA and defining characteristics but haven't found anything yet. I doubt we will."

Saree nodded. "All right. Let's get everyone in seats, fold, and release the escrow. We'll continue the search and investigation after we fold again."

"Assuming we get there in one piece and remain that way after the credits transfer." Ruhger glowered at his holo.

Saree squeezed his forearm. "Where are we going? It's got to be somewhere with comms but not somewhere we'll be noticed."

"I've got Tyron changing *Lightwave*'s designation. Then we'll fold to Sextans." He turned his hand up and took hers. "Not Sa'sa, but the constellation entry. No one would expect us to go there, but they have excellent comms. From there, we'll go to an uninhabited system that I won't specify until we sweep the Command Center."

"Excellent plan." Saree hoped they were ready to go. "*Lightwave*, report if unable to fold. If nothing heard, we'll fold in one minute." She brought up the *Lightwave* Gov Human comms, double-checked that the location reporting was off, and readied the notification to the Sirius escrow. It hurt to lose so many credits to an unknown entity funding some larger plan she knew nothing about, but they'd figure it out, eventually. With her crew, they'd find the individual, the way the person infiltrated, and the larger organization. Then they'd figure out what kind of organization stole from them. Even if they had a good cause, the theft wouldn't go unanswered; that only encouraged more theft, and eventually, it wouldn't be bloodless.

Most likely, the group's cause was destructive or obstructive. Most sentient beings were inclined to cling to the past, rather than embrace the future. While that served them well as hunter-gatherer societies, it could be counterproductive in modern times. As Saree mused, the seconds ticked away.

"*Lightwave*, prepare for fold in five, four, three, two, fold." Ruhger swept the surveillance to the big screen, relegating their intruder to a smaller spot at the bottom. "We've arrived safely in Sextans."

Saree poked the send button. "Message sent releasing the escrow. Our safety cushion is gone." While the casual brushing aside of their security hurt the most, the lack of fallback credits was dangerous, especially with Gov Human actively hunting them. Using Gov Human's comms was slightly risky but more secure. Although, that being might be part of Gov Human. "We'll wait for the confirmation of receipt from Sirius Central Bank. With the comms here, that shouldn't take more than an hour. Be ready to fold if we're discovered."

"Copy that, Clutch Leader." Ruhger pointed at his face. "I've got a selection of emergency folds ready. Crew, if you're not doing anything else, continue manually searching *Lightwave*, but be ready for fold and remain in armor."

"I'm preparing snacks, but I'm ready to secure everything at any moment," Loreli said. "We can't wait an entire hour without sustenance!"

Q giggled. "That's ridiculous. But awesome." She trotted from the Command Center, accompanied by Grant. Tyron and Katryn scrolled through their holos, while Chief and Lashtar hovered near machinery in the engine room.

Saree certainly appreciated Loreli's care. Q was still too thin, and being stunned twice wasn't going to help.

"Don't worry, mon Cap-i-tan!" Loreli, in a small vid at the bottom of the big screen, lifted a platter. "No frying or even any cooking involved, even though it limits my creativity." She placed the platter on the counter and waved off the vid.

It seemed a lifetime had passed, but Saree had boarded *Lightwave* in Dronteim only a few standard years ago. She'd been nervous back then, but in reality, she'd been extraordinarily fortunate. Not only had she escaped capture by Familia, she'd found a family. She smiled at Ruhger. Even with all the difficulties and heartaches, she wouldn't change anything.

Hopefully, these last few hours would turn out the same in hindsight.

CHAPTER FIVE

RUHGER

RUHGER GROUND HIS TEETH. Days of searching and they found no trace of the extortioner. The being left no DNA or other physical clues behind, not even in the IsoSafe. They'd wiped the memory on that medico device clean—the only thing on it was Saree's captivity. There was no sign the being took any medico records the device collected about her, but with the extortioner's obvious skills, that might not be correct.

Tyron and Katryn believed the being might even be a remote, with comms to a sentient elsewhere. Even the best human-seeming remote didn't have speech patterns like that, although a custom job was possible.

At least they'd discovered how the being had infiltrated *Lightwave*. The extortioner's shuttle had already been in orbit, flying just outside their specified path. On their wide area surveillance, the shuttle fired cold thrusters, then cloaked. A smaller cloaked shuttle or pod separated from the main shuttle and matched velocities with tiny puffs of cold gas. Then it slid through their shields at an extremely low velocity. That meant the infiltrator had the highly classified Gov Human shield encryption key. The cloaking was highly advanced, shifting frequencies and methods constantly. They'd back-tracked the pod and shuttle from Lightwave; even knowing the orbits, finding the spacecraft on surveillance was challenging. The origins of the cloaking devices and programming were unknown.

After attaching to *Lightwave*, the extortioner exploited a safety protocol in the bod-pod to open it and get inside. *Lightwave's* original bod-pod was gone, probably moved into the IsoSafe's spot inside the enemy shuttle. They must have destroyed the beacon because there was no sign of it. After leaving the Command Center, the being or remote returned the same way. The pod used tiny puffs of cold gas to glide through their shields and return to the larger, cloaked shuttle. That shuttle moved away equally slowly, at a constant sunward velocity. It had remained cloaked until *Lightwave* folded out. If they'd stayed, they could have found it and destroyed it, but it was likely larger threats remained in the orbit. Or resided on the planet or station. Folding away to fight another day was the better part of valor.

They'd all watched recorded surveillance vid until their eyes bled, searching for other shuttles, pods, and remotes. They'd inspected the entirety of *Lightwave*, examining smaller locations with remotes. Q and Katryn complained of aching knees after crawling through kilometers of ducting. They'd energized the hull several times, burning off their sensors and anything the enemy left behind. Then the crew inspected every square centimeter and replaced sensors. Katryn and Q had also modified *Lightwave*'s shielding to change configurations randomly. They'd also changed the near-view surveillance to search for the new style of cloaking the infiltrator had used, but they weren't sure it would work.

Lightwave, originally a military troop transport, had far too many bod-pods for their small crew. Ruhger ran the odds over and over, but keeping all of them was riskier than taking a second or two longer to reach one. They removed two of every three escape pods, welding the hatches and filling the gaps with cerimetal foam. Getting to an active bod-pod added less than a second. They also changed the release protocol that allowed the being entry. It would slow an emergency escape by a few seconds, but the time was nothing next to the vulnerability. Once in a safe fringe system, they'd sell the extra bod-pods, putting a few extra credits in Lightwave Clutch's empty accounts. At least the being—the enemy—hadn't taken their personal savings.

Grant had analyzed the extortioner's words, sentence structure, and mannerisms. They were mid-level system generic human, without any hint of an origin system profile. He was fairly certain the being speaking was human, rather than some other sentient. The being spoke with a definite superiority; they thought little of the crew's intelligence. Even Saree was treated like a child, although the extortioner acknowledged she had an important role, especially for humanity. The most telling part of the speech was the revelation that the being was part of a group. But the group's goal was unknown.

Grant and Tyron both speculated, based on the overall speech, that there might be a tie to the Humans First movement. Not the idiots they'd battled in the past, but perhaps a smarter group, working more quietly in the political sphere. But the being didn't display true xenophobia, just a declaration of alien unreliability. Which, from a human perspective, was true. The Sa'sa were leaving frontier human system clock maintenance to *Lightwave*, and they could only do one at a time. But the telling part was lumping the Sa'sa into a group as "aliens" rather than a specific species or their more correct designation as Time Guild members. Both men admitted they could be biased in their assessment.

They'd all considered artificial intelligence, too, but AIs probably wouldn't care about humanity's needs. They believed the being was human or trained by humans.

Other oddities abounded. The being was certain that other rich beings would "come within reach" and seemed to think nothing of killing all of them. Folding them into a sun seemed short-sighted. *Lightwave* would be missed; an investigation would bring attention to the system at the least. If the organization would cut their losses by abandoning their assets in orbit, it was no wonder they needed a lot of credits. They speculated that the being might float in orbit continuously, just waiting for the right opportunity. If so, an AI or remote seemed more likely.

Saree shifted restlessly in her seat next to his. "I've written messages for the Time Guild and Gov Human about the theft. I think, even though we don't know how far this individual or organization can reach, that I should also send a message to The Guide™ about the system. They were waiting in orbit, if not for us, other rich beings. Are they still there, or have they moved on to another system that attracts the wealthy? The Guide™ should warn beings about the extortion scheme. Beyond the warnings, the group clearly studied us specifically, so that makes me wonder again if there's a tracker on *Lightwave* we haven't found."

Ruhger offered his hand to her, palm up. She placed her hand in his and he clasped it gently; the physical connection offered relief and reassurance. "We've got to investigate the fold generators and the power system without destroying everything. I'm positive there's a passive tracker at the very least."

"It makes sense. The manufacturers want to know where and how their products are being used."

Ruhger squeezed Saree's hand. "The 'how' would require more than a passive system."

"Not necessarily, but there are a myriad of emitter sources on a fold generator." Chief twirled his wrench. "There are command and control interfaces, status reporting, go-no criteria, and a lot of others. Even under manual control in the engine room, status information is transmitted. It would be easy to bury statistics in that as noise."

"Or not bother to bury it, just transmit in packets." Katryn smirked. "Break it into little bits and no one will notice. And if they do, they'll need a decryption key to read it." She sighed. "It's probably next to impossible to break."

Chief shook his head. "There's really no way to prevent comms leaking from fold generators, either. Not if you want to fold."

"Someday, we'll buy an old fold generator and tear it apart." Tyron sniffed. "But since our credits are gone, that might take a while." He stood and stretched, then gazed at Saree. "We're all tired and battered. Can we take a rest day or two?"

Saree nodded. "That's an excellent idea. We'll get caught up on sleep and spend time in the medico to heal the bruises. Since we cleaned during our search, we can source the replacements we need. Q and I will look at the Time Guild's list, and develop a fold plan with Ruhger. We'll fold in and out fast, tuning clocks, so we can build up our emergency fund again." She held up a hand. "Without decimating our individual savings. I appreciate everyone's willingness to pitch in, but I'd rather not. Those are your credits, not the clutch's or *Lightwave*'s."

Ruhger had a bittersweet finding. "We have one other account that wasn't touched. During our transition into a clutch, we missed a small *Lightwave* maintenance account. It's for emergency repairs. Our parents' company, Security Fold, set it up when we first split into a semi-independent transport. However, it's at a Nexus bank, and I'm sure Gov Human is monitoring Nexus closely. If we need funds, we can get them, but we'll give away our current location."

"We can always use an escrow or another intermediary, but that means fees." Lashtar shrugged. "Worth remembering." She rose. "Come on, Bhoher. I need sleep. The kids can keep hashing this out, but I'm tired." Chief captured her hand and followed her out.

Ruhger rose. "I'm younger than they are, but I'm all for sleep. Come on, maybe something brilliant will infiltrate our dreams."

"Nightmares, more likely." Q bounded from her seat. "See you in the morning!" She ran from the Command Center.

"We've got the watch," Tyron said. Katryn nodded.

Ruhger sighed, wishing Q didn't have a reason for bad dreams. All he could do was support her and he would, no matter how many credits they had or didn't have. Saree tugged him toward their compartment. Sleep might not bring answers, but it couldn't hurt. Especially sleep with Saree.

"All stations, we've arrived in Emma; report issues immediately." Ruhger glanced at Saree, lying on her medfloat. "Like the last six folds, this is a tune-and-fold, unless there's a reason to stay. Ruhger out." Saree had assured him she was fine, that tuning ^*timespace*^ in Carina constellation was easy. Q backed Saree; they alternated between active and observer roles, so both got adequate rest. Still, he couldn't help but worry. They'd been zipping around Carina for four standard days, tuning ^*timespace*^ twice a day. It seemed like a heavy load, even if the clutch needed the credits.

"Retrieving messages now. Gov Human system is pinging like the shell of a bod-pod in a folder explosion." Tyron smirked. "Too soon?"

Tyron surprised Ruhger—he didn't often make tension-relieving quips. "Not at all."

Saree scrolled through the Gov Human messages. "I guess our warning finally got through. A lot of these are yelling at us for informing the media. They forget we don't work for them."

"We'll look at the timing of the return messages—that might tell us who's trustworthy." Tyron tilted his head.

Katryn smirked. "Or who is too busy for the Clocker."

Saree rolled her eyes. "It gives us another data point. The more we compile, the better our chances of figuring out who in Gov Human is acting against us. And humanity, for all that they claim to be pro-human."

Ruhger searched for more news on fold clocks. "There's an uptick in fold clock array purchases, and the price of soothing stones is rising. Governments are seizing soothing stones from people and medical facilities. Is the potential for better clock maintenance worth more than calming those with mental issues?"

"Back to the needs of the many outweigh the needs of the few." Saree grimaced. "But it's hard to say that fold transport outweighs the mental stability of many individuals. Especially when there's no evidence the stones need to be close to the clock. Spreading them across the inhabitable planets might be better."

Chief entered the Command Center. "Some systems must import food, water, or other survival necessities. Pavo did. I wonder, if the Universal Great Farmer's Collective could grow everything necessary for human life, would it have started a war?"

Lashtar followed Chief. "If it hadn't, your life would have been entirely different. Why look back at that?"

"If it offers clues into how our enemy thinks, I have to consider it." Chief sat in his usual chair. "We need all the clues we can get."

Saree pointed at her holo. "Well, we've got a big one here. An official condemnation of our actions informing the media from our old frenemy General Jodl. He's got a lot of nerve."

"It's toothless." Ruhger squeezed Saree's hand. "He's got no authority over you or us."

"A desperate attempt at relevancy and a bid for attention." Grant waved a hand dismissively. "I doubt he's part of Humans First, either, but we'll add him to the list."

Saree swept her hand through her holo. "I'll look at the rest later. I need to back up Q now." She relaxed into the medfloat and quickly fell into the relaxed but strangely alert ^timespace^ body position, matching Q.

It was odd that he could tell when the rest of the crew couldn't. He wasn't always sure about Q. Perhaps Saree and Q had a mental defense while in ^timespace^ but it didn't affect him because he posed no threat. But no one here was a threat, so that didn't make sense either.

Grant turned to him. "Interesting offers coming from Emma, Ruhger. They claim to build fold clocks, available only to humans."

"Fascinating. There are fold clock arrays manufacturers, but I've never heard of one selling only to humans. Let's dig into that." Ruhger brought up a local net interface but hesitated before accepting. "Net connection is expensive here."

"Tourist tax." Grant pushed a message to the big screen. "We have a formal invitation to visit the clock manufacturing plant. They're just getting started and would like Saree's expert opinion on their designs."

"That was fast." Alarm klaxons rang in Ruhger's head. "They must have been watching for us. They have a Sa'sa clock here, right?" He crossed the deck to stand next to Saree's medfloat. She was still in ^timespace^ but showed no signs of distress. He rounded the end of her bed, standing between the two medfloats. Q didn't seem disturbed, either, but he'd stay here until they came out or needed recall.

Grant said, "They do. If they've been tracing our travels—and a lot of beings are, including Gov Human—then they could have been surveilling the fold clock orbit. A folder pops in, they focus visual sensors, and boom, we're identified. *Lightwave* started as a standard military troop transport, but we've changed it over the years. It's unique."

The crew chattered, but Ruhger stopped paying attention. Time ticked away, too slowly. He was about to call Saree when she stirred. He waited for her and Q to awaken.

Q blinked. "Yuck. That is one giant mess."

"Was one giant mess." Saree sat up. "Whatever they're doing here, it needs to stop."

Grant joined them. "We've got an invitation to visit their fold clock manufacturing facility. Sounds like we need to, even though it might not be the best idea."

Ruhger turned to face him. "Any special reason other than the usual security concerns?"

"That's the major one. They have a lot of heavily armed security at their plant when there doesn't seem to be a threat from the local population. They have a lot of political support, because the business brings high-paying jobs." Grant grimaced. "And Tyron and Katryn are having a difficult time infiltrating their net, partially because of the control the local government has over the net in general on Emma, partially because their security is extremely good. I don't think we should accept the invitation."

Tyron spun his chair around to face them. "What if we had backup? Wouldn't General Kerr or Jodl be interested in this? If we can separate them from Doc's father, that is."

"Let's not chance that." Ruhger slashed his hand through the air. "We should forward the request to Gov Human, along with our concerns, and get a report from them. No reason to risk ourselves. And we should fold out now that Saree and Q are done. We'll thank them and tell them we'd be happy to return later, when the needs of the Time Guild aren't so pressing."

"Ooh, so diplomatic!" Q snickered. "You're turning into a politician."

Ruhger shuddered. "Take that back. I'm not some mudhugging FLOB." He extended his hand to Saree. She took it and slid off the medfloat, following him to their usual seats. He opened comms with Loreli, the only one of them not in the Command Center. "Next fold is already planned to Miaplacidus. Any objections to folding?"

"Grant, reply to that invite as Ruhger suggested." Saree sat. "Ask them about security concerns, too. I'd like to know if they can explain their reasons other than normal fears of theft and espionage."

Grant nodded. "Give me a few moments, then we can fold."

Loreli's face appeared in the bottom corner of the Command Center screen. "No objections, but I'd like to remain in place for a few hours after the next fold or two for dinner."

Ruhger smiled. "Of course, Loreli. Suns forbid we interfere with your creative process."

"Don't you forget it! Loreli out." Her beaming visage disappeared.

"Well, that's unpleasant." Grant swept a vid to the screen.

A woman in a scarlet military-style uniform, covered in multihued ribbons and awards, with rank or position cords on her shoulders and a wide ribbon around her neck, stared down at them, her eyes narrowed, mouth pinched. "We insist you remain and lend your expertise to our endeavors. Humanity depends upon it! If you attempt to leave, we will fire and disable your fold transport."

"Clearly, she doesn't understand our capabilities." Saree jogged to her medfloat. "Don't wait. Fold out now."

Regardless of her command, Ruhger waited until she reclined, then brought up ship-wide comms. "Folding in five, four, three, two, fold. Report anomalies and issues immediately."

Tyron raised a hand. "I've got a big one. Where are we?"

Chapter Six

SAREE

Saree returned from ^timespace^ and opened her eyes. Ruhger stood over her, clearly worrying, along with Q and Grant hovering at her feet. "What's the matter?"

"We're not in Miaplacidus. Can you tell where we are?" Ruhger pointed at the surveillance up on the big screen. "Because the computer doesn't recognize the location. We think they hit us with a laser as we folded, imparting a lot of energy or perhaps damaging the fold generators or the fold power generation. Chief's investigating now. He said the fold generator controls are lit up with errors and catastrophic damage warnings."

Saree sat up. "I didn't notice anything odd in ^timespace^, but I wasn't doing anything active for fold, just smoothing ^timespace^ for both systems. It seemed very quiet here, especially compared to the chaos in Emma."

Q bounced in place. "If no one folds into this system, then ^timespace^ won't get disturbed, right?"

Saree smiled and wished she had Q's energy. "True." She turned to Ruhger. "I'm sure I can get the Sa'sa to help bring us back." She'd go back into ^timespace^ and reach out.

"Wherever 'here' is." Tyron grimaced. "Besides the computer not finding anything familiar, I'm not seeing the number of systems and galaxies I should. I also haven't seen any nebula, which seems truly strange. We may have folded very far from our destination."

"We've got bigger problems." Chief's face appeared on the Command Center screen. "The fold generators have been damaged. I think they intended to fire a warning shot but got closer than they should have, glancing the fold field generators. Two of the outer casings are damaged, exposing the interior."

"Or maybe they intended to fry the generators, so we couldn't fold out." Ruhger glowered.

Saree grimaced. "Did the laser energy surge send us to this unknown location? Or was it the breach of the fold generator casing? You've said in the past that breaking the seal created problems."

Chief shook his head. "Unknown. I'm sending remotes out now, but more than likely, I'll have to suit up and go out there. I'll definitely need to do that to repair them, assuming the damage can be fixed."

"Any estimate of how much energy would be helpful, Chief." Ruhger manipulated fold equations on his holo. "I'm assuming we'd fold on the planned vector, but the energy will affect how far, I think. Maybe."

Lashtar appeared next to Chief. "We've got another problem. Charging is very slow. I'm assuming we folded into interstellar space. We've got the engines running, but we should minimize power expenditures where we can."

Q wrapped her arms around her waist, and her shoulders rose. "Hopefully we won't have to feed the wallcoverings to the recycler for food."

Loreli bustled in, towing a tray. At Q's words, she dropped the tray at the table and hustled to them, folding Q into a hug. "Of course not, dahrling! Trust in Chef, she's got your back *and* your stomach." She released Q but grasped her shoulders gently. "I've got a year's worth of emergency rations squirreled away, plus at least a half-year of regular food. I'm prepared!"

"We'll use the wallcoverings for fuel long before food." Chief shrugged. "But we've also got plenty of fuel. One of the cargo holds is full of fuel bladders and another contains water. We have plenty of plas for the printers and kilos of emergency supplies. We'll be fine, Q."

Ruhger stepped next to Q, sliding her from Loreli's hold into his. "We've got you, kiddo. We're very well prepared for every contingency, whether that's theft or fold gone bad."

Q clung to him, no doubt remembering how she'd been trapped on Hal's folder while he desperately fought for survival. Saree rose from her medfloat and hugged Q and Ruhger—at least they were together. "Even if we never get back, it won't be anything like what you experienced. We're in control and can stay that way manually if necessary."

Q turned her head and smiled, a little tremulously. "I know. The surprise got me."

"That's what we're here for." Ruhger released Q, clasping Saree's hand for a moment, then letting her slip away. "But right now, rather than worrying about folding, I'll work with Tyron to find us the closest star and orient us for the best charging. Then thrust along that vector."

Since Q dropped her arms, Saree let her go and frowned at Ruhger. "You don't think we should remain in the same location, so we can reverse our fold?"

Ruhger shook his head. "No. We don't want to return to Emma, and I'm sure you can call the Sa'sa for help."

He had a point—no sense in returning to a place that attacked them. At least not without a lot of firepower behind them. "I'm sure too." But before that, they had to survive. "Let's split our efforts. Ruhger, you and Tyron get us power by orientation—thrust for the nearest star. Chief and Lashtar are working on the fold generator inspection, then building a repair plan. Q and I will dip into ^timespace^ again and get the Sa'sa to help us. Katryn, Grant, you want to help Chief? We'll need safeties for any outside work. Loreli, you can do what you do so well, or if you have time, you can help Chief."

"Hardsuits for everyone working on the fold generators, inside or out." Ruhger pointed at the armor compartments.

"Saree, can I help Chief?" Q turned to her, a crease in her brow showing her concern. "I don't want to go back into ^timespace^ if you're calling the Sa'sa."

Saree smiled at her. "Of course. No reason for you to join me." She should have thought about that; the Sa'sa were still wary of Q's presence in ^timespace^, even though they'd proven she wasn't a threat.

Loreli took Q's hand and towed her to the back. "Come on, we'll help Chief together, then you can minion for me. Lots of onions to chop, chop, chop! Why use powered tools when you have a minion?"

Q groaned, throwing her arms up dramatically. Saree chuckled, joined by the rest of the crew. Grant and Katryn followed them to the armor compartments. Ruhger returned to his seat, enlarging the surveillance screen and speaking quietly with Tyron.

Saree sat on her medfloat, ready to drop in again. But something Q said resonated. ^timespace^ was unusually quiet. If they were in interstellar space, that made sense. There wouldn't be any folders, soothing stones, or stores of transuranic metals to perturb ^timespace^. If they were in deep interstellar space, even the normal disruptions of ^timespace^ by solar flares or other natural phenomenon would be missing.

She swung her legs up and lay back. One other possibility existed. They could have changed planes, or dimensions, or universes; whatever separated their existence from others. If the fold mathematician theories were correct, there were an infinite number of parallel universes or planes that could be reached by fold. But if someone had made it safely to another universe, no one had returned.

Actually, the Sa'sa might have; it was hard to tell what they considered reality. But they'd implied their transitions were consciousness only; not a corporeal body. But their consciousness was shared, so if one clutch of Sa'sa went, then wouldn't all the Sa'sa experience it? Or maybe they did and thought it was normal, unremarkable? Perhaps they lived in many dimensions all the time.

But even if spanning the universes or dimensions was normal for the Sa'sa, it wasn't for humans. At least current humanity.

Future humanity would have to wait—she had her own problem to solve. Saree closed her eyes and concentrated on her breathing. It took longer to clear her mind than normal, but she entered ^timespace^ and ^looked^ at her surroundings.

As she expected, ^timespace^ was quiet, the ripples of their passage almost gone. She ^reached^, expanding her consciousness across ^*timespace*^, seeing everything but nothing. No pools of power, no ripples of fold, no ^*pull*^ of soothing stones; nothing. She ^*reached*^ in a different direction but again, found nothing. No sign of the Sa'sa, either.

A ringing tone sounded, recalling her from the beauty of ^*timespace*^. She had a body, and it was time to return, no matter how little she wanted to leave the serenity. She recalled her heartbeat and breath, anchoring into her flesh, and opened her eyes. The overhead whirled, and she slammed her eyes shut, gripping the medfloat's soft foam.

"Saree, are you okay?" The roughness in Ruhger's deep voice revealed his concern.

"Yes, but I overextended a bit." His big hand enclosed hers. "I'm a little dizzy, but it's getting better." The swooping in her stomach slowed and then steadied. She opened her eyes.

Ruhger glowered down at her. "Perhaps you need to set a more conservative alarm on that singing bowl. I don't like what happens when you get lost out there."

Saree raised the back of the medfloat to a seated position while she decided what to say. Ruhger didn't need any more of her worries, but she didn't want more pain, either. "I'm not really a fan either, but it's hard to define exactly what the medfloat is looking for, other than a period of time or a medical change. And once my medical status changes enough for the medfloat to pick up, I've probably gone too far. But next time we can find a medico we can trust, I'll work with them. Okay?"

Ruhger sat, sliding into her side, wrapping one arm around her and grasping her hand with his free hand. "You constantly terrify me." His glower smoothed. "I don't want to lose you."

She smiled grimly at him, squeezing his hand in return. "I don't want to be lost. But sometimes, you must push your limits for survival."

"I know." Ruhger sighed. "Since you already did that today, did you find anything?"

She shook her head. "No. Nothing. No soothing stones, no ripples in ^*timespace*^ other than what we created, no pools of power, nothing. I think we may be in an alternate reality or parallel universe or whatever it may be. There's no sign of the Sa'sa, either, but I didn't look for them until later. Next time, I'll start with them."

Ruhger's glower changed to a scowl. "After you've recovered. I'll make you a shake since Loreli is in Engineering." He rose. "Stay there." He jogged out the hatch.

She didn't need a shake, but he'd feel better if he did it, so she didn't object. "Tyron, have you found anything familiar?"

He spun his chair to face her. "No. The number of systems and galaxies have dropped significantly. The computer can't match anything in our reality or even as a time-progressed reality so far. If we were in a parallel universe, something should look the same, right? We're in a different reality entirely, I think."

"Are you sure we didn't just fold so far away that nothing looks right?" Her stomach tossed uneasily. Combined with her *timespace* experience, their situation might be rather perilous.

Tyron grimaced. "It's possible. We fold hundreds, thousands, and millions of light-years regularly. But if we folded a billion light-years, then it might be enough. I don't have the math to tell if a laser could add that much energy to our fold." He shrugged. "I think it's more likely the damage caused the fold to go wrong and sent us elsewhere. But when Ruhger returns, I'm done speculating—the math genius can reach his own conclusions." He chuckled.

The hatch whooshed, and the math expert entered, trotting to her with a muddy brown drink in his hand. "I used Loreli's recipe, but I must have missed something because hers don't look like this." He handed her the bev-tainer. "Tastes good, though."

She held up the drink. It looked like a mixture of dirt and sand with bits of green veggies and purple berry bits, but she sipped to avoid hurting his feelings. Dark chocolate hit her tastebuds, but the texture was a little gritty. "It tastes great. Maybe it just needs a little more blending?" He reached for the bev-tainer, and she yanked it away. "It's fine. Go work the math because that's what we need. I'll be just fine here."

"Are you sure?" Ruhger frowned.

"Yes." She put her hand on the back of his neck and pulled him in for a quick kiss. "Go. Figure this out. I'm right here, and I'm okay. The medfloat says so." She felt steady, too.

He kissed her again, then joined Tyron, bringing up a hologram of their universe big enough to walk through and throwing a vector across it. There was a lot of empty space in the model. Additional views of fold math and laser specifications followed, enclosing the two men in a bubble of color and lines.

She knew fold math basics, but what they were doing was far beyond her capabilities. After she recovered, she'd reach out to the Sa'sa. But not ^seeing^ any hint of them in ^timespace^ was troubling. She sucked her drink down, ignoring the grittiness and bursts of different flavors. A little more time on the blender would improve it, but the drink delivered the required nutrition and anchored her in reality. Ruhger would be less anxious once she drank it, too.

Regardless of where they were, Q's concerns were valid. Saree pulled up inventories and confirmed Chief and Loreli had underestimated. According to the computer, they could continue consumption at their current rate for another three years without issue. That was only partly comforting; three years stuck inside *Lightwave* would be challenging. But she was sure they could find their way back. Or if not back, to some place that allowed them to roam, even if they couldn't get out of their suits.

But to do that, they needed fold generators. Saree watched Chief's working group in the Engineering vids. Chief, Lashtar, Grant, Loreli, Katryn, and Q were in Engineering, helmets and gauntlets off. They needed to expand Engineering; there was no reason to crowd everything together and excellent reasons to separate the various mechanical plants for safety. And give Chief and Lashtar a bigger compartment plus more working room.

Chief pointed at a vid; a current view of the fold field generators next to an older view, both fully deployed. Four separate fifteen-meter-long arms ended in cubes, presumably containing the machinery or circuitry generating the fold field. Each field generator cube was five meters square. A meter of space separated the field generator cubes from each other, arranged in a square.

In the current view, corners were missing from two of the field generator cubes. One cube had lost a tiny corner. But the second field generator cube was heavily damaged; much of the corner was gone. The laser had sliced through the cube's entire height and a meter side-to-side, leaving a long, almost pyramidal section missing.

Inside the badly damaged cube, many long tubes filled with bright red ran between a dark gray cylinder on one side and a bracket on the other. The damaged tubes were dark, but the still intact red tubes flickered and sparked. Fine silver tracings—circuitry perhaps—embossed the interior of the cube's shell.

Chief placed a virtual marker near one of the working tube-cylinder combinations. "Clearly, these most important devices generate the fold field. How they work has been a closely guarded secret. Experimenters have drilled into the outer containment boxes and placed vids inside. They power the generators. The red tubes light up, spin, and blink. We assume that's normal. Then the fold transport disappears but doesn't fold into the programmed location; it's gone forever. Therefore, the enclosing container cubes must have a purpose, a part of the fold field generation. I propose we remove the heavily damaged box and bring it into the cargo hold where we can inspect and take it apart. Perhaps we can repair or rebuild the tubular devices and construct new outer box panels."

"There's no perhaps about it, Chief." Katryn's voice sparked with annoyance and worry. "We have to repair it or go nowhere."

"Except into madness," Q muttered. "I didn't like it the first time."

Loreli hip-bumped Q, sending her crashing into Lashtar. "Dahrling! You're not alone with warring AIs. We won't go mad, and we *will* figure it out. Won't we, Chief?" She raised her brows in a challenging stare.

"Absolutely." He nodded sharply. "I'm an excellent reverse engineer, and I've always wanted to get my hands on a set of fold generators. I'm looking forward to the challenge." He rubbed his palms together, the rasp of his calloused hands loud over the comms. "Looking at the dimensions of the containing structures, I think Katryn and Q are the only ones with a chance to get inside and disconnect the box from the strut. But I'm concerned about the undamaged generators. We've shut down the fold generators at the Engineering control interface, but power still runs through them, enough to fry any remote I send in. There must be an internal source. So, we must breach the seal of the fold generator power compartment first and shut that down. Only then will it be safe to disconnect the generator box."

Katryn raised her hand. "Won't we need to disconnect both damaged boxes? Repairing the one out there seems risky."

"It might be." Chief frowned. "But it might be riskier to remove the box than repair in place. We can inspect first, then decide. Remotes show a lot, but there's nothing like the Mark I eyeball." He tapped his cheek just below his eye. "Here's my proposed operation. We'll enter the fold generator power compartment inside *Lightwave* and turn the power off. Then we'll check the deployed fold field generators using remotes. If the power is off, we'll send in smaller remotes to inspect and see if we can disconnect the cubes with remotes. If not, Katryn and Q will inspect from a distance. Then if you two agree it's safe, Katryn or Q will disconnect the box with Loreli and Grant as external safeties. I'd rather be out there, but you're both younger and quicker than me and Lashtar." He huffed, much like Ruhger would in similar circumstances. "If *any* of us think disconnection is unsafe, we'll use remotes and cut through the deployment arm instead. I'd rather fix it later than injure any of us. Things can be replaced. People cannot. Objections and additions, please. Lashtar, you first."

"You'll bring the plan to Ruhger and Saree first?"

"Yes. We'll need approval. Saree's watching, though." Chief winked so fast Saree wasn't sure he'd done it.

Lashtar tilted her head. "That doesn't count. Barring objections from them, I have none of my own."

"Katryn." Chief pointed at her.

"I'm not particularly talented with mechanical devices, but the plan seems reasonable. I concur."

"Q, you're next."

"I'm good with mechanicals, so if someone's going inside those cubes out there, it should be me." She quirked a brow. "Not a huge fan, since you've been frying remotes, but if we can get the power off, I'll do it."

Chief nodded. "If we can't get the power off, we'll have to find a different way. If a remote can't do it, I'm not risking a person."

Grant raised his hand. "That's covered my only objection. Concur with the plan."

Loreli nodded. "Concur with the plan." She pointed at Chief. "Don't you dare damage my minion. Chopping onions is so tedious." Her attempt at levity fell flat. They were all too nervous for jokes.

"Personnel safety is primary." Chief sent a request to her, Ruhger, and Tyron to join them over comms. She accepted, changing from a viewer to participant, and listened carefully to Chief's operations brief. Tyron concurred if he could also be outside as a tertiary safety, nearer to *Lightwave*'s hatch, and Chief agreed.

Ruhger's mouth twisted. "Once we're working outside, I'll join Tyron in the hatch. Full safety cabling, of course, no free flying. We'll have to run additional cables to the generator cubes. We can't rely on remotes alone to bring the boxes inside cargo. Q and Katryn won't have a safety attachment point other than that cube, a remote, or their safety partner. I don't want to risk them attaching to one of the other fold field generator cubes; it could set up a current of some sort."

"Excellent thought. I hadn't considered that, but with the little we know about these things, and the amount of power they use, it's a possibility." Chief nodded.

"I'll be in Engineering when you breach the compartment. Q, for that part, you'll be up here with Saree."

Q nodded, her eyes wide. "I don't want to go into a fold generator power compartment ever again."

Saree smiled at Ruhger, loving his protective streak, then returned her attention to Chief. "Concur with the plan as stated. I'll remain here, ready to adjust any of *Lightwave*'s other systems as necessary, and watch the surveillance." She shrugged. "Just because we haven't seen anyone or anything yet, that doesn't mean there isn't anyone or anything."

"That was my next recommendation, thank you." Chief nodded. "Team, take a break. When Ruhger arrives, we'll enter the fold power generation compartment. Chief out."

Saree swept her connections off and slid from the medfloat. Since she was steady, she crossed the Command Center to Ruhger. He turned to face her. Saree reached and put her arms around Ruhger's neck. "Be careful, and make sure everyone else is careful, too. I don't want to lose you to something stupid."

He smiled, the larger lift of his lips he saved for her. "Of course. I don't want to lose you, either." He pulled her in tight and kissed her passionately, pulling away too soon. "Thanks for watching over us. I know you'd rather be doing." After caressing her cheek, he walked away to don his armor.

Saree plopped down in her usual seat and pushed the surveillance to the large screen. Light-years of nothingness surrounded them, deep in the black. She inspected Ruhger and Tyron's calculations, then sighed. They had to get the fold generators working, or she had to reach the Sa'sa, or they were in for a very long, boring ride to nowhere. Even if they made it to the nearest system, there was no guarantee it would have anything useful or be habitable.

If Chief couldn't fix the generators, no one could. And if she couldn't find the Sa'sa, they'd be stuck, forever.

Chapter Seven

RUHGER

Opening the fold generator power compartment was even harder than expected. They had no trouble opening the hatch into the small area between the outer shielding and the fold power generator compartment. But getting through the second hatch, into the compartment containing the equipment, was challenging. The security pad on the door read, "Critical Damage. Do not enter. See Warnings." The list of cautions was long and mostly about unpredictable power surges in equipment and the compartment, even the decking.

Katryn removed the security pad cover plate and placed a device on top. Sparks flew from her hardsuit gauntlets. Ruhger brought up his hardsuit's tractor beam to yank her away, but she held up a hand. "I'm fine in the hardsuit. Tricky bugger." She manipulated her holo, muttering to Q, who remained in the Command Center.

Ruhger wanted Q safe and sound, far from all fold equipment. She'd miraculously survived Astra's disastrous fold; remembering Enzo's twisted body turned his stomach. Even thinking about Q going outside, working on the deployed fold field generators, made him shudder. She'd survived one fold in between the outer shielding and the fold power compartment. There was no guarantee she could do it again. But there was no reason for her to get trapped, either.

Eventually, Katryn, with Q's virtual help, got through the security, and the hatch cracked open. Katryn turned to Chief. "I've disengaged the external security, but I'll have more work to do inside, I'm sure."

Chief put his hand on Katryn's gauntlet. "Remote first."

"Copy that." She stepped back.

Chief sent a shielded remote inside. Lasers fired, the remote's shields flaring. "Returning fire. Blast and rad! When I fired back, the defenses returned fire *and* fired into the compartment. Slagged a bunch of equipment." He scowled. "What kind of crazy design is that?"

"Those mudhugging manufacturers had to enforce their exclusivity somehow." Katryn's fingers flew through her holo. "Found the lasers and shut them off. But there could be more, hidden somewhere."

"I'll send another remote." He turned to Ruhger, scowl deepening. "I'm sure part of the manufacturer's strategy is blaming whoever enters for ruining the generators." Chief floated a second remote through the hatchway. More lasers fired and he took them out. They repeated the cycle three more times before Chief deemed it safe for entry. "Survey party, when we go in, use your suit grav generator, and watch each other's backs for weapons and traps. Don't touch anything until you check for remaining power, both what you're touching and everything around it."

"Chief, let me go first." Katryn strode to the hatch. "I spotted a panel just inside the hatch, and I should be able to disarm the rest of this stuff. I hope."

Chief nodded. "Concur. Loreli, watch Katryn's six."

Katryn floated inside, Loreli following but facing the interior of the compartment. Katryn yelped. "Scooter scat, that hurt! Don't worry, I'm fine. Electrical charge overloaded my surge protector. Secondaries kicked in, but one more pulse, and I'll have to come out and replace them. But I've almost got it." Between discussions with Q and warnings from Loreli, Katryn muttered curses. Grant joined them, providing another defender for Katryn. Ruhger wanted to go in, too, but that area was cramped. He and Tyron took turns firing from the hatchway, while Chief watched Katryn via vid.

After a half-hour of work interspersed with laser fire, remote attacks, and power surges, Katryn returned to the hatch. "We've eliminated all the net-based security measures we can find. There may be others based on proximity sensors or other factors. Watch for old-fashioned trip wires, too. I've reset all the security codes to six ones, but I may have missed some."

"Copy that, Katryn. Great job, all of you." Ruhger engaged his grav generator. "Team, monitor your suits' power level."

Once inside, Ruhger surveyed the maze of strange containers and devices. Bright red, yellow, and black warning labels about electrical shock, lasers, death, and injury festooned locked cabinets, featureless cerimetal boxes, and tubes. A multitude of conduits ran the length of the compartment above them and along the surrounding walls. Many were damaged by laser fire.

In the middle of the compartment, a meter-tall "Y" shaped component pulsed with white light at the far ends of the Y; the middle was dark. Cerimetal strands ran over and into the Y just before the arms met in the center. A clear cover with a dark seal mated to a cerimetal case protected the component. On top, a red label stated "Shield biological eyes from light."

If the Y-shaped component got that bright, they should encase it entirely in cerimetal. Besides, fold would warp any biological caught in here unless they could use ^*timespace*^ to save themselves as Q had. That idiot child-abusing Enzo had discovered that the hard way, dying for his stupidity, but he deserved every moment of pain he'd received plus more.

Time to get his head back in the game; Ruhger had more important things to do than dwell on his failures. He followed Chief, who bobbed, weaved, and muttered incomprehensibly. Ruhger was fairly certain, from the labels, the size of the conduits going in and out, and the shape of the containers, that most of the large, featureless cerimetal cylinders and cubes were energy storage. Folding required immense power released in a single surge of 1.2 gigawatts, or a multiples of 1.2 gigawatts, depending on the distance. That required a lot of batteries and capacitors.

Chief returned to the middle of the compartment and floated in front of the Y component. "This is all blast and rad! Look at that ridiculous thing! A flux capacitor? For gigawatts of power? Absolutely not. Most of the equipment in this compartment is just flashing lights and Tesla coils. It's all show, no go."

As Ruhger watched, the light in the large Y component faded. "Interesting. I wonder why they'd go to the expense of creating false impressions when everyone 'knows' simply breaking the seal on the compartment means ruining the generators? Especially when the defenses slagged a bunch of components." He continued before anyone else could follow him down that black hole. "That's a problem for another time. How do we shut off the power to the actual generators? If those boxes on arms out there are actually generating the fold field. Or is it something else?"

Chief shook his head. "I don't know yet. We'll have to trace the controls and the power, see what components are necessary and which aren't. I suspect most of the enclosed boxes and cylinders inside this compartment are capacitors, which are necessary but easily replaced. I also suspect there will be small amounts of power going to many of the visible components to provide a show to any being who breaks the compartment seal."

"Chief, Q. Enzo died, his body and suit warped, and I lived, so there's got to be something going on down there."

Katryn's bright yellow suit floated face up near the overhead. "The only thing up here is a lot of tubes with pretty lights."

"Exactly." Chief waved around the room, creating a slow spin. "There's a lot of colorful light emitters and little real equipment." He halted his spin and floated toward the compartment hatch. "I'm tracing the hard-wired command and control. I'm sure it will run through a lot of these bogus components, so it will take a lot of time. If I can shut off the power, I'll do that immediately, so we can get those damaged field generator cubes off the deployment arms. Right now, I don't know how important those cubes are, or how important anything in this compartment might be, other than power storage."

Ruhger recalled the many fast folds they'd done in the past. "Considering the timing, I think the folder generator cubes are important. The fold never occurred until we fully deployed the generators. But that could be simple programming, too."

"Yes, it could be part of the smoke and mirrors." Grant inspected the lock on a secured cabinet. "If I open these locked compartments, it should make your life easier, right, Chief?"

"Excellent suggestion. Do that." Chief's blue hardsuit disappeared through the hatch. "I'll be back shortly."

Ruhger inspected the compartment again. "Let's split up. Grant, you take that side, designated A-side, I'll take this, the C-side. Scan and then open every locked container and compartment, but only the ones with hatches or other access panels. Use your suit's tractor beam to open hatches rather than your gauntlets. Scan the plain boxes, but don't open them. I'll do the same on this side. Katryn, since you're up there, inspect everything on the overhead, the B-side. Lashtar and Tyron, pull floor panels where you can. See what's underneath. Loreli, watch our sixes. Everyone, make notes on what you find—mark them on the cabinet or compartment itself if possible; if not, the bulkhead, overhead, or decking nearby. If the thing seems important, mark it in red. If you're not sure, use yellow. And if it's blast & rad, mark it in green. Try to open things without damaging them, but I suspect that will be impossible. Objections?"

Silence rang loud. Chief said over the comms, "Excellent plan. I should have done that before I left. Execute."

Chief sounded apologetic, not annoyed, so Ruhger didn't worry about his misstep. But he should have discussed the idea with Chief first rather than taking charge. Both of them were stuck in their ways; he was used to command and Chief to working solo. Or with Lashtar.

Ruhger floated to the far side of the compartment. Three big cylinders of plain cerimetal rose from the decking to the overhead. High voltage warnings were the only relief from the dull gray cerimetal, so he scanned them. As they'd speculated, the cylinders were capacitors. He moved to the next, a shallow, three-meter-long compartment with two doors. He scanned; the manufacturer had neatly arrayed low voltage components inside. Extending a stylus from his gauntlet, he entered Katryn's new default passkey. Ruhger opened the lock and pulled the thin plas doors wide. Inside, lights flashed red and yellow; several were black. Some were round, others rectangles, and some held switches. The labels were long strings of numbers and alpha-numeric characters.

Spotting a small rectangular outline midway up the interior panel, Ruhger pushed it. The rectangle popped out. He grasped it with his tractor beam, then pulled. The entire interior panel swung toward him, so he floated back, opening it. As expected, the panel held nothing but light-emitting diodes, and the switches weren't even connected. He examined the entire compartment but found nothing real, so he closed it and marked each lock with a green X.

Moving along the outer bulkhead, he found more of the same. Large cylinders and rectangles that appeared to be capacitors and batteries, and cabinets full of junk. Behind him, the decking team raised a panel, while Grant inspected the far side of the compartment. Katryn floated face up above the central Y component. Plenty of chatter sounded on the crew channel, but it was time for a formal report. He opened comms with Chief. "Time for a report, isn't it?"

"Correct. Thanks for the reminder. Pulling the floor panels inside these cabinets is a real chore. Stand by."

Ruhger sipped water while he waited. With all the misdirection, finding the actual equipment would take a miracle.

"All crew, Chief. Take five and let's report. The decking in the exterior cabinets is extremely difficult to pull, probably by design. I've had to cut, and it's all cerimetal. I may start my trace inside the fold generator compartment instead. Ruhger?"

"Every compartment and container with a lock on the C-side exterior bulkhead is unimportant. I believe the plain cylinders and boxes are power storage, either capacitors or batteries. I'm starting the next row and working back toward the interior hatch."

"Copy all, Ruhger. Grant?"

"Same as Ruhger."

"Katryn."

"Mostly unimportant. There are tubes of coolant, for the engines I believe, but most of the conduits on the overhead run into that shiny Y in the center, and most of them are empty. The few that aren't have low voltage power, probably for the lights. There are tubes with lights up here, too, that aren't connected to anything but power."

"Floor team."

"Tyron reporting. We've found real, high power hard lines and laser feeds in conduits. They may or may not feed the power to the fold field generators. They're definitely channeling power at higher levels the farther we go toward the fold generators. At the midway point, all of the hard wire power is converted to laser. The conduits and lines are broken, though, with pieces missing. They may have pulled into spaces above the decking, inside the above-decking containers and boxes. And some of those are slagged."

He took a breath, then continued. "From what we've seen so far, I believe that we're essentially standing on an enormous laser weapon, and the laser power is converted to fold energy without destroying the generators. It could be a shield that absorbs and transforms the power. But why go to all that trouble? We can channel gigawatts of power without the multiple transformations."

"Fascinating. But if true, that should make finding the actual fold generators easier. I'm coming back." Chief entered the compartment and floated toward the decking group.

Katryn joined Tyron. "Why go to all this trouble? Why not create your giant laser in the compartment, rather than under the decking?"

Tyron pointed at the decking. "First, if I'm right, this is a ring accelerator that converts to a spiral, then to a pulsed weapon. Laying it flat is efficient, and the backside isn't insulated, so space cools it. That's also why a weapon impact to this area is so devastating; there's a ton of power, and if your shielding fails, there's nothing else to soak up the energy. There's water around the rest of *Lightwave*'s exterior. Second, laying it under the decking leaves plenty of room for energy storage, which is definitely necessary. Third, there's also room for all the misdirection. I'm speculating, but I believe the ruse works like this."

He pointed at the hatch. "Near the compartment entrance, there are a series of interrupters. When the hatch opens without the proper credentials, the interrupters cut one part of the power to the laser. Power is still generated, but not at the required multiples of 1.21 gigawatts. Then, as traps are triggered, the accelerator is cut, with pieces rising into hiding places below the huge capacitors and fake components. Most beings, after finding one or two false trails, will assume that those pieces are destroyed. They might be; the capacitor might also power a small laser that destroys that piece, rather than hiding it. And the lasers that fired at our remotes destroy pieces, too. The farther an 'invader' penetrates, the more destruction occurs, until there's nothing but a half-melted pile of cerimetal left. Either way, I suspect the fold generator manufacturers shut down and discredit anyone who does the work and discovers the whole thing is a ruse. And I also suspect that each manufacturer has different security designs, so it's not obvious. They may even kill to keep their secret. But really, all they have to do is say 'the math is well-known. Build your own fold generators' and that will shut up most."

"And those of us caught in a fold-gone-bad will never return, so we can't talk." Q's voice trembled.

"We'll return." Chief projected calm confidence. "Now that we know how it works, we can rebuild it. If Ruhger can figure out the math, we'll return."

The math was a bigger challenge than he'd previously faced. "It's difficult. Since no one has admitted to changing planes or universes and returning, all I have is theory. Theoretical math far beyond what I usually do. It's not instinctive. But we might not have done that. We may have simply folded a very, very long distance." He grimaced. Speculation wasn't always useful. He pressed on, hoping to reassure Q. "But I'll figure it out. If one of you can determine the power involved in the destruction, then that gives me our overall power. I'll figure out why a number that isn't a multiple of 1.21 still created a fold, and that will lead me to our location. So, now that we've figured out the big secret, I'm going to leave all of you here and return to the Command Center to study."

"Ugh. Math." Q's grimace could be heard over the comms.

Ruhger forced a chuckle even though there wasn't anything funny about the situation. "Now you know why I make you study it. You never know when you might need it."

"I don't think it would matter how much I study fold math. I'm not going to be calculating a return from another universe. The concept blows my mind."

"It shouldn't, Q." Saree's voice was thoughtful. "If you go into ^timespace^, there are... layers for lack of a better term. At least, that's how it appears to me. If I go down, then I find the fundamental frequencies of the universe, based on transuranic metal frequencies. Perhaps every element has a frequency, but those are the ones I'm familiar with. But I'm betting that if I keep going or maybe go up or sideways—for whatever that really is in ^timespace^—I'll find alternate realities or universes or whatever it is that we're in."

As she spoke, Ruhger's alarm grew, his heart rate increasing. "Please don't go looking without me there." He didn't want to lose her; she'd come too close too often.

"I won't. If there's any time I'll need a safety line of sorts, that will be it. I'm hoping Q can anchor me like the Sa'sa do. But I'll wait for you to finish down there."

"How about a decent night of sleep, too?" Ruhger desperately wanted to hold her tight before she tried anything that risky.

"Sure. You can probably use that too, if you're going to dive deep into theoretical math."

Ruhger huffed a chuckle. "I'll need all the brainpower I can manage, that's for sure." A fresh start would be good for all of them.

Loreli floated to the compartment hatch. "Well, since you super-intelligent beings have figured this all out, I'm headed back to my domain. I'll be more useful creating delicious dishes to support your brain power than pulling up decking panels and spraying paint. Minion, I hope you're ready for this!"

"Yes, Chef. Right away, Chef." Q giggled. The sound lightened Ruhger's mood.

Chief gazed around the fold generator compartment. "The rest of us will continue our search for the power cutoffs and the laser's target. Probably whatever is in those cubes on the end of the fold generators."

Ruhger floated after Loreli. "Let me know if you need help. I'll figure out the power surge that hit the laser first. We should have a vid of the impact, so that should give me a starting point, maybe."

Tyron said, "I started a file with specs that Katryn and I collected about the defenses and offensive weapons on Emma. With some visual and positional information, you should be able to find the origin of the laser. Hopefully, we'll figure out the details soon, giving you a more solid foundation."

"Thanks, Tyron, that will help a lot." Outside the fold generator compartment, Ruhger touched down on the Engineering decking. "Everyone, when you return your hardsuit to the cleaners, make sure your suits recharge properly. Grav generators take a lot of power." Muttering followed, but obvious reminders were part of his job. After putting his hardsuit away in his armor compartment and showering, he joined Saree and Q in the Command Center.

Saree swept a screen of math to the lower left side of the big vid display and shoved the surveillance to the upper half. The vid of Chief and crew slid to the lower right side. "Q and I worked on the laser energy delivered to the fold generators." She turned to him. "By the way, I think those extended fold field generator cubes must have a real purpose, or the destruction wouldn't have sent us here. Maybe." She shrugged. "Anyway, we believe the power was 0.56 gigawatts, or exactly half the 1.21 normally required for fold. That might be enough extra energy to fold us somewhere past our plane or universe."

Q picked up a thin sheet of plas and folded it in half without creasing, so the plas bent into an oval tube, touching along two lines. "As you told me, folding space means we bring two planes in space together momentarily. What if the half-energy meant the locations didn't quite meet"—she separated the plas sheet so it no longer touched—"or we went too far, or we skewed sideways, along the line where the two planes meet?"

Ruhger nodded. "That demonstration is merely a representation. It's not a completely accurate reflection of the math. However, you're correct, too. Either may be possible. I've got to dig into the research. The problem is, parallel universe math researchers are a mix of eccentrics, theorists, and black holes, and

I'll have to look at all of them." He smiled at Q. "But that estimation you just did makes the job so much easier. Now, any theory that doesn't consider a difference in power by half or a quarter or an eighth can be put aside for later study. The theories with those power differences are far less than others. You two just saved me a whole lot of time and effort."

Saree winked, and Q grinned. "You're welcome. But now that you know, I better go minion, or Loreli will start yelling." She bounded from her seat and out the hatch.

Ruhger smiled. Surrounded by intelligent fun people made life better. But family would be even better closer to the part of the universe they called home.

Chapter Eight

SAREE

After a good night's sleep, Saree reclined her medfloat and sank into ^*timespace*^, reveling in the beauty and peace. Q's power burned bright against the unusually dull background of ^*timespace*^. Saree searched for familiar landmarks, although that term wasn't right, but found nothing. She ^*sank*^ to the fundamental frequencies, looking for the fold clock transuranics. She found the common neptunium and plutonium, but none of the rarer elements. As she contemplated the two elements, the faint echoes of the other elements seemed to shadow the main frequency, rather like a harmonic above a single note.

Wherever they'd ended up, it was very different. Even the common elements were weak, tenuous. Perhaps they were in a much older universe or plane, where the elements had decayed. They could have traveled in time rather than planes. They'd have to ask the computer to time-progress their universe much farther, closer to the "death" of existence. Which, if she was in her body, would be terrifying. But in ^*timespace*^, she floated, serene.

Before the beauty could capture her, she ^*looked*^ for the signature of the Sa'sa. But she found nothing like them. She'd have to go ^*farther*^ somehow.

A bell tone interrupted her. Time to return to her body. She concentrated on the heaviness, the breath rasping in her throat, the rise and fall of her ribs, and returned with a thud. "Oh."

"Saree, come back. Stay with me, Saree, are you okay?" Worry, with an edge of despair threaded through Ruhger's tone. "Saree, come. Say something, please."

"Ugh. So hard." Sucking in breath took too much effort; her chest weighed a hundred kilos and her heart ached as it thumped hard and fast. The thought of opening her eyes was daunting.

"Thank the suns you're back." Relief soaked his words.

Ruhger's hand squeezed hers lightly, followed by a warm breeze, then slight pressure caressing the back—he'd kissed her hand. She'd scared him. "I'm sorry, Ruhger." She sucked in a breath, the weight of her chest a little less but still harder than it should be. "I didn't think I was gone that long or did that much." Already, the experience was fading; she had to tell them before it disappeared. "I think we're in a much older place or universe, where many of the suns and galaxies have died. The transuranic frequencies are weak, fading away, as if their half-lives are over."

"Sunspots. Rest." Ruhger rubbed his thumb over her palm. "Tyron, age-progress our star charts much, much farther. Like to the end of the universe."

"Copy that, Captain. Death of the universe coming up." Tyron's words were dark, but his tone light. "Does that mean we time-traveled?"

Saree wished she knew. "Don't know. Maybe."

"And that's not terrifying at all." Katryn's voice was grimmer than normal.

If they had traveled through time, could they return? Or perhaps they'd crossed multiple parallel universes, coming to one far ahead of theirs.

"It doesn't really matter if we traveled in time or space or both." Ruhger tone had returned to his normal, factual tone. "What matters is figuring out how to return or reverse what we did or was done to us."

"But narrowing it to time or space would make the calculations easier," Chief said.

The hatch whooshed, fabric swished, and a small hand took hers, forming it around a cool cylinder. "Drink, Saree, and anchor to your body." Q's hand guided hers toward her head, and a straw settled between her lips.

She'd forgotten Q had been in *timespace* with her. She must have returned first. Saree sipped gratefully. A sweet-tart-salty taste coated her tongue, the liquid flowing thickly, but not like a shake or smoothie. Cool, but not cold. After several swallows, she pulled the straw away and opened her eyes. Ruhger and Q stared down at her, almost identical creases between their brows. She forced a smile, even though her mouth was tired from the tiny effort of sucking on a straw. "Thank you. I'm okay." Both sets of brows rose quizzically. "I will be okay. I feel exhausted, but this helps." She raised the bev-tainer, aware her hand trembled. "What did you see, Q?"

"Keep drinking and I'll tell you." Q steadied her grip, bringing the straw back to Saree's mouth.

"Yes, keep drinking and stay there. If we need your input, we'll bring it to you." Ruhger kissed her palm. "Rest. Recover." He put her hand down on the medfloat and walked away.

Q grimaced. "You disappeared on me. I searched but had to return. I wanted to go back out, but Ruhger wouldn't let me. Where did you go?"

She shouldn't have disappeared from Q's senses. "Finding the transuranic frequencies was difficult. I had to search and... sink, for lack of a better term, farther than normal. The rarer elements were mere shadows, like echoes of their former existence. And I found no sign of the Sa'sa."

Q's eyes widened. "That's more than a little terrifying. I wonder if any beings still exist. Did Galactica eat the universe?"

Saree shuddered. "That's even more terrifying."

Grant appeared, leaning against the foot of her medfloat on the opposite side of Q. "Maybe that's why Galactica hasn't wiped us out. It's time-progressed the universe and understands that without sentients, it will die of starvation at the end."

Q snorted. "Millions and millions of years later? Would it care?"

Grant shrugged. "Hard to say. We can speculate that it looks ahead, but how far or how is anyone's guess."

"The universe will end eventually, no matter what we or anyone or anything else does." Chief walked into view, spinning his wrench across his knuckles. "Entropy wins in the end, so why worry about it? It's far more likely a natural disaster would kill sentients and Galactica. While we can predict supernovas and collisions and all the other things, oddities happen. Extinction events can happen without warning. So, why waste resources on sureties, like the end of the universe, when you can protect against closer and more likely events?"

"Life endures. Even if humanity doesn't, the non-oxys could thrive for many eons after us. Less competition for resources." Grant smirked. "They're better at conservation, too."

"The computer is working on the time progression but warns that it's less accurate the farther ahead we go." Saree couldn't see Tyron, but he probably sat in his normal chair. "Too many uncertainties. I don't know if we'll get an actual answer to the time-traveling question."

"Is there any non-random electromagnetic noise?" Lashtar joined Chief. "Even way out here in the middle of nothing, waves travel, or we couldn't see any stars."

"Excellent thought." Chief nodded. "Even if it's nothing we can understand, intelligence creates patterns."

While Ruhger and Q probably wanted her to remain flat, she was missing too much. Saree raised the head of the medfloat while sipping the last of her drink.

Q frowned. "Sure you want to do that yet?"

"I'll stay here." She handed the bev-tainer to Q. "Thank you for the drink. It was tasty for an electrolyte solution."

Q grinned. "I'll let Loreli know you approve. If you'd keep from scaring us, you could have a recovery shake like I did. Chef's a miracle worker, but she can only do so much with a fast-absorbing solution of minerals and sugar."

Saree chuckled. "I'm just happy I could drink it rather than have it shoved in my veins."

Q's happiness disappeared. "Uh, hate to tell you this, Saree, but you got that, too. You came close to overloading your heart. That's the reason Ruhger didn't shock you to bring you out of ^timespace^."

She put her hand on her chest. "I guess that explains the ache. Well, I'll definitely stay right here for a while." That also explained why the crook of her left elbow was sore.

"Good choice." Q squeezed her shoulder, then trotted out of the Command Center.

There had to be a better way for her to search ^*timespace*^. One that didn't overload her body. The Sa'sa methods wouldn't work; the hive mind spread the effort so no one being took on the whole task. And they wouldn't care, overall, if a few individuals were lost. Maybe that's why the Time Guild leaders were older, more mature, and physically larger; they'd survived. And perhaps they needed support to reach ^*farther*^ too.

Whether or not she could use their methods didn't matter because they weren't here. Wherever here was. "Ruhger, did you have any luck with the math?"

"Working on it." He turned toward her, holos layered around his head. "Based on the power calculation that you and Q performed, I've created a series of power levels we can attempt to send us back." His mouth twisted for a moment. "The problem is, only the lowest of those levels are something we can produce with our current equipment. And we have to fix what's broken first."

"If it's broken." Chief shrugged. "The initial laser generation is intact. The destroyed part of the accelerator can be reconstructed, although finding enough basic pieces and parts might be a challenge. We can't print cerimetal. We've also figured out how to shut the power off, although doing that means we'll burn through a lot of fuel to fully reenergize the thing when we're ready. The longer it's off, the more power naturally dissipates from the storage elements. The next step is to disconnect the generators at the end, figure out what they actually do, and fix them." He grunted.

"If we can." Tyron shook his head. "Especially without a cerimetal forging capability."

"If we need that, and we can get someplace that used to be inhabited, then maybe there will be something we can scavenge," Chief said. "But we might not need a full enclosure for a single-shot." A brow rose. "And let's face it. If we take more than a single shot to get back, I'm not sure we ever will."

Q entered, towing a tray. "Oh, you mean we could fold through realities, jumping endlessly like that ancient vid, righting wrongs throughout time?" She scowled. "Let's not change bodies, okay? I like mine the way it is now. I worked hard to get it back."

Saree shivered at the reminder of what Q endured. "I'd like to remain intact, too." Besides, her ^timespace^ capability might be tied to her physical body.

Ruhger shook his head. "If it didn't happen during our fold here, I don't think it will happen now."

Loreli bustled inside, towing another tray. "Oh, let's hope not! I'm far too fabulous to leave all this behind!" She swept an arm down her body, dressed in a white pleather corset and tight, shiny white leggings with her usual sky-high platform boots. A white beret sat snug on her head, crushed over one ear, and a belt with both kitchen knives and a laser pistol was slung low across her hips.

Saree grinned at Loreli's version of tactical wear. Wildly impractical, but the leggings would fit under armor. The delicious scents of toasted bread, roasted meat, and sweet berries made her mouth water.

Loreli jabbed a finger toward her face. "You will stay there and eat, while the rest of us eat at the table like civilized beings. We will relax and talk about other, non-emergency things, then we will rest and exercise and relax. In the morning, we'll discuss our next steps. We have no reason to kill ourselves getting home."

Grant jumped to his feet and snapped a salute. "Oh, absolutely, Cap-i-tan and Clutch Leader Loreli. Your word is our command."

Saree snickered, joined by Q. Ruhger glowered, Chief grunted, while the rest chuckled. But no matter who said it, they were correct. "She's right. So, we'll follow Chef's orders. We'll enjoy ourselves, relax and rest, so we can begin fresh in the morning. We'll probably see something we missed today because we're tired." She pointed back at Loreli. "But I'm not eating here. I'm joining you at the table."

Ruhger held up his hand, palm out. "Not on your own. I'll carry you there."

Saree nodded. She had no problem with Ruhger taking care of her. "I'll happily agree to that." Ruhger's arms were always comforting, even under less than ideal circumstances. "Let's eat."

Her chosen family gathered at the table, chattering. Ruhger scooped her off the medfloat and carried her to the table, placing her in a chair, then sitting next to her. "Let me know when you get tired."

"I will." She was so lucky to have him and all these wonderful people on her side. Even if they never returned, they could live happily together. But they'd get back. She was sure of it.

By the middle of the next day, she wasn't so sure. Disconnecting the field generation cubes from the fold generator deployment arms proved extremely difficult. Despite turning off the power, the cubes were still energized. They'd fried several remotes already, but despite the risk, Chief insisted he had to inspect the thing personally. How he could do that and not get fried or shocked when the remotes did had kept him inside *Lightwave* so far, but how long he'd listen to reason was unknown. Fortunately, she could lock down his armor if necessary.

"There's got to be power storage units inside the arms or at the back of the fold field generator cube." Ruhger folded his arms over his chest.

Chief clenched his wrench so tightly his knuckles turned white. "Agreed. But I don't know how we bleed off the power without folding. Or attempting to fold. But that could fold us into nothing, or a black hole, or blow us to pieces. And every moment we delay, more power burns off the interior capacitors and batteries. I need to look at it." Frustration simmered in his tone.

Ruhger took a breath, and Saree put a hand on his forearm to stop him from continuing their circular argument. "Chief, you'll be easier to electrocute than a remote. Suits are far more fragile and you know it. I don't understand what you'll see in person that a remote can't. You won't be able to get any closer; you'll have to rely on your helmet's electronics."

Chief raised both hands toward the overhead. "I can't explain it, but I can't see the patterns via remote. Once I was inside the fold generator compartment, I could tell it was all blast and rad. But I couldn't via remote. My... talent, for lack of a better term, doesn't work that way. I must see it in person."

"We can make this work." Tyron turned to her. "We can hook Chief to a remote. Either Ruhger or I will control it, making sure his suit never touches the generators. We'll attach power level indicators to the exterior of his suit. Katryn can watch those, and if they increase, she can tell us."

"If they increase quickly, I will yank him back, because that will be faster." Katryn tilted her head, giving Tyron a pointed look.

"Concur." Tyron smiled at her, then turned back to Saree. "We can stand next to each other and use dual controls. We'll put two safeties outside with him; probably Ruhger and Grant, and a third in the hatch, probably Loreli. She can watch the surrounding area, while Ruhger and Grant concentrate on Chief and the remote. Lashtar backs Katryn and me. Q has wide-area *Lightwave* surveillance, and Saree, you've got command. Does that make sense?"

It did, but she had a ship full of experts. "Your thoughts on this plan, Chief?"

"I concur. I'll give full control of my suit to Tyron and Katryn. Ruhger will control a safety cable, while Grant and Loreli back him up in the airlock."

"Ruhger?" She squeezed his hand.

"Concur, with a slight change." He grimaced. "Both Chief and the remote will have safety cables. Grant and I will tether to the interior of the airlock and mag our boots so we can pull easier. While Chief is our primary concern, I don't want the remote to fry, then collide with the fold generators, making the damage worse. Or collide with Chief and fry him."

"Any other additions, deletions, or modifications?" Saree met every remaining crew member's gaze. They all shook their heads or said no. "Okay, everyone suit up. I mean everyone, including me, for emergency operations. We must be prepared for the worst."

"Copy that, Clutch Leader." Loreli saluted and marched to her armor cabinet, tugging her chef's hat off.

Saree followed the crew and climbed into her hardsuit, her body still a little fatigued and stiff from overextending the day before. When she emerged, Ruhger waited for her, with his helmet retracted. He bent and kissed her, and she returned his love with interest. He smiled, raised his helmet, and trod from the Command Center.

Saree took her usual seat and adjusted the main vid screen. She placed the wide area surveillance in the upper left quadrant, the near area surveillance in the lower left, and Chief's view in the upper right. Ruhger's view was in the lower right. Crew stats hugged the bottom in a series of smaller windows.

Standing to Saree's left, Q surrounded herself with surveillance holos, zooming in and out to inspect areas of concern. Occasionally, she'd glance at the action on the big screen, but she was clearly concentrating on her mission. Tyron and Katryn sat on her right, Lashtar peering over their shoulders. They watched Chief's remote and suit controls and his helmet vid on their left. On their right, the remote's forward vid and a shot of the fold field generator cubes with power gauges superimposed.

In the Engineering-level airlock, Ruhger attached the back of Chief's suit to a tripod brace. They mounted it on a large remote using a low-power explosive bolt. The bolt was designed to blow so the forces would equalize and not impart a vector. Chief hung suspended from the brace slightly in front of the remote. If something happened to the remote, any of them could blow the bolts and pull Chief back. If the worst happened, and Chief's suit got fried, a loose tether between the remote and Chief would be safer for all of them. But that wouldn't give them the control they needed to get him close to, but not touching, the fold generators.

"Chief, Ruhger. Kick your leg to check the attachment gimbal."

Chief kicked his right leg back, and his whole body swung up, twisting slightly to the left. He countered with a suit thruster, bringing him back to an upright position. "Seems secure, Ruhger."

"Chief, Tyron. Once we're outside the airlock, let us test the controls, please. We'll bring you close to *Lightwave*'s surface and try different thrust levels on the remote and your suit."

"Copy that, Tyron. You have full control."

"Exterior Team, Ruhger. Chief is ready for operations. State any objections now." Three seconds passed, then Ruhger continued. "Command, Exterior Team ready. Objections?"

Q and Chief's control team gave Saree a thumbs up. "Exterior Team, you are a go for operations. Proceed when ready."

"Copy that, Command. Loreli, cycle the lock." Ruhger grasped Chief's safety cable, while Grant took the remote's. The inner hatch closed, and dust swirled in the rapidly dwindling air. The outer control indicators flashed, and the hatch opened into dark space, brightened by *Lightwave*'s exterior lights. Chief's helmet vid showed the cubes of the fold field generators; the deployment arms were hidden by *Lightwave*'s exterior and the engines.

"Chief, Tyron. Testing controls now." Chief's view showed him floating out the hatch, and close to *Lightwave*'s surface. The close-in shields, set to their lowest levels, scintillated as he moved back and forth, then rotated, bent, and swayed. His shields brushed *Lightwave*'s shields a few times, then Tyron and Katryn perfected their control. "Command, Chief, control testing complete. Ready to proceed?"

"Chief ready."

Saree was satisfied with the control, safeties, and plan, even though she desperately wished Chief didn't have to go outside at all. Q gave her a thumbs up, too. "Command, Exterior Team. Proceed with operational phase." She switched *Lightwave*'s close-in shields off, routing a little more power to the next level of shields outside their area of operations.

Chief floated along *Lightwave*'s exterior bulkhead. At the end, they paused, and Chief attached two carabiners to *Lightwave*'s surface, then routed his and the remote's safety cables through them. This would lessen the chance of the cables tangling. Ruhger had argued Chief would be safer if he and Grant were standing on the end of *Lightwave*'s bulkhead, near the engines. Both Saree and Chief agreed the greater risk wasn't worth the reward.

Tyron flew Chief into open space and toward the fold generator arms, inspecting the surface as he went. After a slow traverse parallel to the arms leading to the damaged field generation cubes, they halted him near the least damaged box. "Command, no surface damage beyond the normal wear also noted on the arms. Deployment mechanisms appear complete and unharmed. First generator box has a corner missing." A red line appeared near the generator box. "Missing corner is approximately four centimeters wide by nine centimeters high and nineteen cents long." Chief's view zeroed in on the cleanly sheared corner, and a white light flicked on. "The interior parts appear intact, but it's difficult to tell without sending something inside, which we can't do without frying it. The interior of the enclosure was obviously damaged along with the exterior, but I don't know if the circuitry embossed inside is real or a ruse. Tyron, please move me to the next fold generator cube."

"Copy that, Chief. En route. We'll float by the whole thing one meter away, then you can tell us where you want to get closer."

Chief floated across the gap, then the second damaged fold field generator cube came into view. The laser had sheared off a much larger corner; the red lines appeared again. "Damage is extensive, removing an entire corner of the enclosure, plus interior components. Exterior damage is five meters high, or the entire height of the box, by one and a third meters long, measured straight across the cut line. Again, the interior of the enclosure is printed with circuitry. Inside, the intact tubes remain brightly lit with red light, but most are dark, many sheared off. Tyron, can you get me closer?"

"Copy, Chief, moving you to ten centimeters from the surface." Tyron's finger slid forward in front of his face, and a distance indicator counted down. The surface power indicators on Chief's suit didn't rise. "You're now ten cents away. I can take you closer if necessary."

"Stand by." Chief's helmet flashed reflected light as he inspected the interior of the generator. "Interesting. I believe the tubes with lights are just that, useless tubes of light-emitting diodes. However, the circuitry surrounding the lights may generate the field. Also, I can't be sure, but I think that circuitry extends up into the fold field generator deployment arms."

"Blast and rad," Ruhger muttered.

"Indeed," Chief replied. "That means disconnecting not only the damaged cubes, but an intact box, getting them all inside, and figuring out how to open the intact one so we can copy it. If they're all the same. That may not be true because fold requires coordinates in x, y, z, and time. Four variables, four boxes. But that may be a false speculation."

Saree tapped a rhythm on her thigh. Chief was literally too close to the problem. They needed all four cubes to be sure. "Chief, Command. We'll bring all four inside, or we won't be able to tell how they differ. Also, we'll experiment by opening the most heavily damaged cube first."

"Excellent points, Command. Tyron, can you take me to the back of the cubes, where they attach to the deployment arms?"

"Moving." The remote and Chief lowered below the damaged box, then rose behind it.

"As we could see with the remotes, the cerimetal of the deployment arm isn't welded to the box. Can we get a fiber optic sensor in there?"

Saree jolted inside her suit, alarmed. "Not one on your suit or the remote, Chief."

"No, we have other, smaller remotes," Chief replied. "I've got a few here with me. Let me fly one down there." He plucked a small object from his suit and pushed it toward the intersection of the box and arm. "It hasn't touched the surface yet, and I don't see a power spike. I'll share the vid and lower it to the surface."

A sharing request from Chief appeared in Saree's holo, and she selected it, leaving it in her suit holo rather than pushing it to the large vid screen. The vid showed plain cerimetal surfaces ninety degrees to each other, with a small gap between. The gap grew larger as the remote flew closer. "Touchdown. No power surge." The gap increased and brightened. "Turning on lights, deploying fiber." The view increased, then showed a slightly tarnished piece of cerimetal. The view changed, zooming out, showing a mechanism.

Chief said, "Got it!"

The remote vid sparked and went black.

Chapter Nine

RUHGER

Ruhger tensed but didn't yank Chief away. Chief's suit appeared to be working; only his inspection remote went dark. Plus, Chief's position, between the deployment arms, made action a bigger risk. He and Grant should have moved when Chief did. "Tyron, I can't pull Chief safely from his current position. Can you orient the remote so we have a direct route between the carabiners on *Lightwave* and his position?"

"Blast. I hadn't noticed I moved him between the deployment arms. Stand by."

"Wait." Chief emphasized his words, but kept his tone calm. "I know how to get the boxes off, I think. And I'm fairly certain we can do it safely."

Fairly certain? "Not quite good enough, Chief. We need to be absolutely positive before you touch anything." Ruhger deliberately relaxed his tense muscles, keeping a secure but loose grip on the cable.

"Copy that. I'll test with another mini-remote or two. But the one I set down on the backside of the cube still works. Inside the box, there's a problem, but I believe the backside isn't energized. And the mechanism attaching the cube to the arm is a rotating mechanical interlock. If we rotate the box left-handed and push toward *Lightwave*, it will come loose."

Ruhger's relief at the simplicity of the solution let the remaining tension release from his shoulders. But caution was still critical. "Tyron, make sure Chief doesn't touch the exposed end of the arm after the box releases. We'll need larger remotes to rotate those boxes, capture them, and tow them back here."

"Towing, yes, but I think I can rotate them loose." Chief reached his hand toward the surface.

Chief's vid showed the box receding. "Chief, let's test with remotes first." Tyron's voice was slightly exasperated.

"Sorry. You are correct. Stand by." Chief plucked mini-remotes from his suit and sent them to the backside of the boxes and the deployment arm, two on each. All four touched down without issue. But when he deployed a fiber from a remote on the back of the box to touch the deployment arm, it went dark. "If I connect only to the box, not the arm, then we should be able to use the remote to turn me and the box."

Ruhger huffed. "Turn you into a giant magnetic zero-g wrench?"

"Not magnetic, but the idea is correct. I can touch down with my boots and hands, locking on the cerimetal, then the remote turns both of us. It's not ideal, but we'd have to build a similar tool."

"No, we wouldn't." Tyron said. "Disconnect from the tripod fastening you to the remote, and then disconnect the tripod. Then connect the tripod to the remote using the single connection and the tripod's feet to the box. The remote can turn the tripod, acting like a wrench."

"Excellent. I should have thought of that." Chief motioned for them to come closer. "Someone let me loose, so I don't have to blow the bolt. Then all of you can back off again."

Ruhger didn't like Chief out there alone and unafraid. Especially when he wasn't putting his safety first. "Command, I propose a change to this plan. Before Chief does any of this, Grant and Loreli go to the end of *Lightwave*'s bulkhead, where they can easily move so they can pull Chief loose and not hit anything. I'll use another remote and fly to Chief. That way, I can get him loose from the tripod without blowing the bolt, and I can watch closer for potential problems and help if necessary."

"Objections, Chief?" Saree asked.

"None. That seems smart."

"If no objections from anyone else, make it so. Send some extra remotes, too."

"Good idea. I'll get them." Ruhger energized three larger remotes and sent them out the cargo bay airlock. "Ready, Grant, Loreli?"

"Ready," both answered, their voices remarkably similar with tension. After attaching their safety cables to safety loops outside the airlock, they bounded to the end of the bulkhead. They stepped around the corner to the engine and fold bulkhead.

The new three remotes maneuvered into view. He sent one each to Grant and Loreli, standing on the "bottom" of *Lightwave*, and brought one to himself, attaching a flexible safety cable to it. "I'm going to stay near Chief, with his safety cable in my hand, where I can pull him away quickly with my remote. Let me know if I block your view, Grant, or if something is coming our way, Loreli."

"Copy that, Ruhger," Grant said. "I'll give your cable to Loreli, and she'll pull on my command, so she can continue watching our surroundings."

"Copy all, Ruhger, Grant," Loreli said. "Got all your fine sixes."

Ruhger pushed off the bottom of *Lightwave* and floated to Chief, the remote following him. When he neared Chief, he stopped three meters "below" the deployment arm, so Grant and Loreli had a clear area to pull both safety lines if necessary. "Bring Chief to me, Tyron, and I'll get him loose. Then we'll proceed as planned."

Chief's remote thrusted to Ruhger, Chief facing away from him. Ruhger clipped a line from Chief to his remote, disarmed the explosive bolt, placed the safety pin in it, then pulled the retaining bolts, setting Chief loose. Together, they removed the tripod's feet from the remote, replacing them with strong cerimetal magnets. Then they removed the explosive, rotating gimbal at the tripod's tip and replaced it with a solid connector and attached that to the remote.

Chief magged his boots to Ruhger's remote, standing next to him. "Okay, Tyron, maneuver the remote wrench into place."

"Copy, executing now." The remote floated forward, the three legs fastening across one corner of the five-meter-long cube. All three pressure indicators showed a solid connection. "Remote in place. No sign of power surge."

"Tyron, Chief. You'll need to pull toward the arm and rotate left-handed at the same time."

"Copy that, Chief. I'll start with a small impulse, then increase it slowly."

On the remote, thrusters glowed red momentarily, then lit to bright blue. The remote stayed in place for a few seconds, then moved, the fold generator box rotating below it. At three quarters of a rotation, the box stopped.

"Thrusting away from the deployment arm," Tyron reported.

The cube floated free, and Ruhger sighed, his shoulders relaxing. "Take it to the cargo hold, then bring the tripod back, and we'll do the next one."

"Copy that, Ruhger. Chief, do we want to undo all of the fold field generator cubes or just the damaged ones?"

"Tyron, Chief. Just the damaged ones at this point. We should be able to see enough from the minimally damaged box to fix the other."

Chief disconnected his safety cable from Ruhger's remote. "I want to get started on dismantling the box right away."

Ruhger wasn't surprised. "Make sure you test for residual energy before you do anything to those boxes, Chief. And stay in your suit for now. Also, you'll need a safety in the cargo hold with you. Command, that's your decision."

"Concur," Chief replied.

"Chief, Command." Saree's voice conveyed her relief. "I'll send Tyron to the cargo bay. Since personnel are no longer in danger close to the fold generator cubes, Katryn can handle the remote and unfasten the next box by herself. Ruhger, remain at a safe distance."

"Copy all, Command." Ruhger was more than happy to stay out of the way. He sent his remote to the side of the newly empty deployment arm, taking vid of the connector. Shiny fingers of deliberately twisted cerimetal, embossed with circuitry, extended into space. Ruhger recorded vid from all angles and tested with small remotes. At a few millimeters from the connector, the power levels spiked, then the remote died, sparks occasionally flying off to die in the vacuum. They'd have to use compressed air to blow any debris off those connecting fingers before reattaching the fold field generator cubes. Ruhger huffed. Assuming they could fix them.

Ruhger stared into the mostly dark space, galaxies and nebulas glinting in the distance. If they couldn't fix the cubes, they might be on a long, slow trip to nowhere. But he had faith in his crew, his family. Between all of them, they could solve the problem and return them to their universe or plane or time. Eventually.

Katryn floated the remote into place and twisted the less-damaged cube off the deployment arm. Ruhger followed the box and remote into the cargo hold, while Grant and Loreli coiled and fastened the safety cables to the bottom of *Lightwave*. They'd need those cables when they reattached the cubes. If they could fix them.

Inside the cargo hold, Chief had already disassembled the heavily damaged box, the sides lying on the decking like a flat packing box before assembly. Circuitry glinted in the lights. Chief floated above the flattened box, muttering. Tyron hovered nearby, but not over the box.

Ruhger received a message from Chief—a vid and instructions for disassembling the box. "Katryn, I'll take the remote controls from you and take the cube apart." He sent "his" remote to the recharging station.

"Copy that, Ruhger. Releasing controls to you."

In his holo, the remote's controls showed his change in status, switching from secondary to primary. He moved the fold generator box into the empty area of decking Chief specified. After lowering the box, he sent the remote to recharge, leaving the tripod "wrench" in place for the reinstallation. Or to remove the intact cubes, if necessary.

While Tyron closed the big cargo bay hatch, Ruhger tested the box for residual energy but found nothing, so he proceeded with Chief's instructions. Along the side of each corner, pressing and rotating half-centimeter circles unlocked the sides. Using his suit's pinkie, he pressed and rotated, the box unfastened, and he unfolded the sides into a lopsided cross shape with corners cut off on three ends. One side held the once-bright red cylinders upright, the tubes dark; they'd easily slid out of their brackets.

Chief had energized portions of the decking just enough to hold the box sides flat. Ruhger adjusted his suit, latching his mag boots to the decking alongside the most-damaged portion. The orderly patterns of gold and silver circuitry, interspersed with small components, told him nothing. He'd be better off returning to the multiverse fold math. "Chief, Tyron, I'll leave you to it." He released his mag boots and pushed off the decking.

"Copy that, Captain," Tyron replied. "I'm pulling replacement cerimetal sheets and printing new interlocking fasteners for the sides." As Ruhger floated by, Tyron frowned, the expression exaggerated by his helmet. "Even if we can fix these generators, we'll need a target. Good luck."

"Suns." Everything relied on his so-called genius with math. But fold math was complex for regular travel in their time and space. The theories on folding to other realities, planes, or universes were even more difficult. They had too many variables, including a lot of imaginary numbers. As usual, the key was to change only one thing at a time. But that was almost impossible. Each alteration created a cascade of changes. Determining whether they'd traveled in time versus distance versus planes would help. But until then, he had to go down all the rabbit holes.

Ruhger waited for the airlock to cycle. A rabbit was a small rodent, and it lived unground. But why that equated with a series of possibilities, including false paths, would have to wait for another day when his brain wasn't fried by math. He entered the Command Center, waving at Saree on his way to his armor compartment.

After he removed his suit and showered, Ruhger surrounded himself with equations and theories. When his stomach rumbled, he swept it all away. Frustration simmered at the waste of time and energy down the many false trails.

"Ruhger?" Saree put a hand on his arm.

"I'm okay, just annoyed. Since no one has ever returned from a fold-gone-bad, I have no way to know if any of the theories are right. Francois van Lieugen y Ongkowijaya hinted that his theory *has* been successfully tested, but he hasn't provided proof. Most other theorists think he's blasting rads, and no one's successfully repeated his test. But they're all using programmed remotes, not doing it themselves. What if the fold fries the remotes? They can't return."

Saree's brows rose. "Do you think he's blasting rads? Because it doesn't sound like you believe that."

"No." His answer shocked him. "Well, maybe not."

Saree wagged her finger in front of his face. "No, no, no. No second-guessing. This is how your genius works." She tapped his forehead. "Whatever you do, it happens partly in your subconscious or unconscious mind. So, I'll follow up. Why is he right, and where is he wrong?"

Ruhger concentrated on Saree's smile, trying to keep his mind on the problem but not van Lieugen's specific conclusions. "I think he's right that there are parallel universes, rather than differing existences or planes. I think most of his math is correct, although his brother Wilmer, who is well-respected as a theoretician, has some valid criticisms."

Saree raised a brow. "Are they, though? Has either one done a successful experiment?"

"Wilmer refused to try because he's a theorist, not an experimentalist. But that seems like a weak excuse. Someone must have tried both."

"Someone might have a reason to suppress both the theories and the experiments."

Ruhger nodded and squeezed Saree's hand. "Probably. There's a lot of money in keeping the secrets behind fold generators."

Saree chuckled. "Besides, university politics are cutthroat. You wouldn't think a bunch of soft-bodied, giant-brained people could be so horrible to each other, but they are. One of the reasons I did most of my advanced degree work off-world was to avoid the backstabbing and politics. Even in my completely obscure field of ancient Old Earth folk music, other Old Earth music specialists were insanely jealous. They tried everything to stop me from getting my thesis study approved. I had to track down every single person on the committee and explain I was funding the research myself before they'd approve it. All these academics were sure I was stealing potential funding from their projects. Even after I explained, a lot of them asked me for credits or called me a liar, but not to my face. The vote was really close. Those people are expert rad-blasters."

Ruhger couldn't believe what he was hearing, but Saree never lied to him, and her mannerisms showed no hint of joking. "Good thing I never had to study, then, because I'd be shooting people."

"One of many reasons I was glad we escaped Old Earth. Academia is a cult, already. Being trapped inside an academic cult with an AI leader was a nightmare." She shuddered.

Ruhger pulled close, holding her tight. Saree returned his embrace. It wasn't a popular opinion, but he was glad Old Earth was gone, the Librarian version of Galactica dead. Humanity could fully focus on the way forward, rather than the questionable, twisted history of the past.

"Command, Chef Loreli. Dinner will be in thirty minutes. Don't be late. Chef out."

Saree laughed. "Well, we have our orders. Let's go pull Chief away from his puzzle because you know he'll never go willingly." She pulled away, taking his hand and tugging him to the hatch.

Ruhger followed gladly. Unlike Chief, he was more than happy to stop working on his problem. Plus, if Saree was right, and she usually was, his back brain would keep thinking. He could do something more enjoyable while a miracle occurred.

Chapter Ten

SAREE

After a good meal and conversation followed by a lovely sleep period, hope buoyed Saree's spirits. They'd find the solutions to all their problems before extreme measures or desperate chances were required.

Entering the dining compartment for breakfast, her certainty took a plunge at the worry line between Q's brows. After gathering a plate full of pastries, Saree sat next to Q and wrapped her arm around the girl's still too-thin shoulders. "Hey, what's with the long face?"

Q shivered ever so slightly. "I don't like being trapped in interstellar space, no matter what time or place we might be in."

Saree pulled her tighter into a side hug. "I don't blame you. I don't like it either. But we've got a few tremendous advantages. One, no warring AIs. Two, a couple of certified geniuses."

"More than a couple." Q turned to face Saree, pulling from her hold. "You're one too."

Saree chuckled. "Well, star, meet sun."

"Huh?" Q's nose wrinkled.

Saree pointed at her. "If I'm a genius, you are too. You can do everything I can in ^*timespace*^; the only difference is experience." Except that strange interlude on Sa'sa. "And the weird Sa'sa ancestor ritual. I wonder if you need to experience that?" No chance of it happening any time soon, since she couldn't reach the Sa'sa. Besides, Saree went there with Ruhger, her mate, as part of a queenship ceremony, and Q didn't have a mate. The Sa'sa would try to split them up again, too. "I'm not certain the ritual had any effect on me, though."

"Can't chance it." Q's mouth twisted and her eyebrows rose in a comically quizzical expression. "Who knows what they'd do to me if I went back to Sa'sa without a human mate? Never mind that I don't really need one to have children." She wrinkled her nose. "But I'm not ready for that kind of commitment. I need to be the cool aunt first."

"Well, for that to happen, we need to find medico supplies because I'm not live-bearing kids." Saree shuddered, remembering her foster mother's glee, sharing the "horrors" of natural childbirth. The woman was such a rad-blaster; plenty of women had children naturally with no problems. Fortunately, Saree was fairly certain her "kindness" had been repaid. Gov Human sent her foster parents to a frontier world on a hard labor sentence for child abuse. After they departed, Saree hadn't tracked them; she'd only cared that the couple never had control over children again. She made a note to check when *Lightwave* returned to civilization. They'd both been good at influencing people in all the wrong ways.

"I guess I could ask Grant to be my fake mate, but then he couldn't be your speaker." Q snort-chuckled. "And the Sa'sa would separate us again." Her smile died.

Saree nodded. "Well, if we're here a while—and I don't think we'll be too long—I'll work on recreating that ceremony. No reason I can't, without the creepy dead body. And Ruhger played no role, so you shouldn't actually need a mate." One more reason they had to return—Q needed interaction with people her age. "But I'll have to find the Sa'sa hive mind. And I haven't found any trace of it yet." She'd have to keep looking. Even if they were in a far future time or a different universe, she should be able to reach the Sa'sa mind. But perhaps the Sa'sa had moved on to another plane of existence. If it was a long time ago, the hive mind might not exist.

She'd keep looking; it seemed logical that some trace of it would exist, even without the Sa'sa. She was a part of it, and so was Q; future ^*timespace*^ maintainers must touch the hive mind to do the job. Or maybe they didn't. If all they did was smooth

^*timespace*^, like the Travelers, then they didn't need the hive mind. Or the Sa'sa.

Or a fold clock.

Didn't they? Saree's mind spun. "Ruhger, if ^*timespace*^ is smooth, do we still need a fold clock?"

He stopped pacing and stared at her, his brows wrinkling. "Of course. There are four dimensions, and we specify a target for each one." His expression deepened into a glower; deep thought, not anger. "But if we didn't care 'when' we arrived, then no, we wouldn't need a fold clock. That would mean time-travel, though, and no one's proven that works. I'm fairly certain, from the theories and the math, that we can't time-travel. I believe that when we specify something other than our time, we fold to a future or a past that differs from ours. Changing the time factor also changes the universe, existence, or plane we fold into." He huffed. "Well, that clarifies that. Thanks. I still don't know if *Lightwave* folded into time and space or just distance, but I can now discard some theories and speculations."

"Interesting, because I'm getting indications from the computer that we are in a far future universe, rather than a far distant one." Tyron turned his chair to face them. "But it's hard to tell; the models are nebulous."

Ruhger shook his head. "I think we folded into the far distance. It only looks like time travel because the light from our current universe hasn't arrived here yet."

Tyron looked at the overhead with a huff equal to Ruhger's, then returned to them, relief on his face. "Of course! Why didn't I think of that? Sure, we time-traveled, but only by appearances, not reality."

"I didn't think about it either." Ruhger shrugged his massive shoulders. "And I should have."

"Or the computer should have." Katryn pointed at the big vid screen. "The speed of light is constant, other than around black holes, so it should have considered that. The fact that it didn't makes me suspicious of the results."

Saree nodded, agreeing with Katryn. "Garbage in, garbage out. Tyron, try running the navigational programs, allowing for relativity." She chuckled, but there was nothing funny about it. "With fold clocks, we never worry about relativity. We go, magically appearing at the same time we left. Of course we don't consider it."

"I've been chasing a hyperbolic comet." Ruhger shook his head. "Ridiculous. Stupid on my part. I should have started with the simple solution and checked to see if it fit, rather than spinning through the theoretical multiverse."

Saree wagged her finger at him. "None of that. That's not how your brain works. You've got to work with your process, not against it. Just like the computer, you need input, good input, and we didn't have that."

Chief and Lashtar entered, retracting their helmets. "Besides, there are four fold generator cubes. It makes sense to consider all four dimensions. Lashtar and I are speculating, but we believe each box creates a different field, and the combination creates the effect that folds space. I can't tell what those fields are or what they do, just that they're different. Does that agree with any of the math, Ruhger?"

He nodded. "It does."

Which was great, but not the most important issue. "Can you fix the generators, Chief?" Saree held her breath while Chief grimaced.

"I can't recreate them perfectly. We can replace the panels and recreate the circuitry for the least-damaged box. But without a model for the most-damaged box, there's no guarantee what I make will work. Or work correctly." His grimace deepened into a scowl. "Plus, there's more blast and rad in these things. Those tubes with the bright red lights are all show, no go. They're just pretty distractions. Without them, the boxes could be much smaller."

"Chief, could you build those from scratch?" Ruhger's tone was unusually hopeful. "If you can, we've got an alternative source of revenue when we return. Relying on the Time Guild alone makes me ping like an asteroid field on a single use suit. If we can build fold generators, that's a potentially huge income source."

Was Ruhger uncomfortable with the single source of income or the source of that income? Saree knew Ruhger didn't trust the Sa'sa, and therefore, the Time Guild, but she hadn't realized how much it bothered him.

"We'd have a hard time holding off the current suppliers of fold generators while we got a manufacturing plant up and running." Tyron mimed an explosion. "Sabotage is guaranteed."

"And someone would certainly steal my ideas and create cheaper, more dangerous versions." Chief shrugged. "The only reason we didn't destroy everything when we entered the fold generator compartment was Katryn and Q got around the safeguards."

"We could only do that because of the specific damage to the fold generators." Katryn shook her head. "If it hadn't been for that, and Q's sharp eyes on the net, I think the whole thing would have melted into a slag heap before we circumvented the fold generator security net."

Tyron put his arm around her shoulders and kissed the top of her head. "It was a little too close to melting you into a slag heap, too."

Katryn shivered. "Not something I want to try again."

Saree waited. "I'm not sure copying is such a bad thing. Why shouldn't fold generators be open source?"

Ruhger huffed. "How many would fold themselves into oblivion?"

"Self-solving problem, Ruhger." Chief shrugged one shoulder. "It would decrease the number of fools in the universe."

Saree frowned at him. "Not a great business model, Chief. But let's not get ahead of ourselves. First, we fix the damage and try to return. Then we can build an improved model. Maybe we license it to a manufacturer rather than build it ourselves."

"We should do the same with fold clocks," Grant said. "If we're expected to take care of all human ^*timespace*^, why not supply them with our own fold clocks, too?"

Saree shook her head. "We're members of the Time Guild. I don't want to leave the organization behind, Grant."

"Maybe not now, but it might come to that later, Saree."

"No." Saree shook her head slowly, trying to emphasize her feelings on the subject. "Even if the Time Guild becomes all human, I think it's important to keep the institution. Supplying quality clocks and tuning them based on need, not politics, is important."

Grant raised both his hands, palm out. "Okay, you've got a point. But part of my job is devil's advocate, remember?"

"Maybe when we're not fighting for our lives, Grant." Ruhger raised a brow.

"When are we not fighting for our lives?" Grant rolled his eyes. "But fine. I'll table that discussion for a few years. Maybe."

Saree frowned at him, but it was hard to stay annoyed at Grant even when he pulled them out of orbit. "How can we help rebuild the fold generators, Chief?"

Chief pulled his wrench from his armor's exterior pocket, tossing it from hand to hand. "Tyron's got the printer going for the containers and connectors. I think I've got enough electronic components and circuitry metals to recreate the boxes, but I don't know what the most heavily damaged one looks like." He slapped the wrench into his armored palm with a thwack. "I think I need the other two fold generator boxes to figure that out. Removing the undamaged boxes is chancy, because there could be another failsafe ready to slag the whole thing."

Q chuckled. "If it helped, we could take a tiny corner off of each with a laser." Saree echoed Q's chuckle, along with the rest of the crew.

Except Chief, who pursed his lips and nodded. "That's a pretty good idea. If we damage the right place, it won't do a lot of harm, and losing continuity should prove to the failsafe logic that damage has occurred. Then we can open them safely." He nodded at Q. "Brilliant idea."

Q laughed. "I was joking. But I guess only half-joking?" She shrugged.

Ruhger held up a hand. "Are you sure? All the cubes have different circuitry, right?"

"Yes." Chief nodded once. "But if we take off a tiny corner, we should break the circuit but not destroy too much. We can go a half-centimeter over the thickness of the cerimetal."

"I can do that with remotes," Katryn said. "I'll send a couple out, fry off whichever corner is best, Chief, and remove the boxes. Tyron can lay them flat for you. We'll take detailed scans and have the computer run a comparison. That should help with the reconstruction."

"Great ideas, Katryn." Chief nodded once.

"Agreed, on all points." Saree smiled. "Make it so." She turned to Ruhger. "Now that you clarified the math, what's our destination? Should we fold to an empty system first to recharge?"

Ruhger shook his head. "Not sure yet. Let me go through all the models and see what I can get rid of now and what needs more investigation."

"Dinner in two hours!" Loreli caroled. "Minion, come help. Grant, you're helping too."

Grant's lip stuck out in a pout, and he blinked his ridiculously long lashes. "You don't need me with the fabulous Q!"

"Nice try, Speaker." Q tugged him from his chair. "If I'm going, you're going."

"Besides, you don't want to miss my reward!" Loreli pointed at Grant, then Q. "Special just for you two!"

"Give me a couple of seconds, Chef." Q shoved Grant toward the hatch, then smiled at Saree. "Are you sure we didn't time travel? Because if we only traveled in distance, we should be able to reach the Sa'sa hive mind, shouldn't we?" Her brows lifted, then she spun on one toe and ran through the hatch.

"By the egg of Zarar! She's right." A mixture of exasperation, annoyance, and fear swept through Saree. She shouldn't have lost sight of that fact.

"Is she?" Tyron shrugged. "Just because distance seems immaterial in ^timespace^ doesn't mean it is. We've never folded outside the Sa'sa sphere of influence, right?"

Ruhger rubbed Saree's tense shoulders. "He's right."

"And that means more time in ^timespace^ for me." She hadn't found the Sa'sa, but that didn't mean they weren't there.

Ruhger's fingers tightened, then released, and he rubbed rather than massaged. "Be careful, that's all I ask. Don't go without letting me know, and we'll set timers."

Saree had no desire to get lost in ^timespace^. "Absolutely. I may do some exploration without Q in ^timespace^ because she doesn't have my reach, for lack of a better term. Also, I don't want to accidentally pull power from her like a soothing stone."

"Would having a soothing stone help?" An odd mix of expressions flashed across Katryn's face.

She was hiding something. Saree didn't sigh or show any emotion of her own, despite her instinct to yell at the woman. "Yes. Even a small soothing stone could boost my power, especially if the rest of you activate it."

The crew's expressions revealed their distaste. Katryn bounded from her seat and out the hatch, demonstrating her disdain. Saree sighed out loud.

Ruhger returned to his massage. "Don't worry about it. We'll do it, no matter how much we might not like it."

Saree twisted to look up at him. "We don't have a soothing stone, so it doesn't matter."

Tyron took over Katryn's remotes, maneuvering them into place near the remaining fold generator cubes. He aimed the remote's laser.

The hatch hissed and Katryn entered, carrying a large container. "Here you go. A soothing stone."

If there was a soothing stone in there, the case must be heavily shielded. Or someone had sold Katryn a fake.

Ruhger released Saree's shoulders and stepped in front of her, blocking Katryn's approach. "Why do you have a soothing stone, Katryn?" His voice was low and ominous, with a threatening edge.

Katryn stepped around Ruhger and carried the box to the conference room table. After letting the box thunk on the table, she turned to face them. "Because I bought it after our first trip to Aljanah. It's no secret that I didn't trust Saree or her talents, and I especially didn't trust your reaction to her, Ruhger. I wanted a safety switch of sorts if things went wrong, so I took a chance on buying one of these." She shrugged one shoulder and looked down at the decking. "Quite frankly, I'd forgotten I even had it. It was in the back of my shielded storage container in the cargo hold."

Katryn met Saree's gaze. "I trust you now, and I believe you have Ruhger's best interests at heart, along with the rest of ours. So, I'm turning the stone over to you, to use as necessary." She put her hand on the top of the box and entered a code, then turned back to Saree. "I've cleared the security. Put yours in or leave it unsecured." Katryn walked to Tyron. He gathered her close, shooting a raised brow look at Ruhger, who only glowered.

Her action, apology, and explanation took a lot of guts. "Thank you, Katryn. I appreciate the stone and your trust. I won't let you down." She grabbed Ruhger's hand. "Please secure the case. I don't want to touch it."

"Rad-blasted right you're not touching it." Ruhger strode to the table, inspected the box, and entered a code, then put his hand on the top. He turned, glowering at Katryn. "I can't believe you went this far." Ruhger's fists clenched, and he leaned forward, his body quivering.

Saree rose to stop him. If he wanted to attack badly enough, he'd avoid her easily. But she couldn't have such dissension in her clutch, especially after Katryn's sincere apology and atonement.

Chapter Eleven

RUHGER

Anger tightened Ruhger's hands into fists, and it took all his willpower to stay where he was, rather than shaking Katryn. Certainly, she'd known soothing stones might be deadly to Saree, that's why she'd bought it. But she'd kept the stone in a heavily shielded case, or Saree would have discovered it. Plus, Katryn had apologized, and that was just enough to prevent him from doing something terrible.

That, and Tyron would kick him from one end of the compartment to the other. Since Katryn had explained, he'd deserve the beating. Besides, from the defeat in Katryn's slumped posture, she probably wouldn't fight him, and that would make the entire situation worse. Trust couldn't be forced. And all of them tended toward worst-case scenarios. He closed his eyes and ran through a meditation sequence, controlling his overactive emotional response.

By the time he opened his eyes, everyone was gone except Saree, standing next to him but not touching.

She grasped his hands. "Better? If it helps, I'm not upset. I know Katryn has mixed feelings about me, and I understand her reasoning. And I understand why she 'forgot' about the stone. It's easier to shove our failings away, hiding them from ourselves, than to deal with them."

Ruhger gently squeezed her fingers. "I'm okay. I'm angry, but I understand. Katryn's always had a quick temper and trust issues. She doesn't believe fully in any of us, except Tyron. And she doesn't always understand how cutting her words can be. Or until after she's done the damage."

"I get it." Saree smiled at him. "We both have trust issues, too. That's why it took so long for us to get together. I'd probably have attacked with words, except I had to hide my true identity for a long time. Otherwise, my personality might be much closer to Katryn's."

Ruhger chuckled, pulling Saree into a hug. "I'm glad it isn't. One of her is enough." He relaxed his arms enough to look at her face. "But I'd love you anyway."

"I love you, too." She rose on her tiptoes.

Ruhger gratefully drew her up, bringing his lips to her soft mouth. He wanted to keep kissing her, but they were in the middle of the Command Center; anyone could come in. "We should go."

Saree giggled. "Yes, but not to our compartment. It's almost dinnertime, and you know how Loreli will be if we're not there. The honeymoon is over." She pulled away but took his hand and led him to the hatch.

Just before the hatch opened, he stopped and pulled Saree back into his embrace. "The honeymoon will never be over, you know."

She smiled and put her hands around his jaw. "Of course not. Not for us. But for Loreli?" A laugh burst from her. "The grace period is over."

"Attention, *Lightwave*. All hands report to the dining room immediately. Now!" Loreli bellowed the last word.

He winked at Saree, then yanked her off her feet for one more deep kiss. After Saree flushed pink, he relaxed his arms and took her hand in his, leading her to the dining room. But he was looking forward to their personal dessert more than Chef's undoubtedly fabulous meal.

The next morning, they gathered in the Command Center around the conference room table. Saree tapped a rapid rhythm on the table. "Chief, how's the reconstruction going?"

Chief tapped his wrench on the table. "We're making progress, but not as quickly as I'd hoped. Katryn's been a tremendous help. She removed the remaining fold generator boxes off the deployment arms and ran image comparisons between the four boxes. But the missing corners of the most-damaged box are where many of the differences seem to be. Also, the bright red tubes running through the middle aren't blast and rad after all. They guide and modify the laser blast, changing it into electricity that surges simultaneously, surrounding the box. I think those tubes are the key to generating an even field and might be part of why we ended up here, rather than somewhere else. Or oblivion." The tap of Chief's cerimetal wrench on the plas table thudded ominously. "So, not only do we have to recreate the circuitry, we also must recreate those tubes. I've asked Tyron to take the lead on that, while Lashtar does the circuitry inlay on the cerimetal." He sniffed. "She's got a steadier hand than I do, and a good eye for the individual circuits."

Lashtar put her hand on his, halting the tapping of the wrench. "But you can see the big picture. I can't tell what the thing does, only where the next logical tracing or component goes, based on your direction." She turned to Tyron. "Grant's been extremely helpful, identifying the individual components. Q's good at connecting them to the traced circuitry. We're not going as fast as any of us want, but we're making progress because we make a good team."

Ruhger wished he was a part of that team; it would be easier than banging his head against impossible math.

Of course, Saree turned to him next. "How's the math problem going?"

He didn't hold back his exasperated huff. "Not well. I'm concentrating on distance only, and I've discarded the most obviously wrong theories. I'm even more certain that the energy from the laser raised the amount by point six-six gigawatts, a half of the usual 1.2 gigawatt multiples for folding. If I can't find a theory that really fits, I think the best thing we can do is reverse our fold, using the same amount of power. We'll have to store enough to fold out immediately to an emergency fold where we can recharge."

"That's a problem because some capacitors got fried." Tyron grimaced. "In normal circumstances, we would easily replace them. Or we might not need them at all. We're fairly certain that some are overload or feedback safeties. But some of the critical capacitors got taken out, too. Depending on how much energy we need, we might make it all the way back. But we might not, and I'm sure we won't be able to fold until we recharge. Chief and I believe it will take thirty-six hours without engine charging. Twenty-eight with. And that's only if we don't fry more capacitors on the way back."

Saree rocked back in her seat. "That makes my part even more critical. I've got to find the Sa'sa or be sure that they don't exist in our current reality." She sighed. "Let's set a time so you can all help energize the soothing stone." She turned toward Q, sitting next to her. "Q, you're in charge of that. I don't want you in ^*timespace*^ when I'm pushing that hard. I don't want to take you that"—her fingers fluttered in the air above the table—"far, for lack of a better term. I could pull you out of your body. Plus, your power should energize the stone a lot. Don't touch it, though." She wagged her finger in front of Q's face. "And if I don't come back, don't you dare go looking for me. That's an order. I'm stronger than you are in ^*timespace*^. If I can't get back, you won't come close to finding me. Understood?"

Q nodded, her face solemn. "I understand. I don't like it, but you're right. I need to work on developing my abilities, rather than hiding from them because the circumstances are scary. That's not going to change, and the only real protection I have is enhancing my talent."

Ruhger smiled at Q, proud that his kid was taking her gift seriously.

Saree hugged Q. "Well, I still can't reliably create that shield you generated, so you've got me beat there."

Q snickered. "I can't do it reliably either. I'm guessing that we both could under threat, though." She frowned. "Either way, I understand my orders and will comply. After you return—because you will, I'm sure—we'll work on an improvement plan for me." She shrugged. "I'll follow through this time."

Saree grinned. "Agreed." She hugged Q again, then released her and turned back to Chief. "How much time do you need to finish your work before I call you to help with the soothing stone?"

Chief placed his wrench on the table. "I'd rather not start and stop. Let's do this hoodoo now."

Saree spun her chair to face him. "Ruhger?"

"Agreed. Let's get it over with." He cupped her cheek and ran his thumb across her soft lips. "Listen to me, and come back when I call, please." Terror surged, but Ruhger controlled his fear. Channeling his emotions into his voice helped bring Saree back; otherwise, he was only hurting himself.

Saree put her hand on his, turned her face, and kissed his palm, then smiled. "I will. I'll listen." She pulled his hand from her cheek, pulling so his palm landed over her heart. "You're here, so I'll listen wherever this might go." She tapped the top of her head with her other hand.

Ruhger desperately wanted to pull her into his arms and tell the rest of the crew to get lost, but they had a job to do. He stood, took her hand, and walked with her to her medfloat.

Saree climbed on, then squeezed his hand. "Don't worry. I'll be fine."

"Worry is my middle name." Not that anyone in his family ever had a real middle name. Most spacers didn't; their fold transports and shuttle designators were more important than personal names. Mercenaries didn't either, taking on the identity of their company. They'd add it to the designation of their original world or parents if they kept the connection, but often, new mercs were outcasts, homeless, and unwanted. But none of that mattered—Saree did. "How long should I give you?" He caressed the back of her small hand with his thumb.

She shrugged. "How long did it take me last time? Take five minutes off of that."

He'd take ten. He set an alarm on his e-torc. "I'll try the singing bowl first, then call you back with my voice." He suppressed a shudder. "I'm not going to use an electrical shock unless I absolutely have to. I think your heart rate and distress drew you back last time because nothing I did worked." He pressed his lips together so he wouldn't beg her to stay. She had a job to do, and he couldn't hold her back. Not if they were going to return to their part of the universe safely.

Saree smiled gently. "I'll come back." She lifted her head. "Q, is everyone ready?"

"Ready when you are." She met his gaze. "Ruhger, you can help from there. Just think positive thoughts, sending energy and emotions into the stone."

Loreli bustled into the Command Center, placing a bev-tainer into the cup holder on the medfloat. "Ready when you come back, Saree." She sashayed to the table, resting her hip on top and placing her fingertips on the rock. "And I'm ready to energize this stone like no one ever has!"

Ruhger chuckled, then nodded to Q and turned back to Saree, resting below him. "Everyone's ready. Trust yourself, Saree. Don't overthink it."

"I'll go into ^timespace^ and wait for the energy to build, then use it. Don't touch the stone, Q. Everyone else can, but if you feel an energy drain, pull away. Go, Q." At Q's wry frown, she closed her eyes and dropped into ^timespace^.

Ruhger couldn't blame Saree for the unnecessary reminder. He was worried about both of them.

"Focus on the stone. Send your hope, love, fear, whatever you feel into it." Q's volume and tone dropped as she spoke.

Ruhger clicked his timer on, then tried to send his terror for Saree into the sandy, oblong rock on the table. Wait—that box was keyed to him, but Q got it open. He shook the annoyance away; that was a problem for later. He sent his annoyance and fear for Q into the rock, too. And his embarrassment about the ridiculousness of thinking into a rock.

"Hands off! Keep focusing." Q leaned on the table, hovering perilously close to the soothing stone. Ruhger left Saree on the medfloat and grasped Q's shoulders, pushing her into a chair. He couldn't lose both of them. He shoved all that fear into the rad-blasted rock, too, and recalled his anger with Katryn, pushing that as well.

His alarm chimed, recalling him from a meditative state. His hands rested on Q's chair; the rest of the crew stood around the table, their eyes closed, hands on the table. On the table, the soothing stone had turned to dust. Ruhger let go, returned to Saree's medfloat, and stretched his fingers. He picked up the singing bowl's hammer and then surveyed her medico data. She was in a deep meditative state with no sign of distress. He could wait five more minutes.

Two minutes later, her heartbeat spiked, but resettled. He gripped the hammer but didn't ring the bowl. Then her pulse rose slowly and her brain activity increased—she was returning without his intervention. Ruhger's heart sang, his heart tempo rising with hers. He placed his hand over hers and squeezed gently. His crew stirred, coming out of their trances. Q and Loreli joined him at Saree's medfloat, while the rest relaxed.

Saree blinked rapidly, seizing his hand. She smiled, wonder and happiness both clear. "I found the Sa'sa!"

"Thank the seven suns of Saga." Ruhger squeezed her hand again, while the crew gathered around the medfloat. "Can they help?"

She grimaced. "Sort of. I barely made contact. I don't think I conveyed much to them except relief, and they mostly sent me alarm and the command to rest. But I know"—her nose wrinkled—"*where* they are in ^timespace^. I can find them again." Loreli handed her the recovery drink, and she sipped.

"Did you recognize the individual?" Chief asked.

Saree chuckled. "There are no individuals. But I recognized the gathering or clutch. I reached the Time Guild clutch. I believe they were looking for me because I got relief and a sense of triumph, then concern." She shivered.

Ruhger pulled a blanket over her body, even though he wasn't positive her trembling was a physical reaction. "So, are we in our time and universe?"

"I don't know for sure. It's always hard to tell what time it is with the Sa'sa because their hive mind carries the past and can show different futures. I've never seen the future possibilities, though. I only know they are there."

Saree had excellent instincts; she had to trust herself. "What do you think the most likely possibility is? Actually, don't think. Tell me what your first thought was when you contacted the Sa'sa and when you returned to your body."

Saree's shoulders rose toward her ears, then relaxed. "If we changed universes or planes, we're in one that's close, perhaps connected by ^*timespace*^. If we traveled in time—no." She shook her head. "I don't know how I know, but I know we didn't travel in time. I'm almost positive we didn't change planes, either."

Ruhger smiled, tension releasing from his shoulders and back. "That helps a lot. Ruling out time travel drops the number of crackpot theories and mathematical conundrums by half. More like two-thirds. Great job." Distance, even millions of light years, was a matter of power, not next-to-impossible math.

"That helps us, too." Chief's head bobbed, his expression thoughtful. "If we're not traveling in time, we can make some assumptions on the damaged circuitry." His head tilted and his lips compressed. "I shouldn't know that, but I do. Come on; we've got to get this down before it leaves my brain." He towed Lashtar away.

Tyron grinned. "Great job, Saree. We'll go help Chief." Tyron, Katryn, and Grant followed Lashtar. Loreli tagged along, muttering about celebration dinners.

"Katryn!" Saree called. When Katryn turned back, Saree continued. "Thank you for the stone. I wouldn't have made contact without it." Katryn smiled and trotted after Chief, Tyron flashing a grateful look back at Saree.

Q pushed the bev-tainer in Saree's hand back to her mouth. "I'm sure Loreli will call me shortly, but can you tell me anything more about what you saw?"

Saree grimaced. "You know how hard it is to describe anything in ^*timespace*^. But rather than searching in all directions, I did what Ruhger suggested. I rested and gathered energy from the soothing stone, listening passively. Then I searched in the direction, for lack of a better term, that I thought the Sa'sa might be. As I got closer, the mass of thought created by the hive mind pulled me in and let me make contact." She smiled ruefully. "I always thought there was no true distance in ^*timespace*^ but I was wrong. It's so strange to have actual distance and direction, rather than a concept."

Ruhger nodded. She knew where the Sa'sa were physically, too. She simply didn't realize it, so he'd help. "Saree, what direction is that? Point." He snapped the last word, and her arm flew up behind her head, slightly to her left. He smiled at her. "I knew it. Stay there. Trust your instincts, Saree." He swept up the navigation controls in his holo and placed a vector parallel to her arm. "Okay, you can bring your arm down. Good job."

She chuckled and shook her head. "We make a great team, that's for sure. I had no idea I could actually give you a direction."

"I believe in you." He had all the faith in the universe for her. "Drink. Rest. Then you and Q can work on a training plan while I do the math. Thanks to your abilities, I'll have estimates rather than ridiculous guesses to feed into the equations." He kissed Saree quickly, then stepped away to bring up the math he'd been working on. But first... "Q, we'll be having words about how you opened that security box."

He returned to his holo, loving the laughter of his favorite people. The support and intelligence of his family would get them home.

Chapter Twelve

SAREE

Saree stood next to Chief. He pointed at the reconstructed box on the cargo hold's decking. "They're not pretty, but they should work." Rough ridges of cerimetal stuck out on the outside, so the box couldn't lie completely flat, but the circuitry and tubes inside were bright and shiny. He gripped his wrench tight, his knuckles whitening. "I think."

"No way to know until we try." Ruhger shrugged one massive shoulder. "Between all of us, our best guesses are pretty decent, but it's all theoretical."

"Command, surveillance." Q's voice held urgency.

Saree couldn't help thinking *what now?* "Go surveillance."

"Incoming. An entire fleet of something. The thruster signatures are strange."

The ghostly glow of holos lit her crew's faces. Saree leaned on Ruhger's shoulder, sharing his holo, rather than bringing up surveillance.

"Might be non-oxys," Tyron said.

"Or remotes." Chief stabbed at his holo. "Galactica, maybe."

"Time to intercept or attack?" Saree would rather leave than make first contact—or last contact.

"Not enough data; just spotted them." Q's voice conveyed her puzzlement.

Saree spun on her toe. "I'm coming. Chief, get that last box reattached. Let's fold before they get here, whoever they are."

Ruhger trod alongside, fingers flashing through his holo. "They probably folded in, that's why we didn't spot them until now, Q."

"Oh. Of course."

Saree flashed Ruhger a smile, but he was busy manipulating his holo. They entered the Command Center and sat.

Ruhger swept away most of his holo screens and manipulated the surveillance on the big screen. "We'll need another minute of observations, but I'm fairly certain they're not moving any quicker than we can—yet. We'll see if they continue acceleration. With their thrusters facing directly away from us, it's hard to get a good calculation of velocity without waiting. We should have put out observation remotes after all."

Q snorted. "Why? We're deep in interstellar space. Nothing and nobody around us. Somebody spotted us and they're coming to look."

"Or attack." Ruhger shook his head. "Never assume intent, good or bad. Plan for bad and hope for good."

Grant joined them. "Be polite, be professional, but have a plan to kill everyone you meet." He lifted a brow. "Some Old Earth general. Maybe."

"Real person or not, they were right," Ruhger rumbled. "Also, engage your brain before you engage your weapon."

Saree rolled her eyes. *Military types.* "Well, edifying as all this is, I'd rather leave before either occurs. We can tell Gov Human about this location when we get back, and they can talk to the other species about sending emissaries. Or not. Either way, it's not our job. We have enough difficulties doing ours without taking on someone else's."

Ruhger nodded. "Agreed. I'd rather avoid than engage."

Saree kept an eye on the remote towing the last box to the end of the deployment arm. The sooner the thing was attached, the better.

Q turned to them, a deep crease between her brows. "How about I go into ^timespace^ and see if I can pick up intent? You know I can sometimes."

She definitely had some sort of empathy. "On a medfloat, please."

"Of course." Q jogged to hers and jumped on it.

Grant rose, following her. "I'll watch her."

"Thanks, Grant." Saree turned to Ruhger. "Got an equation for us? A fold destination?"

He nodded. "I do. It's a system in Cepheus, the closest destination I have coordinates for. The Garnet Star is uninhabited; a red star on the verge of collapse, so it's a bit chancy, but the last readings showed it intact. Despite wildly fluctuating radiation profiles, scientists believe it will be at least another hundred standard years before collapse, and probably much, much longer. But that's the whole reason we have coordinates for something so far from civilization; scientists are observing the star with remote platforms." He grimaced. "It's not ideal, but the next closest target is almost a thousand parsecs farther, so it would take a lot more energy to get there."

A chance worth taking. A star collapse was a long, drawn-out process until the very end. "We'll look for runaway fission indicators when we arrive, then. Will we have enough power to make another fold?"

Ruhger sucked in a long breath through his teeth. "Unknown. Probably. I've got the next fold destination selected, but as I said, it's a thousand parsecs farther. Unfortunately, chances are good that we'll burn something out on this fold. If we make it to our destination in the first place."

"Command, Chief. Box locked and loaded. Continuity testing in progress. Approximately five minutes until completion."

"Copy that, Chief. We've got a fold target, so once you report testing is successful, we'll attempt fold." Saree tapped a rhythm on her chair arms, trying to calm her nerves.

"Command, I'd like to do more testing but understand your decision. I can't guarantee further tests will be useful."

"And they could cause more problems, like break a fragile connection." Ruhger locked their fold destination into navigation. "You know that risk is always there. Since there's no way to truly test the repairs other than fold, I'd rather do that than meet whoever's coming." He maximized the surveillance. "They're coming in hot. They've got grav generators, or they're tolerant of high gravity, or they're remotes. Sooner is better, Chief."

"Sooner *is* better, Chief." Q sat up on her medfloat. "I don't know who or what they are, but they're not friendly." Her nose wrinkled. "They're not hostile, exactly, either but I'm getting an impression of fear and determination. A 'go away or we'll make you' kind of feeling."

Saree smiled at her. "Good job. All the more reason not to do anything extra, Chief."

"We're not. I'll report status when I'm done. Chief out."

The race was on. Unless the unknown forces had capabilities far beyond theirs, *Lightwave* would fold before laser fire reached them, let alone whatever ships or remotes were out there. "Q, does your feeling mean those are sentients or AIs?"

"I'm not sure." Q wrapped her arms around her waist. "But whatever or whoever, they don't want us here."

Saree didn't want them to stay any longer, either. "Chief, sooner is better."

"Acknowledged," Lashtar replied. "Going as fast as we can."

"Saree, we should probably get into armor, preferably hardsuits, but soft is better than nothing. The Garnet Star blasts a lot of rads." Ruhger rose, walking to his compartment. Grant and Q followed him.

Chief's team was already in hardsuits. Saree brought up comms with Loreli. "Chef, armor up ASAP, please."

"No! My sauce will curdle!"

"Better your sauce than your brains, Loreli." Saree muffled the snort-laugh that wanted to burst free at Chef's dramatics.

"Fine. I'll be right there." A few moments later, she swept through the hatch and ran to her armor compartment, sniffing disdainfully on her way. But when she thudded back out in her hardsuit, she tossed a salute.

Ruhger stepped up next to Saree in a hardsuit, Grant behind him. "Go, I've got command."

"Command is yours." She ran to her armor compartment and struggled with the hardsuit's plumbing. Once finished, she fastened the suit, leaving the helmet retracted, and joined Ruhger. Q was there, her face flushed.

"You two need practice." Ruhger raised his hands to his holo. "Chief's testing is complete and successful, so I'll keep command. All personnel, any objections to fold, raise them now." Saree gripped the back of her chair while Ruhger waited three seconds. "Fold in five, four, three, two, fold."

Navigation changed; stars popped into view. They'd survived fold. Saree couldn't hold back her relieved smile.

"High radiation on most bands," Grant reported. "Fluctuating."

"We appear to be on target." Ruhger pointed at the navigation screen. "We're on the outer edges of the Garnet Star's system. We should charge quickly here, without too much radiation, if the star remains stable."

Q poked at her holo. "There are a number of stations nearby; I assume they're scientific monitors, since none are inhabited."

The silence from Engineering was worrying. Saree brought up a vid in her holo; Chief, Lashtar, Tyron, and Katryn huddled around a holo. "Engineering?"

"Assessing damage," Chief said. "We've definitely fried something in fold systems, probably more than one component. Main batteries are charging, but the fold generators are throwing warnings with damage reported by all subsystems. With the way we rigged this thing, it's not surprising. But we should be close enough to civilization that we can get replacement parts if necessary."

"Chief, we don't want to tell anyone we've successfully deconstructed and fixed a fold generator," Tyron said. "We'd be folding from a supernova into a black hole."

"If this supernova's rad levels keep rising, we might be better off in the black hole," Grant said.

"Q, help me find something we can shelter behind and still get power." Ruhger manipulated his holo. "Sorry, Saree. Command is yours, again."

"I accept." They were two halves of a whole, but the crew needed to know who was in charge.

Q shoved a vid to the big screen. "What about one of the experimental monitoring stations? Some of them are massive. I'm sure they're heavily shielded. And maybe we can siphon power from them rather than generating it on our own." The screen displayed a gigantic circular gold sun shield with solar arrays and a smaller square box attached to the back. "They must have to do a lot of orbital maneuvers to keep a sun shield that big in place. It would act like a sail under the pressure from solar winds, and this star is one enormous storm."

Of course a child used to scrounging would consider stealing power normal, while the researcher in Saree's head screamed about destroying science. But scientific knowledge was far less important than their survival. Besides, with that big of an array, there should be power to burn. "Q, have you found one big enough to shelter *Lightwave*?"

"Almost. The fold generators and shuttles might stick out, but we could maneuver *Lightwave* back and forth to even the exposure."

"Command, Chief. The fold generators can take it. We can leave them exposed unless we're repairing them. And we can stow them, although I'm not sure how that will impact continuity testing. Q, that solar shield might be perforated. Plus, most of the power generation is most likely going to orbit-maintenance thrusters. That's why it's not acting like a giant sail. We'll have to avoid those thrusters because they'll be strong enough to burn through our shields."

"We'll have to return to a fold orbit to fold out, too, or risk destroying the station," Ruhger said. "If we have to, I'll do it, but I'd rather not."

Saree was grateful for her crew's intelligence and cunning. If they relied on her rule-following self, they'd be dead. But she made a good clutch leader because she knew the rules, or could figure them out, and would break them when necessary. And she never assumed she was the smartest person in the compartment—with the geniuses surrounding her, she definitely wasn't. Together, they were unstoppable. "Ruhger, take us there. If we destroy something on our way out, we'll find a way to buy the replacement. Chief, keep me informed, please. Grant, write, but don't send, a message for Gov Human about what we found out in the back of beyond. Facts about the location and the drive signature recordings, but nothing about why we were there. They don't need to know. Katryn, Q, get us access to that station, then return to researching Medico Holloway and his organization, unless Chief needs you. Safety of crew and *Lightwave* is our top priority. Second is staying hidden. Fold generator work is third. Questions or comments?"

Ruhger's fingers danced through his holo, creating orbital traces. He leaned toward Q, discussing their potential destinations.

"Scientists are terrible about net security, so we should be able to tunnel through the research net and hide the origination of our net queries," Katryn said. "But any data we need from inhabited space will have a big delay because I'm sure the experimental data is folded out periodically, not daily. It will be easy to ask the questions, but getting the answers and staying hidden via fold message is much harder. We may have to ask the questions, have the answers sent to message boxes, and retrieve them disguised as orders to the research stations. Or wait until we've got better comms. So, stick all your queries into a folder in priority order. We'll figure out how transmission will work later."

"Understood." Saree shrugged. "Do your best." They were stuck until they could fix the fold generators. "Ruhger, after you fly us to a safer location in this system, find our next fold destination. Somewhere with good comms that's relatively safe."

"And has replacement parts," Chief said.

Ruhger leveled a sardonic glower at her. "Finding the holy grail of fold locations isn't likely. Hiding from Gov Human, Medico Holliday, and his extremely wealthy clients will be difficult. Adding in deliveries?" He shook his head. "If we can get equipment sent here, perhaps through the experimental station's maintenance program, that's our best bet. But I doubt we can do that without sentients showing up to fix things."

Q leaned forward in her seat. "Maybe we can pull some components from the experimental stations. They might have spares stored here, or we can find one that's been damaged or is at the end of life, or..." She shrugged, lifting both brows.

Q's life experiences were coming in handy again. "Excellent ideas. Get on that." Saree smiled at her, trying to convey her approval.

"We have to break into their net, so it should be easy to find what we need if it exists." Q flashed a grin and turned away, pulling up a holo. "Once we're in, Grant can help us search."

He saluted sharply but ended with a silly wave. "Your wish is my command."

Q laughed. "Sure it is."

Saree smiled, grateful for Grant's attempt to lighten the mood. The crew was fully tasked. Sourcing replacement parts, fixing the fold generators, finding their next fold destination, and discovering more about Holliday was a big load. And she had to pay for it all—they needed credits. Saree pulled up the last Time Guild priority list. But rather than searching through it, she sat back. In the flurry of disasters, finding gestation devices got pushed to the bottom of the priority list. As it should be; they had to survive or nothing else mattered. But since they'd decided, her arms ached to hold a child, to feel a baby's heartbeat next to hers.

While survival was paramount, having a child wasn't entirely selfish. She didn't want to mandate her child's future, but having children showed humanity that she was taking their concerns seriously. Although, she was sure there'd be plenty of detractors no matter what. "Grant, how can we make it clear that my children must be raised by me to have any chance at accessing ^timespace^?"

Grant turned, frowning. "I don't know that we can. You were surrounded by the Sa'sa, but Q wasn't. Neither were most of the other trainees."

"But I've gotten so much better working with Saree." Q raised her hands high and then dropped them dramatically. "If I'd been raised by her, just think how much farther along I'd be. For one, I wouldn't have all these doubts about my ability carved into my brain."

Grant shrugged. "Okay, so I can sell that. We need to find out if the trainees from the human colony on Sa'sa are better than those from Aljanah. And how the Travelers raise children."

Saree shook her head. "We already know that. Every Traveler is raised to believe their God smooths the infinite road, and their prayers on the soothing stone altars enhance that. They help with worship as soon as they understand the basic concept. Smoother candidates are chosen after puberty by other smoothers. It's probably based on power levels, but none of the leaders could tell me exactly what they're looking for."

"I can definitely craft a message that works for us, then. The challenge will be rejecting younger trainees. Some parents will try to force their children on us or *Quantum Fold*."

"They're already doing that." Q brushed the idea away. "Doc turns them down because it's outside the stated experimental parameters, and more importantly, it's unethical. If someone leaves their kid at *Quantum Fold*'s hatchway, they're turned over to local social services and law enforcement. However, they've been discussing allowing trainees' families on board *Quantum Fold*, similar to Los' family. Doc knows younger minds are easier to teach. He doesn't want to essentially orphan children for an experiment, though, and until we can test reliably, how would he know who to pick? Even the Travelers don't know until after puberty, and they watch their children for years."

"I suspect they have a good idea long before puberty but haven't bothered to measure or determine how or why," Grant said. "Why would they? The kids aren't going anywhere for a few years."

"I'm into the experimental station net," Katryn said. "Got a time stamp and it's confirmed. We didn't travel in time. Or if we did, we time-traveled both ways." She snickered.

Talking to the Sa'sa made Saree fairly certain that was true, but evidence was a relief. She had enough trouble with the talents they had, she didn't need to add time traveling to the list.

Ruhger turned to her. "Got our destination. I'm taking it easy, so we can keep working underway." He brought up comms. "All crew, low thrust in five, four, three, two, thrust." The impulse was so low the grav generators compensated perfectly. "I'll increase the velocity slowly, but not too slowly, hopefully minimizing our radiation exposure while maximizing our energy generation.

We should arrive in approximately two hours and ten minutes. Exceptions for emergencies, of course."

"Of course." Saree smiled at Ruhger. "I'll want a status report from all teams after we dock or initiate station keeping."

"After dinner, Saree!" Loreli's warbled between command and joy.

"Of course." Saree chuckled. "Wouldn't miss it for the universe."

Chapter Thirteen

RUHGER

IN THE BETA SHUTTLE airlock, Ruhger turned to face his team. "Final buddy check now." He inspected Tyron's hardsuit, while Chief and Lashtar checked each other. "No leaks."

Tyron twirled his finger in the air, so Ruhger turned. "No leaks."

"No leaks, Ruhger," Chief reported.

"All suits reporting clean and green," Saree said over the comms. "Net and surveillance ready. Outside team, you are clear to proceed."

"Copy that, Command." Ruhger opened the airlock to the main experimental station where Q had found an inventory with a few spare parts. As a bonus, the station had a rudimentary personnel capability, with standard shuttle clamps and airlocks. Getting inside was relatively easy. Katryn had successfully broken through the station's minimal security and captured all outgoing security alerts.

The station's outer airlock hatch opened. Ruhger stepped inside, his mag boots snapping to the plas-covered floor, his team following. The hatch cycled, allowing them entry. Lights flashed on, one flickering and dying, illuminating a cramped compartment with four human-standard chairs in front of a large, dark screen. Narrow corridors extended to the right and left.

Ruhger took two steps, leaned over the chairs, and brushed a hand through the display area. Station status appeared. A flashing red warned there was no breathable atmosphere inside, and seven radiation scales fluctuated in different bands. General status displays reported on the other nineteen experimental stations around the Garnet Star. The station closest to the star, flying a deliberate spiral orbit into the sun, was yellow; Katryn had reported several systems had failed, probably due to radiation. "I don't see any security warnings, Katryn."

"Copy that. Didn't think you would, but I wanted to be sure."

"Acknowledged. As planned, let's split up and search for spare parts." Ruhger turned to his left, following Tyron, while Chief and Lashtar went right, toward the most likely storage area.

Tyron, laser rifle in hand, opened and cleared the first compartment. "Bunk room and sani-mod."

Ruhger glimpsed four bunks with storage shelves attached to the compartment walls and a sani-mod beyond. He followed Tyron to the next compartment, a cramped kitchen with a dining table for four. After that, a compartment with two chairs, a couch, a vid screen on the wall, and game controllers hanging on the wall. At the end of the corridor, bright red and yellow emergency labels told them to stay out unless evacuation was necessary. Their exterior inspection had revealed a large bod-pod with just enough power and control to get the crew to the far side of a rocky planet, hopefully protecting them until rescue arrived.

Without bothering to open the shuttle's hatch, Ruhger turned away. "Command, Tyron and I have found crew quarters and the emergency evac bod-pod. Joining Chief and Lashtar."

"Copy that, Ruhger. Chief?"

"We're checking the inventory against what's here," Chief said.

"Don't bother, just find what we need, get it, and move out." Saree scowled. "We'll send replacements after we arrive at a safe location."

Ruhger passed the control area and entered a large compartment. Plas bins in a variety of sizes were attached to the bulkheads. Crowding the center of the compartment, veg plas boxes on pallets and stronger plas crates were attached to the decking with Velcro straps.

"I'd like to make up for our intrusion by leaving it better than we found it, but understood." Chief pointed his finger at a label on a box and checked his holo. He moved to the next, scanning and reading the codes. "Ruhger, start at the far end of the compartment on the floor items. Tyron, take the bins on the bulkhead opposite of Lashtar. You can work front to back and meet in the middle of the rear bulkhead. Q's adjusted our label readers based on what we've found so far, but if there's any question, scan with sensors, then open the container and check."

"Copy that, Chief." Ruhger trod to the far end and brought up the label reader Q had modified to use the fiber optic built into his hardsuit's forefinger. He almost skipped the first pallet labeled emergency rations but followed protocol. Chief would double check any entry not fully supported by data. And probably some things Ruhger didn't miss, because that was how Chief operated.

The label scanner beeped, reporting the expected pallet of emergency rations. His scanners agreed, except one box contained vacuum bottles rather than plas packages. He opened the box, finding long tubes labeled Russe Standard Vodka. Why anyone would risk smuggling that space junk was a genuine mystery. He'd rather drink rocket fuel.

Moving on, he found more emergency personnel supplies. Next were station repair kits, including a tall stack of cerimetal repair plates wrapped in plas. He tagged those for Chief. They'd used several of their smaller hull plate patches repairing the fold generators, but he wasn't sure if they needed replacements.

"Found some capacitors," Tyron said. "Mostly smaller, but we could link them, right?"

"Correct," Chief said. "Send those to *Lightwave*."

A meter-square bin floated out the hatch, one reason they hadn't bothered to make the station habitable. Transferring equipment was easier in zero-g.

Eventually, Ruhger met Chief in the middle of the compartment. "Tagged a couple for your inspection, Chief."

"Got them. Can you start on the bins at the end?" Chief pointed behind Ruhger.

"Wilco." Ruhger returned to the far end and scanned bin labels. He found more emergency personnel supplies, including a bottle of Pristine Platinum Vodka, a much, much better brand. Good thing Loreli hadn't joined them, or that flask might float out the hatch, too. He reached the end of the bulkhead. "Survey complete. Nothing useful."

"Copy that, Ruhger. Start at the other end from Tyron."

Ruhger followed Chief's orders but found nothing else on the list. A few containers and boxes had floated past him while they searched, but not nearly enough to fill what they needed. "Chief, is the search complete?"

"It is." His tone was glum.

That meant finding and stealing parts from the experimental stations. None of them were happy about that. "Okay. Outside team, let's return to *Lightwave*, rest, and refuel. We'll start scavenger operations when Katryn's team locates what we need." Ruhger pointed at the hatch, making his team go first, then plodded behind them. After cycling through both airlocks, he retracted his helmet and scrubbed his hands across his sweaty head. He desperately needed a shower. He flew the short distance to *Lightwave* and docked.

Following his team to the Command Center, he held off Saree's attempt at a hug with a raised palm. "I stink. After a shower?"

Grinning, she jumped and climbed his hardsuit, kissing him quickly, then dropping to the decking. "Looking forward to it. Loreli should have a meal by the time you're all done, so we'll debrief in the dining room."

Ruhger nodded and plodded to his armor compartment, removing and placing it in the cleaner, then showering. Clean and dressed in a fresh *Lightwave* shipsuit, he joined Saree, waiting in the Command Center. Kissing her came first; even though the mission was low-risk, going into an unknown, potentially hazardous environment was always dangerous. Particularly if there was more security than originally found.

Eventually, Saree pulled away, took his hand, and towed him to the dining room. "Loreli's been inspired. All the food is red."

Good thing Loreli always made taste her priority, because red food could be horrifying. No matter how safe it was, raw meat was not one of Ruhger's favorites. But the dining room didn't smell like iron; the scent of toasted cheese made his mouth water. He seated Saree at the head of the table and sat next to her.

Loreli swept out of the kitchen, dressed in a poufy white skirt covered with sparkling red crystals. Above that, a shiny red corset and a white beret with a red ribbon perched jauntily on her head. "The first course is a cheese course with a selection of red berries, red jams including a pepper jam, and garnet crackers, accompanied by a berry basil gin and tonic! Enjoy!" Loreli and Q placed glasses and plates covered with red and pink in front of each of them, then sat at the end of the table.

More courses followed, including a shredded Aurigian spiny rooter with blood citron sauce, a shaved red beet salad with creme fraiche, a pomodoro stuffed ruby pasta from Serpens Six with a toasted pink hoofer sauce, and a dessert of Genevian raspberry sorbet with Genevian chocolate coffee mousse, accompanied by a Troi Chocolate Obsession martini. Every bit of it was amazing, and Ruhger desperately wanted to lick the dessert plate clean. "Delicious, Loreli. You've outdone yourself. I hate to—"

"Spoil your delicious meal, but we need to plan." Loreli had dropped her low tones even farther in imitation. The crew laughed, Q's high giggles standing out against Chief's guffaw.

Ruhger pointed at Loreli. "Yes, that. Saree?"

She looked at Katryn. "What did you find?"

"Grant reconciled what the outside team found versus what we need. Katryn, Q, and Grant found most of the rest, except the large capacitors. There are a few in surge protection circuits on some of the experimental stations. Unfortunately, those stations are all much closer to the sun. There will be a greater dose of rads no matter how much shielding we use. Plus, taking those components increases the chances of an experimental station failure."

Saree grimaced. "Better an experiment die than we do."

Ruhger squeezed her hand. "But I know it hurts your scholar's soul." Before she could answer, he turned back to Katryn. "Locations?"

She threw a holo to the middle of the table, displaying the Garnet Star, the experimental stations, and their location. She flicked her fingers, highlighting three stations approximately halfway between them and the innermost experiment, death-spiraling into oblivion.

Grant said, "I've been tracking the sun's blast and rad and looking back in the records. When they began tracking, the star had a twenty-two-standard-year cycle of highs and lows. Then that decreased to eleven, and it's been decreasing exponentially since then. That's one reason the researchers believe it's close to supernova. But the decrease isn't an even curve." Grant moved his hand up and down in front of his face, unpredictably rising and falling. "It jumps up and down randomly, only averaging to an exponential curve. Plus, it varies by location on the surface of the sun. We can predict sunspot formation to some extent. But we don't know how long they'll last or how many rads they'll blast, or even if it will be a coronal mass ejection or a flare. So, we can try to time our raid for a low point in the cycle and avoid sunspots, but there's no guarantee." He shrugged. "It could cycle from a new record high to a new low in the time we take to fly there. I've done some calculations, but they're worth the plas they're not printed on."

He pushed a spherical graph into the center holo, overlaying the system. The overlay was yellow for low rads, rising to a purplish-red for the highest, and the levels shifted over time, rotating around the star. "I can't find the safest orbit through all that. Even the computer threw up its metaphorical hands." Grant grimaced at him. "I'm hoping you can do better, Ruhger."

Ruhger's mind spun with the sun, crafting orbits and throwing them out just as rapidly. "This might take a while. Even then, I'll only be minimizing the rads with a best-case scenario. We'll end up traveling through some high spots. There's simply no way around it, even with a powerful shuttle like Alpha."

Chief shook his head. "We need to take Beta shuttle. The engines are almost as good, but the shielding is much, much better."

Ruhger had forgotten that. The orbits in his head shifted and changed. "Well, it's not ideal, but the safest orbits are highly elliptical, where the highest altitude matches with the orbit of the station." He threw a few variations on the main holo.

Saree sucked in a breath. "The low-altitude portions of the orbit are awfully close to the star, aren't they?"

"Yes. That's why I'll have to time them carefully, so we're not over a sunspot or other high-rad formation. Even with the velocities being much higher, crafting the orbit will be tricky. I'll need constant status reports, Grant, and I'll add multiple bail-out points. But a highly elliptical orbit is extremely difficult to change on the close-in, high velocity portion."

Tyron frowned at the holo and pointed. "To make these orbits work, you'll have to drop crews off under velocity, then pick them back up while you keep flying, right?"

Ruhger sighed. "Yes. I don't like it. But that's the safest for everyone."

Saree shook her head. "I don't like it at all. Hardsuits have very little margin for error. With the way the solar winds shift, and the changing of the sun's surface, I think the possibility of fatal rads is too high."

"It is very high." Ruhger threw a new orbit on the holo. "But this is the safest docking scenario I can come up with. Look at the rad doses. They're much higher for the entire crew and the shuttle. So, we may fry one or two individuals, or a shuttle and a team." He shrugged. "Which is better?"

Saree closed her eyes and dropped her head. "None of them."

"Then we're not going anywhere, and we'll all die slowly," Chief said.

Saree raised her head, staring at him. "Can we all think about this tonight and find some alternatives? For example, using the smaller capacitors and linking them?"

Chief nodded, but his lips were compressed tight. He didn't think that would work.

Loreli said, "Absolutely. Everyone needs rest, especially after my epic meal. No one can calculate odds properly when they're tired and sated. You need hunger; a drive for survival." She shook her fists in the air.

Grant snorted. "Like you'd let any of us suit up for a big expedition without feeding us first."

"But of course, darhling!" Loreli flung her hands out dramatically. "But the right fuel, designed to enhance action, rather than recovery."

Ruhger was fairly certain resting wouldn't change anything, but he'd happily take another night with Saree.

Especially when he was the one most likely to die.

Chapter Fourteen

SAREE

Saree closed her eyes, attempting meditation again, even though it hadn't worked the first, second, or third time. Crouching in a hardsuit inside a cobbled-together cerimetal container wasn't particularly comfortable, even with the suit holding her in place. No one wanted her on the scavenging team, but she had distinct physical advantages over the rest of the crew. Her DNA tolerated radiation much better than most humans, and she'd safely stored her reproductive material outside her body. Plus, Saree had more hardsuit time than anyone but Ruhger, Chief, and Tyron.

Chief and Lashtar both insisted they were the next best choices, and Saree agreed. Fortunately, *Lightwave*'s medico suite could bank male genetic material. Tyron could join the team and Ruhger could fly without jeopardizing their reproductive capability. Q and Katryn wanted to come, but they were more vulnerable to rads. Loreli and Grant had volunteered, but they had less hardsuit time.

They'd all taken pre-exposure meds. Loreli was prepping the medico pod for their return, knowing all five of them would need treatment. Saree had to badger Ruhger, but eventually, he admitted he'd get the largest dose of rads. He'd designed the flight path to minimize exposure, and he'd adjust for flares on the fly, but he'd receive a lot. They'd leave *Lightwave*, zoom through the perigee of the orbit far too close to the star for comfort, then slow as they neared apogee. The experimental station orbited in a circular orbit just below their planned apogee. Ruhger would continue orbiting, his exposure increasing with every revolution.

Saree's team would work in the much safer environment on the far side of the experimental station's sun shield.

Just before reaching the high point of the shuttle's orbit, their team would launch. They'd ride inside a shielded container on a pallet using a pair of remotes for orbital adjustment thrust. They'd programmed the orbital thrust but anticipated switching to manual control. The remotes were too vulnerable to rads. They could shield the computers but not the connections with the sensors. Humans were better than their available electronics in the hostile environment. Chief had added high-rad tolerant remotes to his shopping list.

For additional shielding, cerimetal plates and plas water bladders surrounded their transport container. Anticipating complete remote failure, they towed two more shut-down remotes, covered in more shielding, to use on the way back to the shuttle. In the best-case scenario, they'd rejoin the shuttle on its first return orbit. But Ruhger would probably orbit two or more times before they'd completed their mission.

Chief had stacked additional shielding around Ruhger in the shuttle, but each orbit increased his radiation exposure. They all agreed that if he had to orbit more than twice, Ruhger would return to *Lightwave*. The scavenging team would shelter on the experimental platform while he received treatment and rested. Then he'd fly again, picking them up. They'd strongly considered putting Grant on the scavenging team so Tyron could fly the return trips. But he couldn't make real-time adjustments the way Ruhger could. Plus, Tyron was better than Grant with mechanical and electrical components, especially in zero-g.

"Command, Team, Beta Shuttle," Ruhger said. "On my mark, ten seconds to launch point...mark."

"Team copies, go for launch," Tyron replied. As the next-best pilot, he controlled the remotes. Tyron also commanded the scavenging team. Saree and Lashtar didn't have enough experience. Chief could get stuck in minutia, especially with mechanical and electrical devices to puzzle over.

"Command concurs," Grant replied. "Go for launch."

"Five, four, three, two, launch." Ruhger's calm voice reassured Saree. "Safe flight."

A small lurch signaled the release of the remote's clamps, then gravity surged, pushing Saree's body against her suit. As their team separated from the shuttle, their orbital traces spread on her display.

"Safe flight, Beta," Tyron said. "We're on track. Radiation nominal."

Nominal for the Garnet Star. Anywhere else, the rapidly increasing dosage would alarm Saree. She tried to relax again. They had a twenty-four-minute transfer if everything went as planned. Grant, Ruhger, and Tyron reported status every five minutes, but each nano-second crawled by.

"Deceleration thrust in three, two, thrust." Saree's body pressed against the front of her hardsuit. After four minutes and seven seconds, a vibration shuddered through Saree—they'd landed on the experimental station.

"Team, stand by." Tyron shared the map of the station they'd studied. "As planned, Chief and Lashtar will disable the surge circuits, then place the jumper cable to bypass the capacitors. Saree and I will test for remaining power, then disconnect three of the four capacitors. After disconnection, Chief will test each capacitor, and if it passes, Lashtar will tow and attach them to our pallet for transfer. Chief will test the pallet remotes and replace if necessary. Saree and I will remove the hardwire bypass, then enable the surge circuits. Personnel safety is first priority. When your tasks are complete, return to the shielded pallet. Any objections?"

They'd all agreed on the plan. Saree controlled her breathing, the rasp of air loud in the silence.

"Hearing none, exit in order after me. Attach safety cables ASAP. Avoid the station-keeping thrusters at all costs."

Saree checked their route on the station map, then pushed the display to a corner. Tyron released the front of the pallet, duck-walked out of the box, and stepped on to the station's surface. His suit lights speared bright white beams through the pink-tinted gloom of the giant sun shield. Where vents allowed the star's solar winds to pass, pillars of brighter red rose from the backside of the sun shield in circular patterns. Each shining beam was larger than their shuttle; the sun shield was two kilometers wide.

Saree followed Tyron, with Lashtar and Chief behind her. She turned her suit lights on and searched for an empty safety bar on the station's surface. Each of them would anchor to separate loops, so a failure wouldn't affect all of them. Taking two steps, she latched on and followed Tyron to the edge of the station, each of them attaching their cables with carabiners along their route. Chief and Lashtar walked parallel to them, attaching their cables to another set of loops. The jumper cable rode on Chief's back, and Lashtar towed a small remote with tools and spare parts.

Tyron stepped around the corner to the side of the station, and Saree followed, standing parallel to the sun shield. He found the removable plate covering the surge circuitry and used a zero-g driver to unfasten the bolts. Chief and Lashtar continued to the power subsystem control panel. With any luck, they'd disable the surge protectors and the jumper would be a backup. Using a jumper on a live circuit, especially if a surge occurred, was risky; there was easily enough power to fry a suit. They'd all practiced attaching auxiliary life support from their suits to another's. But sharing air and heat meant shortening their stay on the station with an increased workload.

Tyron lifted and rotated the five-meter square cerimetal top plate out of the way. He'd left it loosely connected on one corner, so it didn't float away. "Command, exterior plate loose. Equipment appears to match diagrams. No obvious signs of scorching or other damage."

Below the heavily shielded cerimetal plate, four one-meter diameter by five-meter-long cylinders were attached with massive copper springs to a copper-plated tray. The tray was secured to the station with more bolts. The springs and tray absorbed shock and acted as a tertiary surge director. A five-centimeter-wide flat platinum cable connected the tops of the four capacitors.

"Command copies." Grant's voice was unusually stern. "Beta shuttle nearing orbital far mid-point, rads within expected limits."

Saree breathed a sigh of relief. Ruhger hadn't been hit by a coronal mass ejection or radiation blast from a sunspot. But it could still happen—they had to hurry, but without taking unnecessary chances.

"Team lead, Chief. Surge equipment electronically disconnected. Enroute to you."

"Lead copies Command and Chief." Tyron turned toward Chief and Lashtar. The jumper cable, a ten-meter-long copper wire with multiple clips, was coiled on Chief's back. "Standing by for jumper placement."

Saree extended the probes on the multimeter she carried, testing for voltage, amperage, and resistance. The readings confirmed Chief's statement. But since the circuit was used only when the power system was overloaded, there was no way to know for sure until a power surge hit. "Team Lead, reading confirms no power."

Lashtar unfastened the jumper cable from Chief and took one end, handing the other to him. They walked to opposite ends of the capacitor bank, crouched, and placed the connectors on the ends of the flat platinum cable. Each connector clamped across the top and bottom of the cable, and a blade would slash through the cable, severing the original connector. The jumper also included a clamp, so Chief could connect it to the remaining capacitor when they were done.

"Team Lead to Lashtar and Chief. Sever the cable in three, two, now." Tyron slashed his hand down in front of his body.

The blades slammed down and the flat cable separated. Chief and Lashtar pulled the jumper to the side and temporarily fastened it to the far side of the capacitor compartment. That gave them working room.

Saree tested again. "No power, but the capacitors may contain residual energy." They all knew that, but safety reminders were important.

Chief and Lashtar kneeled and pulled the original platinum cable off the tops of the capacitors, handing it to Saree. She slapped a temporary safety loop to the surface of the experiment, breaking the two-part adhesive on the end of the temporary loop. After waiting five seconds, she fastened the platinum cable to the new loop.

Chief and Lashtar extended zero-g drivers into the capacitor compartment. Chief said, "Lashtar, the tray is connected only at the corners. We'll take the whole thing out all at once."

That was the fastest solution but not the right thing to do. Rather than waiting for Tyron, Saree spoke up. "Chief, we need to leave one capacitor in place."

"Once they're out of the compartment, we'll take one off and replace it. It will be faster." His tone betrayed his annoyance.

Saree scowled at him. If Chief didn't want her to second-guess, then he needed to explain changes to the plan completely. "Copy." They'd discuss it in the debrief. She turned away, watching for debris or other hazards.

"Bolts free on this side; ready to raise," Lashtar said.

"Working on the last one," Chief replied. "Free. Raise on three, two, now. Not too fast! I'll bring it toward you, Lashtar."

"I'll adjust your safety cables," Tyron said.

Chief walked along the edge of the compartment, pushing the giant, shiny copper tray with the tall cylinders inside, bringing them to Lashtar. Saree took a few steps back, attaching her safety cable to a loop out of the way. Tyron adjusted Chief's, then Lashtar's safety cables.

Chief and Lashtar turned together, bringing the entire unit to a stop about a meter away from the open compartment. "Use a temporary tether and attach your safety cable to the tray, then we'll unfasten one of the end capacitors." Chief slapped a loop to the copper tray, then attached his safety cable.

Saree alternated between checking on Chief and watching for space junk, while Tyron did the same for Lashtar. After many muttered curses, they freed one of the end capacitors, the springs on the bottom of the cylinder sticking out oddly.

"Team, Lead," Tyron said. "We're running close on time for Beta Shuttle's return. Chief, Lashtar, take the capacitors to the remote pallet and get them attached. Saree and I will reinstall the remaining capacitor and attach the jumper, then enable the circuitry. Everyone understand the changed plan?" He pointed at Chief, Lashtar, and then Saree, each of them affirming in turn. "Saree, get the capacitor, and I'll get inside the compartment."

"Copy that, Lead." She took the capacitor from Lashtar and towed it to the edge of the compartment. She was thankful for zero-g because otherwise, moving something bigger than herself would be difficult even in a hardsuit.

Chief said, "Lead, I know we don't want to leave the station weaker, but with our lives on the line, don't you think we should?"

"No!" After her outburst, Saree clamped her lips shut. That wasn't her call, even though the possibility of destroying an entire research station for their gain made her sick. But Ruhger's life was most at risk. She should have kept her mouth shut.

"Chief, Lead. I've got a cutoff time programmed. Command is watching. We'll stop at that point and return."

"Copy that, Lead." Chief's normally unemotional voice was relieved.

Hoping she hadn't pushed Tyron and Grant into a stupid decision, Saree pushed the big cylinder down to Tyron. Then she pulled herself into the compartment.

"I'll bolt the springs on this side of the capacitor where the tray was fastened," Tyron said. "If there aren't any holes there, use a couple more of the temporary safety loops on that side."

"Excellent idea." Saree placed one across the end of the closest spring, then using her hardsuit, bent the spring's attachment piece over the loop to hold the spring to the loop. Then she pressed the glue side to the bottom of the compartment. It wasn't perfect but should be good enough for zero-g. She pulled a second safety loop and attached the second spring.

Tyron kneeled above her, at the edge of the compartment's opening. "Saree, I'm ready to attach the capacitor."

"Copy that, Lead." She pulled herself out of the capacitor compartment, joining Tyron.

"Saree, Lead. Ready for reconnection?" Tyron kneeled on the edge of the station, above the capacitor, the jumper cable connector in his gauntlet.

She tested the capacitor, then both sides of the cable with the multimeter but registered no power. "Ready."

Tyron shoved the connector onto the top of the capacitor. Sparks flew and died in the vacuum. Tyron jolted and his suit went dark. He separated from the jumper, jolting against the end of his safety cable.

Blast and rad! Saree bounded to him, connecting her safety cable to his suit. She pulled a power connector from her suit, opened the receptacle on Tyron's, and shoved the cable in, pulling him closer with her other hand. The cable seated, but Tyron's suit stayed dark. "Command, Saree. Tyron's suit fried. Employing emergency measures. Chief, if I can't tow him back in time, launch without us. That's an order." Without the capacitors, none of them would live.

"Saree, Beta Shuttle. Join Chief, and we'll come back and fix the station." Fear raised Ruhger's bass tones to a tenor.

Saree extended an auxiliary oxygen tube from her suit. "I've got to stabilize Tyron first." If it was an easy fix, she could do it. But knowing the likely damage and how long it took to run the entire emergency checklist, they couldn't make it back in time.

"Station Team Lead Saree, Command." Grant's words snapped. "Continue with life support actions. Chief, new assignment is Transport Team Lead. Detach your backup remotes. Cover them with all the excess shielding. Beta Shuttle, if Transport Team remotes fail during transfer orbit, pull them in with the Beta tractor. Transport Lead acknowledge."

"Transport acknowledges," Chief said. "Will configure the remaining remotes into best transfer platform possible with time available."

"Command concurs. Beta Shuttle."

"Beta acknowledges. Stay safe, Saree."

To break comm protocol, Ruhger must be terrified. So she replied, "Wilco, you too." Saree pried Tyron's emergency O2 connector open and jammed her auxiliary tube in. Her suit reported a small rise in CO2 and the air pressure increased. The returning air was already colder; without heaters running, Tyron's suit was losing heat fast. She opened the exterior control panel on his suit and entered the emergency code, but the display remained dark. Prying the control panel up with a fingertip screwdriver, she flicked the manual switch for the secondary systems, but nothing happened. The suit was completely fried. "Command, Station Lead, secondary electronics not booting. Initiating repairs." Using a short cable, Saree connected Tyron's suit to hers, so the O2 and power couldn't pull away. Since three separate connectors tied his suit to hers, she disconnected his safety cable from the station. She needed to reach all parts of his suit.

"Copy, Station Lead," Grant said. "Keep us informed."

"Transport, Beta, launch in thirty seconds." Ruhger's voice had returned to his usual calm.

"Transport acknowledges Beta. Break, break. Station, Transport Lead. If you get inside the capacitor compartment, you may be able to seal it enough to hold pressure and heat. Reengage the station's surge circuitry first. Don't touch anything but the compartment lid. Break, break. Command, find a safer compartment. If none, once Saree gets the surge circuitry hooked up, see if you can route a small amount of power through it to warm that area. Or turn off the cooling near that compartment."

Saree listened but kept working on Tyron's suit. Getting inside with the remaining capacitor seemed like a way to get both of them fried. But Saree would do it to save Tyron. And Chief was right; they shouldn't be at risk if they only touched the lid of the compartment. But the remaining capacitor could blow, or the original platinum cable could flex under load and touch them. Or something else could go wrong, since it already had once.

"Transport, Command considering options. Ready for launch? Transport and Beta, you have comms priority."

"Command, Beta shuttle, Transport Lead. Ready for launch." Chief's voice had dropped lower. "Launching in three, two, launch."

"Beta copies," Ruhger said. "Got you tagged. Intercept in four and a half minutes."

"Station, Command. Katryn says you'll have to turn the circuit on where you turned it off. Since it was done manually, there's no way to reengage it via net. It's a safety issue." Grant's voice held determination with a touch of fear. "Looking for a better location for your stay."

"Copy that, Command." She pulled the spare suit controller from the toolbox.

"Station, Command. No other suitable compartments on station. Stabilize Tyron, then reconfigure station and secure yourselves behind best shielding possible. Katryn sending location tags."

"Command, Station. Concur." Saree pulled the emergency suit controller from the tool box and deployed the flexible connector. Flipping Tyron's suit controller out of the way, she plugged in the connector. The controller's screen lit. "Command, Station. Emergency controller attached; diagnostics started. O2 levels are good, but my suit is cooling."

Sharing the air meant circulating it through Tyron's, and that meant the air returning was the temperature of his suit. Too much colder and he'd lose feet and fingers. She could increase the heat on her suit, and she'd have to, soon, but that meant using more power. If they had to wait eight more hours, powering both suits might become an issue.

"Transport, Beta." Ruhger's voice was calm. "Employing tractor beam in five, four, three, two, now."

"Station, Command. Acknowledged. Beta Shuttle will make one more orbit. If pickup is unsuccessful, Beta Shuttle will return to *Lightwave*. You'll have to stay on the station while the pilot is treated and the shuttle examined for damage. Another attempt will occur approximately eight hours later."

"Command, Beta Shuttle," Ruhger growled. "Negative. Rads are lower than expected. The shuttle can orbit twice before refit is required. Also, Chief and Lashtar are on board safely."

"Copy Transport Team retrieved. We'll reassess after the next perigee, Beta Shuttle," Grant said. "The shuttle might make it, but you might not."

Saree wanted to yell at Ruhger, but she had more immediate problems. While the suit controller booted, she peered into Tyron's helmet. His face was lax, with his eyes closed and mouth open. From the CO2 levels reported by her suit, she was fairly certain he was still breathing. The skin at the base of his neck flexed—he had a pulse. She timed the flutters of life. "Command, Team Lead. Tyron appears unconscious but alive. Pulse is fifty-two." Which seemed low, but Tyron was in extraordinary physical condition.

An alert flashed on her suit's status. The emergency suit control had finished booting and was attempting to connect to Tyron's suit. "Command, you seeing the emergency suit controller status?"

"Affirmative, Station Lead."

Good; she wouldn't have to report what she saw. The suit controller reported the right arm and shoulder of Tyron's suit were inoperative, but it successfully connected to life support. Heaters in his torso, legs, and left arm came on, and his O2 system booted, plus most of his batteries were working. The load on her oxygen system dropped almost immediately. Two minutes later, she disconnected the emergency O2 tube from his suit but left the shared power connection in place. Tyron's power system wasn't stable.

"Command, Station. Medico data confirms Tyron is unconscious but stable. Other than upping the oxygen level, intervention not recommended until transport to medico suite. Try to warm the right arm with the external heaters."

Blast and rad! She'd forgotten all about those. Saree pulled the emergency heat packs from the tool kit, wrapping a flat self-adhesive pad around his gauntlet and then four more along his arm. Designed for vacuum, the pads were simple insulated electrical heating elements with thin flexible batteries. "Heat pads attached. Let me know if I need to remove any, Command."

"Wilco, Station," Grant said. "If you can secure the station's surge compartment easily, do so. If it takes too much effort, don't. Get to one of the shielded locations Katryn sent you and rest. We'll monitor Tyron, and warn you when it's time to go to the remotes for pickup in approximately eighty-five minutes. Good job."

Saree used zip ties to secure the compartment's cover rather than screwing in all the bolts. Then she towed Tyron with her to the station power control unit. Following the instructions, she reengaged the surge circuitry, turning to watch the compartment. No sparks flew; a good sign. Or the surge through Tyron had fried the remaining capacitor already. "Command, Station. Power system energized." Grant acknowledged. She checked the station schematic; one of the tagged locations was on top of the station's power control unit.

Securing her safety line to a loop above the power control unit, she pushed off and floated up. A smooth cerimetal plate gleamed. She grabbed three long Velcro loops from the tool bag and fastened Tyron's suit to the top.

Then she commanded his suit into sleep mode; everything configured correctly except his right arm, but it was under the chest strap, so it shouldn't be terribly uncomfortable. Then she placed another loop, sliding her legs underneath, and put her suit in sleep mode, too. "Command, Team Lead. Both suits in sleep mode. I'll meditate to reduce suit power requirements, but I won't enter ^*timespace*^."

"Copy all, Station Lead. Will give you a fifteen-minute warning when it's time to move and alert you to any change in Tyron's status. Will monitor conditions on Garnet Star carefully." Grant's cadence was slower and his tone quieter.

"Copy all, Command. Station out." She brought up a direct comm connection with Ruhger's messaging system, not wanting to distract him when his flight path was so dangerous. "Ruhger, stay safe, and I'll see you soon. I'm meditating through the wait. I love you." She sent the message and concentrated on her breathing, knowing they'd make it back to *Lightwave* and the love of her family.

Any other outcome wasn't acceptable.

Chapter Fifteen

RUHGER

Ruhger released and rotated his jaw, loosening the tight muscles. Tooth damage wouldn't get Saree and Tyron back on board. At least Chief, Lashtar, and the rad-blasted capacitors were safe-ish, but three out of five wasn't good enough. Not even close.

Shaking out his hands, he reviewed navigation and Q's improved sunspot tracker. Along with current sunspot activity, it displayed the location, type, and predicted size of the effects from previous sunspots, all of them labeled. Using it, he could avoid some of the worst blast and rad. He bumped their velocity up, widening the orbit slightly to avoid a coronal mass ejection the star had previously spewed. That change meant a slightly longer orbit intercept for Saree and Tyron, but the magnetic effects of a geomagnetic burst on the other side might bring their orbit back to the original path or a little lower.

Dancing through the sun's crazy effects and trying to predict the next sunspot and what it might spew kept his mind mostly occupied, but dread for Saree and Tyron lurked, making him question his decisions. But fear wasn't all bad; he was completely alert and ready for anything, despite fatigue and the radiation bombarding his body. It was only a matter of time before those impacts would take a toll. He only hoped the pre-exposure drugs kept him flying safely.

During a lull in sunspot activity, he listened to Saree's message and sent her an "I love you" in return. "Transport lead, Beta. Doing okay back there?" They'd stayed inside the shielded cerimetal box to reduce their rads.

"Beta, Transport lead. We're fine. Also, we lashed the remaining remotes together, making a sled of sorts. Saree and Tyron will lie on top of the remotes, under layers of shielding, with a few layers underneath the remotes, too. But you'll probably have to pull them in with the tractor beam."

Ruhger rolled his shoulders, grateful for Chief's reassurance. "Copy that, Transport, and thanks."

Every five minutes, Grant reported Saree and Tyron's status, which was reassuring and worrying. Tyron should regain consciousness and if Saree had drifted deep into ^timespace^, Ruhger couldn't easily bring her back. He'd have to try over the comms, and that method hadn't worked yet. He bumped the thrusters, accelerating and avoiding a dense mass of gamma rays.

By the seven suns of Saga! "Command, Beta Shuttle. Gamma rays from sunspot G-four-two will impact the outside team's station in approximately three seconds."

"Copy that, Beta. We'll monitor." Grant's voice tightened with tension.

Ruhger shouldn't have told him; they couldn't do anything to help Saree or Tyron. Besides, the stations were designed to endure radiation, geo-magnetic effects, and solar winds, with multiple lead and cerimetal layers built into the sun-facing side. The sensors and controllers were all heavily shielded. The power systems had even more. Otherwise, the station would have stopped working long ago.

He concentrated on the flight, minimizing the impacts of the sun on his passengers, himself, and the shuttle. They sped through the perigee, unable to avoid radiation and the remains of coronal mass ejections in the low point of their orbit. Nearing the orbit's mid-point on their return toward the station, they slowed. "Command, Beta. Close mid-point achieved."

"Understood. Notifying Station team." A singing bowl rang over the comms, hopefully recalling Saree. "Station Lead, proceed to remotes. No change in Tyron's status. Recommend leaving his suit locked in sleep mode."

An intelligent choice; Tyron might wake confused and thrashing, disrupting Saree and their return to Beta Shuttle.

"Station Lead acknowledges," Saree said. "Disengaging straps now."

Ruhger concentrated on his orbit and the sun effects; if he didn't reach intercept, Saree couldn't return to *Lightwave* and safety. But even busy with adjustments, every word from Saree reassured him and soothed his heart.

"Command, Station. Tyron and I secured to remotes. Pulling shielding over our suits on sun-facing side. Orbit loaded, ready for launch." Saree spoke in her normal calm command mode.

Ruhger brought Saree's orbit into his navigation; they'd fly through the remains of a mass ejection. "Command, Beta. Recommend orbital adjustment for Station Team." He manipulated the orbit and sent the revision to command.

"Command copies, Beta. Team Lead, implement orbit one point one."

"Acknowledged and input," Saree said. "Standing by for launch."

Soon, he'd intercept, and she'd be safe. A wave of nausea crashed through him and sweat burst from his forehead—his cumulative radiation had reached the danger zone. Risking a few more rads, he retracted his helmet and swiped his forearm across his head, but more sweat sprang forth. His stomach turned and twisted, but he forced water down his throat. Staying hydrated was necessary for efficient and effective brain function. "Command, Beta. Radiation side-effects beginning. Sweating and nauseated but operating at one hundred percent." He pulled a sweat band from an exterior suit pocket and snugged it across his head, just above his eyebrows, then raised his helmet and took an anti-nausea med. The tumbling in his stomach lessened, but then heat flushed his entire body.

"Command copies, Beta. Let us know if you need us to fly from here."

The interference with the signals made that riskier than his about-to-be reduced skills. "Wilco." Ruhger lowered the temperature in his suit and upped the air pressure, but it didn't help much. Time passed too slowly, but finally, the moment arrived. "Station Lead, launch in fifteen seconds."

"Copy launch in fifteen seconds, Beta," Saree replied. "Go for launch. Thrust in five, four, three, two, thrust."

Ruhger watched her orbit and the intersection with Beta Shuttle. "Right on target, Team."

"Command, Tyron waking, appears distressed. Suit remains locked in sleep mode. Tyron, it's Saree." Her tone changed from calm and collected to urgent but still controlled. "Tyron, you're safe. You're in a hardsuit. Don't struggle. You're safe. Tyron, can you answer? Acknowledge you are safe." Command snapped through the last sentence.

"Acknowledged. Safe. What happened? Where am I?" Tyron sounded confused and bewildered.

"Station Lead, Command. Katryn will talk to Tyron off main comms." Grant made the correct decision again; Katryn's voice should calm him better than Saree's.

"Acknowledged, Command. On target for intercept."

Anticipation and relief reduced Ruhger's nausea. He brought up the tractor beam, calculating the most effective use without changing Saree and Tyron's velocity and vector too abruptly. Their hardsuit grav generators were limited to low-g's.

He closed his watering, burning eyes, calculating the orbital intercept. He could literally fly with his eyes shut, except he needed the sun effects display. Rapidly blinking his eyes every thirty seconds, he checked the graphs through the strobe-like effect of his fluttering lashes and watery shimmer. "Team, engaging tractor beam in five, four, three, two, engage."

"Ack—Tyron, no. Stay with me! Stop! Stop now! Tyron, I order you to stop!" Saree panted into the comms.

"Station, Command. Tyron's suit is under control." Grant's voice snapped. Ruhger was grateful Grant had acted because it would have taken him too long to find the crew suit interface. He had enough to do.

"Copy, Command. Good thing Beta Shuttle had us in the tractor beam, or we might have lost him." Saree was angry and Ruhger didn't blame her. Katryn probably let Tyron loose. She should have known better.

"Apologies, Station Lead." Katryn's tone was exasperated and terrified. "I thought he was okay, but he's not. I think he's hallucinating. I'll keep his suit in sleep mode."

"Do so. That's an order." Saree's annoyance and fear snarled through her words.

As they neared the intercept point, Ruhger pulled Saree and Tyron into the shuttle, keeping the acceleration low and the change in vectors minimal. Eventually, he deposited them safely on the cargo hold decking, closed the hatch, and breathed a sigh of relief. Opening his eyes had become useless; they were watering so much he couldn't see. "Initiating thrust for return to *Lightwave* in five, four, three, two, thrust."

"Beta, Station Lead. Strapping Tyron's suit to the cargo bay bulkhead. Joining you shortly."

He swallowed, trying to wet his dry mouth, but gave up and sucked on his water straw. "Sooner is better. Can't see. Flying blind."

"Suns," she muttered. "Command, Station Lead. Tyron secured. Checking pilot."

Ruhger concentrated on his orbit, blinking every thirty seconds to check the sun effects. Movement to his right made him jump. The temporary wall of water and lead shielding receded, and Saree's face shield almost touched his. Her brow was creased in concentration, deepening into concern. "You don't look so good. Put your suit in sleep mode. I've got the return flight."

Thank all the suns. He'd continue flying if there wasn't an alternative, but it was risky. "Copy that. Love you." Unable to remain alert, Ruhger configured his hardsuit and took another anti-nausea dose.

"Command, Beta Shuttle. Saree assuming pilot in command. Enroute as planned. Will arrive in twenty-five minutes and ten seconds. Engage anti-radiation medico procedures in Ruhger's suit."

"Copy all, Beta Shuttle. Starting radiation treatment now." Grant's voice had turned grim again.

A hiss and pressure at his elbows and neck signaled injections. Within a minute, his eyes would no longer open, and he fell into sleep.

Blurry words and numbers strobed on a bright holo above Ruhger. He shut his fluttering eyelids. Despite every muscle aching and every inch of his skin burning and sore, he turned his head and peered through his barely-cracked lids. Saree slept on a narrow cot next to him, her hand under his. An intravenous line ran into the back of her other hand, but she seemed to sleep peacefully. Hopefully, her modified DNA had resulted in less radiation damage.

Looking down his body, he saw he clearly hadn't fared as well. Tubes ran into both elbows and sensors pulled at the skin on his chest and pressed against his head. He blinked up at the medico data, grateful his eyes weren't running like a faucet, and the smeared lines coalesced into words and numbers. The diagnosis was radiation poisoning, of course, but response to treatment was designated adequate and would last at least another twenty-four hours. Since his body felt like he'd been pushed through a black hole and fried under a main thruster, the prescription wasn't surprising. He'd probably be here longer than that.

He turned his head to the other side. Tyron rested flat inside the IsoSafe that had previously imprisoned Saree, with as many lines as he had. Katryn slumped in a chair next to the IsoSafe, listing against the side. From her breathing, she slept. Chief and Lashtar weren't in the medico compartment, so he hoped they'd recovered faster. Or maybe there just wasn't enough room; they were probably receiving treatment elsewhere.

Rustling preceded Loreli's entry. She wore white leggings topped with a shiny white corset, topped by a remarkably plain light green medico coat. But her towering headgear, a fluffy, layered mass of white and green translucent material decorated with medico symbols, made up for the simplicity of her main outfit.

She bent over him, her eyes widening when they met his. "You're awake!" Her words were uncharacteristically quiet but full of enthusiasm. "Wonderful. The treatments are working better than expected." She lay her hand on his shoulder, then pulled it away. "Sorry, I forgot your skin is tender. Don't move too much; let the medfloat do the work. The radiation means you'll bruise easily and your skin is fragile." She focused above his head. "But the medico reports you are improving rapidly and predicts you'll be out sooner than expected. Thank all the suns." She put a hand over her heart.

"How's Saree?" Knives sliced Ruhger's throat and his voice rasped.

Loreli slid a straw into his mouth. "Drink. She's doing very well. Her body endured the ordeal much better than the rest of you, but she's exhausted. She helped us get the rest of you into treatment before she agreed to her own." She sobered. "Tyron's not recovering nearly as well. The electrical shock combined with the radiation is a tough combination. The IsoSafe and medico pod tell us he needs professional care." She shrugged, but she was clearly worried. "Chief and Lashtar are doing good; they're taking turns on the other medfloat. A little more treatment and rest, and they'll have *Lightwave* fixed. Then we can fold out of here and get Tyron the care he needs." Her shoulders slumped. "I rather wish we hadn't bolted from *Quantum Fold* so fast. Doc would fix all of you right away. But hindsight is always twenty-twenty, isn't it?" She shrugged and then frowned. "How are you feeling?"

"Not horrible. Everything's sore, bruised, and burning, but better than I expected." The water helped, but his throat stung.

Her lips flattened for a moment and her head tilted. "Well, you'll feel better soon. Go back to sleep. The more you rest, the better you'll feel. Next time you wake, I'll have a recovery shake for you." She wiggled her fingers and twinkled. "Nighty-night."

Ruhger closed his eyes and followed Loreli's orders. Knowing Saree was okay and the rest of his family under proper care let him drop into sleep.

He woke several more times, Loreli bustling in with a delicious, soothing drink, Saree asleep next to him still, but the IV gone from her hand. Loreli assured him she had woken, eaten, and was doing well. When he opened his eyes again, the medico holo was gone and the room dim, with a faint glow to his left. He turned his head, relieved his pain didn't make him wince.

Saree sat next to Katryn, both reading on their holos. Tyron lay on his side in the IsoSafe, red warnings scrolling across the surface.

He raised his hand to scrub the sleep from his eyes. The IVs were gone, and his skin no longer blazed but still smarted.

Saree bounded out of her chair, peering worriedly at him. "Ruhger. How do you feel?" She reached her hand toward his but then pulled back, gripping the edge of the medfloat.

He lowered his arm, covering her hand with his. His palm ached a bit with the pressure, but no worse than he'd had with other tissue injuries. "I feel a lot better. Hold on, let me do a self-check." He closed his eyes and assessed his body from his toes to his head, then opened his eyes. "My skin feels slightly bruised, like the grav generators couldn't compensate for high-g's, and there's a slight singed sensation, too. My muscles ache, my head is throbbing a bit, and I feel like I competed in a seventy-two-hour marathon, but overall, I'm in pretty decent shape, I think."

Saree's relief showed in her smile. "That's excellent. You'll have to take it easy for a while. No workouts for at least two weeks, treatments three or four times a day for at least a week, and you've got to move very slowly, to avoid bruising and tearing your skin. Soft clothing, nothing binding, no suit time, no armor, limited holo use." She raised both brows. "Understood?"

He smiled up at her. "Understood. I'm sure you'll have to remind me, often, but right now, I'm in no hurry to do anything. Unless I can help get Tyron treatment."

She shook her head. "We've got it covered." She raised her forefinger, wagging it back and forth in front of him. "Remember, I've had a traumatic brain injury, and part of your protocols are very similar to mine. So, don't push it."

"Payback is here, huh?" Ruhger squeezed her hand gently.

She smiled ruefully. "No, I just want you to recover fully. Speed isn't as important."

"I understand. What about Chief and Lashtar? Where are we at with *Lightwave*?"

Saree nodded. "Progress. Chief and Lashtar are both two days ahead of you. They're down to twice-daily treatment, with no strenuous activities and mandated rest. Q and Loreli did the capacitor installation under Chief's direction. Now he's testing circuitry from the comfort of a chair. Q's acting as his hands. Lashtar is helping Loreli with kitchen duties when she feels up to it. Unlike Chief, she's good about paying attention to her body and the medico prescription, and she hauls him away for treatments and rest." She sighed. "Tyron hasn't changed much. He needs expert care. Katryn and I are trying to figure out where we can get treatment without the rest of us getting thrown into some horrible experiment. But we'll take the chance if we have to."

"You can drop us in Beta Shuttle and fold out." Katryn joined Saree. "I think that's the only way we'll make this work." She tugged on Saree's arm, and she turned to face Katryn. "And yes, I know that will get us captured and used against you. But it's better than all of us getting taken right away. If we pick the right place, we can ask for asylum. Plenty of worlds are happy to thumb their noses at Gov Human and the super-rich body modders. We'll be grounded, possibly for life, but better that than the alternatives."

Mudhugging forever? Ruhger shuddered. But if that's what it took to stay with Saree, he'd do it. Tyron felt the same about Katryn, and since she'd been raised planet-side, she'd adapt quickly and help him.

Saree squeezed Katryn's shoulder once and let go. "We'll keep looking, Katryn. But Tyron's health is my priority for a fold location, not our safety."

Ruhger added his opinion. "I agree. I owe Tyron my life, several times over." If it wasn't for Tyron, he'd have died long ago.

Katryn smiled grimly. "You know he'd say the same about you. You're even." She grimaced. "If I have to, I can sell being disenchanted with Saree's takeover of *Lightwave*. Tyron's in no shape to say anything, and I can dismiss anything he says as a hallucination or maybe that I'm taking this chance while he can't object."

Ruhger's heart hurt. "I don't want you two to leave *Lightwave*. Especially after we agreed to raise children together."

Katryn shook her head. "I don't want to, either. But I'm afraid we might not have a choice. It will depend on what's happened while we've been gone."

Saree nodded. "What the press knows and speculates, and what Gov Human, the Sa'sa, and the medico community have done since we disappeared will definitely impact us. We've got to fold in, get news, and fold out. Or fold into a safe system where we can get news and not draw attention."

Ruhger cleared his throat and regretted it when pain knifed down his esophagus. Saree spun and placed a straw between his lips. He sipped. "Thanks. Perhaps the Cassiopeia constellation entry? Or Lisse, that gray station? Or even Bonfanti? Although we'll pay for that one." Goldie had said that even though *Lightwave*'s crew had helped take control of the station, they wouldn't get a free ride. They'd get discretion, but since it was popular with bounty hunters, they might get caught.

Both women nodded. "We've considered all of those, along with Polarissima Aus, Lacerta, Nexus, Pavo, and a bunch of others. No matter where we go, we'll change *Lightwave*'s designation first, but that won't protect us from visual recognition. We've removed almost all exterior markers, but you know there are databases that track folders of note. We've made ourselves into celebrities of a sort. And we've made too many changes to *Lightwave*'s exterior that will confirm our identity."

"The fold generators will draw attention, too," Katryn said. "Those repairs will be pretty obvious if someone gets a vid while they're deployed."

Their arguments sounded pretty well rehearsed. Ruhger wracked his brain for some place quiet, where no one would notice them if they paid the fees. "Dronteim. Right where you joined us, so many folds ago." He pointed at Saree. "Good comms, no one cares about folders if they pay the fees and stay out of local politics, and the clock was updated not all that long ago." He smiled but quit when the skin around his mouth hurt. "From all reports, no one was upset about Lady Vultan's disappearance."

Katryn snickered. "No, we heard even her family didn't miss her. The son said all the right things about her presumed death, but he didn't look very hard for her. Rumors say he's gotten rid of the Thymdronteim plantations and moved on to mining instead. The plan was to make all the credits he could, then move his family back to a core system."

Ruhger huffed. "Good luck with that. I don't think nickel is that valuable."

Katryn shrugged. Saree tilted her head from side to side. "They might make it if they only care about themselves. But regardless of them, you're right. No one would expect us to return there. I don't think their health care is great, though, so we'll leave them on the list. I'd prefer to fold into a location with good healthcare for Tyron, in case our fold generators blow again."

Ruhger agreed. "But I also know they've got good repair facilities there for sophisticated equipment. We wouldn't have to raid for capacitors."

Saree swept her hand through her holo. "I didn't know that. I'll add it to the list of pros. Along with a lot of Familia, at least back when I was on station, as a con."

"Check with Chief, in case my brain got too rad-blasted." Ruhger blinked, his eyelids heavy.

"I'll do that." Saree patted his hand once. "You go back to sleep."

He smiled at her. "I will." He closed his eyes and faded into black, secure in her love and her care for their family.

Chapter Sixteen

SAREE

SAREE DIDN'T RECALL HER childhood very often, but she breathed a prayer to her parents' God. They had to survive fold, get information, find Tyron an outstanding and safe medico facility, and fix the folder again if necessary. All while not getting caught. At least they wouldn't be tracked entering the constellation; they were folding straight into Dronteim's most distant small folder orbit. With all factors considered, it was the best choice, if not exactly safe.

Once there, they'd test the fold generators, and if they were operable, they'd retract the extensions and order replacement parts. Meanwhile, they'd gather news about *Quantum Fold*, Chief Medico Holliday, and Gov Human and download messages. Saree was certain they'd have hundreds of messages from all three parties and the Time Guild. Once they got parts for the fold generators plus spares, they'd fold somewhere with better healthcare and no Gov Human interference. The plan was good, but plans often changed on the way to orbit.

"All stations, fold in five, four, three, two, fold." Ruhger's voice rumbled lower than normal. "We've arrived safely in Dronteim. Contacting fold controller payment system now."

"Querying major news sites," Grant said. Saree slid her forefinger from Grant to the big screen, asking him to put the critical articles up, and he nodded in acknowledgement.

"Downloading messages," Katryn reported. "Checking on medico facilities."

Q bounced in her seat. "Downloading Time Guild messages."

"Command, Engineering. Initial inspection shows the fold generators have survived intact. Retracting now and will continue testing."

Saree opened comms with Chief. "Excellent job, Chief, thank you."

"It's a shared victory. Lashtar's looking for parts. We'll monitor the conversation so you don't have to repeat things later."

Saree smiled. "Thanks, Chief." J'ker Hanty's face appeared, covering the big screen, his meter-tall mouth hanging open. She jumped.

Grant snickered, then sobered. "As expected, this guy is creating a big conspiracy theory around the authorities on Emma firing at us and your disappearance, even though it hasn't been that long. Gov Human and *Quantum Fold* have stated that Lightwave Clutch was in Emma, folded out, and our current location is unknown. Gov Human asked the public to report sightings and got thousands of messages." He chuckled. "Of course, they have no idea those reports are wrong. I feel bad for the people assigned to go through all that blast and rad."

Saree frowned at his radiation reference. With Tyron sedated, his comment was in poor taste.

"Too soon, I guess. Sorry." Grant grimaced. "Anyway, lots of theories, no answers, and Gov Human and *Quantum Fold* have stopped answering queries. Major news outlets corroborate we were attacked and then folded because there were at least three independent folders in orbit who left after we did. They told authorities and reporters they weren't sure why we were being fired on, but they didn't want to be next. Meanwhile, Chief Medico Holliday is busy refuting rumors of cloning. He's gotten death threats from extremists and is currently holed up in his principal residence, behind stringent security measures. Plus, many of his medico locations have shut down due to lack of business, and he's being investigated for financial irregularities." Grant smirked. "Couldn't happen to a better guy, but I think the pressure will only make him try harder. The reputable news organizations are also offering rewards for sightings of us and Holliday's clones, so we can't stay here long. Amateur fold transport watchers are probably taking vid of us right now."

As expected. Many systems had satellites near fold orbits, watching for threatening or unsafe folders. Fold transport spotting was almost a sport in some systems. "Keep looking. I'm sure there's speculation about a fold gone wrong. Also, find *Quantum Fold*'s location and General Kerr's fleet, please." Grant saluted. She moved on. "Q, what do you have?"

"Message from the Time Guild, asking for a location report. Then a follow up with a retraction, after you contacted them in ^timespace^." Q raised her brows. "They've updated the fold clock prioritization list a couple of times, but I haven't found anything unusual there yet."

"Don't bother." Saree brushed Q's concern away. "Once on the list, the priority is changed automatically by a number of factors. Find out if the Sa'sa have answered questions from Gov Human about us. Because I'm certain Gov Human is asking."

Q bowed. "As you wish."

"Hey, Ruhger." Grant waved. "A pandemic is winding down in a chain of islands on Dronteim. See if our favorite medicos are here."

"Good idea." Ruhger brought up a list; probably shuttle records from Dronteim Station.

A tendril of hope bloomed in Saree's heart. "Excellent idea, Grant. I'm sure they'd say Tyron's issues aren't something they specialize in, but if we can provide them transport, and they help us, it could be a win-win."

"Saree. Got something for you." Katryn's grim tone was alarming.

Dread churned in her stomach. "Yes?"

"One of the newest radiation exposure therapies is body modding." Her lips flattened momentarily. "And guess who's the best and how they do it?"

Her stomach stopped churning, dropping to her feet. "Chief Medico Holliday on *Beautiful Perfection*, right?"

Katryn nodded. "He doesn't have a lot of experience with electrocution, though."

"Who does?" Saree frowned. "Maybe the medico school on Cygnus Secundus?" A frontier world with substandard construction—electrocution and other trauma was almost guaranteed.

"But they don't do advanced radiation treatments. I think we'd have to cure the electrocution first, though. Fix that tissue damage, and you'll fix some of the radiation damage." Katryn's head tilted to one side. "Maybe? I'm guessing that's the theory behind body modding for radiation."

"Keep looking." Saree squeezed her eyes shut for a moment and breathed, trying to blank all the problems from her mind. But meditation was far beyond her. "If we have to use Holliday, then we will. Hopefully, Gov Human will protect us, because of the publicity." But she doubted it.

"Not a chance," Ruhger growled. "I'm not trading you and Q for Tyron. Sorry, Katryn, but he wouldn't want that either."

Her shoulders drooped. "I know." She straightened and scrolled through her holo.

Saree's spirits fell along with Katryn's. Too many people wanted them for too many reasons.

"There's a significant number of systems protesting the attack on the human clocker." Grant pushed another vid to the big screen, replacing Hanty's florid face with a written news report. "Particularly the fringes. Systems are banding together into loose coalitions to get more attention. Several think your disappearance after the attack is part of a Gov Human conspiracy to control where you tune clocks. A protective custody that goes too far." He flipped one hand up through the air in a careless gesture. "But that rumor has always existed; it's just getting stronger. Others are blaming Emma's leadership and demanding Gov Human investigate them. Dronteim is one of those." He smirked. "Takes one monarchy-dictatorship to know another."

"Pandemic medicos are a no." Ruhger turned toward her, glowering. "According to Dronteim's ministry of health, they'll be here longer than we want to stay. We could still ask for help, but I'm not sure they'd know anything more than we can get from our medico pod. Also, they're still trying to control this pandemic."

Saree squeezed his hand. "We knew it was a long shot."

"Saree?" Q bit her lip, then released it when Saree nodded. "I've got a kind of risky idea, but if it works, it would be perfect."

Such a relief that Q 's confidence and creativity were returning. "Anything we do will be risky."

Q shrugged. "True. Here's my idea. If Doc's father is closing some of his locations, they're the locations farther from his home system, right?" Grant nodded and put a star map on the big screen with the shut-down shops in red. Q flashed a thumbs-up, then focused on Saree again. "What if we used one of the temporarily closed locations? I'm sure Katryn and I can get around the station and compartment security. Then we could get inside and treat Tyron using their equipment. Since it's a medico facility, we'd have everything we needed to live for a few days. Beds, sani-mods—there's probably even clothing left there because he'll be hoping to reopen once the bad publicity dies down. We can bring ready-to-eat meals." She glanced around their group, half-smiling, half-questioning.

"That's not a bad idea, Q." Ruhger nodded. "It's the last place anyone would look for us."

Saree frowned. "But if he found us there, it'd be bad. We'll have folded straight into a black hole. And everyone would recognize *Lightwave*, even in a crowded core system."

Katryn held up her forefinger. "But if you drop Tyron and me off, we can stay in the facility and Q"—frowning, she turned her chair to look at each of them, stopping on Grant—"and Grant can monitor from a shuttle. Everyone else stays on *Lightwave* and folds out. Q can deal with the net security, including the utilities we'd use, like power and air, and Grant can deal with station or system authorities. He can sell ice to non-oxys, so if we got caught, he's got the best chance at talking us out of the situation. But I've got to check something first." Using both hands, she scrolled through multiple screens on her holo.

"And I can bribe people, if we have enough credits by the time we get there." Grant scrolled through his holo. "The Time Guild has paid us for all our pre-attack tunings, so unless we buy a lot of extra supplies here, we should be good."

"Grant, I'll be wiping out a lot of that." Chief's face appeared in the lower righthand corner of the main screen. "Large capacitors and other high-power components aren't cheap. I'm sending an order for authorization."

Grant scrolled and pushed through his holo. "Got it, Chief." He whistled. "You weren't kidding."

"We need all of that and more, Saree." Chief waved his wrench in front of his face. "I've got the bare minimums listed."

Saree wasn't surprised. "Copy that, Chief. Buy it, Grant." They didn't have a choice. If *Lightwave* couldn't fold, none of them would survive. "We can pay bribes out of my personal funds."

"And mine," Ruhger added. The crew chimed agreement.

Saree put a hand over her chest, the warmth of family love lifting her spirits. She'd been so fortunate to find her *Lightwave* family. But relying on luck got people killed. "Okay, assuming we can get into a core system unnoticed, and fly a shuttle to wherever the medico spa is, and break in unseen, and stay unnoticed—do we need a medico? Because I doubt radiation treatment is a menu choice on a body mod float."

Q grimaced while Katryn sighed. "It's not. I just checked. It's a special protocol and takes specific programming and equipment. So far, Holliday's done the radiation treatments on only his folder. It's an experimental treatment, so the programming is on two specifically modified medico pods. The protocol and results are monitored by Gov Human's drug approval authorities." Katryn scowled. "If we could get into the same system as his folder, I'm sure I could break his net and get the protocol. But that's just the radiation poisoning. The electrocution is more critical. The IsoSafe has repaired the major damage to his body, but there's so much it can't do. Nor can our main medico pod. So, we need an expert, not just a pod and a protocol."

"We know several trauma medico experts." Q raised both hands. "The medico school on Cygnus Secundus is full of them, but we can't risk that. Doc is the obvious choice. That's his specialty. The question is, can we trust him?" She squeezed both eyes shut and screwed up her nose, then scowled. "I'd trust Doc with my life; he's saved it several times. But family complicates loyalty."

Saree reached and squeezed Q's hand. "It's not just family. It's Gov Human and the potential impact on the Time Guild research. The Time Guild is paying for everything, but without Gov Human's support, Doc's research and training of humans won't be legitimate. And since the two of us are human, that's the logical species to start with. We haven't been terribly successful teaching humans, so teaching other species, even close to human DNA species, like the Grus, seems like a fold too far. The Travelers won't even attempt it; it would be anathema to many, I think. Or close enough that they'd have a revolt. We've put them through enough religious debate, so I wouldn't ask."

Q winced. "We should probably send messages to the Travelers' leadership on *Tobar*, and let them know we're alive, if they haven't figured it out."

She was correct. "Do that, please. I'll send a message to Doc. We've got several alternate email services set up for emergencies, and I'm sure he's monitoring all of them."

Q held up both hands, palm toward Saree. "He's not good about net security. If he's been checking, Gov Human's seen him and is watching those services."

Grant shook his head. "Los would make sure that didn't happen."

"Good point. I'd forgotten." Q's smile seemed tinged with relief. "Probably because I wanted to forget about Bevan Astra. Sorry."

Poor Q had been through so much. "No need. It's been a bit bizarre."

Ruhger snorted. "More than a bit. And it's not getting better, because I have an even wilder idea."

Surprised, Saree turned to him. "*You* have a wild idea?" Ruhger's decision-making was unparalleled, but out-orbit ideas weren't his strong point.

Grant chortled. "Oh, we've got to hear this."

Ruhger nodded, glowering. "Ruth gave me the idea. We reverse thrust and hijack Chief Medico Holliday's folder. Preferably with him or another expert medico on board."

"You're kidding." Saree couldn't believe those words came from Ruhger's mouth.

Grant pumped his fist. "Yes! We'll go back to our beginnings and fly a pirate's flag!" He snickered. "Well, I'll raise the flag while you invade." He frowned at Ruhger. "Actually, doing that kind of complex military operation without Tyron might be difficult."

Ruhger nodded. "I know. Tyron's the one who points out all the flaws in our plans, provides solutions, and is key to execution. I'm not sure we can pull off a folder capture without him."

"But you have me and Q," Katryn said. "Depending on his net defenses, we might make it happen without firing a shot. Look at what happened to us. And Lashtar's no slouch with military operations." She held up her fist and counted, raising her fingers. "But one, we have to find him. Two, we need to do a lot of preliminary research, and that might mean folding into his home system or paying someone a lot of credits. Three, we have to get him somewhere that's minimally inhabited and defended, so no one interferes if he gets the word out. Four, we've got to make sure there are very few people on board, so when you go in, there's less chance for problems. Five—"

Ruhger lifted a bushy brow. "Maybe you should let us worry about the infiltration part, Katryn. We've done it before. Also, if we can prevent him from crying for help and firing, the defenses in a system aren't important. We grapple on and fold out." He shrugged. "Easy."

Saree stared hard at Ruhger; he wasn't going to like her idea. But she didn't much like his idea, either. "You know the easiest way to get them close enough to grapple on, right?"

He glowered at her. "Using you as bait."

She nodded. "Yup." The notion didn't thrill her either.

"Why would he do that?" Q asked. "Wouldn't he want Saree and me to come to him in a shuttle?"

Grant sniffed. "If he wants the bait—Saree's eggs—then he's got to agree to our terms. The problem is, I think he'll anticipate this scenario. He's not stupid, just arrogant. If we contact him with terms that include linking folders, he'll either say no or have Gov Human military with him."

"But if we caught him off guard, it might work." Q stared into the distance, her eyebrows almost meeting. "If we could find him in his folder and spring the requirements on him, he'd either accept or make excuses to wait, and if he delays, we fold out."

"That would only work once," Grant said. "After that, he'd be traveling with security."

"I don't think it will work at all." Ruhger shook his head. "He'll be too suspicious. No, the only way to do this is a surprise first strike. We fold in, isolate his comms and net, board, take over, and fold out. Fast. But as Katryn said, we'll need to do a lot of target research. But Ruth gave us a good start." He shoved a document to the big screen.

Saree didn't like anything about the idea. Plus, why would Ruth gather intelligence for them? She worked for *Quantum Fold* and enjoyed the challenge. She read the message.

"Ruhger. I hope you, the crew, Saree, and Q are free to read this message. I'm sending this via a personal contact on Aljanah Station to one of your old message addresses because I don't trust Gov Human. I think they're intercepting everything from Quantum Fold. I'm not happy with Doc's father or Gov Human's support of his plan. Saree and Q are people, not tools, and their self-determination is just as important as anyone else's. Their procreative ability belongs to them.

I'm not the only one upset on Quantum Fold, especially after Q's terrible experiences, so we're doing something about it. I've attached specifications for Beautiful Perfection, along with known modifications, a fairly complete vid of the interior taken during several tours by various Quantum Fold personnel and at least one Gov Human medico. Plus a full, detailed vid of the exterior with known and speculated offensive and defensive capabilities, and a preliminary workup on net capabilities and defenses with recommended attack profiles.

I've also attached a personnel roster with background checks; more than one of the folder's crew is personally beholden to Holliday for helping their family's medico needs. Despite this, he's had significant personnel turnover, because he's arrogant and demanding. I've got feelers out for his full records from the Gov Human Medico Association because those will include vid of his various businesses, his folder's medico pod specifications, and profiles on him. But medico nets aren't always easy to break. On a personal note, if you can pick me up before any counter-action, I'd love to help. But I understand if you can't.

One final note: Doc is extremely unhappy. Every message from Gov Human and his father concerning Saree, Q, or Lightwave gets displayed for everyone in command to see, even the stuff marked 'eyes only,' and his answers include the bare minimums of public information. He's turned down every request for psychological profiles and notes and all other personal medico information on you and Q. As you folded out, Doc told all his medico personnel to wipe their files of any information concerning any of you and asked Los to make sure those files are unrecoverable. Which is good because Gov Human's highest courts levied a search warrant. When Doc turned them away because they need the approval of the Time Guild, the net infiltration attempts ramped up.

We suspect an armed attack next. Doc's already sent objections to Gov Human, including the fact that we have children on board and the unknown reaction of the Sa'sa. He's offered everyone paid vacations on an entertainment planet, but most of us are staying. I'm staying unless I can help you. He's informed the Time Guild about the search warrant but hasn't gotten a reply. Don't reply to this message. We're deleting the account immediately.

Stay strong, Ruth."

"Ruth seems to think we'll have to rescue one or both of you at some point. I'd rather take the fight to Holliday before that happens. Consequences can fly straight for a big black hole. These specifications are exactly what I need to do that. I'll send a link to Chief and Lashtar."

Saree reached over and squeezed his forearm. "Ruhger, this is a big decision. I'm not comfortable with piracy."

He turned to her, taking both of her hands in his. "But government-sponsored abduction and medical experimentation are okay?"

"Of course not. But one doesn't mean the other is okay. It's a false argument, and I have no intention of falling to that level." Ruhger knew all of these things. Fear had to be driving him.

His mouth twisted. "You are right, but so am I. This guy is not going to walk away. If we have to stay on the side of the law, even when it turns against us, I want to be ready to act. So, we'll plan an invasion, whether we use it immediately or not." He quirked a brow. "Fair? Since it's Q's and your lives on the line?"

"Very well. Study away. But I reserve the right to say no." She met his gaze.

Ruhger smirked. "If you're still on board, sure." He turned away and scrolled through diagrams of *Beautiful Perfection*. Katryn and Q peered into a holo together, muttering net terms that sounded more like magical incantations to Saree. Grant chuckled at a personnel record. As usual, her family had joined forces and faced the threat head on, each one taking the area of their greatest strength.

Saree wasn't getting involved, yet. She'd check the Time Guild messages, since Q was diving into net stuff. Doc's message to the Time Guild had been sent on to her without comment. Not surprising. "Grant, the Time Guild forwarded Doc's message to us for action. Would you draft a response, please?"

Grant laughed. "It would be my great pleasure, Clutch Leader. I will say absolutely no in the floweriest, most obnoxiously pleasant words you've ever read, citing their own laws against them. This will be fun!" He stood and bowed deeply. "Thank you for this fabulous opportunity, oh most wondrous *Lightwave* Clutch Leader!"

Saree rolled her eyes but couldn't help laughing, too.

"Saree, this means we've got to avoid Gov Human military at all costs." Ruhger reached out and squeezed her hand. "If they didn't before, they will now believe they have the authority to capture all of us without consequences."

"I'll add something about interference with the only human clock maintainers being a direct attack on the Time Guild to our official reply." Grant typed in the air, then pointed at the overhead. "And after you approve it, I'll send this reply to the Time Guild for official transmission to Gov Human."

Of course Grant had considered the proper routing of the message. "Perfect, thanks. I'll review *Beautiful Perfection's* personnel folders while you work on that, Grant."

He smirked and focused on his holo.

Saree connected to the file storage, opened the folder captain's file, and read. Even knowing little about Chief Medico Lorcan Holliday, she was certain there'd be plenty of weaknesses to exploit in these files. Rats didn't employee knights in shining armor; they employed other rats, or even lesser lifeforms; those who wouldn't show up the big boss.

And Chief Medico Holliday wasn't just a rat. No, he was an emperor with no clothes, and if he shoved them into a black hole, they'd show him the way to a supernova. Her vehemence surprised her. Maybe she shouldn't oppose Ruhger's plan after all.

Chapter Seventeen

RUHGER

"Ruhger, ^timespace^ is surging." Saree ran to her medfloat, in the back of the Command Center. "We should leave. Now." Q followed, jumping on the other medfloat.

The unexpected benefit of being invaded and held for ransom—the IsoSafe kept Tyron alive so Q and Saree could both get medico support while in *^timespace^*. When they found a safe place to buy more medico equipment, a custom medfloat for Q was at the top of the list. Ruhger opened ship-wide comms. "All stations. Incoming. Fold in thirty seconds or less. Objections to an uninhabited system? This one was safe at last check." He brought up the verified emergency folds, selected the system, and checked the math. "Chief, *Lightwave* is ready for fold?"

"Ready for fold when you are," Chief replied.

"All stations, fold in five, four, three, two, fold." Surveillance and navigation changed, and he checked both. "We've arrived safely. Cross-check and report issues." The overall fold generator status showed green. A few subsystems remained yellow; components or connections that hadn't been repaired yet. As Chief and Lashtar replaced components, they'd added sensors, too, getting better status information.

"Captain, Engineering. Fold capability intact. Full power regeneration in sixteen hours."

"Copy that, Chief. I'll leave comms open for your input." Ruhger checked the power available against the distance to his next emergency folds. They could fold if they had to, but giving Chief the time to finish the replacements and repairs would be better.

Saree sat up. "I smoothed *^timespace^* here but left Dronteim alone. No sense in confirming we were there."

Ruhger turned his chair to face her. "Can you tell who was folding in?"

She shook her head. "*^timespace^* doesn't work that way. I can tell a Traveler folder, but not the specific folder. But from the size of the wave pushing through *^timespace^*, I think it was probably a Gov Human fleet."

"Makes sense." Ruhger released his death grip on his chair's armrests and stretched his fingers. "They need to leave us alone." They could do so much more if they weren't being hunted.

Grant grimaced. "I added that to my Time Guild response to Gov Human. 'If you continue to harass our clock maintenance clutch, we will no longer maintain fold clocks in Gov Human systems.' That should be plain enough for them to understand."

Saree slid off her medfloat and joined him. Q followed, sitting on his other side. Saree leaned forward. "You'd think, but my guess is they're not going to give up. It's a chance for them to control clock maintenance completely, outside the Time Guild."

Q rolled her eyes. "A non-existent chance. If we can't teach people how to do it, they can't. Especially if they raise the kids in some sort of weird school. Lashtar already told us that doesn't work very well. I may have rebelled against the Sisters' rules, but at least I knew they loved me, if not exactly like a parent." She grimaced. "Being raised by employees? Yuck."

Saree nodded. "Absolutely. The problem is, Gov Human is full of egotistical control freaks. They're not going to let go of the idea unless we can prove it doesn't work, or we force their hands in some other way."

Katryn entered, her shoulders slumped. Ruhger didn't need to ask; Tyron hadn't gotten better. "I'm going to Engineering to help Chief. The faster we get the full repairs done, the faster we get Tyron help. Katryn, any luck on a location?" He stood.

She shook her head, her eyes downcast. "No. Not that won't get us captured."

Ruhger sat back down. He couldn't bear leaving Katryn in such a defeated state of mind. "Then I guess we've got no choice but to capture Daddy Holliday. Where are you and Q on infiltrating his net defenses?"

Katryn turned to him, still grim, but determined. "It's hard to tell until we attempt it, of course, but if the information Los gathered is correct, it's doable. But it will take testing and time. It's not something we can fully prepare for, fold in, and implement. Especially since we've been out of touch, so some of our systems don't have the latest upgrades. We did what we could in Dronteim, but they're frontier, so they're not going to have the newest stuff either." She flopped back in her seat.

Q leaned forward. "I'm pretty sure we can infiltrate quickly. Holliday's systems are mostly manufacturer's standard, with some commercial add-ons. If we could find another folder like his, we could break in for practice. We'd also need to find practice nets with his additions or build our own, but I've been a part of some net testing boards in the past." She poked Katryn's arm. "Actually, why didn't we think of merc net? You can bet someone's looked at Holliday's folder even more than Ruth. It's a perfect target—a rich medico making credits on the uber-wealthy. That's probably why he only folds to core systems unless he's got Gov Human military or mercs with him."

Katryn snapped her mouth closed. "Of course. I should have remembered that, but we've been on the straight and narrow for so long..."

Q snickered. "Don't worry, I'll yank you off. And speaking of that..." She turned to Saree with a wicked smirk. "After we get the folder, we should dump his people someplace in the back of beyond but safe, like Circinus, and sell the folder. Giving it back is risky, and if we dump it, someone else will take it and sell it, and probably the crew. If *we* sell it, we get a decent return on our efforts, and we make it clear that messing with us will cost big time. Make it hurt where it counts—his credit stash."

During Q's speech, Saree's face was a study of mixed emotions. Appalled, disbelieving, and finally, thoughtful.

Ruhger chuckled. Q's lawlessness and Saree's reaction were funny. He had no trouble with Q's idea. It might be technically illegal, but what Holliday was attempting was legal extortion.

When enemies wrote and enforced the laws, there weren't a lot of great choices. "You know, I think Q is right. We'll be telling the wealthy that they're not the only ones who can play dirty and get away with it. Consequences may be delayed, but they will happen."

"It's not dirty; we've got the law on our side," Grant said. "The Time Guild has a wide range of actions available to them that the Grus added. Gov Human signed those accords. All the signatories ignore those lesser actions because the Sa'sa don't usually fight that way. They're an all-or-nothing species. But we're not." Grant waggled his brows. "So, we go in, capture the folder, dump the people on a gray station, scrub and sell the folder somewhere else, and go about our business. If we get confronted with evidence someday, we show them the provisions about self-defense in the Time Guild charter and tell them to fold into a supernova." His mouth twisted. "The Garnet Star would be perfect."

Saree nodded. "If the Time Guild can send a bill to a system for a fold clock they've destroyed, we should be able to confiscate an asset used against us. Especially if they attack us." She sniffed.

"They haven't attacked, yet, so it's shaded gray by human standards, but I like it." Lashtar entered, limping slightly, Chief by her side. They collapsed in the soft seating between his chair and the medfloats.

"Are you okay, Lashtar?" Q frowned.

Lashtar waved her hand. "I'm fine. Just doing a lot of squatting. It's good for me but tiring."

"I can do that for you, you know." Q scowled.

Chief shook his head. "Your net skills and flexibility are needed here. With the help of hand tractor beams, we're more than capable of the physical labor." He turned to Saree. "And I agree. We capture it, it's ours. Take a medico pod, and sell the rest. Karma is real."

Saree frowned. "Karma could bite back." She shivered. "It's not the way I prefer to operate. It's definitely iffy."

"Not by the Time Guild or Sa'sa standards. Holliday is attacking. He's egg stealing. That's an attack against the clutch." Grant raised his brows, staring at Saree until she nodded. She wasn't entirely happy about the prospect but wouldn't object. Ruhger was happy she'd given in and that he wasn't the one who forced her to see the possibility was real.

"We need a location where we can access merc net without excessive delays and not get caught." Katryn spread her hands apart. "Ideas?"

"A constellation entry," Saree said. "Good comms, no one stays long. We'll get noticed and reported, but we can stay long enough to get the information we need and fold out."

"Unless we break." Chief waved his wrench in the air. "Our fold generators work, but they're not a system. It's a patched-up mess masquerading as a capability."

Ruhger snorted. "You built it. It's not a mess. It might not be packaged neatly, but I have no doubt in your abilities to make a system work."

Chief shook his head. "I've got a lot of doubts. Especially about the fold generator cubes. Who knows how long those will last? We need new fold generators, from a recognized manufacturer."

"We can't afford that, Chief." Q cackled. "But you know who can? Chief Medico Holliday."

Ruhger smiled. "Of course. We take the fold generators and put them in *Lightwave*."

"Or we transfer to Holliday's folder entirely." Q shrugged. "I know you all have an emotional attachment to *Lightwave*, but it's old."

Lashtar snorted. "So am I, but I'm not headed to the bone yard yet."

Chief scrolled through his holo. "Maybe we can combine the two folders into one. The fold generators on *Perfection* are more than it needs. Why not connect the two permanently and give us room for expansion?"

"An excellent idea, Chief." Ruhger couldn't help smiling. "That gives us a whole medico level and room for ^timespace^ students, if we can't rely on *Quantum Fold*. But we can't do that on our own, can we? We need a shipyard."

Chief nodded. "We do. I can connect the two folders permanently, but I can't seamlessly integrate them, which would be much better. It would hide both folders better, too, especially if we give the combination a new designation."

There had to be some downsides, though, beyond the morality of the action. "While we charge, let's consider the negatives and the positives. I'll start a shared document." Ruhger held up his right hand, palm out. "We're brainstorming, so just put your ideas and thoughts down, no matter how far a fold they may be. We'll go through and look at the ramifications later. Understood?"

"Excellent idea," Lashtar said. "Because you're right. There are negatives, and we'll think of more as time goes on."

Everyone appeared to agree, except maybe Katryn. But she was in a fragile state, and her anger at Holliday was justified. If it hadn't been for his greed, Tyron would be fine. But some beings never learned that credits couldn't buy happiness and that control was an illusion.

"I like the idea of going on the offensive, though." Lashtar mimed a roundhouse punch. "Bullies believe running is weakness. If we take the fight to Holliday, we're making our position clear."

"We'll also be angering some very powerful people in the core systems," Grant said. "There are other medicos to the stars, but since we're certain Holliday is doing off books experimentation on humans, there's a lot of credits involved. His investors may have cut him off, but if we attack him, we give them an additional target for their anger. Some of them probably want his folder in exchange for the funds he's already spent, but they haven't been able to confiscate it quietly."

Q shrugged. "You snooze, you lose. They should have done it already. I'm sure they all have contacts in the gray or black, along with their own mercs. Besides, to those people, a folder is nothing. They have dozens."

"But what they don't have is a challenge." Lashtar grimaced. "That's what many ultra-wealthy beings are looking for—the next risk that gets them a big payoff. It's not the credits, it's the thrill, the excitement. That's why they do illegal things. They're risking getting caught, even if they can buy their way out of trouble. The human clocker is a challenge, one worth taking."

Ruhger nodded. "And they wouldn't care if the Sa'sa punished all humanity because they'd be safe in their little enclaves. Or so they think."

"That safety is an illusion." Grant shook his head. "They should study history. Mob rule, violent overthrows, those all happen regularly. If the core human systems were cut off, it would get ugly fast, and the masses would look for someone to blame."

"The wealthy would pin that blame on me." Saree glared at the navigation display. "People are already scared of me. Twisting the narrative would be easy."

Ruhger put his hand on hers and squeezed lightly. "I'm sure we can get ahead of that."

"Especially if we find mindless clones." Q shuddered.

Ruhger slashed his hand across his body. "Negative. We're not invading his medico experiments. If we can take his folder, we can send information we find to the Medico Association and Gov Human, but there's no reason for us to go there. It's not our job."

Saree turned toward him. "But it might be the only way we can prove that it won't work."

Ruhger shook his head. "Put it all in the document. Grant, it's your job to organize it into categories in... three hours."

Lashtar raised her hand. "Give that to me. I'm less personally involved."

The hatch swished open, and Loreli sauntered in. "You're all personally involved in our next meal. Let's go!" She spun on a toe, her long white gown twirling with her and trailing on the decking behind her as she sashayed out.

Ruhger stood and held his hand out to Saree. "You heard Chef. It's time for dinner. You've got three hours for comments after we eat, then Lashtar will organize, and we'll discuss. But while we eat, let's focus on the food. Loreli's creations deserve our attention."

Saree slid her hand into his, and they left the Command Center together. Ruhger smiled at her. No matter what happened, if they were together, he'd be happy.

Chapter Eighteen

SAREE

On her medfloat, Saree stayed on the edge of ^*timespace*^, remaining close to the Vela constellation entry, ready to dive in and smooth their fold out if necessary. Using Familia's home constellation entry for their information gathering and war gaming was a bit risky. But after Lightwave Clutch's previous smack down, Familia was suitably wary. Plus, a Sa'sa Time Guild clutch with supporting Warriors wasn't far away. Adding to the risk, Chief Medico Holliday might attack them without Gov Human backing. He had plenty of supporters in Vela who'd love to have Saree under their control. If Holliday folded in with a mercenary fleet, they'd fold out, but if he was solo, they'd take the fight to the enemy.

They were more concerned that Gov Human military would join Holliday, enforcing their illegal edicts. But any supporter, merc or government, would wait until Holliday yelled for help. Shutting down his comms and other net capabilities was crucial to their success. They needed a realistic simulation, which required fast net connections. The risk was worth taking.

While Katryn and Q ran net scenarios, Ruhger, Grant, Lashtar, and Loreli war-gamed the infiltration. Before folding to Vela, Ruhger made all of them practice firing weapons, both in auto and manual modes. While the computers made targeting easy, there was always the chance their net could be infiltrated; cutting those connections and shooting accurately were necessary skills. Saree had also noticed that manual practice made checking and correcting the automations faster. It also gave all of them a better grasp of strategy, rather than focusing on the simple tactics of putting overwhelming firepower on every target. Since they wanted the folder, not shooting it to pieces was important, too.

Good strategy would also make a difference if Holliday brought one or two mercs with him, but not an entire fleet. Fortunately, Ruhger was a strategic master, and Chief was almost as good. Both could fire lasers and other weapons while controlling the battle. But with their current mechanical issues, Chief had to concentrate on *Lightwave*'s systems. Lashtar could back Chief on both, but they all hoped that wouldn't be necessary.

Folders popped in and out, but none of them were Gov Human military, and Saree hadn't detected any big surges in ^*timespace*^ signaling a fleet. But, if *Quantum Fold* came, she still hadn't decided if they should stay and talk or fold out immediately, avoiding the situation entirely.

Saree needed to go through *Lightwave*'s messages, but Q and Katryn needed to work. It was more important for Saree to remain aware of ^*timespace*^; she'd check after they folded out.

"Bad news," Grant said. "Holliday's offering big bounties for our capture. Merc net is churning. Some big names have implied they're taking the job. Others are objecting strenuously, saying it's a stupid idea to take out the only clocker keeping travel stable in the human fringe."

"Awesome." Q rolled her eyes.

An odd surge in ^*timespace*^ made Saree submerge fully. She ^*reached*^ to the smooth bubble—a Traveler folder. She resurfaced enough to talk. "Travelers incoming."

Q spun, wrinkling her nose. "Wonderful."

"Checking identity," Grant said. "It's *Tobar*. I'll find out what they want."

"Thanks, Grant." Saree reentered her half-meditation, watching for pursuit. Galactica might be actively following the Travelers, but coming to Vela was unlikely. A group of Sa'sa darted to her, and she sent a greeting. They welcomed her, then returned to their ^*timespace*^ smoothing; probably Valentia system, since that was the declared destination of most of the folders entering Vela.

"Saree, I'm working with *Tobar* to find a system we can fold to," Grant said. "They have information for us, but they don't want to stay here. Familia isn't friendly to Travelers."

Sunk in ^*timespace*^, Saree didn't reply. Grant knew what to do, and they'd fold out when they decided or when Katryn and Q were ready. Or more folders entered.

"Chief, can we fold?" Ruhger asked.

"Still no issues, but no promises either," Chief said.

"All stations, unless there are objections, we're folding to the Lepus constellation entry in thirty seconds," Ruhger announced. "Secure and crosscheck for fold."

Time counted down, and Saree dropped fully into ^*timespace*^. Linking with the Travelers, they smoothed ^*timespace*^ on their way from Vela to Lepus. After checking for disturbances and anomalies, Saree dropped back into her body and opened her eyes.

Ruhger's slight smile lit, and he took her hand. "Welcome back. Ready for this?"

Saree sat up and stretched. "Probably not, but when did that matter?"

"Grant's telling them about the attack and how we fixed the fold generators." Ruhger huffed. "They didn't sound surprised about any of it, so I'm guessing they modified their fold generators a long time ago." He led her to the conference room table.

She sat at the head, facing the screen with *Tobar*'s leadership sitting at a similar table. Theirs had an elaborate tea set, and brightly colored art and green plants decorated the compartment. Before Saree could say anything, Loreli entered, towing a tray with a tea set, delicious-looking desserts and snacks, and a recovery shake. Winking, she set the shake near Saree's right hand, placed the tea service on the table, then sat, fluffing her white satin skirt. Saree's nose twitched; caramel and chocolate made her reach for the treats, but she stopped. Business came first.

"Greetings, Clutch Leader Saree." Listraba, the Speaker for the Infinite Road, stood and bowed, her layered gold necklaces tinkling.

Taking her cue from the formal greeting, Saree stood and bowed in return. "Safe folds, Smoother of the Infinite Road Listraba. To what do we owe the pleasure of your company?"

Listraba smiled. "Ah, for that, you must thank Speaker for the Ship, Ruslo." She turned, sweeping her hand toward him.

Ruslo stood and bowed but sat again before speaking. "Greetings, Saree. Since you warned us of the possible attacks on our women and procreation, we've reached out to clients we've assisted in the past. Our first message was to the medico school on Cygnus Secundus. We got an acknowledgement, but they denied hearing anything about the matter. They reassured us they'd never agree to assist human cloning, although they can clone animals."

Patriarch Kein flipped his hand away, as though shooing a fly. "Animals don't have souls, so there is no problem with that."

Ruslo raised his brows, then returned to gazing at Saree. "Agreed. Forewarned, the Sisters insisted that the medicos and everyone else on their compound delete everything to do with you, Q, or *Lightwave* so there would be nothing to find. The medicos had already purged their databases, but some other organizations were more reluctant. Fortunately, those records are immaterial to your health or personal status. Since then, we've received multiple messages warning us that Gov Human sent investigators to confiscate genetic material and records concerning you, Q, and the rest of your clutch. Reportedly, Chief Medico Lorcan Holliday is livid about his people's failure to find anything. The Secundus medico school has filed a complaint with the Medico Association against Gov Human and Holliday. They're threatening legal action if the harassment continues, and other medico schools are joining their complaint. They believe government interference in medico matters is wrong. And that cloning human beings is wrong."

"We will sign on to such efforts as well," Pater Kein added. "Human cloning is evil, and evil must be stopped."

Saree couldn't agree more. "Absolutely. Thank you for letting me know." She sighed. "I guess it was too much to ask that they not attack others in their fervor to get to me." She wouldn't tell them about their plans to go on the offensive. As a peace-loving religion, the Travelers wouldn't be helpful and might even think they had a duty to report what they knew to Gov Human. Although, most likely not, after the authorities hounded them. Still, she'd never ask them to choose which decision was the greater evil.

"It shouldn't be." Ruslo scowled. "And to aid your defense, we are sharing information we wouldn't normally share. In the past, our construction clans have built medico compartments for Holliday. He doesn't pay on time, or sometimes at all, and often threatens us with blacklisting or worse. So, I have compiled every scrap of information on these deals. We've included subcontractors and associates, vulnerabilities because of his cheapness and lack of concern for others, and other items of interest. It's not a Gov Human intelligence report because we don't have those kinds of analysts. But I think you'll find several areas interesting."

Saree stood and bowed deeply, just missing the table. "Thank you. We truly appreciate your help." It was a generous offer, definitely skirting their non-violent beliefs. But it added a deeper layer to their knowledge.

Ruslo shook his head. "You have helped us just as much. Your warning allowed several of our folders to leave before they'd have to use extreme escape measures."

"Plus, as Pater Kein said, evil must be stopped." Listraba tapped the table. "Our speakers for the future are listening diligently. They've warned three folders of danger, allowing them to fold out before any action. We've warned clients we may need to disappear if Gov Human folds in. Most understand, some are very unhappy, and others see this as an opportunity. I believe you may be familiar with one of those systems. We've done work on Emma Three in Carina before, but with their recent change to an authoritarian military government, we won't risk going there. They sent a message asking us to relay their offer of protection."

Ruhger huffed. "Conscription isn't protection."

"Precisely." Ruslo nodded. "Therefore, we no longer accept work there. That, and our smoothers of the infinite road don't want to draw the attention of the Sa'sa. Working in systems with non-Time Guild fold clocks is inviting unwelcome attention."

Saree held up her hand and waggled it back and forth. "Sort of, but not really. Because the Sa'sa have abandoned the frontier human systems. They're leaving all of those to us and you."

"Interesting. Humans to smooth human space." Listraba tilted her head. "But not the core, right?"

Saree shook her head. "No. I'm not capable of that. I don't think you are either, or you don't want to be."

"Travelers must travel." Ruslo nodded sharply. "It has been seen."

"And while there would still be travel, a single constellation would be too confining." Listraba held up both hands, palm out. "We can't risk it. And speaking of risk, while we're avoiding Gov Human at almost all costs, the Guardians and people of Aljanah are not so lucky. The medico facilities on the planet and station have destroyed what they can and hidden much of the rest. But there are plenty of reproductive-capable humans on the station and the planet with Traveler heritage. Plus reproductive material storage facilities on the planet. DNA testing will quickly confirm that we are different in several ways. And different can be targeted."

Q waved a finger in the air. Saree nodded. If Q had something to share, it would be relevant. "I don't know if it's true for your people, or the Guardians, but I can't enter ^*timespace*^ on a planet. I have to be in space. Saree can do it on a planet or anywhere, really. So, if Gov Human has some way of screening for ^*timespace*^ ability, encourage the Aljanah government to make it happen on the planet." She shrugged, scowling. "Although if *Quantum Fold* hasn't figured out how to screen for ^*timespace*^ ability, I don't know how Gov Human can."

"Interesting." Listraba nodded slowly. "We don't live on planets, so training a smoother of the infinite road on one would never occur to me. I've also never attempted smoothing on a planet. Why would I? Planets can't fold, and asking God for the impossible is testing God. We don't do that."

"We try not to do that." Pater Kein smiled gently at Listraba. "You know we all do that every day without thinking about it."

"Of course. Still, my point is I've never tried such a thing, and I don't see the point of doing it." She shivered.

Saree didn't have a dozen smoothers with her, just Q. "I understand. Sometimes we must both be on a planet, but we need to watch ^timespace^, too. It's a handy talent for us."

"I can see that." Listraba nodded.

Ruslo raised a finger. "I believe that's all we had to tell you. We've sent the data. If you have questions, send a message, and we'll do our best to answer."

"Thank you, Ruslo. Thanks to all of you. If we find out anything else, we'll let you know. Is there anything we can do for you?" She surveyed her crew and the Travelers, but no one had anything to add. "Safe folds. *Lightwave* out."

"Smooth roads. Go with God. *Tobar* out." The screen turned off.

"Interesting." Ruhger shrugged one shoulder. He pushed the recovery shake closer to her.

Saree sipped. "It is. Also useful. Lashtar, you, Katryn, Q, and Grant can pile through the documents. Split it up as you see fit. Let's see how it helps. Any reason to leave here before we do anything else?"

"No, and this is as good of a place as any to charge fully." Chief chose a savory bread and cheese creation. "Besides, I'd like to eat."

"Works for me." Ruhger scooped up a skinny green pepper stuffed with a pale creamy filling. "Let's stay here for at least twenty-four hours, maybe more."

"Agreed." Everything smelled wonderful, but browned butter and dark chocolate called her. Saree grabbed a mini-chocolate cupcake with a giant swirl of dark chocolate ganache and took a bite. "Delicious as usual, Loreli."

"Thank you, dahrling. Enjoy!" She hustled away, towing an empty tray. "Don't ruin your appetite completely. We'll have a full meal in two hours."

Saree grinned, then took another bite. They might have grim work ahead of them, but at least Loreli had sweetened the deal. She finished her cupcake and poured tea for all of them.

Ruhger selected a piece of bruschetta, then stopped with it suspended in front of his mouth. He put the bread down. "Once we're reasonably certain we can take Holliday's folder, rather than looking for him, why not lure him someplace? We tell him not to bring additional folders, and if he does, we'll leave, and he'll never get another chance."

Chief snorted. "Didn't we already talk about this? He'll never agree. Or if he does, the mercs or Gov Human will fold in five minutes later."

"It's possible." Ruhger turned to Saree. "Could you do an extended fold with another folder?"

Saree realized her mouth was hanging open, and she snapped it shut. "Someday, you'll ask a ^*timespace*^ question that won't astonish me to the point of incoherence."

Ruhger huffed. "But not today."

"No. The problem is, I don't know what the limiting factor or factors are on extended fold. Distance is definitely a factor. When we retrieved Q before she made it to *Quantum Fold*, enclosing Beta Shuttle in the bubble of ^*timespace*^ so far from us took more effort than normal. But I don't know if mass makes any difference."

"We could test, maybe." Ruhger glowered at the table. "But no matter what, if we want to fold with his folder, we'd have to latch on."

Lashtar shook her head. "You're thinking like a mudhugger. While you're talking, you send a small force to take the folder over. That is the way."

"Still might take too long." Grant shook his head. "If we're only talking, then he's got every incentive to stay far away. He knows we used to be mercs."

Saree had the answer. "So, we give him what he wants. My eggs." She held back a shudder. She'd never allow her children to be in the hands of that unethical medico.

"No." Ruhger turned to her and gripped her hands. "We're not giving that black hole anything, let alone our children."

"Of course not. But we can fake him out. Tell him we'll split out a few for him, in exchange for him leaving us alone and calling off Gov Human and the rest of his wealthy supporters."

Ruhger shook his head. "He'll know it's a fake out."

Lashtar chuckled. "Not if we let it slip that we're desperately in need of credits and show him the real thing. A container of frozen eggs, waiting for him. He'll have no way to know they're not human."

Chief grinned at Lashtar. "You're so smart." He faced Saree. "He knows we were attacked in Emma, but he doesn't know about the organization that ripped us off. Nor does he have any idea what we're paid for clock maintenance because all that is handled by the Time Guild, and he can't get into the Sa'sa banking system, right?"

"When we got on merc net, that was one of the things I checked. No one's made any sense of the Sa'sa nets, and the Time Guild bank is on the Sa'sa nets." Katryn rested her chin on her fist. "Go on. I can't wait to hear the rest of this."

Q chortled. "Loreli should have made popcorn."

Chief snorted. "We let our financial woes slip—that's your job, Grant—and when we contact Holliday, we not only ask for a one-on-one meeting but a massive amount of credits." Chief raised his wrench above his head. "Like ten years of operating costs. Then we negotiate down to five years or so. He puts the credits in escrow, but we don't take them. Not ever, because the beings who can fund such capital are not the kind we want on our tail."

"That could still get us attacked by those beings," Grant said. "They'll see it as a broken promise."

"They will." Chief nodded. "But we put a whole bunch of stipulations on the contract, including contradictory terms. Make it so he'll inevitably break it somehow. Many of those will get weeded out during negotiations, but we can create a bunch of fake stuff that Q needs for reproductive health. Because you know he'll want her, too. We'll set up a swap in person, but you know he'll bring a shuttle full of mercs or remotes and try to take us over and get everything. But the whole thing will be a ruse. While he's enroute, we'll send a cloaked shuttle to his folder, infiltrate, and fold it out. Then *Lightwave* follows, leaving him stranded on his shuttle. The biggest issue is orbital velocity, because we'll have to fly much faster than he does, so we're ready to invade before his shuttle latches to *Lightwave*. If we can't, we latch him to our cargo bay hatch and we keep him there. They'll eventually blow the hatch, but we'll set up a laser crossfire. Then Katryn takes over his shuttle, we blow the latches and clear the cargo bay. Meanwhile, we take over his folder."

Ruhger stared into the distance, then refocused on Chief. "The biggest issue I see is Gov Human or other mercs folding in halfway through the process. If both shuttles are enroute, our shuttle gets left behind, too. If our forces are in the middle of infiltration or takeover, and a force folds in, they could destroy or invade our shuttle."

"We put a failsafe on the eggs and I hold it." Q held up her hand, clenching a napkin. "If they get that far and stun me, the whole thing blows, taking me with it. I can't be in armor, or they'll fry my armor, and the chances are fifty-fifty if my hand will release."

Saree wasn't about to let Q take that risk. "No. I'll do it."

"That won't work. Your eggs aren't in your body." Q pointed at her chest. "It has to be me."

Ruhger shook his head. "None of this will work. We don't have enough people. We'd need full merc teams."

Saree agreed with Ruhger. "He's right. Q and I have to be on *Lightwave* or Holliday won't believe any of it. We'd all have to prove our status with proof of life measures. Katryn and Q will be needed for net work on Holliday's folder and shuttle. I'll be needed in ^*timespace*^, too, to watch for incoming folders. We'll need Chief on *Lightwave*'s fold generators. What if they fail after we fold into the exchange destination? That leaves Ruhger, Grant, Loreli, and Lashtar. We need someone to run defense for *Lightwave*, plus offense if they break in. Then we need a team capable of taking on Holliday's folder."

"That's true, under normal circumstances." Lashtar smirked. "How do you feel about betrayal?"

Chapter Nineteen

RUHGER

Ruhger's shoulders tightened, and he rolled them, his hardsuit shifting smoothly with his movements. The plan was perilous, but every time they folded into civilization, they risked fold generator failure and getting caught. If they folded into a system like Emma, who wanted the Clocker, or a system gunning for Holliday's bounty, the locals could fry their fold generators upon identification. Sadly, some systems were probably taking out fold generators on every small folder using the more remote fold orbits, just in case they were *Lightwave*. The bounty was big enough that some would risk the back blast. Most small folders of their type weren't well connected—no one would notice if they went missing.

They'd chosen Caldwell 88 in Circinus for the meeting. Full of debris from the previous battle, Holliday's pilots would be cautious. Since Ruhger could out-fly anything but a full Artificial Intelligence, and Holliday would never put one of those in control of his life, they could intercept *Perfection*'s shuttle long before it reached *Lightwave*.

The size of their attack and defense force was inadequate, but they didn't dare involve anyone else. Chief sat in the co-pilot's chair, but rather than flying, he, Grant, and Loreli searched for smaller debris intercepting their orbit that surveillance might miss. Saree was half in ^*timespace*^, and Katryn was attempting infiltration and takeover of *Perfection*'s net.

The strategy had taken weeks to implement. They couldn't tell anyone exactly what they planned. First, Lashtar sent carefully crafted messages of growing discontent to the Sisters of Cygnus leadership. She complained about low pay, long hours, little contact with civilization, falling out of love with Chief, and a general lack of respect from everyone on *Lightwave*. She also included references to things that had happened on Secundus, pointing toward their plan. From Nan's responses, they were fairly certain that she understood it was a deception, but there were no guarantees. Gov Human was certainly intercepting every message and parcel in and out of Cygnus. Lashtar sent slightly different messages to Ruth, telling the tale of an unhappy person, short on credits, looking for a way out. After her first dismissive reply, Ruth hadn't answered the following missives.

As predicted, one of Holliday's personal assistants contacted Lashtar through an anonymous messaging system. Lashtar replied with suspicion and denials but ever so slowly agreed to betray the clutch in a system of her choosing.

They knew Holliday would be even more suspicious than Lashtar, and there'd certainly be a double-cross. But with a bit of luck, they'd take over Holliday's folder before his shuttle could latch onto *Lightwave*. They'd recorded vid and medico telemetry of Saree and Q secured to medfloats, with the rest of the crew stunned and hog-tied on the decking surrounding the two women. Saree's egg storage container was there, too. Tyron remained in the IsoSafe in the medico pod; his status had been key to convincing Holliday the whole thing was real. Faking Tyron's complex injury would have been difficult. Lashtar complained to Holliday that Saree and Ruhger were lying to Katryn; they weren't looking for advanced care, just waiting for Tyron to die.

Despite their careful planning, Ruhger had literally dragged his feet departing *Lightwave*. Leaving Q, Lashtar, and Tyron behind was grueling. Once they latched on to *Perfection*, they'd need Saree, so Q would be stuck on her medfloat dropping in and out of ^*timespace*^, watching for an inbound fleet. Q had wanted to come with them, but she had so little experience with battle and none with their team. Ruhger couldn't put her in danger like that. Leaving Saree on *Lightwave* would have been better for many reasons, but she had plenty of live fire time with their team. If they ended up in a battle, they'd need all the fire power they could get.

If everything went to plan, Katryn and Q would take Holliday's folder through the net without firing a shot. They'd shut down the weapons and take over the command and control. According to the information they'd gathered from merc net, they should be able to do it easily. If they took over the net, Saree could remain in ^timespace^ and Q could assist Lashtar with defense of *Lightwave*. If Holliday somehow pulled off his own miracle and invaded *Lightwave*, Q and Lashtar were the only live defenders. They had to avoid that at all costs.

Ruhger wanted to leave more people behind, but with just six, the invasion of *Beautiful Perfection* was idiocy; less meant certain capture or death. Success relied on surprise and the design of Holliday's folder. He'd built the folder to impress high society, not to defend against anything but minor attacks. Even folding into the fringe was pushing *Perfection*'s defenses. Holliday's choice had been logical—he had to appeal to the upper crust of society, and few in the fringes could afford his fees. If they could, they could provide full space defense, too.

"I'm in the folder's operations net," Katryn said. "We should be able to latch on and enter without notice unless there's some other physical sign, like a vibration. I'm not in their life support, offensive, or defensive capabilities yet."

"Can you create a distraction when we latch?" Chief pointed at a shuttle status display. "Like activating the latches at a hatch at the far end of the folder or some sort of alarm?"

"I've got that, Chief," Q said over the comms. "I'm not dropping into ^timespace^ until Saree leaves Beta Shuttle."

Ruhger pointed at the operation checklist on the lower right corner of the shuttle's main screen. "First, get into the folder and shuttle's interior vids. If they have attack remotes, or a significant number of troops, we'll have to disengage."

"Sorry." Katryn's fingers flicked through her holo.

"Ruhger, Q. I've penetrated *Perfection*'s shuttle vids. Shuttle is full of remotes. They can't latch, or we're dead."

"Suns. Lashtar, hold them off." It wasn't unexpected but still unwelcome.

Lashtar said, "Shuttle *Perfection, Lightwave Fold Transport.* You're in violation of our terms and will not be allowed to dock. Return to your folder, or I fire."

"*Lightwave, Perfection.* We are not in violation."

Lashtar snorted. "I just took down a bunch of former mercs. I'm not stupid. Your shuttle is full of remotes, and Holliday isn't there. The agreement was we exchange in person. You're not the only one willing to pay for these people. I'm folding out."

"Please listen, Gentle Lashtar." A different male voice.

Katryn said, "The voice print says that's Holliday himself. Of course, that's not hard to fake. He might still be on the folder. Q, have you spotted him on the shuttle yet?"

"I think he's here." Q shared a picture with an arrow pointing to a hardsuit in the seat behind the pilot. "But his helmet is up, so I can't be certain."

"Why? You intend to attack and take, not make an exchange." Lashtar's tone was hard; she played her role perfectly.

"Katryn, the folder's interior vids?" They had to know what was on the folder. If it was full of remotes too, their plan wouldn't work.

"The remotes are merely self-protection and patient transport." Holliday spoke in the typical calm, "I know best" voice effective for many medicos, except for an edge of arrogance he couldn't hide. "As you said, you took out a crew of very smart people. Why wouldn't you betray me?"

"Because there's only one of me? I can only do so much. But I can leave. Now."

"Wait! I'm sure we can work out an exchange method." Holliday's words flew out of his mouth. Something was driving him because he was risking a lot—if he was on the shuttle.

Katryn pointed at the orange dots on the schematic of Holliday's folder, displayed on the upper part of Beta Shuttle's main screen. "I've got some interior vids. Remotes in the cargo hold and stationed throughout the folder, including outside piloting. Maybe inside piloting, too, because I haven't gotten in there yet. Unless

I can break into their command and control, I recommend we disengage."

"Ruhger, Q. I know this remote model. I can disable them."

Ruhger adjusted thrust to match the folder's velocity. "Standing by." If Lashtar had to leave, they'd be stranded. They'd brought extra water, food, and air, but it wasn't ideal. Especially if *Lightwave*'s fold generators broke.

"Can we? I don't think you're playing fair, Holliday." Lashtar's tone was skeptical.

"I am," Holliday said. "There are always ways to work around problems."

"And rules and laws, right?" Lashtar's disdain was probably a little too strong.

"I don't think you have much of a right to criticize me on that, *Sister*."

They continued throwing thinly-veiled insults at each other. Despite the perilous situation, the exchange was amusing. Lashtar had perfected her style at the Sisters of Cygnus' orphanage; teen girls and egotistical idiots would wither equally under her dry snark. But nothing penetrated Holliday's superiority.

"Ruhger, Q. I can power down the remotes on the shuttle. They can be rebooted, but only manually. I've sent Katryn the vulnerability information."

"Copy that, Q. Stand by." Ruhger turned to Katryn. "Can you get to the remotes on Holliday's folder?"

"Working on it." Katryn stared into her holo, her fingers flying. "Give me a few... ready on your command."

"Q, Ruhger. Don't let Holliday's shuttle latch. Use the tractor beam—shove them away. Then fire if necessary." He input thrust to match velocity with Holliday's folder. "Be ready to fold. Q, Katryn, disable all the remotes in five, four, three, two, now. Latching to Holliday's folder." Hopefully, disabling the remotes would distract the crew enough that they wouldn't notice the vibrations. He slid Beta Shuttle alongside the folder's locked clamps, closing their boarding clamps around *Perfection*'s, then pulling them in tight enough to seal the hatch.

"Q, *Perfection*'s fold generators are powering up!" Saree said. "Fold *Lightwave* now!"

"Q, Saree. Shuttle firing at our fold generators. Folding in three, two—" Static hissed.

Blast it all to the giant black hole of Andromeda! No time to fly Beta Shuttle clear. They hadn't planned on *Perfection* folding so early in the exchange. "Offense is our only chance. Raise helmets, prepare to breach. Katryn, stay here and get control of that net. We need C2, now." Unlocking his hardsuit from the seat, he raised his helmet, engaged his shields, and thudded to the hatch, with Grant, Loreli, Saree, and Chief behind him. He smacked the hatch release, and it slid open, revealing *Perfection*'s outer hatch. "Katryn, figure out where we are and what forces are nearby." He pried the hatch control cover open, popped off the decorative cover, and attached an electronic lock picker below the button.

"Remotes disabled," Katryn said. "Clear beyond the airlock. Working on airlock controls. Working on C2."

The outer hatch opened, and he stepped inside. When the rest joined him, he cycled the airlock. It opened without delay—blast and rad, they were walking into a trap. Ruhger raised his rifle and peered around the edge. Grant did the same on his right. Five remotes bearing a plethora of weapons waited in the shiny white corridor with pinstripes of medico green and tasteful artwork. Red lights shone on the remote's panels—Q's codes had worked. "Chief, if you can permanently disable those remotes fast, do it." He didn't want to leave a threat behind them.

Ruhger's heart pounded and his mouth dried; he slowed his breathing. Watching for movement through the sights of his rifle, he scanned the entire corridor and stepped forward. A crunch of plas and cerimetal made him jolt. In his rear view holo, Chief smacked his fighting axe into a remote's control panel. He continued. Grant stepped in sync on his right, Saree and Loreli behind them, walking sideways to cover their six. After finishing the remotes, Chief took the rear guard.

Just before an intersection, Ruhger stopped. Grant stepped close to the inside corner, raised his arm above his head, and crooked his pinkie vid around the corner. "Clear."

Ruhger kept his left shoulder to the outer bulkhead and trod forward, the rest following. They'd chosen the airlock nearest to the piloting compartment, but it was a hundred meters away.

"Ruhger, Katryn. Live forces inbound, soft armor. Five ahead, five on the intersecting corridor. They're launching remotes. Attempting shut down."

"Copy, Katryn." The defenders chose the perfect location. Unlike *Lightwave*'s cube, *Beautiful Perfection* was a long oval, a graceful but pointless shape in the vacuum of space. With each step along the curve, their line of sight shortened. As they proceeded toward the end where piloting was located, the bend sharpened.

"Missed one remote, inbound on intersecting corridor, high," Katryn said. "Trying again."

Ruhger raised his rifle, firing when the remote appeared. It fired a single blast, splashing harmlessly off his shield. The remote crashed to the decking, the front a smoking hole. Katryn must have disabled it as he fired.

"Rolling EMP grenade." At the corner, Grant crouched and tossed an object down the intersecting corridor. He backed away three steps, Ruhger copying him, so their suits didn't get fried by the electromagnetic pulse. If they'd been wearing soft armor, they wouldn't risk using EMP.

After the electric-blue flash and bang, they ran forward. Grant and Loreli peeled off to the intersecting corridor, while Saree and Chief followed him, going straight. As they rounded the gently curve, rifle barrels appeared. Ruhger fired before he saw anything but hands and arms, aiming at the rifles. Laser fire splashed off shields. Saree's beam joined his, and they penetrated a shield, taking out one defender.

"Fire in the hole." Chief stepped between them, rolling another EMP grenade on the decking. They all backpedaled but continued firing to keep the defenders away.

Another flash and bang followed. "Charge!" Ruhger ran forward, still firing, Saree beside him, Chief between them. The remaining four armored beings stood frozen, the electromagnetic burst frying the armor's control and power. Ruhger stopped firing but kept his weapon raised. When they reached the troops, Chief and

Saree yanked weapons from hands and belts, putting them in their backpacks. Then they secured each person with special armor cuffs around their wrists and ankles. It was safer to peel them out of the armor, but that took time. "Grant, Katryn, one attacker down, four secured."

"Ruhger, Katryn, Grant. Two attackers down, three secured. We'll see you on the other side." Smart of Grant to remind them he'd appear in front of them shortly. Friendly fire was an oxymoron.

"All forces, Katryn. No more personnel or remotes detected. Unable to penetrate security around piloting compartment. Recommend gas through air vents first; they run below the decking just past the entry hatch. Marking the location on *Perfection*'s schematic. We've folded into the Vela constellation entry, Hotel One orbital slot. Messages have been sent; I don't have enough power to block all comms."

They were running out of time. In Ruhger's holo, a black X appeared on the map of the folder. He passed an airlock on his left. At the virtual mark, he stopped and scanned the decking with infrared and x-rays. Katryn was right; the air system ran below the decking. Rather than messing with tools, he turned up the magnification on his helmet and found a seam, then stomped, using the power of his hardsuit to break the decking tile.

Chief kneeled at the hole and burned an opening in the plas tube. Grant and Loreli joined them, standing on the other side of the broken tile, facing away. Chief pulled a fist-sized object from his weapons belt, pulled the pin, and rolled the object into the tube. Opening his first aid kit, he slapped a bandage over the opening.

A clever choice; that bandage was designed to seal a punctured lung. If they were in soft armor, Ruhger would have objected. But in hard armor, if one of them punctured a lung, the suit would seal it or they were dead.

"Katryn, Ruhger. Vid in piloting shows two beings in soft armor. No effect from gas. Working on entry."

"Negative. If we can't talk them into opening it, we'll breach it. Go to next priority." He strode to the hatch.

Grant passed him and placed charges around the exterior of the hatch. Ruhger activated his exterior speaker and pressed the intercom. "Piloting. We're breaching your hatch. Surrender now and live." He didn't want to kill them, but breaching charges were shaped, creating massive shockwaves inside compartments if the hatch wasn't heavy enough to soak up the entire blast. Depending on the over blast, they might survive in soft armor, but there was no guarantee.

"We don't get paid enough for this." The hatch slid open.

Ruhger entered, his rifle up. The pilots stood with their hands raised and pistols holstered, but in soft armor, that meant nothing. "Helmets down."

They retracted their helmets. Knowing the knockout gas remained in the compartment, Ruhger told the two, "Breathe deep."

Scowling, the two wavered, then collapsed, their armor slowing their fall. Loreli secured their ankles and wrists, then dragged them to the side.

Moving to lean over the pilots' seats, Ruhger brought up surveillance and navigation.

Saree joined him. "Ruhger, ^timespace^ is surging. Incoming. I'll try to push them out." Saree's face went slack, her hardsuit keeping her upright.

Could she do that? He entered the coordinates for the emergency fold they'd chosen. "Folding in three, two, fold." Navigation didn't change. "Katryn, are there biometric controls on fold?"

"I don't know. I can't penetrate the C2 net."

"Grant, Chief, Loreli, go for the fold generator compartment." They thudded away; the fold generators were in the middle of the folder at the bottom, not in the tail. "Katryn, these controls look real, but they could be fake."

"I'm on my way," Katryn said. "Maybe I can jack into the system from there."

"No. Not without someone to watch your six. Keep working and watching surveillance. Find the weapons, too."

"Copy that." Katryn was surely scowling, but they needed her working in a secure location.

Ruhger kneeled. The piloting consoles stood on pillars. Using the power of his suit, he pinched the material covering the pillars and yanked. No fiber, no electronics, nothing but a beam of plas. While pilots could fly the folder from anywhere in the ship, piloting compartments usually had hard line backups. The compartment was a fake; probably a show for investors and patients. Katryn had to get control of C2. If they couldn't fold out, they were in big trouble. Ruhger returned to the hatch. He'd remove the charges; no sense in making it easy for whoever was inbound. But he wasn't sure it would help. Holliday and his Gov Human support had anticipated their every move so far. Perhaps they should join Chief in the fold compartment.

Ruhger yanked the disarmed breaching charges off the bulkhead and replaced them in his backpack. Crossing to their captives, he kneeled and pushed one of them into a seated position, so he could look over the man's shoulder. His holo was still up, but he was reading a novel, not flying. Ruhger slid him to the side and checked the next man; he was playing a vid game.

A couple of nobodies inside a fake piloting compartment with some pretty holos created a great distraction. "Chief, Ruhger. Report." Chief didn't answer. "Katryn, Ruhger. Status?" She didn't answer either. "All crew, report."

No answer. Comm blockers or Holliday's forces had captured them. Ruhger couldn't go looking for them; he had to protect Saree. He closed and secured the hatch, then spot-welded it shut. If he could get outside the ship, he could tow Saree back to their shuttle. And if he had to, he'd blow a hole in the exterior hull of the ship. But they were probably safer on the folder than the shuttle—it was easy enough to force the shuttle away with a tractor beam and blow it to pieces.

Instead, he'd break through an interior bulkhead with the breaching charges and find Chief and the rest of the crew. If Saree hadn't returned from ^timespace^, he'd activate her suit's grav generator and tow her. He dropped the fake pilot and turned to Saree.

Astonishment blasted through him. Saree's eyes were closed and her face serene—she was in ^*timespace*^. But her suit hovered half a meter above the decking—without the grav generator engaged.

Chapter Twenty

SAREE

Saree dropped into ^timespace^. Out of time, space, and better ideas, she formed the bubble of ^timespace^ she normally used to keep a tractor beam from latching onto *Lightwave*. Preventing a folder from entering the system didn't seem likely, but she'd try. It was theoretically possible—folding appeared instantaneous; but it wasn't. Perhaps a large bubble or bow wave in ^timespace^ in the correct place could block the fold. But it had to be in the correct orbital location.

While she fed more power to her bubble, she realized Holliday must be on *Perfection*. The medico to the stars would never risk getting stranded in a back-of-beyond system, even for a short time. When his planned double-cross of Lashtar failed, he didn't want to chance *Lightwave* counter-attacking, so he abandoned the shuttle.

But if Holliday was on the folder, he had protection—more remotes and personnel were certainly near. Katryn had disabled the remotes in the cargo hold and in the public corridors, but Holliday could reboot them manually. Or more likely, order a flunky to do it. Hopefully Ruhger considered the possibilities because she couldn't drop out of ^timespace^, not even to protect herself.

Since she had to remain in ^timespace^, she'd make the bubble stronger. Holliday might have soothing stones; she'd steal power from them. If she couldn't get enough power to keep folders out, then she could call the Warriors. But she didn't want to deprive Vela's clutch of protection, even if the threat against the Sa'sa was low in Vela. Familia wasn't stupid; they knew Valenti and the surrounding systems weren't a top priority for Saree. They'd probably protect the Sa'sa.

Maintaining the bubble, she ^searched^ for power, finding small pools nearby. As expected, Holliday had smoothing stones. Saree smirked. They'd be a lot smaller, soon. She ^pulled^ energy from the pools, expanding and strengthening her bubble, then ^looked^ for more.

Time Guild Sa'sa darted to her, questioning. Holding the bubble and answering them was challenging, but she firmed her resolve. She projected her fear of capture by the egg-stealer Holliday, fear of more forces, and her solution. The Sa'sa, the usual chaotic mix of melded individuals she couldn't count, spat ideas and thoughts at each other, then split. Half sped away, the other half remained and pushed power to her, astonishment emanating from them.

Shocked, she fumbled but then funneled the Sa'sa's power into her bubble, expanding and strengthening it. The Sa'sa slowed their power to a trickle. If she expanded it too far, she might prevent fold for the entire constellation, and they didn't want that. She held the bubble, but maintaining it wasn't easy. They had to fold out soon.

She longed to check on Ruhger and her crew, but she had to maintain the bubble. The alternative was capture, followed by "necessary" medical torture and permanent incarceration. Death would be the only way out, and even that might not release her fully.

If ghosts were real, she'd haunt Holliday forever.

Power sparked from the fold generators. She had no way to know the fold target. Saree waited for the moment of connection, the Sa'sa brimming with anticipation and wonder. When the fold connected, multiple pools of power, small and large, waited on the other side—a wealthy core system. She ^reached^, ^pulled^, and ^energized^ her bubble, pushing them beyond the intended target to a location without soothing stones. The Sa'sa recoiled, astounded, then surrounded her, siphoning excess energy from her and then darting ^away^.

Saree ^looked^ at the chaotic bow wave she'd driven into ^timespace^ and smoothed it, then returned to her body. Her back slammed into her suit, driving the breath from her lungs. Air pressure forced her lungs to expand, and oxygen made her lightheaded; her medico status flashed red warnings, then settled to yellow and green. Looking beyond the alerts on her helmet face shield, she met Ruhger's worried gaze.

"Saree! Say something, please."

"Oof." Every muscle ached, her back smarted, and her head was fuzzy. A straw shoved between her lips, and she drank. The lukewarm sweet and salty mix of an electrolyte solution made her nose wrinkle, but she kept sipping until the flow slowed. If she didn't, the suit would inject something similar into her veins, annoying her. "I'm okay." She rose slowly, letting the suit do the work, hopefully preventing any vertigo. Despite that, she was panting when she achieved vertical. "What happened?"

His brows raised. "I was hoping you could tell me that."

"We folded, and I pushed us somewhere other than the intended target because we were headed for a core system." Saree shuddered. "Probably Valenti."

"You pushed us somewhere other than the intended fold?" His forehead wrinkled and white showed around his deep chocolate irises.

"Yes." She huffed, just as amazed. "Huh. I didn't know that was possible. No wonder the Sa'sa were surprised."

"The Sa'sa came?" He shook his head. "Never mind. I've lost contact with the team. We need to hide and regroup. Let's go." He turned to the hatch. "I'm sure Holliday is here, and he's got more remotes or people with him."

"Stop right there or I fry you both." Holliday's voice rang through the compartment. "You've gotten soft, Captain Ruhger. I'd expect better of mercenaries of your supposed caliber. As for you, Saree of Jericho, I don't know why you're with such a basic individual, when you deserve someone like me. You've got thirty seconds to surrender."

Nausea rose, but Saree swallowed it down. "He's disgusting. Let's get out of here."

Ruhger gazed at the decking, then stomped, breaking a tile in half and firing. "Saree, fire!"

She raised her rifle and aimed near his target, then squeezed the trigger. A mesh of cables disappeared, then cerimetal glowed yellow and red, melting. Laser fire splashed around their shields from weapons hidden in the compartment.

"Faraday cage." Ruhger drew his pistol with his left hand and fired, enlarging the opening. "It's a trap—he was going to fry our hardsuits. I think we got lucky—we must have hit the main power cable right away. We'll go out the bottom, wherever that ends up. I don't trust anything about the schematics we've got. I think the merc net information was a plant; a good one to fool Katryn and Q. Keep firing, but scan outside the compartment."

Saree locked her rifle to her arm, commanding the hardsuit to spiral outward. Her scanners proved Ruhger's supposition. "People and remotes outside the hatch. I think they're placing breaching charges." Saree drew her pistol, too, and kept firing until a hole wide enough for Ruhger's shoulders appeared. She stopped shooting; her rifle was down to a half-charge. Ruhger's was probably lower.

"Follow after I'm through." He stopped firing, pointed the rifle and pistol straight down, and dropped into the hole, then stepped away.

Saree jumped, bending her knees to signal the suit to soften her landing, and scanned for enemies. An empty compartment; possibly a cargo bay from the three-meter-square hatch on the exterior wall and the attachment points on the bare reinforced bulkheads.

"Energize mag boots in case they blow the exterior hatch." Ruhger jogged to the nearest interior hatch. "We've got to find our people."

Saree engaged her grav generator and pulled a cable from the front, hooking it to Ruhger's backpack. "Tow me. I'll jump on Katryn's net."

"Good idea. I'll let you know if I need anything." He pressed the hatch release, but nothing happened. "Blast and rad. Cutting through these bulkheads will take too much time."

Rather than watching Ruhger, Saree pulled up Katryn's profile but was unable to connect to her suit. Saree rerouted the request to the shuttle but couldn't connect there, either. "Comm blockers. Disconnecting." She disengaged the grav generator and undid the cable.

Ruhger fired into the hatch's controls, but predictably, it didn't open. He raised his arm, scanning the bulkhead to the side. "Maybe we should go outside and return to our shuttle." White noise crackled over his words; the comm blockers, probably.

She put her hand on his back. Connecting them would strengthen their comms. "Maybe, but they could detach it and blow us to pieces."

"Except they need you." He looked over his shoulder.

"No, they don't. If they can find *Lightwave*, which I doubt, they'll use any of us to pressure Q into giving up."

Ruhger snorted. "Not going to happen. Q's been through too much, and she knows the result is death for us and captivity for her. She'd rather die fighting, and she'd make sure she went out in a blast so Holliday would get nothing."

Saree squeezed her eyes shut for a second against the pain. "I know you're right. I hate that this selfish, horrible person would kill someone so good and talented, someone who could benefit the entire universe, just for credits."

"It's not for credits, it's for immortality." Holliday's voice came from outside her suit. He'd intercepted their comms, but he hadn't penetrated their controls yet.

A boom sounded, then debris rained from the overhead and the decking vibrated. The enemy had breached the fake piloting compartment.

Saree returned to the hole they'd created, raising her rifle. She turned on her exterior speaker. She'd distract the pompous windbag while Ruhger kept searching for an escape. "You're an idiot. There is no immortality. Human clones are mindless, and it doesn't matter who you misuse, they'll always be mindless." An armored foot appeared above her, and she fired.

"That may be true. But the cloning and immortality are two different things. Cloning you is the first step."

Saree huffed, putting all the derision into the sound that she could. "You're not even cloning or doing anything remarkable. You're trying to take my children. You're nothing but a kidnapper."

"You don't know everything." Holliday's tone was that unique mix of self-centered derision and superiority that the wealthy did so well.

"I know enough. If you steal my children, you'll raise them in slavery. You're using a child to fulfill your selfish desires and ruin humanity's chances to expand safely. You're an evil abductor, slaver, and child abuser."

"Who cares what you call me? Your opinions are uneducated and immaterial." Despite Holliday's words, his tone was offended.

After examining the hold, returning every few seconds to join her in firing through the hole in the overhead. Ruhger stepped close to her and jerked his chin up, looking at the jagged void. She nodded, understanding his plan. He fired continuously, stopping just long enough to toss an EMP grenade through. Then he jumped, flying through the hole. Hopefully, he knocked a bunch of them over. Saree strengthened her suit's top shield and followed, using her grav generator. They sprinted through the crowd of armored beings and remotes, bowling them over. Their shields crackled with deflected energy. At the hatch, Saree spun back and fired with her rifle and pistol. The beings and remotes were so crowded, they shot each other as much as they hit her and Ruhger.

Ruhger slammed the hatch and fired several shots, spot welding it shut again, but it wouldn't hold long. "We've got to find Holliday." Ruhger spat his name. "Take the fight to him. Or fold out. Or both." He spun and hurled an EMP grenade at the forces thundering down the corridor on their left. Then he sprinted to their right, along the outer corridor, returning toward the middle of the folder.

Saree ran behind Ruhger, putting her suit in automatic defensive fire to the back. Where would a big coward like Chief Medico Holliday hide? Probably in the medico bay; he'd feel comfortable there. Or he might have a true safe room. Or maybe even a two-seat folder—he had the credits and influence to get one.

Near the first intersecting corridor, Ruhger skidded to a halt and around the corner. "Here." They ran toward the central lift tube. Just before they reached it, he kicked through an interior wall. "Stay to the side, don't use the rungs." He rolled another EMP grenade back the way they came and turned to her, rustling in her backpack. Taking two of the enemy's pistols, he grabbed a sticky tab and slapped the pistol against the bulkhead. Engaging the trigger on full, he did the same with the other pistol, firing into the lift tube. Orange lightning crackled as the pistols' laser energy disrupted the lift field. Then he ducked through the opening he'd created in the decorative wall.

Saree followed. In the narrow space between the lift field and the decorative wall, bright orange glowed along a column. It rose far above them and descended below, but it wasn't smooth. Bursts rose from the column intermittently; the pistols' lasers playing havoc with the field. Plain cerimetal rungs stuck out on the side of the column; a maintenance ladder. Ruhger raised his gauntlets to hover on either side of the rungs and flew up the column. Saree copied, staying a half meter below his feet.

A text message appeared in her holo. "Use subvocal voice to text. Second shuttle above. Holliday could be there."

Maybe. Saree subvocalized, "Suit, communicate using secure text to Ruhger. Holliday might be in the medico area or safe room."

"Possible. Let's check the shuttle first."

Halfway up, laser fire splashed against the shield below her feet, and the surges in the lift field stopped. Shield power had automatically routed to her feet; she'd have to equalize it after they got off the ladder.

After three seconds, Ruhger stopped; he'd reached the top. Saree hovered below his feet, but she couldn't stay there long. Her power was draining and shields eroding. The columns powering the lift tube split, bending to the left and right above their heads, glowing orange. There would be more columns, placed in a circle and connected on the top and bottom. When energized, the giant cage formed the lift tube field. At the top of the cage, a small gap existed above and behind the energy conduits, allowing maintenance. Although, they usually turned the field off before attempting to come near the conduits.

Ruhger bent and slid into the cramped space above the top, floating face down just above the flowing brilliant orange. Again, Saree followed him and at the end of the lift field, she bent to curve around the next column, going down headfirst.

But they only went a few meters before Ruhger stopped and punched his pinkie finger through the decorative wall. He twisted his arm, then continued through, kicking a lower hole, then stepping out.

Saree followed, emerging into a narrow, plain corridor. In a cerimetal grid above their head, water was stored in pods—they were in a maintenance corridor at the top of the folder. Twenty meters in front of them, an old-style hatch with hinges blocked the passage, a keypad flashing "locked."

Ruhger twirled a finger, and Saree spun. He grabbed another pistol from her backpack and attached it to the column, firing down. Then he trotted to the hatch. Saree followed but stopped when ^timespace^ surged. She engaged her grav generator—her suit power was at two-thirds—and attached her cable to Ruhger's suit again. "^timespace^ disturbed. Dropping in."

In ^timespace^, *Perfection*'s fold generators powered up. Firming her resolve, Saree surrounded the folder with a bubble, holding them in place. If the fold generators fired, she'd meld that power into her bubble and hope it didn't shatter.

Or shatter her.

Chapter Twenty-One

RUHGER

"Blast." Ruhger needed Saree's help, but if they folded, they'd end up in Valenti or Antlia, so she had to stay in ^timespace^. He had to find Holliday or a secure hiding spot. He placed breaching charges on the hatch hinges, then ran back to the hole he'd created near the lift tube, Saree floating behind him. During the short countdown, he fired at the forces in the maintenance space. Then he stuck another confiscated weapon to the decorative wall, firing into the lift tube and creating havoc again.

After the charges fired, he grabbed the hatch off the decking and stepped into the narrow passage, turning and shoving Saree behind him. Holding the hatch in the opening, he fired short bursts to spot weld it on the three remaining sides. It wouldn't last long; the hinge side had head-sized gaps. He searched for an open spot in *Perfection*'s schematic showing Holliday's safe room. Saree was right—Holliday would feel too vulnerable in a shuttle. But in a medico suite, he was in charge, in command. He'd feel safe, even if he wasn't.

As Ruhger thudded along the corridor, he focused on the medico suite design. Holliday's surety would be his downfall—Ruhger would make it so. When he reached the next hatch, the flashing keypad switched from locked to open. Expecting enemies, he stepped to the side, raised his rifle, and kicked the heavy hatch open. But the corridor was empty. He towed Saree through and closed the hatch. It locked behind him.

He was being herded. Or if he was extraordinarily lucky, Katryn was helping him. Holliday's forces could easily block comms, but if Katryn was free, she'd dig deeper into their net. Either way, he was heading in the right direction, and he had few choices. If Katryn couldn't take over *Perfection*'s command and control, Ruhger had to capture Holliday. But Holliday wouldn't herd Ruhger toward him. He could use the breaching charges, but he'd reserve those for an emergency. His current path was good enough.

The next hatch unlocked. Ruhger cleared and crossed through. At the next intersection, he turned toward the rear of the folder. Each hatch opened and secured behind him without incident; the folder's upper level was eerily empty. Even if Holliday didn't have many people capable of military-style operations, remotes should hound him. Either overwhelming forces were waiting at the medico suite to take them down, or someone was assisting Ruhger.

Above a blank spot on the folder's engineering drawings where a secure compartment could easily exist, Ruhger stopped. He had time to plan. If Holliday's forces had captured his crew, they'd be sending him threats. Perhaps they'd confined his crew to a compartment but didn't have them fully under control. That could explain his progress but not the lack of enemy forces. If Katryn had locked Holliday's forces out of this level, they should be going through the empty spaces like he had, so she must be creating problems elsewhere. Or Holliday had set a trap.

Either way, he could count on forces guarding Holliday's compartment. They'd know he was above them, so going straight down wasn't smart. If he could get into the folder's vids, then he could figure out which approach was best. Definitely not the obvious hatchway. But Holliday almost certainly had an emergency escape route from the safe compartment.

A text flashed in his holo from Saree. "Warriors inbound."

He pulled her suit close, peering through her helmet, but she was still in ^*timespace*^. She must have surfaced just enough to message him. Perhaps she could no longer hold the incoming folders away.

He returned to the folder's architectural drawings. If he'd designed the safe compartment, the secret escape would end inside a shuttle. But Holliday didn't have piloting credentials, so it might go to a bod-pod. Plus, there wasn't a shuttle near the possible safe room, but there were bod-pods nearby. One of them was much larger and on the level below the medico suite; probably Holliday's. He highlighted it, chuckling. He'd borrow the Keere extortionist's playbook and break into the bod-pod hatch from the outside.

Subvocalizing, he said, "Text highest priority to crew, continue sending until receipt. Located possible Holliday safe room. Possibly connects to four-person bod-pod on bravo side, level ten; location marked. Going in through bod-pod. Assistance welcome. Stay safe."

That task completed, Ruhger continued to the folder's exterior bulkhead. The enemy hadn't found him on *Perfection*'s upper level, but they might reach him if he went to the next level down. Or while he searched for a way into the bod-pod. Going outside wasn't a great idea, either; they'd vaporize him and capture Saree. But remaining stationary would only get them captured. The Warriors would make a great distraction, though. Then they could go around the exterior of the folder.

He pulled Saree around his body and touched his helmet to hers. "Saree, return! Saree! Saree, come back!" She blinked hazily at him. "Tell the Warriors we're going outside. We need protection." She nodded, then closed her eyes and returned to ^*timespace*^.

Ruhger searched for an airlock in the schematic. There should be an exterior access at the end of each of the maintenance corridors, but there wasn't. Eventually, he figured out the correct symbol, but reaching the nearest airlock meant returning the way he came. He ran back, but the hatch didn't open. Perhaps his helper was telling him there were enemies on that side. Or the enemies didn't want him going there.

He returned to *Perfection*'s map. On closer inspection, two narrow vertical tubes ran the entire height of the folder, each one halfway between the main lift tube and the ends of the folder. They hadn't existed on the schematics they'd gotten from merc net. The verticals were probably bare-bones ladders allowing maintenance personnel access to all folder levels. The verticals were only a couple of meters wide; coming from the top, he'd have the advantage in a firefight.

He turned and ran, returning to the center of the folder. Hatches unlocked in front of him, including the unmarked entrance to the maintenance stair. He slipped his pinkie finger inside, turning it, but the ladder appeared empty. He towed Saree inside and closed the hatch; it locked. Tromping would make too much noise, so he enabled his grav generator and tried to ignore the power drain.

Zipping down the steep, zig-zagging stairs, he turned his suit slightly sideways to maximize his view of the tall, narrow space. His suit's scanners watched for weapons and personnel above and below him. Using his grav generator was not only quieter, but safer. The barely-wide-enough, very steep stair had no interior railings. If someone fell, there was little to stop them as they bounced from level to level.

If Holliday's forces planned a trap, the ladderway should be it. Something or someone was keeping them away.

After descending three levels, his sensors pinged—movement two levels below. Ruhger stopped and sent a tiny remote flying through the small central gap. A flash and the spy remote view went black. Ruhger pulled up the remote's last bit of vid—a blue hardsuit. It might be Chief. Whoever it was, they knew he was here. He turned on his exterior speakers. "Chief? KITT."

"Tricorder."

The correct response, but the delay between challenge word and reply was longer than it should have been, and he'd almost groaned the word. If that was Chief, he was under duress, or someone else was in his suit. But if it was Chief, he should have used the duress word. All their codes must be compromised. Ruhger turned off his exterior speaker and put his helmet to Saree's. "Return! Danger! Return."

She shivered and her eyes shot open. "I'm here."

"We're on a ladder in Holliday's folder. Someone below us has Chief's suit. Or he's under duress or drugged."

She nodded. "Plan?"

"Lock his suit. If it's not Chief, drug, peel, and secure; take the suit. If it is, tow him, find out what we can."

Saree's lips clamped together for a moment, then she nodded. "*Lightwave* Clutch Queen to Chief Engineer Bhoher capture duress zero-zero-zero-delta-echo-sierra-tango-roger-charlie-zero. Initiate." Her voice, booming from her exterior speaker, echoed in the tube.

"You're kidding me." Saree's command combination was the most obvious code ever.

"What?" She held up both hands. "It's a classic."

"Exactly." He didn't want to know what she'd programmed for his suit.

She frowned. "But the destruct command is completely different."

"Reassuring." Not. But rather than reply, Ruhger continued down the ladder, rifle raised. Saree continued floating behind him and pointed her rifle above them, guarding their six. He reached Chief's suit, which surprisingly contained Chief, but sweat beaded his forehead, his eyelids sagged and jerked, like a man desperately trying to stay awake, and his skin was wan. Stepping around Chief, Ruhger locked the hatch behind him.

Saree unhooked her suit from his and jacked a hard line into Chief's suit. "He's been drugged. Administering antidotes now, but it won't be a quick recovery. Attach his suit to mine, and I'll command his grav generator on. Hope I don't have to go back into *^timespace^*."

Ruhger agreed, because towing two hardsuits would be awkward and difficult to protect under attack. "We go down one more level, then outside on the skin of the folder. Someone, probably Katryn, has been helping us, unlocking and securing hatches. Or we're being herded."

"Copy it's a trap." She smirked. "What else is new? Let's go while they're distracted by the Warriors."

He flew above the stairway and stopped at the next hatch, but it didn't open. Nor did the next one down. With no alternatives, he went to the lowest level of the folder. Before emerging into the bottom corridor connecting compartments with air handlers, cargo storage, and power generation, he put his helmet to Saree's. "I love you. This is almost certainly a trap, and we'll end up captured or killed." He didn't care about himself, but Saree's freedom was critical for the universe.

She smiled. "I love you too. I can ask the Warriors to enter the folder and rescue us."

"Do it. Because we've probably been played. Whatever's out there is likely more than we can handle." Saree pursed her lips in an air kiss, then closed her eyes and faded into ^*timespace*^. His hope and love warred with despair because he couldn't follow where she went, and he had no way to retrieve her other than his voice.

Her eyes popped open. "The Warriors are gone. Their clutch is under attack."

"Of course it is." They had a choice—retreat or charge ahead. But it probably wasn't a real choice. Soon, all the hatches would be locked and they'd be stuck. Ruhger retrieved *Perfection*'s schematic. The maintenance ladderway above them was a long oval tube of cerimetal bulkheads, but he still had breaching charges; they could create their own exit. He grinned. They could go directly into Holliday's safe room. He went back to secure text. "Up three levels, then we'll go out the back."

Saree's brows raised. "The back—oh. Copy."

"Stop a level below me." He'd wasted a lot of time already, so Ruhger used his grav generator, slaloming up the stair treads. He reached a spot level with the "store room" that was the most likely location of Holliday's safe room. After placing the breaching charges, he retreated, joining Saree down a level. The ladderway jolted and shuddered, debris raining down the stairs. Then he zoomed up, shoving through the hole he'd blasted and straight into a waterfall. His hardsuit kept him upright, and the water slowed.

Above him, a shredded water bladder dripped, the top hanging at least three levels above and the bottom attached to the level below him. Directly in front of him, another cerimetal bulkhead; the struts bent from the force of the breaching charges but not broken. The water had soaked up a lot of the blast. Ruhger placed two more charges into the bulge left behind and fired them off, then used his laser rifle to enlarge the hole.

As he pushed into the compartment, laser fire splashed against his shields. Squinting against the scintillating energy, he adjusted his shields and helmet. Two laser beams fired at him; he had to move or get fried. He shoved through the hole and charged the hardsuited person firing at him but rebounded against a shield.

Soft armored beings sprawled around the room; they were most likely dead, but if he could end this quickly, they might save a few. He matched his shield to the enemy's and pushed, backing the person—most likely Holliday—to the corner of the compartment, and fired his pistols point blank. A civilian hardsuit; it was no match for his armor or weapons.

In his rear holo, Saree's heavy boot smashed into the bottom of the hole he'd created, enlarging it. Then she emerged, towing Chief. She stepped to the side and raised her pistols, joining Ruhger's efforts.

The hardsuited being tried to shove past Ruhger. "Suit, lock arms. Energize interior tractor beam controls." With his fingertips, he used the suit's tractor beam, reaching out and yanking one pistol from the hardsuit's grip. The being tried to use both hands on the remaining pistol, but Ruhger reacted faster. "Lower your shield and surrender, or die." He had no mercy for the man who tried to steal his children.

The being raised their hands, raising Ruhger's suspicions. Holliday wasn't the kind to give up even when outmatched. Especially when he still had defenses in that hardsuit. "Show your face."

A grim woman stared back at him. "If you're going to kill me, do it quickly."

Ruhger shook his head. "I'm not Holliday. Where is he?"

"Not on the folder. Too risky for the likes of him." Her brows rose and lips twisted. "Before you ask, I don't know where he is. None of us do. We're here to do a job and get paid."

"Are you in command? And what is the job?" Because whatever the job was, it wasn't winning. Ruhger's certainty the whole thing was a trap rose.

"No." She smirked. "And we're merely a distraction. I think it worked."

Wonderful. "Congratulations. You're helping an AI speed the death of humanity." He turned away, then spun, punching through the woman's helmet and into her face. He probably shattered her jaw, but he didn't care. "Let's go. I think our only chance is the fold generators, but it'll be nearly impossible."

"We'll get there." Saree grinned at him. "You're good at the impossible and we've got too much to lose."

They were probably surrounded. Ruhger was certain they couldn't go back to the maintenance ladderway. But no one had followed them into the safe room. He put his helmet against Saree's. "We'll take the way of water."

Her brow wrinkled, probably in puzzlement. "I'll follow wherever you go."

Her trust was a precious gift. Ruhger returned to the hole into the safe room and then tossed his last EMP grenade into the ladderway. Before it blew, he fired his pistol into the water bladder below the one they'd already destroyed. A jet of water and steam rose, and he dropped a breaching charge into the hole he'd melted. Backing into the safe room—which from the shelving really was a storage room—he waited until it blew, then jumped into the shredded, dripping remains.

Dropping to the bottom level of the folder, he smirked. Half-hidden by sloshing water were the shattered remains of two twenty-centimeter diameter plas pipes, for filling and emptying the bladders. Those pipes connected to the water bladders on either side of the one he'd destroyed; automated shut-offs must have activated, or they'd be swimming. In front of him, a valve lay in the pile of plas, with an access hatch in the cerimetal bulkhead in front of it—a manual shut-off valve. And their way out.

Saree and Chief landed behind him, Saree raising her rifle. Ruhger fired at the latching mechanism, then kicked the small hatch open. Using his pinkie vid, he searched for movement and heat. Both existed, but not in the shape of humans or remotes. He switched to visual; a mechanical room; probably water pumps. Using his rifle, he sliced through the bulkhead, enlarging the hatch, and shoved through.

They'd have guards at the fold generator hatch and more forces inbound; they'd be easy to find. He jogged around the water pumps and piping, scanning for movement and heat signatures, Saree right behind him, towing Chief. The pipes rose through the ceiling, and then the hum of fans surrounded them. The mechanical level appeared to be one vast area. A terrible design; the air handlers ought to be separated from the water pumps by full bulkheads. If a leak occurred, the air handlers could easily be swamped.

"Ruhger, fold generators are powering up. Hooking up." Saree attached a cable from her suit to the back of his.

Blast and rad! He'd have to tow both of them and somehow keep them safe. Remotes zipped over the air handler cabinets. Hiding between the mass of water pipes converging before entering the pumping station, he tucked Saree and Chief behind him, aimed, and fired. Evidently, the remotes were programmed to avoid damaging the infrastructure because they attacked from only one direction. Using the weapons in Saree and Chief's suits along with his, he quickly downed six. Then he left the scant cover, sprinting ahead through the air handler fans, and into oxygen generation.

No one would risk firing around pure O2—if a fire started, it would swell into a conflagration, risking the entire folder. He stopped and tossed a knockout drug into the main O2 line. With the enemy in armor, it wouldn't affect most living beings, but it might get a few if the filters were inadequate. Then he ran through the machinery and storage tanks, a faint orange glow emanating ahead.

The tangerine glimmer had to be the lift tube. *Perfection*'s design was anything but—only a ridiculously overconfident idiot would allow a lift tube to the main engineering level. Not only would any problem in engineering penetrate the entire folder, but it was almost impossible to defend. The schematics they'd obtained of *Perfection* didn't reflect reality. Holliday must have bribed the shipyard or made after-sale changes.

Remotes and beings in soft armor massed around the tube, and shifting shadows signaled the arrival of more. With the fold generators on the far side, the enemy was smart.

Ruhger grinned. He'd have to do something stupid.

Chapter Twenty-Two

SAREE

GRITTING HER METAPHORICAL TEETH, Saree formed her bubble of ^*timespace*^ again and waited for the split nanosecond when space folded. Shoving with all her might, she ^*pushed*^ them beyond the point of connection. As they passed, she snatched energy from the abundant pools of power at the intended destination. ^*timespace*^ roiled, the waves she created raging around her, threatening to pull her under.

Sa'sa flocked toward her, smoothing the waves while sending insistent demands and queries. Chaotic conversations flew in the clutch too fast for her to understand.

Saree ignored the Sa'sa but joined the effort to smooth ^*timespace*^, recovering and soothing herself. Then she envisioned what she'd done. At her thoughts of egg-stealers, Warriors flew to them. Some of them disappeared momentarily, then arrived again—a cohort had folded to meet them, wherever that might be. She still couldn't connect her position in ^*timespace*^ with reality—yet.

Saree surfaced, while remaining aware of ^*timespace*^ and the Sa'sa. "Ruhger?"

"Busy." His rifle, pistol, and suit fired lasers at weaving remotes, and he tossed grenades.

She opened her eyes and slammed them shut, then added more filters to her face shield—the auto-darkening wasn't enough.

Ruhger had locked her suit and engaged defensive auto-fire. Unable to move, she looked out the side of her helmet—Chief's suit blazed, too. "Just listen. *Perfection* folded, but I pushed us beyond the intended target. Sa'sa Warriors folded into our current location. I'm sure they'll come in and help us if I ask. Do you want me to?"

"No. Gonna overload the lift tube. Probably blow a hole in the bottom and top, so tell them to stay clear."

She couldn't have heard that right. "Didn't we want this folder?"

"We'd take it apart, anyway." He spun, firing a laser beam millimeters from her faceplate. "Got that one. I'll release your suit. Fasten Chief to me and take our six. We'll charge for the bottom of the lift tube."

Ruhger's inventiveness might kill them. "Or I can have the Warriors disable the folder. They can target the engines without destroying the fold generators. I think."

He snorted. "You're taking all the fun out of it. But if they can do it without killing the fold generators, the sooner the better. Because my plan is desperate."

"Leave my suit in auto-defense. Be right back." Saree sank into ^*timespace*^ and ^*called*^ the Warriors; their attention was immediate and intense. Focusing hard, she thought about disabling *Perfection* without destroying the fold generators and showed them her location. She cautioned them that several of her clutch were missing, and their clutch shuttle was attached to *Perfection*. Reluctantly, she added Ruhger's idea of overloading the lift tube.

The negation was immediate—the Warriors weren't in favor. Instead, they withdrew their connection but left the surety of protection behind. Saree returned to her body, surfacing just enough to speak. "They're going to protect us, but I don't know how."

"Perfect. Can I release your suit, or do you have to drop back in?" He turned and twisted, firing deliberately, then spraying a wide beam. Inside his helmet, sweat ran down his face.

She detached from ^*timespace*^. The Warriors were going to do what they thought best. "Release. I'll help while we wait." Saree's suit unlocked. She left the auto defense firing, unhooked her cable from Ruhger's suit, and moved Chief between them. Raising her rifle, she targeted one remote after another. Too bad she couldn't manually fire a rifle and pistol accurately at the same time like Ruhger.

Her shields took constant hits, and her power levels dropped steadily. No matter how many remotes she killed, more appeared. In front of her, a yellow and black warning label showed her how desperate Ruhger had been; they sheltered between tanks of pure oxygen. With the folder's fire suppression system already working overtime, holing the tanks was likely to send fire flashing across the entire lower deck. But it was the only reason they hadn't been killed or captured yet.

Beyond their questionable shelter, the amber glow of the lift tube flickered and died, followed by all the lights. Ruhger's suit went dark. Saree flicked her suit lights off, then Chief's—no sense in highlighting their position in the dark, although their laser weapons did that, anyway.

Jagged blue lightning speared the black, sparks flying from dying remotes—the Warriors had arrived, using their spears. Saree locked her suit and sank deeper in ^timespace^, but the Warriors were focused on their task, so she returned to her body. Sapphire spikes arrowed through the dark, remotes crashing to the decking in front of them.

A phalanx of Warriors appeared, splitting to go around obstacles, then rejoining into a single, unstoppable force. The cerulean blue targeted the enemy without hesitation. When they reached her, they turned, facing outward. They continued firing their spear-like weapons until all the remotes were gone and the enemy ceased firing. Five of them turned to face her, while two groups of five split off from the larger group, walking deeper into the folder's mechanical level.

Saree sank back into ^timespace^, expressing her gratitude. The Warriors conveyed they would clear the rest of the folder of their enemies. They'd secure all sentients and leave them in the corridors, while destroying remotes. Saree agreed and thanked them again, but her appreciation seemed to fall on deaf ears. The

Warriors had a mission to protect clutches, particularly queens, and feelings weren't relevant.

Returning fully to her body, she shivered. The Warriors were sentient, but like the rest of the Sa'sa, their individual survival wasn't important compared to the clutch. It made them seem machine-like, but of course, they weren't. They were living beings, trying to survive in a hostile environment, just like the rest of them. Even though it was normal for the Sa'sa, the submersion in the clutch would probably always horrify her to some extent. "Ruhger?" She unlocked her suit and lowered her rifle.

Leaving his rifle raised, he looked at her. "Looks like they've saved us again. What are they doing now?"

"They're clearing the rest of the folder. They'll leave people and other sentients in the corridors and kill all the remotes." Saree winced. "Blast, I hope they realize who's a member of my clutch because the rest of the crew is here somewhere."

"Ruhger? Saree?" Katryn's voice sounded in her helmet.

Relief let her shoulders relax. "We're here."

"Got you five by five," Ruhger said. "Status?"

"I'm in a return air tube at the top of the folder." Her nose wrinkled. "Been helping when I can, but I had to move a lot to avoid detection."

Saree breathed a sigh of relief. "You can come out. The Sa'sa Warriors are clearing the folder. I don't know if they'll recognize you, so don't fight if they put restraints on you."

"That will be fun. I'm glad you're both safe, though. Where's everyone else?"

Ruhger finally lowered his rifle. "Chief's with us, but he was drugged. Probably interrogated. Grant and Loreli are unknown."

"We're just fabulous, dahrling! Is Chief okay?" Loreli appeared in Saree's holo. She didn't look so fabulous—sweat matted her hair, her makeup was gone, and her lip bled in multiple places. Grant peered over her shoulder, looking even worse, with black eyes and cuts dripping blood across his pale face. Neither wore their hardsuits.

"You don't look fabulous. Can you walk?" Ruhger glowered.

"Yes, of course." Loreli circled her hand around her face. "A few hours in a med-float, and this will be gone. They just wanted us to give up. Unfortunately, Chief's previous experience with the hypnotic drug seemed to make him more susceptible to whatever it was they gave us. He did his best to ramble on about everything and anything, but he couldn't tell lies, and their questioner was very, very good."

"Don't worry, the guy is dead." Grant's tone was unusually grim. "He got arrogant, gave me an opening. But we couldn't get out of the compartment. Been trying to contact you for hours."

Saree put her hand up to rub her aching heart, but she met only the exterior of her suit. "I'm sorry, Grant. The Warriors are clearing the folder. Don't fight them. Just tell us where you are."

Loreli's eyes widened and her lashes fluttered. "Oh, something to look forward to! I so love big, powerful guardians."

Grant smirked. "We don't know where we are. They held us in tractor beams, fried our armor, peeled us, put bags over our heads, and floated us somewhere. We're using the enemy's comms."

"I've got control of the net, now, so I'll find you and let you out." Katryn sounded distracted.

"Any sign of Holliday?" Ruhger snarled the name.

"No. I don't think he's on board."

Saree agreed. "I don't think he is, either. He's too big a coward to confront us in real life. He sent someone in his place with a voice generator."

"Agreed." Ruhger nodded. "Katryn, can you get a message to *Lightwave*?"

"Already sent to all the usual message boxes, but it may be a while before they contact us." She grunted. "I'm out of the air return and into the corridor. Oh! The Warriors have surrounded me, and they're leading me someplace."

Saree smiled; her exhausted, abused crew wouldn't suffer further. "They must recognize you as a clutch member."

Grant said, "That's why we put the clutch logo on our hardsuits."

"Good point. Anyway, we're in the lowest level of the folder, heading for the fold generators." She pointed in that direction, and Ruhger nodded. "I'll ask the Sa'sa where *Lightwave* is."

"Perfect." Ruhger turned his suit lights on and walked through the dark mechanical level, kicking dead remotes out of their way. They crossed the bottom of the dead lift tube and found a hatch. Ruhger attempted to open it, but it was locked. "Katryn, when you get here, we need to get inside the fold generator compartment."

"I'm coming. Grant, Loreli, I'm releasing your hatch now. You're in the medico suite."

That was a good place to store inconvenient people. As much as Saree hated Holliday, she admitted he was clever. "Find a medfloat and climb in, unless there are unsecured people wandering around."

"Not sure that's wise, Saree," Katryn said. "Holliday might have done something to them."

"Copy that," Grant said. "I can reboot one to factory settings, unless you think Holliday's capable of specialized programming."

"Reboot it," Katryn replied. "Let me get into the fold compartment, then I'll check them."

"Saree, I found our suits and weapons, too," Grant added. "After Katryn clears them, we can take turns in a medfloat and guard each other until the Warriors clear this level."

That was the safest plan, and she'd make it better. "Excellent idea. Stay connected, so we'll know if something goes wrong."

"Wilco. You first, Loreli."

"No, you look worse than I do, dahrling!" She winced with every word.

"Only because I'm whiter than an ammonia snowflake in the vacuum of space. You got the worst beating. I don't regret killing that evil thing in a human suit."

Saree grimaced. Grant didn't need more death on his soul; none of them did. "I regret you had to, Grant. Loreli, he's right. You go first." Steady thumping grew louder; the Warriors coming their way. When they appeared, Katryn's bright yellow helmet stood out among the dark Warrior armor.

One Warrior motioned them away from the hatch. Another pointed his spear at the keypad, a tendril of blue piercing it, then enlarging to cut through the bolts securing the swing-door hatch. When it swung free, the Warriors entered, spears at the ready, leaving Katryn behind. Her fingers flew in front of her face, and she squinted.

Ruhger entered, still towing Chief, and Saree followed, Katryn behind her. Inside, two people in hardsuits stood with their hands raised, the Warriors securing them in wrist and ankle shackles and placing hardsuit unlockers in the proper place on each person's chest, unactivated. The Warriors marched on, checking the rest of the compartment, while Saree followed Ruhger to stand in front of the captured crew.

"Who's in command, and what were your orders?" Ruhger barked the words. The two people stared up at him, mouths clamped shut.

Katryn said over their internal comms, "Probably vaccinated against drug interrogation. I've checked the medfloat Grant rebooted. Comparing it to the Life Loom and ours, the programming appears standard. There's still a small chance one of Holliday's people could have hidden something tricky."

Saree nodded. "Discuss with Grant and Loreli, please." She turned on her external speaker. "But we could use whatever drug they used on our crew member. If they die, oh well."

"Selfish, bottom-dwelling mutant," the person on the left spat. "If you'd give up your genetic material, humanity could be free."

Saree glared at the slimeball but didn't bother arguing. True believers weren't worth the time and effort. "Humans First? Figures." She moved to the next person. "You too?" The woman kept her mouth tight. "Doesn't matter. We'll just dump them on a gray station and fold out."

Both glared, but Saree didn't care. They weren't Holliday, and they probably didn't know where to find him. She left them standing there and joined Ruhger at the fold controls. "Can you fold us?" They'd eventually find someone who'd talk.

Katryn's fingers flew. "Give me a few. I'm double-checking the medfloat."

Ruhger raised a brow. "First, where are we going?"

Saree chuckled. "Guess that's my job. Hold on." She sank into ^timespace^ and ^reached^ to the nearest Sa'sa clock maintenance clutch, asking where her clutch's nest was located.

At first, the Sa'sa were horrified and alarmed—a queen kicked out of her nest was dead. She reminded them that she was human, not tied to her nest, and that she'd ordered the clutch to flee. Approval came to her, along with puzzlement over her lack of ability. Eventually, they told her *Lightwave* was in Horologium, one of their many emergency folds. "*Lightwave* is in Horologium and safe. I'll take Chief to the medico suite and let you know when the Warriors are done. Then we can fold out and meet them." She unhooked Chief from Ruhger's hardsuit.

Ruhger nodded. "Good plan. Katryn will be through with the medfloat by then. She'll break into the fold controls and fold us. I'll find some hand tractors. That way, we can move all of Holliday's people somewhere until we can dump them someplace safe."

Saree scowled at the two on the decking. "Safe-ish. I'm not too worried about their comfort."

"Agreed. Then we'll find Holliday. We've got to stop his plan now." Ruhger walked toward a pile of humans at the end of the corridor, Katryn trailing him, checking their six.

Saree left the fold generator compartment, towing Chief. One way or another, they had to neutralize Holliday. Preferably without alienating humanity further. Using her grav generator, she zipped up the dead lift tube, entered the medico level, and towed Chief toward the suite.

Unlike most of the corridors on *Perfection*, high-end coatings covered the walls in soothing shades of gray and white with medico green accents. The decking was soft and slightly bouncy, and tasteful art alternated with pics and vid of beautiful people displaying Holliday's best work. But some were more sinister; outrageous body mods into animals, birds, and aliens. Each ad stated the person remained human even though their appearance was radically different. Saree would bet that many of the modifications made these people more alien than actual aliens. Which should prove the theory behind Humans First was ridiculous, but the cult they'd formed left no room for reason.

She crossed the perfectly decorated waiting area, heading for Grant and Loreli. The emptiness seemed odd. She couldn't imagine that Holliday cared about his medico staff enough to leave them somewhere safe. But with his credit problems, perhaps his staff had abandoned him. Well-trained medicos were in high demand; they had no reason to put up with Holliday's behavior and every reason to leave a difficult boss and controversy behind. Especially if he couldn't pay them.

Her map showed Grant and Loreli beyond a hatch marked "Treatment One." The map showed shuttle bays directly connected to treatment compartments nine and ten; undoubtedly for those remaining incognito.

The compartment hatch opened on a short corridor. Hatches on both sides were marked consultation, then two offices, and two treatment rooms at the end. "Grant, Saree. Coming in."

The hatch opened, revealing a bruised and battered Grant leaning against the end of an enclosed medfloat, a laser rifle pointed at the decking. Loreli lay inside the medpod, her body relaxed, her face covered with a treatment hood. "How is she doing?"

Grant grimaced. "Good enough that the medfloat isn't sending warnings." He passed Saree, leaving Loreli's medpod behind. "Come on, let's get Chief in the other medpod. Katryn told me how to copy the programming over from the first medfloat, so it's clear."

Saree followed him into the treatment room next door. She untethered Chief, pulled his suit over to the medfloat, and commanded it to unlock and disrobe. "You've got him?"

"Yeah. You're going back to Loreli?" The upper part of Chief's hardsuit split and peeled away. Grant caught the unconscious Chief under the arms, holding him upright while he waited for the bottom half to come off.

"Yes. We'll block these hatches open or move the medfloats so we can watch both." There were too many ways into these compartments.

Grant sniffed. "Just break down the wall between them. I'm pretty sure it's decorative, and who cares if it isn't?"

"Great idea." Saree brought up the folder's schematic and raised her arm, bringing up a laser cutter.

"Saree, Katryn. The Warriors just turned and ran! Everything okay up there?"

Saree sprinted from the compartment and into Loreli's—empty. "No! Loreli's medpod is gone!"

Chapter Twenty-Three

RUHGER

BLAST AND RAD! RUHGER sprinted for the lift tube, then used his hardsuit's foot thrusters to fly up to the medico level, leaving scorched plas below him. He flew along the corridor, scanning for hidden passages. He landed just inside a ridiculously fancy but empty lobby. Then he crashed through the seating arrangements, leaving broken furniture in his wake.

At the end of the Treatment One corridor, Grant towed a medpod from a compartment. Inside the compartment next door, Saree stood behind a group of Warriors. One fired blue lightning at a biometric lock pad, wall coverings shredded around the outline of a hatch. Saree pointed at the hatch. "This goes down a few levels to a shuttle hatch. Holliday's got another extra-large bod-pod there, but I'm worried it might be a shuttle or small folder. I'm also worried that using this passage might cause decompression, so Grant's moving Chief."

Saree was smart; booby-traps were almost guaranteed in a secret escape passage for Holliday's personal use. He wouldn't care about collateral damage.

"Saree, Katryn. I can fold us out if the Warriors are okay with that. Unless that's a one-person folder, he'll be going nowhere."

"I'll check." Saree closed her eyes but didn't fully immerse in ^timespace^. "Yes. They agree. Where?"

"I've got us set to join *Lightwave* in Horologium." Katryn's tone was factual, but fear ran under it. "No way to track us unless *Perfection* sends a message folder. And *Lightwave* can destroy that."

"Hold one, Katryn." Saree's face relaxed, but within seconds, her eyes opened. "Agreed. Fold now."

"All stations." Katryn's voice boomed from the speakers in the medico area and in his hardsuit. "Fold in five, four, three, two, fold. We've arrived safely in Horologium. Contacting *Lightwave*. You find Loreli."

"We will." Saree's tone mirrored Ruhger's grim mood.

The hidden hatch opened, and the Warriors tromped single-file into the narrow passage. Ruhger followed. "Saree, warn the Warriors that Holliday might have a small folder. Get them to fry it if it separates from *Perfection*. Because this escape route isn't on the folder's plans. There's probably a lot of these hidden ways and who knows what's at the end?"

"Clutch Saree! Stop or the chef dies. Painfully." The male voice, tagged as Holliday, gloated through the folder's speakers.

Ruhger's fists clenched. The man was such a rad-blaster. Or his double was.

Saree kept moving. "Katryn, Saree. Is Loreli's medpod airtight? Can you get eyes on him?"

"Saree, Katryn. Got vids of the passage you're in. Holliday is probably watching. You want to put a hole his folder or shuttle or whatever it is at the end?"

Saree's mouth twisted and she sniffed. "Exactly."

"Saree, Grant. Her medpod is the same model as Chief's. I'm checking."

If there was anyone who deserved a rapid decompression, it was Holliday. Guarding Saree's six, Ruhger brought up his comms and pulled Q and Lashtar into their loop. "Lashtar, get a tractor beam on anything emerging from *Perfection*. Holiday's got Loreli in a medpod; he might be in a bod-pod, shuttle, or folder. Grant's checking if the medpod is airtight."

"Copy. Tractor beam ready. Q's adjusting lasers for precision fire and shield penetration." Lashtar's voice snapped.

Ruhger wanted to tell Lashtar about Chief, but the details would have to wait. She'd already know something was wrong from his suit data. He pulled up *Lightwave's* offensive controls, watching Q work. She knew the weapons but had only practiced precision strikes on simulations, space junk, and remotes.

"Warriors folding in," Saree said.

"Well, do I need to prove what I said?" Holliday—or his doppelganger's—arrogance was crystal-clear.

Saree straightened, her fists clenched at her sides. "Holliday, this is Saree of *Lightwave* Clutch. You will release Chef Loreli immediately, unharmed. We've folded to a distant, unoccupied system. The Warriors and *Lightwave* are ready to act. You cannot escape. Anything you do to Chef will be done to you. And if you're a body double, not only will we take Loreli's damage out on you, we will take it out on Holliday himself, too. Because wherever he might be, we'll find him. Is that clear?"

"You can't get to me before your Chef dies!" Holliday snarled.

"If she dies, you will suffer a thousand cuts before I kill you."

Ruhger had never heard so much menace in Saree's voice. His heart ached for the decisions she'd have to make and the actions she'd be forced to take in the future, because she'd have to carry out any threat she made.

She continued. "Then I'll send the vid to your enemies so they can watch you beg for your life. I'll make sure everyone knows how you broke your medico vows, and you'll be reviled forever."

If that was Holliday, Saree couldn't have come up with a better threat than utter humiliation and the ruination of his legacy. If it was a double, he'd hear the certainty in Saree's voice and surrender.

"The woman who can't even properly punish systems that steal Time Guild property is going to torture me? That will never happen. You're a musician, a weakling, not a leader. An utter failure. Completely unable to see beyond your plebeian future to the triumph of humanity, and equally unable to profit from your talents—uh!" A thud followed.

"Got him." Loreli sniffed. "What a fool. Seriously, did no one teach you that gloating always gets the evil genius in the end?"

"Loreli? Are you okay?" Saree pushed past the Warriors and sprinted. The Warriors fell in behind her, and unable to get through them, Ruhger took up the rear.

"I'm fine, dahrling! Woke up and saw Holliday waving his arms around above me. So, I waited until he was practically frothing at the mouth and slammed the lid into his face. He dropped like an undercooked souffle. Perfection!"

Saree chuckled. "Of course it was. You couldn't do anything less."

"Saree, Grant. I couldn't find any documentation that the medpods were airtight, and Loreli's not in a critical condition, so I used the master medico controls and woke her early. Sorry, Loreli, but I figured you'd rather act."

"Of course I would, dahrling! You know me! When Saree and Ruhger get here, I'll go back into treatment. Easy as pie. Although, I don't know why that's a saying, because a good pie crust takes a lot of practice!"

Saree stopped at a hatch. "Loreli, can you open the hatch? If you can't walk, we'll break in."

"Not a problem." The hatch slid open, and Loreli stood to the side. "Welcome to Holliday's escape. Enjoy." She swept her arm to the side but then slumped against the bulkhead. A torn medico jacket partially covered her.

Saree stood aside, letting the Warriors enter first. Ruhger followed them and put his arm around Loreli's waist, hauling her back to the medpod. "Great job, Loreli. You saved yourself and us. Go back to sleep. We've got it." He helped her recline and lifted her legs, settling her inside.

She yawned. "Sleep sounds lovely. I think I added a few bruises." Her hands went to the buttons of the jacket.

Ruhger turned his head. "I'm sorry. We'll do a better job guarding your recovery." And he would. He should have prioritized the crew's safety over everything else. They didn't have enough people to do everything, so they had to focus on what mattered most—family. He held out his hand, grasping the medico jacket. Then he closed the lid and restarted the healing program.

He turned. Holliday lay face down, his wrists and ankles tied together behind his back with strips of his jacket, forcing him into an uncomfortable arch. His mouth was stuffed with something shiny and red—an apple? Loreli had outdone herself again.

The Warriors turned and marched out of the hatch, allowing Ruhger a better view of Holliday's secret escape. Loreli's medpod was shoved into the cramped area behind four ruby-red velvet acceleration seats. A large screen in front of the seats displayed a navigation view of the system. To his right, a hatch revealed a tiny sani-mod and, next to that, a simple galley. Fruit had tumbled from a small basket next to an autobev.

Ignoring the grunts from Holliday, Ruhger shoved between the seats, bringing up the ship's specifications. "It's a small folder." Perfect. They'd needed one of these for a long time.

"Excellent." Saree stood between Loreli's medpod and Holliday, frowning at him. "That will come in handy." She crouched. "For crimes against *Lightwave* Clutch, your folder and its contents are forfeit. You—or the real Holliday—are personally responsible for any debt remaining."

Holliday struggled against his bonds, then sagged, his nose flaring rapidly. With a stuffed mouth, working hard enough to pant was a bad idea. After everything he'd done, Holliday deserved to pass out. Depending on who owned his loans, death might be kinder. But with Gov Human on Holliday's side, they had to tread carefully. He turned off his suit's external speaker. "Don't forget he's got friends in high places."

Saree's brows lifted. "Oh, I remember. But once we reveal everything he's done, I'm wondering if that will remain true. How much of Gov Human will support him? Besides, I suspect there's someone behind him, pulling a lot of strings."

"I agree." Ruhger turned, looking for secured compartments or data sticks. "We need to search the entire folder. I'd bet there are more hidden compartments. Maybe some of them have real evidence of what Holliday has done and who's paying for all of it. Starting here seems logical."

"We can start here, but unless there's another hatch into the folder, this is clearly a last-resort emergency escape." Saree turned, examining the craft. "I'd bet there's another compartment where Holliday works; something easier to get in and out of, with an expensive workstation."

She was right. "But his electronic records will be copied here. If Holliday had to escape, he'd want access to his data and his credits."

"True. But the bigger question is, what do we do with him?" Saree squatted and pointed at him. "Whether he's Holliday or not, keeping a prisoner is a hassle. Dumping him in a core system is a bigger risk than I want to take. We can dump him at a gray station, I guess."

"Let's give him a few credits, just enough for a fold out, and see where he goes." Ruhger chuckled. "That might tell us a lot."

"Risky. I'm sure he's got credits he can access. Maybe a backwater fringe system would be better. Some religious community with limited access." She turned to him, snickering. "Or, we could drop him on Bonfanti. I'd bet Goldie would tell us what he does and where he goes."

"If we pay her enough." Goldie wouldn't pass up easy credits. Assuming she was still in charge...

"We take it out of his credits. Let's use him while he's trussed up. Maybe we can grab enough credits to make his life difficult, although I'm sure he's got stashes that aren't accessible here." She picked him up by the rope tying his wrists and ankles together and brought him to Ruhger.

Ruhger configured one of the acceleration chairs into a lounge. Saree dropped him on to it. He swept through views on the main screen until he got to the net security and found the credentials. "Holliday could have duress words and actions set. If this is him, they could be activated by seeing him bound. But if we let him go, then he can use duress words. If it's not Holliday, then his DNA might trigger failsafes, too." Ruhger shrugged. "Anything we do now might backfire. Since we're in suits, we've got a decent chance of surviving, but it's not a guarantee."

Saree poked at the holo. "I don't think he'd activate anything deadly. He'd know someone would catch him and he'd rather live, sure he'd be able to escape." When the security routine asked for confirmation, she grasped the back of his head and made him look up at the screen. Then she turned him and put his hand on the sensor pad that appeared. It flashed green. "Or he's too confident to think anyone could capture him."

"Maybe so." Ruhger created new security profiles for him, Saree, Katryn, and Q. "Katryn, Q, we're in Holliday's personal security profile. Maybe. Want to check it out?"

Q snickered. "Let me at it. You know how much I love using other people's credits!"

While the Sisters might object, Ruhger had no problem with the idea at all. Especially from someone causing so many problems for them. "Good."

"I'm still going through the command and control," Katryn said. "Originally, it was straightforward, but there have been multiple modifications recently, and the code is very odd. Almost something Hal or Maxine would write—suns! This is AI-generated code. You know what that means, right?"

"Galactica." Saree's word dropped like a shuttle into a black hole.

If Galactica was controlling Holliday, so many things suddenly made sense. And the danger had just radically increased. Blast it all to the giant black hole of Andromeda! Of course a person like Holliday wouldn't think twice about selling out humanity because he'd make a deal and stay alive.

But no living being got the best of Galactica.

Chapter Twenty-Four

SAREE

Galactica. Saree shuddered. Of course, it all came back to Galactica. It must have realized it needed humans for clock maintenance. It could DNA-modify most of humanity into happy slaves, keeping some "wild" humans to provide the creativity Galactica lacked, and grow clones for clock maintenance. Except clones weren't viable yet, so using Holliday, the foremost authority, to make the scheme work was the perfect solution. Especially when controlling Holliday with small things like credits and accolades was so easy. He was no threat to Galactica—the perfect proxy, until he got greedy and went off script. "If it's Galactica, then what did it do to the folder? Because you know there's some sort of failsafe."

"I just took out a message folder," Lashtar said. "We've lost control."

"The net is fighting me and Q, trying to kick us out." Katryn's words were muffled, like she was speaking with her jaw clenched. "Let's get back to our shuttle, just in case."

"Or the fold compartment?" Ruhger asked. "We can control the entire folder from there."

"I thought I had full control, Ruhger. Get to the shuttle!" Katryn's urgency and strain came through in her voice.

Retreat was the only choice. "Let's go. Ruhger, I'll tow Loreli. Grant, you've got Chief?" Saree tied a cable to Loreli's medpod and virtually leashed it to her suit.

"Got him," Grant said.

"See you on Beta Shuttle." Ruhger towed Holliday with his suit's tractor beam.

Saree wouldn't leave anyone behind. "Katryn, where are you?"

"I'm on my way." Katryn's breathing sped.

"Lashtar, Q, take out the fold generators if they spin up." Saree slowed to negotiate the corners with Loreli's medpod. The passage wasn't designed for large objects. At least it was a ramp, rather than stairs. She could wake Loreli, but she'd be a sitting duck without armor.

"Remotes are coming back to life." Laser fire sang in Katryn's comms.

"I'll deactivate them," Q said. "If I can. Suns!"

They ran into the medico facility, lasers turning their shields into shiny glare. Saree focused on Ruhger's back until her face shield adjusted. They thudded along the long corridor decorated with patient portraits. Or victims, perhaps. Certainly, there were humans who wanted to look like animals, but Holliday surely would have tested his body mod programs before trying it on high-status or wealthy individuals. Perhaps that's what he did with the clones. Her stomach twisted, but she pushed the nausea aside—they had to reach the shuttle.

"Generators are deploying," Lashtar said. "Ready to fire. I've got the tractor beam on the shuttle."

She couldn't let them fold into Galactica's maw. "Ruhger, can you tow me?" She followed him into the lift tube.

"Power's almost gone."

Blast. "Trade me Holliday for Loreli." She couldn't let them fold.

Ruhger slowed. "^*timespace*^?"

"Yes." She could form the bubble and push them past again, or do something. Anything.

He shook his head. "Wait for the shuttle." He bounded upward, thudding onto the decking hard enough to dent it.

Saree followed, hoping Loreli's medpod would generate enough lift to join her. She could use her suit tractor beam if she had to, even though her power levels were reaching the mins, too. Rising, she almost shot past Ruhger, but he caught her with his gauntleted hand, redirecting her momentum to send her shooting down the corridor. In her rear-view holo, Lorelie's medpod floated up and trailed her. She sprinted ahead to their shuttle, Ruhger running behind her, Holliday bouncing in his wake. Saree didn't feel bad about the bruising he'd receive.

Reaching the shuttle bay, Saree entered the codes, but the shuttle bay hatch slid open before she finished.

"Firing," Lashtar said.

Ruhger passed her. She followed him into Beta Shuttle, mag-locking Loreli's medpod to the decking next to Chief's, then dropping into the seat behind Grant. Katryn pounded inside, stopping against Loreli's medpod, then throwing herself into the chair next to Saree's. Once in the shuttle's seats, their hardsuits began recharging.

Grant stabbed the shuttle clamp release. "Glad you could join us."

"Brace for thrust." Ruhger input power, shoving away from their perch on *Perfection*.

"No need to fly too far," Lashtar said. "You're not folding."

Q laughed. "Nice one, Lashtar!"

"I thought it solved the problem neatly." Lashtar chuckled. "With what we know now, we can fix them easily enough."

A vid from *Lightwave* appeared on Beta's main screen. *Perfection*'s deployment arms had been neatly bisected and the fold generators floated nearby, tumbling slowly. "Perfection indeed, Lashtar." Saree grinned. She was so lucky to have these smart people surrounding her.

A groan drew her attention to Holliday, curled in a ball on the decking. He'd bitten through his apple gag. "Help. I need a medpod."

Saree rose and retracted her helmet. "Well, you'll have to wait because others need them more. Enjoy the pain you've inflicted on so many." Even if he hadn't caused physical pain, which she truly doubted, he'd created a huge emotional load for them, and certainly many others.

"Saree, let's go back to *Perfection*." Grant smirked. "We'll use one of his medpods. I'm sure he's got some interesting options."

Saree scowled at Holliday, thrashing against his restraints. "I'd bet you're right, but let's make sure no messages got out, or we might have company we don't want arriving soon." She turned back to the main screen and returned to her seat. "Lashtar, Q, any sign?"

"I smoked the one message folder I saw." Lashtar frowned. "If they had cloaked message folders, one might have gotten away. Can you tell from ^*timespace*^? I need to catch the fold generators before they bang into each other."

"I didn't see anything, either, but I've been working the net." Q bit her lower lip. "The defensive net program is slippery as a Secundus slimer."

"We'll probably have to zap all the hardware and start from zero." Katryn scowled. "We've isolated command and control, but communications is a disaster zone, and the rest of the net isn't any better."

"What about the med suite?" Saree snickered. "We've got the perfect test subject."

Holliday's eyes widened and his mouth dropped open. "But..."

Katryn snorted. "Don't know. Not my priority. Can we go back and power everything down? If we wait, we may not get the chance."

"Brace!" Ruhger roared. "Lashtar, fly *Lightwave* away! Max shields!"

Saree's body surged against the side of her hardsuit until the grav generators caught up, flying away from *Perfection* at max impulse. She raised her helmet. On the main screen, orange and red fire blew from the bottom of *Perfection*, near the fold power generator. Smaller plumes appeared at thrusters around the exterior. The blast grew, splitting the huge folder into pieces, fire blooming, then dying when the remaining oxygen dissipated into the vacuum of space. The pieces of the destroyed folder headed toward them.

"Stand by for emergency maneuvers." Ruhger's fingers danced. "Blast and rad. I wanted that folder."

Saree double-checked her suit was secured to the seat and endured the velocity changes until the grav generators caught up.

Holliday rolled, hitting the bulkhead with a yelp. She'd lock him to a seat after they avoided the debris.

After some fancy flying, Ruhger announced, "We're clear." He retracted his helmet, blowing out a big breath. "That was close."

"Maybe we can salvage some of it?" Grant shrugged one shoulder. "Those are big pieces."

A view popped up on the screen—*Perfection*'s fold generators snugged close to *Lightwave*'s bulkhead. "I'd already locked on to these, so at least we've got them," Lashtar said. "I imagine the fold power section was the primary detonation source, so we'll have to integrate them into *Lightwave*'s system, but I'm sure Chief and I can do it."

Saree rose, inspecting the medpods. Treatment continued with a positive outcome expected for both. In the medpod windows, Loreli and Chief seemed to slumber peacefully. "Excellent, Lashtar. The medpods show treatment is going well. I'm sure Chief will be on his feet shortly."

"Lashtar, once you get the fold generators secured inside *Lightwave*, let's set up a plan of attack for rescue of sentients and section recovery." Ruhger turned to glower at Holliday. "Your failsafe just killed a lot of people, you greedy mudhugger."

Holliday moaned, but if he was in physical pain, Saree didn't care. Ruhger was right. The Warriors had secured all those people in the corridors of *Perfection*—most wouldn't have reached the bod-pods. She closed her eyes, her stomach rising, and clenched her teeth. Throwing up wouldn't help. "Priority on sentients, of course." She should have asked the Warriors to place the prisoners into bod-pods or compartments. She hadn't considered the possibility that Holliday would blow up his fancy folder. Actually, he probably hadn't; Galactica programmed a failsafe.

"Absolutely." Ruhger turned back to the main screen, bringing the rest of the crew into the search plan.

Saree returned to Holliday. He lay on his side facing the bulkhead, wriggling and moaning. Probably trying to get free, but he was doomed to disappointment. "Why would you make a deal with Galactica? It's out to kill all sentient life."

Holliday swallowed several times and licked his lips. Sweat rolled down his face, and his fancy dress medico uniform shirt was wet with drool. "Sentient? You think humans are sentient? They're barely alive. Simple organisms no better than the monkeys they came from."

Another arrogant rad-blaster, sure he was better than everyone around him. "But you are, even though you're human, too?"

"Not for long." He slammed his mouth shut.

"Ah." Ruhger huffed. "I get it now. Immortality, but not in a clone. Galactica promised you an AI body, didn't it? You give it Saree's children to smooth ^*timespace*^, and it gives you a way to live forever. You're an idiot. Galactica won't create a competitor. It's lying. It feels no emotions, has no moral code. You're stupid *and* gullible."

Once again, Ruhger's brilliance led him to the most logical conclusion. And no wonder Holliday wasn't deterred by clone failures. He didn't care. He'd raise Saree and Q's children as slaves, giving them to Galactica, and gain an AI body so he could live forever. Then he'd have plenty of time to work on the cloning problem, keeping Galactica from killing him until he was strong enough to win. So sad his plan was doomed to fail.

"Galactica? I'm not dealing with that thing." Despite his bonds, Holliday's tone had returned to the medico ultra-calming mode. "My research proves I can transfer consciousness to a new body through ^*timespace*^. But you, Saree of Jericho, are the only human who can work there effectively. Therefore, I require your full-time assistance, immediately."

Saree didn't hate many beings, but she despised Holliday. Even bound hand and foot, his arrogance was unmatched. "I can't transfer my own consciousness, let alone anyone else's. Neither can the Sa'sa. And no one's successfully transferred to a machine interface either. If Galactica told you it could, it lies. It has no reason to tell the truth, not ever."

"But the Sa'sa themselves speak of changing states of being and moving on." A slight waver in his tone seemed to signal some uncertainty.

Saree couldn't help her exasperated huff. "You clearly don't understand what the hive mind is like. Sure, when their bodies die, their consciousness lives on in the hive mind. But not as individuals. Their thoughts and experiences merge into the hive mind, available to all, but a sense of self is gone. Because of that, I can't understand the hive mind. It makes no sense to a human brain. If your consciousness entered the hive mind, which it can't, because the Sa'sa would reject it as an aberration, you would lose all sense of self. For someone who's supposed to be intelligent, you sure jump to conclusions. Non-humans don't think the same way humans do, and the Sa'sa are farther from us than most. Individuals mean nothing. The clutch is everything. If they're using ^timespace^ to move on, it's not as individual beings." She couldn't access the Sa'sa hive mind, but she'd gathered a lot over her years of exposure. And she was even more certain that when they moved on, it wasn't to another corporeal body. It was to another plane of existence.

"You simply aren't applying it correctly. With my guidance, it will happen." Holliday raised his chin. The superior pose was difficult to pull off when trussed hand to foot, but he certainly tried.

"No, it won't. You don't know what you're asking for. Plus, the Sa'sa don't care about your credits or your influence. They will care that you've made a deal with Galactica. They'll care a lot about that." She shook her head. "Ruhger is right. You're an idiot."

"Could you stick that gag back in his mouth?" Katryn glared at Holliday. "I'd like to concentrate on the search, and his ridiculous fantasies are distracting. Free loading oxy breather."

Saree held back a laugh. Katryn was correct. Arguing with Holliday was a waste of time. "I've got something better." From a storage compartment, she grabbed sticky tape and wrapped it around his head three times, then cut a breathing slit in the middle. He'd eventually enlarge that hole, but before that happened, he'd be in confinement or not her problem. And getting it off his hair wouldn't be fun, either, which was petty, but satisfying.

But she'd wasted too much time already. Saree cut the tie between his cuffed arms and legs, then used her tractor beam to maneuver him into a bunk and strapped him down. She left the hatchway between the sleeping and main compartments open, so they could monitor him, rather than just use vids. Astra had taught all of them a hard lesson.

After she sat, Ruhger shoved a view to her holo. "Here's your search area. Tag and move on unless there are life signs."

"Copy that." Saree started with the computer-generated list of large pieces.

"Ruhger, Q. I've commanded the few functioning remotes inside *Perfection*'s pieces to gather all the people into airtight compartments. Then I'm adding air. I've tagged the pieces with life signs. How fast can you get there?"

Ruhger's fingers flew in his holo. "Eight point two minutes. All personnel, secure for thrust in five, four, three, two, thrust."

Saree closed her eyes and breathed. They might salvage something from this fiasco, caused by yet another human determined to live forever. After eons of negative consequences, it didn't seem logical to keep working on such an idea. Enjoying the present and doing good for others seemed far more important than merely extending life. But so many beings would rather worry about what they didn't have than celebrate their current lives, forgetting it could all end in a nanosecond.

At least they'd cut off one man's quest for immortality at the expense of all other life. She'd enjoy the success they made and hope that their search for survivors would bring them more joy. Later, they'd review and plan the next steps.

Loreli's medpod chimed, the lid rose, and an unblemished Loreli sat up, stretching and yawning.

Saree stared; she'd never seen Loreli without makeup on. The cosmetics must be a shield because she was just as gorgeous without the paint.

Loreli glanced around the shuttle, then pouted. "Dahrlings! I thought we'd be back at *Lightwave* already. I was looking forward to creating a proper celebration." She twisted, putting her feet on the decking.

"Slow, Loreli." Saree held up her hand, palm toward Loreli. "Dizziness is common after release." She'd been in so many medfloats and pods, she knew exactly how her body would react. "I'm afraid we've got a search and rescue to run first. Take a seat, rest, then get a drink or a meal."

"Oh, by all the fallen souffles! Can't we catch a break? Let me get snacks, and I'll be right there." Loreli stood, leaning against the side of the medpod and sliding Holliday's battered medico coat on. Then she strode to the galley, entering auto-bev orders.

Trust Chef to make food the main priority during a disaster. But Saree smiled, grateful for Loreli's single-minded joy in her craft. Enjoying the small things and celebrating their successes rather than dwelling on the grim result of greed would be more and more important as the hours wore on.

Saree was so fortunate to have her chosen family, her crew, her clutch. If one of them sank into despair, the others rallied, raising them again. Their complementing mindsets and skills, combined with cooperation and love, rather than competition and hate, ensured their success in the short and long run. She'd do everything in her power to encourage and nurture these people, and they'd do the same for her.

She returned to her assigned search area, secure in the love of her family.

SAREE

SAREE CHECKED CREW MEMBER locations. Chief and Lashtar were monitoring *Lightwave*'s engineering section, Loreli was in the kitchen, and Ruhger and Q were in the cargo bay. "All crew, folding in five, four, three, two, fold." She scanned the navigation and surveillance—a perfect fold. "We've arrived safely in Antlia. Report issues, then execute the plan." Since they were in a core system, Saree didn't have to smooth ^timespace^.

Grant sent their carefully crafted messages with attached vids to Gov Human, while Katryn retrieved the messages waiting for them. Ruhger and Q pushed the largest airtight section of *Beautiful Perfection* they'd recovered away from *Lightwave*. They shoved it into a descending spiral orbit with an emergency beacon spewing requests for help with warnings. With Saree's top priority message to General Kerr, Gov Human would quickly rescue the remaining personnel and Holliday.

They'd put him in one of *Perfection*'s bod-pods and pushed it out next, but without the extra-strong emergency beacon. He'd be rescued, but it would be after the big, multi-compartment section. He deserved to wait forever, but in Antlia, it wouldn't take long for Gov Human to retrieve him. With any luck at all, their vids showing Holliday's delusions about Galactica would discredit him. He'd certainly be detained for detailed questioning.

After retrieving the giant piece of *Perfection* with twenty-six souls still alive, they'd decided speed was more important than dealing with Holliday. Gov Human probably wouldn't share any information they got from him, and there was no guarantee that they'd do anything at all; they might even let him go.

But Saree had specified consequences if they did that. And if Gov Human continued to interfere and hound her, those consequences would increase.

"*Perfection* is safely away, and so is the bod-pod. We're clear of the cargo bay and ready for fold," Ruhger reported.

"Time Guild messages sent and retrieved," Grant said. "Ready for fold."

"Gov Human and other messages sent and retrieved," Katryn said. "Ready for fold."

"*Lightwave* operating nominally; ready for fold," Chief said.

Saree smiled. She'd love to stop at Antlia Station for a puffer sandwich, but that wasn't going to happen until Gov Human stopped treating them like the enemy. "Let's go before the demands reach us. Voice objections to fold now." She waited five seconds. "Folding in five, four, three, two, fold. We've arrived safely in Ara. Cross-check and report issues." They had to get help for Tyron. Even after salvaging several more of Holliday's medpods and using the best one, he remained comatose but stable.

"Saree, I'm not sure this system was the best choice." Katryn pointed at the surveillance on the big screen. Three Gov Human folders orbited near the third planet.

Grant shook his head. "Or Gov Human's influence was wider than we thought."

"Either way, we're not staying here." Saree grimaced. "Chief, what's our range?"

"We can make this list, but we'll need eight hours of regeneration time." Bright yellow highlighted a section of the emergency folds list. "These will take four hours." Neon green lit another section.

Saree closed her eyes and pointed at the green section. Opening one eye and sighting down her arm, she selected Equuleus. "Folding for Equuleus in five, four, three, two, fold. Report issues." Surveillance showed a blue sun in the distance, no sign of sentient life in space, and an icy marble in the distance, surrounded by a ring of space junk.

Not the expert medicos they'd hoped to reach, but since the only sign of sentients appeared to be long gone, they were temporarily safe. They'd rest, recharge, and fold, hoping Gov Human regained sanity and they'd be safe in the known universe again.

Ruhger squeezed her shoulder. "Plan for the worst, hope for the best. It's all we can do."

The Command Center hatch slid open. "And eat a fabulous meal!" Loreli leaned in the hatchway, her ocean-blue skirt tied up on one side, showing multiple fluffy white skirts underneath. Twisted hemp ropes laced through black hardware on her shiny white corset. A replica of an Old Earth sailing ship captain's hat was pulled low across her forehead. A black patch covered one sparkling eye, anchors dangled from her earlobes, and more twisted ropes formed a belt around her middle, a saber thrust through it. "Ahoy mateys, it's time for a pirate's feast. We'll hit them broadsides and loot the booty. On to the grog!"

Saree laughed and followed her crew from the Command Center to the dining hall, remodeled in dark wood and simulated iron lanterns. The salty scent of seafood and rich butter made her stomach rumble. Whatever might happen, they could always count on Loreli to feed them excellent food while lifting their spirts and reminding them life was fun.

But she couldn't help wondering and worrying about the next hit.

The End, for now...

Time Guild 2 is coming next! While you wait, sign up for the Scott Space newsletter for free short stories and more!

Cast of Key Characters and Locations

SAREE OF JERICHO, QUEEN of Lightwave Clutch, fold clock maintainer, and Scholar of Ancient Music (under the alias Cary Sessan). Saree's ability to find and use *^timespace^* to tune the fold clocks and smooth *^timespace^* itself is very rare among humans. She's the first known "Human Clocker" but despises the rude term.

Ruhger, Captain of Lightwave Fold Transport. Raised as a mercenary in Phalanx Eagle Mercenary Company. After a violent mutiny, he helped his parents build Security Fold Transport. When surviving Phalanx Eagle members actively hunt for them, his parents insist he and his childhood friends leave the company. Ruhger forms Lightwave Fold Transport, folding small shuttles around the fringes of the universe. He meets Saree of Jericho during the Jericho Colony Rescue (although neither remember the encounter) and later, in Dronteim when Cary Sessan contracts a series of folds with Lightwave. Expert pilot and math genius.

"Doc" Holliday, Chief Fold Clock and *^timespace^* Researcher, headquartered on *Quantum Fold Research Transport*. Former Gov Human Military elite rescue team member and expert medico, he left the service to help find and train more fold clock maintainers. He originally entered Gov Human military to avoid his father's body modding to the stars business.

Grant Lowe, Speaker for Lightwave Clutch, purser for *Lightwave Fold Transport*. Raised as a mercenary with Ruhger. A reformed playboy, he is extremely persuasive and engaging. Loves Ruth of Jericho, and was devastated by her death. Since discovering Ruth survived, he's attempted to rekindle their romance with little success.

Q (aka Quinn of Cygnus), fold clock maintainer, ^timespace^ smoother, net expert, and escape artist. Raised by the Sisters of Cygnus, her intelligence and curiosity often gets her in trouble. It also helps her escape. Part of Lightwave Clutch, although the Sa'sa want her to start her own clutch.

Tyron Phazeer, Chief of Security for Lightwave Clutch and *Lightwave Fold Transport*. Weapons, y'ga and combat expert, competent at net security. Calm and logical. Raised as a mercenary with Ruhger; contracted with Katryn of Cygnus.

Katryn Phazeer, Lightwave Clutch and *Lightwave Fold Transport* net security. Raised by the Sisters of Cygnus, she leaves to pursue a career in net security. Hired by Tyron Phazeer for *Lightwave*, she forms a personal contract with him. Hot tempered but extremely intelligent, an expert in y'ga, most weapons and net infiltration.

Chef Loreli, Lightwave Clutch and Lightwave Fold Transport. Raised as a mercenary with Ruhger, transitioned to female as a student at Culinary Institute Sirius. Expert with food and weapons, she is often underestimated because of her flamboyant personality and clothing.

Chief Bhoher, Head Engineer, *Lightwave Fold Transport*, contracted to Lashtar. A former member of Phalanx Eagle Mercenary Company, Chief was key to Ruhger and the others surviving the mutiny. He is a mechanical genius and has a reputation as a berserker with a fighting axe. Survivor of a Sa'sa fold clock maintenance destruction event started by the Universal Great Farmer's Collective on Pavo. He is a father figure to Ruhger, Grant, Tyron, and Loreli.

Lashtar, *Lightwave Fold Transport* Engineering, contracted to Chief Bhoher. A former member of Phalanx Eagle Mercenary Company, after the mutiny she left and became a Sister of Cygnus. After Mother Ferra's betrayal, she leads the Sisters until they recover. After turning over leadership to Nat, she helped Q, then joined *Lightwave Fold Transport* and Lightwave Clutch. She's rekindled her former relationship with Bhoher. Y'ga and weapons expert, has a prosthetic leg.

The Sisters of Cygnus, a reclusive, militant female only religious organization worshipping the Mother. Run a well-respected orphanage. Originally based on Cygnus Gliese, they move to Cygnus Secundus after Mother Ferra, their leader, betrays them and Galactica Corporation strip mines Gliese. On Secundus, the Sisters become more inclusive, creating a haven for many religious organizations and the Cygnus Secundus Medico School. Expert instructors in y'ga, a mix of Old Earth yoga and many different martial arts. Orphans receive y'ga instruction from an early age. They are also taught net skills and other vocations, creating opportunity for the orphans. The Sisters raised Katryn and Q.

Ruth Jericho. Rescued by Ruhger and his team from Jericho Colony Station, she is raised as a mercenary with Security Fold Transport. Captured and tortured by the remaining Phalanx Eagle members, she eventually takes command. After attempting revenge against *Lightwave*, she's captured. The crew convince her that they didn't know she was alive. She finds a refuge with the Sisters of Cygnus, then the Guardians of Aljanah. Joins the crew of *Quantum Fold* as their Chief of Security. Grant Lowe's girlfriend before her capture.

Quantum Fold Research Transport. A former luxury cruise fold transport upgraded by the group of Artificial Intelligences named The Consensus. Home for the researchers and students of fold clock maintenance and ^*timespace*^. Doc Holliday, Ruth, Los Lopez, and Porter (Captain) reside on *Quantum Fold*, among many others.

Lightwave Fold Transport, home of Lightwave Clutch, Saree, Ruhger, and crew members. A former military troop transport, *Lightwave* was part of Transport Charlie in Phalanx Eagle Mercenary Company, then part of Security Fold Transport. See Ruhger's entry above.

Sa'sa, a species of hive mind aliens responsible for the manufacture and maintenance of fold clocks and ^*timespace*^.

Fold clocks are key to the safe folding of space for faster-than-light travel. Individual Sa'sa have independent thought and personalities, but are unimportant in comparison to the clutch (family group) and the species as a whole. Each clutch is led by a Queen, and is divided into classes. Only some clutches have ^*timespace*^ Maintainers, but all Sa'sa are connected to the hive mind through ^*timespace*^. All clutches have Warriors, the protectors of the clutch. Appearance of all Sa'sa is similar to Old Earth velociraptors, but with elaborate clothing and head coverings; size and intelligence varies according to class.

Time Guild. An organization created at the insistence of non-Sa'sa, including humanity, to ensure fold clock maintenance is appropriately distributed across the known universe. Run by the Sa'sa, the Guild ruthlessly protects clock maintenance clutches and fold clocks. Deliberate destruction of a clock maintenance clutch or fold clock results in the destruction of all parties involved. There are rare instances where this is not true; see *Lightwave: Short Stories* 1 for an example.

^*timespace*^ The underlying frequencies of the universe. Fold clocks use transuranic metal frequencies, ensuring that each folder arrives in the same time as they left. Fold generators use transuranic frequencies to bring planes of space together for a split nanosecond, enabling faster-than-light travel.

Chief Medico Lorcan Holliday, body modder to the stars, father to Doc Holliday, expert medico with questionable morals. Owns *Beautiful Perfection*, a medico fold transport.

Mensians, an intelligent but xenophobic heavy world species with massive bodies and four arms. Known for body modding without limits, they are skilled, but are risky for other species.

Medico Pancea, Lead Medico for Pandemic Medicine. Her medico team specializes in crossover native diseases affecting humans on newly colonized worlds.

Travelers. A religious organization that continually travels the universe, known for construction skills and decorative arts. Outsiders are distrusted, particularly planet dwellers. Many humans despise the Travelers, because their contracts are convoluted. Despite that, cheating a Traveler isn't wise. Part of their religious ritual is using soothing stones to help them fold space and smooth what they call The Infinite Road, which is actually ^timespace^. Each folder is led by a group of Speakers, and all Travelers folders are guided by the speakers and religious leaders on *Tobar Fold Transport*. Ruslo is the Speaker for the Ship, Listraba the Speaker for the Infinite Road, Patriarch Kein heads the Traveler religion. Friend to Lightwave Clutch.

Aljanah Guardians. An offshoot of the Travelers, they guard access to the soothing stones on Aljanah Five. Soothing stones help the Travelers smooth space during fold, and energize their escapes when necessary.

Non-oxys. Collective term for non-oxygen breathing species. Generally, they interact very little with oxygen breathers, such as humans. But they will assist efforts to hold back Galactica.

Hal, a Sa'sa created Artificial Intelligence. Once Saree's virtual assistant, now an independent AI helping contain the Librarian version of Galactica on Old Earth. Other AIs involved are Frost and Maxine. Since the destruction of Old Earth, they search for other instances of Galactica.

J'ker Hanty, a human vid star of a "news" show with unprofessional reporting.

Familia, an organized crime family based on Valenti in Vela. Justice Fatima, with Enzo as her enforcer, ensured Familia obeyed its own rules. Q destroyed much of Familia's influence with *Lightwave's* help. Bevan Astra was also part of Familia, then came to *Quantum Fold*. He betrayed Q and *Quantum Fold*. Redeemed himself with a suicide attack on Justice Fatima's folder, *Indomidito*; his survival is possible, but not probable.

Gov Human, responsible for protecting human worlds and ensuring joint species standards, accords, and treaties are upheld. Largest organization is Gov Human Military, tasked with defense of humanity. General Kerr leads the Laniakea Fleet which is usually supportive of Lightwave Clutch. The rule-driven General Jodl leads the Gov Human Military Inspector General.

Humans First, a xenophobic organization determined to ensure humanity's survival. Many members strive for the destruction of all other species. The Sa'sa are favorite targets.

Merc Net, a network designed to help mercenary companies find work. Also includes bounty hunters and other associated military and security-related jobs, along with many informational boards. Legality and morality are not a consideration, so jobs also include assassination, insurrection, and other aggressive actions.

Galactica, an ancient xenophobic artificial intelligence. Driven to survive, it created Galactic Corporation to exploit species of all kinds, including humanity. Capable of destroying all other sentients, it knows it needs the creativity of corporeal life. Attempts to control other species to ensure its survival, and desperately wants a fold clock maintainer. Uses arrays of fold clocks to maintain timing.

The Guide™, a guide for humans traveling the universe. Don't forget your towel!

Antlia; home of Gov Human and Gov Human's Laniakea Fleet. Antlia is also home to a floating non-oxy species; their food is popular with humans, especially the Puffer sandwich.

Aljanah, see the Guardians above.

Ghost Nebula; a dangerous emergency escape fold.

Bonfanti, a gray space station run by Goldie, a former slave in the Bonfanti Arena. Arena fighting has been disbanded; the station serves anyone who can pay.

Old Earth, humanity's birth place. A nuclear exchange made it uninhabitable, leading to the exodus of humanity with the help of the Sa'sa. Old Earth eventually became a research station and a repository of human history. Galactica took it over, becoming the Librarian, and turned the researchers into a cult. Destroyed when the Librarian blew up the planet.

Reane, a planet hosting the Atlas Challenge, a competition designed by *Lightwave's* crew to bring Q home safely.

Valenti in Vela, home to Familia.

Cygnus; a constellation with three human-inhabited systems. Cygnus Prime aka Deneb, home to adventure travel; Cygnus Gliese, the original home of the Sisters of Cygnus, then strip mined by Galactica Corporation for transuranic metals, and Cygnus Secundus, a jungle world and the new home of the Sisters of Cygnus.

Caldwell 88 in Circinus; home to the traveling Madras, a religious institution of higher thought.

Nexus Station, a well-known space station near Canis Major, Canis Minor, Lepus and Orion. Many folders are registered on Nexus. Almost everything is available on Nexus for a price. Nexus Below runs the workings of the station, such as air and water.

Acknowledgements

I've done a lot of these, and the list of people to thank is getting longer, which is a marvelous problem to have. While I've numbered these, there's not a true order—everyone on this list is key to my success and sanity!

The biggest thanks goes to The Amazing Sleeping Man for supporting me wholeheartedly through this wild business.

Second to Julia Huni, also supporting me wholeheartedly daily and by critiquing my works. And revising my book blurbs! And entertaining me with her writing, the hilarious Space Janitor and Former Space Janitor series, among many others. You're the best!

Third, to my sprint group who keep me on track and make writing fun. Marcus Alexander Hart, Hillary Avis, Paula Lester, Lou Cadle, Kate Pickford and Tony James Slater are all fabulous!

Fourth, everyone else who helps authors succeed. There's a huge list of author services that make life easier, and I highly recommend the Facebook Group 20Booksto50K to find the right ones.

Fifth, the lovely folks who run the Facebook Group Kickstarter for Authors. Primarily Anthea Sharp and Thorn Coyle, but also many others. It's been an interesting experiment!

Sixth, Deranged Doctor Design for another wonderful cover and Polaris Editing for proofreading. Thank you!

Seventh, my ARC team. Jim, Neil, Kirk, Jon, Maria, Carlos, Manie, Aviraj, and everyone else who responded and reviewed. Reviews help a book get noticed! Thank you!

Eighth, my readers. You all ROCK! See the next page for the extra special people who brought this project to life on Kickstarter!

Last, but most important, God. Thanks for keeping me on this writing journey!

Awesome Kickstarter Supporters!

THANK YOU SO MUCH for bringing this project to life! You are all amazing, awesome Gentle Beings!

B. Edward Held
Gary Chappell
Sean Wilson
Christian Meyer
John Idlor
Anonymous Reader
Richard Challis
John Stephenson
Joel Williamson
Gary Olsen
MEENAZ LODHI LODHI
Carl Overmiller
DragstarSteve
Alice Hickcox
Ginger Booth
Patrick Hay
E.C. Eklund
Herschel Blackburn
Robert Parker
derawill

Bridget Horn
E.R. Paskey
Karen O.
Duane Stafford
J.J. Green
CarlosBA
Julia Huni, Author
Rog
Monika L
Regina Dowling
Eron Wyngarde
G.S. Jennsen
C. Gockel
Irene
Dead Fishie
Stephen Ballentine
Kate Sheeran Swed
Donna J. Berkley
Mike Welch
The Creative Fund By BackerKit

About the Author

AFTER TWENTY YEARS AS a US Air Force space operations officer, AM now operates a laptop, trading in real satellites for fictional spaceships. She writes classic-style science fiction for today's world, full of adventure, hope and heart.

AM's writing cave is deep in the mountains of western Montana; check out Montana, The Amazing Sleeping Man, Zoe, their slightly crazy German Shepherd and Shepherd Book, their new puppy, on Instagram. AM is also a volunteer leader with Team Rubicon Disaster Response.

Sign up for the Scott Space Newsletter and get free short stories, *Lightwave: Short Stories 1*.

The Folding Space Series is complete and ready for binge reading! Start with *Lightwave: Nexus Station* (free on all retailers) or *Lightwave: Clocker*. The Quantum Fold series is complete, too. Start with *Quinn of Cygnus: Lift Off!*

If not out adventuring, find AM in all the usual places:

Website: www.amscottwrites.com

Instagram: https://www.instagram.com/amscottwrites/

Facebook:

Twitter: @AM_Scottwrites

YouTube: youtube.com/@theamazingsleepingman

Email: am@amscottwrites.com

I love to hear from readers! If you find errors, please let me know at the email address above. I'm on all the normal social media, but somewhat irregularly, so if you ask a question or make a comment, please don't be offended if I don't immediately reply. I'm particularly difficult to contact when I'm on Team Rubicon operations or out backpacking—cellphone towers don't exist in disaster zones or the wilderness!